LINE OF BATTLE

—— No. 1 ——

First Command

BY W.P. BROTHERS

FIRST COMMAND

Line of Battle No. 1

Published by Alena Publishing, 2017

Cover Design by Brutal Disorder Logos

ISBN 10: 0-9977394-1-X

ISBN 13: 978-0-9977394-1-1

DEDICATION

This book is for anyone who gets lost in dreams of impossible things. To the hours of children playing make-believe with friends and siblings. To the arguments and fights over imaginary worlds, full of fake people, and the larger-than-life heroes whose sacrifices are worthy of stories. Follow those dreams, enjoy that magic, and treasure those stories.

ACKNOWLEDGEMENTS

In the more than four years it has taken me to complete this project, there have been many people who have supported me. I'd like to extend my heartfelt thanks to the following individuals.

To Angela, Wesley, Mallory and Oliver for supporting me day in and day out while I worked on this novel, hunched over my keyboard. You bunch lift me up when I'm down, and make life worth living. I am thankful daily to have you in my life.

To Lee, Josh, and Boo. Your friendship and many geek sessions have inspired and motivated me. I am not sure where I would be without my heterosexual life partners. Friendships like ours are a rare thing these days. You three gents have helped me craft my ideas, hone my skills, and generally kept me focused. I don't know where I would be without you three.

To Chris and Ben, whose technical expertise helped me create a more realistic framework for my characters to live and play in.

To Reggie, Zack, and Merry for your thoughts and suggestions. Your honesty and time were invaluable.

To all those people in my life that I can't mention by name — family, colleagues, and acquaintances who have inspired or supported me: you have my thanks.

IN ALLIANCE YEAR 836…

The grueling cold war between the Royal Alliance and the Milipa Empire engulfs the known galaxy. The Alliance stands virtually alone against the Milipa, its powerful Royal Navy the last defense against the forces that seek to destroy humanity. A small force of technologically superior ships, the Navy strains to stand guard against the chaos that surrounds it and defend its few remaining allies. Alongside the Navy's other great capital ships — each one unique, a masterpiece of military engineering — the crew of the *RAS Verdun* will dare to confront the enemies of humanity. Her men and women fight and die over planets with no name, in skirmishes that don't officially exist. But far from the Milipa frontier, other terrifying enemies wait for their chance to strike…

PROLOGUE

Here we go.

Lieutenant Kim Morden brought her rifle to rest snugly against her shoulder, racking the bolt. "Do it."

The young sergeant in front of her pulled the control box off the door and began to key in the override sequence. The room was dark, her helmet's night vision visor highlighting his form in light green. His hands worked furiously, yanking and connecting wire after wire, trying to force the airlock open. Morden could feel her team's tension growing, the moments stretching on, one into the next.

Morden met Holsey's gaze, shared a small smile. She was happy her friend was here. They had been so excited to be placed on the same fire team. It wasn't often you were lucky enough to serve in the same unit as your best friend.

The door slid open, hissing as the atmospheric pressure of the centuries-old station equalized with that of the corvette. Morden glanced at the tactical display built into her multi-function watch, confirming what the intelligence data had indicated: no heat signatures, nor any signs of electrical power in the immediate area of the docking bay. She willed herself to relax, releasing the breath she hadn't realized she'd been holding.

Get a grip, Kim.

She spoke quietly into her ear piece. If something nasty was waiting, she wouldn't give their position away. "Egstine, you have point. Brevel, cover the rear. Baker, Holsey, check the corners and doorways. Greene, Lefebvre, Xu, stay here and keep the porch light on for us."

Morden stepped forward and hurried through the hatch right behind Egstine. The rest of the team followed in the tight formation that exemplified the expertise of the Royal Marines, leaving Greene, Lefebvre, and Xu behind to guard the hatch.

The atmosphere was heavy and reeked of the stale, musty, un-circulated air for which these older stations were infamous. It was unnaturally cold, and the icy air burned her lungs as she swept the room with her rifle. Her team spread out, checking the corners.

"Clear." Hansen's voice crackled over Morden's headset.

With a deep humming, the automatic lights started to flicker on, blotting out her night vision. Morden deactivated her visor, blinking in the sickly yellow of the emergency lighting, the automated response to their presence, driven by the damaged AI core.

At least something on this Godforsaken station works.

Despite the thick condensation and weak lighting, Morden could make out the black body armor of her companions against the light gray of the surrounding walls.

She tapped her radio mike. "Recon Team Echo to Ajax. Station breached. Proceeding to check point Alpha One."

"Echo, Ajax, acknowledged." The destroyer's response was barely audible. Obviously, whatever was making it hard to get clear scans was also fouling up communications. "Proceed with caution. We still have no readings out here."

Morden glanced to her left. "Hansen, get an additional repeater up."

He dropped to his knees, pulling the radio pack off his back. Hansen was built like a marine — broad shoulders, massive arms, and a square jaw. He had a handsome face, or Morden had always thought so, although she could never get herself to tell him. His technical prowess made him more than a little arrogant, but she liked that hard-charging attitude.

Then again, dating between fire team members was frowned upon by command, and Morden wasn't as willing to break the rules as Holsey and Brevel. Morden saw Emma and Glen share one of their discreet looks. It had been the talk of the ship when they had announced their engagement. She had expected the captain to come down on them, but to her surprise, he hadn't. Morden wouldn't risk jeopardizing her career, even though it meant putting her attraction for Hansen aside.

Morden took one last glance at the tactical readout, looking for any obvious signs of foul play. She couldn't see any. The distress beacon that had called the *Ajax* here was routine. These older AI cores often suffered breakdowns. The communications and sensor problems were odd, but not unheard of. The five-person crew was likely stuck somewhere below deck trying to fix the 800-year-old AI computer.

The routine nature of the operation didn't make it easier. This was Morden's first time leading a shore party, and she'd be damned if she'd let the captain down. She had always been a perfectionist, and anything except perfection was failure. That drive had propelled her to be first in her class at the Naval Academy.

That was then, this was now.

The captain had given this command to her. Anything but complete success was unacceptable. Morden took another deep breath, ignoring the tingle running up her spine, the animal instinct that allows ordinary people to respond savagely to danger. She refused to let those feelings control her. She wanted to lead with intelligence and skill.

A real leader has no place for fear.

Hansen stood up, finished with the repeater. Morden nodded to Brevel, who was waiting by the entrance to the lower levels. He popped the lock, and the team moved silently down into the station's habitation decks.

M orden growled, entering yet another empty hallway.
Hansen spoke from just out of sight, his voice low. "All the doors are welded shut."

Holsey leaned into her. "Something's fucking wrong here, Kimmy. These tin hulks are used for storage—"

Morden waved her hand, glancing at the time on her watch.

This was taking too long.

They had been snaking through the bowls of the station for just under an hour, funneled through the empty corridors like mice trapped in a maze. The hairs on the back of her neck prickled.

She shook it off. "Hansen, are communications still down?"

He nodded his head. Morden tightened her grip on her rifle.

Fucking technology.

She wouldn't let this happen. If she were to go by the book, she would have to pull out in the next five minutes to reestablish contact. She would have to admit failure. Unless...

Morden thought back to the station's schematics. The AI core was only a few decks down, and they could access the station's transmitter from there. They wouldn't be more than fifteen minutes overdue, and that would be better than slinking back to the *Ajax* in failure.

This corridor should lead to the recreation room. From there, it would be an easy matter to blow the emergency hatch and drop directly into the AI core.

Morden keyed her mike. "Squad, move down by twos."

The narrow passage was claustrophobic, the six door frames that lined its sides the only available cover. Baker and Holsey were in the lead, sweeping each door with their rifles.

The light was improving, her team's pace increasing. Morden started breathing hard, her nerves tightening with each step. The only sound besides their footfalls came from the circular automated door at the end of the hall. It was opening and closing slowly, knocking rhythmically against its frame.

Morden's heart leapt as Baker and Holsey jumped through the damaged door. They were close to the station's core, close to their objective. She could taste it.

The rest of the strike team followed Baker and Holsey through, then skidded to a halt just outside what looked like the recreation room.

Morden waved to catch her squad's attention. "Bachmen, Valmar, Glover, cover our six. Everyone else, clear the room."

The three men turned, taking positions to cover the door.

Morden crossed the threshold into the recreation room. Circular with a high ceiling, it was the largest space they'd encountered so far. Unlike the rest of the station, it seemed to have partial power, bright light flooding from a service window on the left.

Good. The crew must be alive.

Against the wall next to her was a ladder that led up to a long catwalk suspended above the length of the room. At the end of the catwalk was a door that looked like it might lead to environmental access or gravity control.

The walls were plastered with photos of centuries-dead people, the family and friends of every person who had served on this station. Wiring was exposed everywhere. Clearly the crew had worked on fixing the problem before the AI went off line.

Holsey shouldered her rifle, wrinkling her nose. "Am I smelling eggs?"

Brevel nodded. "If they left the kitchen robots on, shit happened fast."

Holsey caught her eyes. "Kimmy, I've got a bad feeling."

Morden brushed her off. "Not everyone likes food as much as you, Em."

She ran her gaze around the rest of the room. Emma was right — two large tables resting next to the service windows still held half-eaten plates of food.

In the room's center, the station's inhabitants had set up four jet-black holochairs, their silver trim glinting against the clean white light. No wonder these idiots hadn't fixed the station — they were clearly more concerned with relaxing in a virtual play world than doing their job.

Morden walked towards the control station opposite the dining area. Its screens were on, though they showed only static. The console's cool white color made it stand out from the rest of the dingy station, clearly a modern addition to the old facility.

She stopped, catching sight of the hatchway to the station's bowels. "Baker, get that hatch open. The rest of you, spread out, cover Baker. We don't want anything ugly interrupting her."

Morden backed up, taking a knee by on one of the holochairs. She aimed at the door Baker was wiring. Hansen and Holsey took up positions on her left, while Brevel, Ditirk took her right. Egstine was standing behind them near the dining area, his eyes fixed on the catwalk.

"Egstine, get in position."

He tensed, raising his rifle to his shoulder. He opened his mouth as if to say something, but never did. Several bursts from some hidden weapon tore into his torso from above, splitting him in two as their explosive rounds detonated inside him.

He collapsed, dead.

Those aren't Milipa weapons.

The room lit up as barbs hit all around the strike team, splintering metal walls and floors. The intense light from the weapons fire was blinding.

Morden spun, firing controlled bursts up at the unseen enemy. She heard several other rifles opening fire nearby.

Who the fuck is firing at us?

"Ajax, Echo. We're under attack." Morden tried to keep her voice calm as she spoke into the hand mike clipped to her shoulder. If there was even a chance someone could still hear them—

The holochair next to her came apart, sending debris clanging against the deck. Morden screamed as hot shrapnel hit her, cutting through her armor and tearing into her right arm.

Baker turned and ran towards her, firing wildly, her Enfield breaking large chunks out of the wall and catwalk as her rapid shots went wild. She skidded to a halt and hung in mid-air before flying forwards, a deep bloody hole in her back.

Brevel and Holsey had gotten to their feet, laying down accurate suppressing fire at the shapes moving above, the shadows falling back as the catwalk shook under the impact of gunfire.

Morden had seen one massive body fall, cut down by their volley, but she couldn't see it from where she was. Her mind raced through the possible identity of their attackers, drew a blank. She strained to see the body, but her gaze landed instead on Baker.

She struggled to her knee, pain searing through her shoulder. She had nothing to stop the bleeding. She reached up with her good arm, pressed her hand against the wound. Her vision blurred as she squeezed the wound as hard as she could, sending bolts of agony through her body. She used her injured arm to draw her Colt M7A1 pistol.

She shimmied towards Baker, blood escaping her fingers, pooling in her gauntlet. If Baker was alive, Morden wouldn't leave her.

The hatchway door blew off its hinges, and Hansen and Ditirk jumped out of the way of the falling metal. She raised her pistol, emptying her magazine into the opening, biting her lip against the pain.

Morden's jaw dropped, her heart hammering against her breast bone.

The Frontin.

The smell of rotting flesh and rancid blood turned her stomach, forced bile into her throat. Her skin erupted in goose bumps, cold sweat trickling under her armor. The Frontin's clawed arms and ten legs pulled its hideous, stinking body into the room. Her heart hammered against her armor. She had seen them only in training videos, knew of the horrors they brought to bear against their enemies. The drone was easily seven feet tall, eight blood-red eyes set in an arachnid's head. Its black, pock-marked armor was covered in grotesque markings of disfigured human forms, written in what looked eerily like blood. It locked eyes with her and opened its mouth, revealing a row of rotting teeth and razor sharp pincers.

We are so screwed.

Morden slapped a new magazine into place, letting the blood run freely from her wound, ignoring the pain. The pistol kicked in her hand as she fired it repeatedly. The .45-caliber bullets split the creature's head, a wave of green blood covering the wall as its body fell.

Hansen tossed a grenade after it. An explosion tore from the corridor beyond, heat and debris washing over the room.

Holsey pulled another grenade. "We need to get the fuck out of here!"

Morden loaded a fresh magazine. "Great observation, Em. Any other gems for me? "

Holsey was right. Frontin were pouring into the room from both sides of the catwalk, shimmying down the wall. With the emergency shaft open, they were surrounded on three sides. If the Frontin got behind them, cut them off from the door, they would be trapped.

Morden's stomach did somersaults. "Pull back. They got us by the short hairs. Holsey and Ditirk first, then Hansen, Brevel, and me." She glanced at Baker's still form. If she was still alive…

If you don't leave her, we all die.

Holsey and Ditirk bolted toward the door, but one of the Frontin jumped off the wall, landing in front of them. Morden couldn't believe how fast it moved, and neither marine had time to react as it kicked Holsey in the side, sending her flailing to the deck.

Ditirk shrieked as the drone's blade stabbed through his torso. It opened its mouth and laughed. Morden shivered at the deep, throaty, unbearable sound. Ditirk tried to pull the blade free of his body, but the Frontin grabbed his shoulder.

Ditirk stopped fighting, staring up at his killer's eyes. He shook as he was lifted from the ground. The Frontin jerked its arm, rending the sword out the left side of Ditirk's chest and letting the disemboweled body fall.

Morden looked up as fresh barbs slammed into the floor next to her. Two more Frontin had reached the edge of the walkway, firing their scatterguns at the deck below. One barb grazed Morden's knee, then burst as it hit the floor. She wobbled and fell, but her return fire hit one in the chest, and green blood dripped from the walkway.

Morden's knee felt numb. Her arm pulsed as she reached for her weapon. Holsey had regained her footing and was driving her bayonet into her attacker. The Frontin roared, grabbing her by the leg. It yanked her off the ground, raising its sword for the final blow.

Lying on her back, Morden raised her pistol, aimed quickly, and squeezed the trigger — only to find that the slide had locked back on an empty chamber.

Her heart stuck in her chest. "You fucking fuck! I'll rip you apart."

The Frontin lanced Morden with its eyes, its grotesque mouth twisting at the corners, as if it were was smiling.

Holsey fired her rife at point blank range. The Frontin's torso cracked, its body shattered by the round. Holsey fell, landing on her back. She rolled to her feet, firing behind Morden.

Hansen and Brevel had come up next to Morden, no doubt forced from their position by the intensifying fire. If it wasn't for the men holding the door, they would have already been dead.

Rounds were whizzing by Morden's head, bursting against the rear wall, disintegrating the ancient photos.

Morden waved her arm toward the door. "Move, jarheads. Time to get the hell out of Dodge."

No one objected.

Morden tried to stand up, her arm and knee screaming as she tried to transfer weight to her shattered limb. Her head spun at the excruciating bolt of pain. Swallowing down bile, she let her pistol fall from her numb hand.

It was out of ammo anyway.

Hansen reached down, grabbed her by the shoulder, and dragged her to her feet. "This isn't nap time, ma'am!"

Rounds exploded all around her as they approached the door. Holsey and Brevel were firing towards their pursuers, the Frontin's anguished screams proof of their effectiveness.

Glover and Valmar stepped out of the doorway to let them escape back down the hallway towards the *Ajax*, rifles firing past Morden's head.

Bachmen signaled them to hurry. Morden caught his eyes just in time to watch the left side of his head disappear, a scattergun blast hitting him from behind.

Morden gasped as the private fell out of sight. Hansen let go, freeing his weapon to fire. Morden's knee buckled, pain lacing through her as she broke her fall with her hand. Hansen's Enfield sent round after round back down the narrow hall.

They were trapped.

Glover's body was lying beside her, neck bent at a horrific angle, eyes blank. She hadn't seen what got him. She reached out, pulling his pistol from its holster. If they were going to die, it wouldn't be quietly.

Morden desperately searched the room, firing at the Frontin swarming past the kitchen.

The kitchen!

It only had the one door, and the service window, it would funnel these bastards towards them, give them a shot at holding out.

Morden fired again. "Go for the kitchen! Holsey, grenade! Cut us a path."

Holsey had perfect aim, the grenade's detonation clearing a path through the charging Frontin. Hansen scooped Morden up, every inch of her body aching.

Brevel was in the lead, clearing one of the Frontin bodies with a leap. A barb winged his leg, but didn't explode. The corporal started to stumble, dropping his rifle as he tried to break his fall.

"Glen! Stay down!" Holsey screamed, emptying her rifle on the advancing enemy, trying to provide cover.

Valmar stooped to pick the corporal up, a decision that cost him his life. A Frontin barb hit an exposed energy conduit behind them. It exploded, reducing them both to ashes in a hail of shrapnel and plasma.

"Glen! No!" Holsey's voice shook, and she started forward toward the charred mess that had been her fiancée.

Sergeant Hansen left Morden propped against the wall, used one hand to grab Holsey by the shoulder, pulling her back. Holsey fought him, yelling and cursing, struggling to reload her weapon.

"He's gone, Em!" Morden pulled herself along the wall toward the galley door.

Holsey responded by shaking Hansen's grip off and firing down the hall, walking backward in an orderly retreat.

Hansen took hold of Morden again and helped her the last few feet to the kitchen door.

They entered the galley, Hansen dragging Morden with him as they charged through the dining area and toward the wide service window. Hansen placed Morden on the window's counter, letting her scramble over to the other side. A second later, Holsey jumped after Morden, followed quickly by Hansen. The two silver cooking robots whizzed back and forth with full plates of food, seemingly confused.

Scattergun bursts slammed into the room, the two robots erupting in a shower of sparks and fragmented metal.

How many Frontin are there?

Holsey dropped to one knee and fired, cutting down attackers one after another. A grenade landed beside her. She cursed, kicking the explosive away. It detonated in mid-air, lifting her from her feet and slamming her into the wall. Morden looked over at her, the effort of turning her head making her grimace.

Holsey was covered in lacerations, blood flowing from her nose. Morden reached out and touched her neck — she was alive, but barely.

Morden rested her back against the wall, drew Holsey's pistol from its holster, and fired at all the targets as she could see. She only had ten rounds, but she'd make each one count. She willed herself to focus on the pistol's sights, the pain in her shoulder and leg unbearable.

She fired quickly, knocking down at least six more Frontin before the last round passed through the barrel.

"Stay with me, Lieutenant."

Hansen was looking down at her, his face white, terror covering up the handsomeness she had grown accustomed to.

Morden dropped Holsey's pistol. "I'm sorry, Robert."

He smiled. "We can still do this, just stay with me."

He fired another burst towards the oncoming enemy. She could only see one more, moving quickly along the base of the wall towards them. Hansen saw it, firing. The marine's round went wide.

The Frontin's didn't.

Its scattergun blast hit Hansen squarely in the chest, showering the wall behind him in gore. His body twisted in place, his mouth open in a silent scream, his glazed eyes staring accusingly down at Morden as he crumpled, slack and lifeless, at her side. Morden's nostrils burned with the smell of blood and burnt flesh.

Her stomach churned, sick.

The Frontin warrior roared. It smiled broadly, picking Hansen up off the ground and tossing him aside like a rag doll. It grabbed Morden by the chest plate, lifting her up in front of it. It looked her in the eyes, a low growl emanating from its lips. She saw it slowly pull a sword out, scraping it across her armor, clearly relishing the moment.

Morden's head spun. She had heard tales of Frontin eating the hearts of their living enemies.

Not today, asshole.

Fear and adrenaline focused her, cut through the pain searing her nerves.

She pulled her combat knife from its sheath and slashed at its eyes. It howled, falling back over the counter as it stumbled in pain. Morden hit the ground, landing directly on her shattered knee. She tried to stay conscious, but spots danced over her vision as pain consumed her. Her eyes closed, and everything went dark.

CHAPTER 1

Aboard the RAS Verdun

Docked at Arnhem Station

"Incoming transmission, Commander." Isabelle's familiar voice rang in Commander Kim Morden's ears, pulled her from her sleep. She cracked open an eye, saw the screen on her desk flicker on, illuminating the room.

Always when I'm sleeping…

Morden begrudgingly pushed herself into a sitting position. "Accept communication."

Admiral Knight's face appeared on the screen. "Commander Morden, good morning. I didn't wake you, did I?"

Morden rubbed her eyes, fighting off the fatigue that drew her back towards the warm covers. "Admiral?" She put on her best smile. "Uh, no sir, you didn't."

This was highly irregular. Admiral Knight should be contacting the captain, his brother. How often was it they were even in range for face-to-face visual communication?

The man before her was wearing much too large a smile for this early in the morning, an annoying habit she'd come to expect from the admiral. His hazel eyes set in his warm, pale face, contrasted with the crisp white of his dress uniform. Despite his infectious joviality, she respected him. He exemplified duty and service, having commanded servicemembers on the front line of every major battle of the past four decades, including the Black Star Campaigns that had taken the life of her father. Admiral Knight was a naval officer through and through, and his family had served as long as the

Royal Alliance had existed. He was older now, in his prime, probably his late fifties, judging by his receding hairline and silver-gray hair.

"Well, get used to it. Captains are rarely known for their well-rested lifestyles, trust me."

She blinked, staring at the screen. "Captains?"

"You heard me, Captain Morden. I am promoting you, effective immediately."

Leave the *Verdun*? The room spun around Morden's head as she tried to understand.

She braced herself on the edge of her bed. "Sir, leaving the Verdun isn't my first choice, I don't want to abandon Captain Knight."

"I admire your loyalty, *Captain*." His smile crept further across his face. "We know you love the Verdun, and that's why we selected you for the job. And before you ask, Captain Knight has just accepted command of the McQueen. He should already be gone."

Morden felt her draw drop, stared at the image on the view screen. She must have heard wrong. Her commanding officer and close friend had accepted promotion and left without saying a word to her. Not that sudden reassignments were unusual. She knew logically that the key to surviving the Milipa Cold War was bluffing — making one ship look like ten, keeping their defenses air-tight. She also knew that, with the Royal Navy's current rapid expansion project, experienced officers were often being siphoned off to crew new ships and to season green crews. In this environment, time was a perilous indulgence. That didn't make accepting rapid-fire changes any easier.

She became suddenly aware that she had been staring at the admiral for a good ten seconds, the older man holding her gaze quietly.

Morden straightened herself. "Sir, don't we need a change-of-command ceremony? This isn't by the book."

The Admiral laughed. "Captain Knight's expertise is needed elsewhere before he takes command of the McQueen. He has selected several other officers from the Verdun to join him." He paused to take a slow drink from a royal blue porcelain mug. "The political situation since the Ardaugh incident is tenuous at best. The McQueen's presence on the border will show the Milipa it's business as usual, and, frankly, we need the Verdun for another mission as soon as she can get underway. Your replacement officers will be arriving at the station in just over two days. Your new executive officer has your briefing packet. Use whatever time you have until then to inform the crew of the change."

"Admiral." She worked to keep the frustration out of her voice. Not only the captain, but several other members of the senior staff, her friends, were leaving too. "The Verdun has just completed a strenuous mission. The crew is tired, and this will be quite a shock. Captain Knight is loved by the crew. More time would—"

"I'm sorry, Captain, but we need you en route immediately. You have two days, and then you'll leave for Derek's Triangle. More details will arrive shortly. Admiral Knight out."

The screen winked off. Morden sat on the edge of her bed, trying to rein in her emotions. Command of her own ship was the dream that had driven her since she'd been a child. She'd curled up on the couch and listened for hours to her father's stories of his adventures, the wonders of space, the glorious battles against the ancient foes of the Alliance.

How could she replace Captain Knight? He was more than just her commanding officer. His patience had softened her edges. She had been so angry when she'd arrived here, fighting to overcome her mistakes, wrestling with her past. He had been supportive and understanding, making her feel at home, finally on solid ground.

And why Derek's Triangle? The region was a dump, a backwater, not even part of the Alliance.

Morden pressed the light pad. The lights located in the center of each of the room's four walls flickered to life, adding a faint buzz to the silence.

She blinked, breathing deeply, trying to compose herself.

She stood up, walked quickly across the room, past the walk-in closet on the left, to the restroom. She tapped the faucet, turning on the water flow. She cupped her hands and splashed water on her face, the cold liquid washing away the desire to return to her sheets.

Mechanically, Morden organized her shoulder-length black hair back into its regulation position, her mind running through what the admiral had said. SSShe knew she had the technical skills to run a ship, but was she really ready?

Being a captain was more difficult than simply understanding operations. A captain was the ship's leader, teacher, and spirit, a representative of the Alliance on foreign ground. It took years to be ready for that responsibility. Was she equal to the task?

Her eyes swept the quarters that were no longer hers. For years, she had embraced simplicity. The regulation, slate-gray walls were blank except for the obligatory image of the *Verdun* against its coat of arms. Had it not been for the pile of papers on her desk, someone looking in would assume the room was unoccupied.

She couldn't help but feel unready, the enormity of the situation pressing down on her. She took a deep breath and closed her eyes, quieting her thoughts and steadying her body. Her eyes slid open again, her discipline restored. The only sign of the tension inside her was her hand unconsciously gliding over the only visible blemish on her skin, a faded scar on her right arm.

She spun on her heel and crossed the room to the closet, pulling out her uniform. At least she would look the part, even if she couldn't feel it.

"Isabelle?"

The soft voice of the AI filled the room seconds before her holographic image appeared in front of Morden. "Captain, your morning report is available in your office. I have a few robots standing by to move you to the captain's suite."

Isabelle appeared as a young woman, her long, wavy brown hair falling well past her shoulders. She spoke with a light French accent, her pale skin, blue eyes, and light, feminine build speaking to her gentle, resilient nature. Each AI was rewarded for its decision to serve others with the selection of its own self-image — gender, ethnicity, skin color, every minute physical detail. Isabelle had chosen well, connecting herself to the cultural heritage of a ship named after an ancient battle.

Morden noticed that Isabelle had reduced her height to match her own, the fleet minimum requirement of five feet even. Morden had never really thought about her height — she'd always had enough tenacity to make up for her size. Apparently, Isabelle was trying to make her feel more comfortable, show respect for her new commanding officer. Morden appreciated the gesture.

Good AI were vital to the Alliance. They allowed ships to react faster in combat, processing information faster than any human could. The very survival of the Alliance rested on the strength of its navy, and the AI contributed greatly. The last few decades had weakened that strength as unforeseen enemies ate away at it. The Quaggar, the disappearance of the Black Star Empire, and the Ardaugh Conflict, among other incidents. Friends melting into enemies. Alliances crumbling. Innocents crying out for protection.

Things were not quieting down.

As the cold war with the Milipa dragged on, decade after decade, the pressure for top-notch AI was growing. The *Verdun* was a warship, a battlecruiser, but Isabelle made her personable, giving the ship a living, tangible personality. She was the soul that ancient sailors, braving the sea on wooden vessels under wind power, had ascribed to their ships.

Morden straightened her uniform. "Have one of the senior officers meet me here in fifteen minutes. Then have whichever of the senior staff remains on board ready in the forward conference room in a half hour. We have a lot to do and no time to do it."

Isabelle's image wavered and faded "Yes, Captain."

This is going to be a very long day.

Aboard the SS Baron

Derek's Triangle

Officer Justin Fray forced himself to sit still. "Helm ready, Captain"

This was it, the opportunity he had been yearning for. His family had doubted him, mocked him, reminded him that people like him shouldn't go to space. Few people had earned this moment as he had, fought for it, bled for it. Most from Panthos IV bought it, trading money for power.

His hands shook slightly. It took all his self-control and focus to keep his face straight and look like the perfectly passive and dignified officer he was determined to be. This would be his maiden voyage.

Fray could still hear the disdain and judgment that had accompanied the booming laugh of his grandmother when he'd told her he dreamed of going to space. It had been the only constant in his life since childhood. He'd lost himself reading history book after history book about the great deeds of larger-than-life captains and admirals dueling with death. He couldn't remember a time when his imagination hadn't burned with those stories.

Constant discouragement and negativity had surrounded him. The grandson of a diplomat, of one of the colony's leaders, a space jockey? His grandmother hadn't been able to stomach that idea, but her belittlement had backfired. It had driven him, fueled him for the challenges and long and lonely nights it took to get into the merchant marine.

Fray couldn't blame his grandmother. Most people saw his position as a joke, a glorified cargo clerk. It may not fit his lofty background, but it fit his heart.

The rampant rumors of people trading personal favors for positions for their least gifted sons had made the ridicule worse. He had lost count of the number of times people had asked him what Grandma had done to get him there. It never bothered him.

The corruption in the Triangle wasn't his problem. As long as he could feel space surrounding him, it didn't matter what backdoor deals went on.

Fray took a deep breath, slowly taking in the glow of the helm and of the other four officers' consoles, which overpowered the soft yellow wall lighting. The consoles were arranged in a semicircle sunk into the deck below the captain's station. He could smell the musty air pumping out of the centuries-old ventilation system. It had almost made him sick the first time he had come aboard the freighter.

"Helm, take us out. Dead slow." Captain Victor Stover's gruff, deep voice snapped Fray out of his euphoria.

Fray's hand started across his console. "Aye, aye."

He let his breath out slowly. He had to focus. This was the asteroid belt. It was difficult territory to navigate for even the most experienced of the Triangle's pilots. The thunderous hum of the *Baron's* engines reverberated through his chest as they cycled up to active thrust. The deck strained and lurched beneath him as the bulky ship fought to gain speed against its own inertial mass. The engines slowly won the conflict, the artificial gravity compensating for the force.

He could feel the entire ship through his controls, from the smallest thrust to the rapidly spinning sections of the hull that produced gravity, a throwback to the century when the old ship had been built. Fray felt like he was the ancient and noble *Baron's* heart as it slid into the darkness of the asteroid field.

Fray's heart pounded against his chest. He had trained on many freighters, but the feeling of actually commanding its movements, controlling it dangerous, beautiful dance, was indescribable.

Fray worked to keep his voice even and professional. "Sir, helm reports successful launch. Running dead slow. Navigation locked on beacon 38-A3 to exit the asteroid field."

Stover sounded pleased. "Excellently done, Fray. You might have some hope yet. Once we're clear of the field, switch to beacon 1-2 and head to the Underwood Colony."

Fray felt a rush of pride. "Aye, sir."

Expertly and gracefully, he maneuvered the *Baron*. It gained speed, pulling out of the protective cover of the port. The ship picked its way slowly through the asteroids, dodging the drifting rocks. Fray smiled.

He was one with the ship, finally dancing among the stars.

His soul was contented.

So contented, he missed the small blip on the outer edge of his sensor readouts

Morden stepped out into the hall, shutting the door behind her. Thomas Stetler, the ship's senior deck officer, was standing just outside her quarters, holding a data pad. He was very young and very bright. Morden respected his enthusiasm, even if his idealism was overwhelming from time to time.

He turned, smiling at her, saluting. "Congratulations, Captain!"

She returned the gesture. "How gutted are we?"

"Badly. The incoming TLS transport will be dropping off five new flag officers to replace those who left with the captain."

The tension in her gut began to mount again. "Five? I knew he wouldn't go alone. Who's gone?"

Rebuilding the command staff wouldn't be easy.

Stetler pointed down the corridor. "Lt. Commander Moreau was promoted to the McQueen as a second officer, Commander Driscoll laterally transferred as his chief medical officer, and, of course, his wife, Air Wing Commander Pintar, followed as well."

She frowned. "You said five. That's four, including the captain. I know counting can be difficult at your age. Who else left?"

The pair set off towards the nearest conference room, two decks above Morden's quarters.

The hallways were crowded, various crewmembers hurrying about their business. Each of them, 5500 men and women serving on the *Verdun*, were her responsibility now.

This was a warship. That meant combat. She would decide who would live and die for goals she might not agree with. This was the basic responsibility of any military leader. She'd always known this, but to have that in her hands so suddenly…

It's lonely at the top.

Her heart started pounding again.

The energy in Stetler's intense hazel eyes was apparent. "Your replacement — the new executive officer — and a new senior navigator are coming aboard as well. Captain Knight had me promoted to the helm. Blake took my spot."

She smiled. "Congratulations. I'm surprised Mr. Wilcox didn't get the executive officer's spot."

"Captain Knight left most people in their respective positions. Basically, we are just getting a new navigator, executive officer, doctor, air wing commander, and chief engineer. That's five, by the way! Otherwise, only Blake and I were promoted."

Morden took in another deep breath, grounding herself in the moment. The familiarity of the situation helped her maintain her composure. She had had operations briefings daily. These were the same blue-gray halls she had walked for five years. The access hatches were still spaced every fifty yards, the smooth faux-granite accent strips every five, the double doors to the officer's mess were still the same rich polished walnut — the small refined touches that distinguished ships of the line. It was still her home.

She nodded. "Do we have any info on the mission or the incoming officers?"

Stetler laughed. "Nope, it's business as usual. The new executive officer was briefed. There were no drones available to bring it out this far."

She wasn't surprised. He handed her the slate with the day's briefing on the state of repairs aboard the *Verdun*.

"I can't operate in the dark."

Stetler laughed, his smile breaking through his professional guise. "Told you it was business as usual."

Morden shot him a sideways glance.

They finished climbing the final stairwell to the command deck. Just to her right was the conference room. She stopped, straightened her uniform, and took a deep breath. Stetler walked forward, opening the door.

Isabelle was flickering at attention just inside the room. "Captain on deck."

The traditional boatswain's whistle sang loudly, breaking up the sound of discussion that greeted Morden and Stetler.

Morden was desperately hoping that the embarrassment and nervousness she felt wasn't showing on her face. "People, let's get started."

CHAPTER 2

Morden slammed her fist onto the table. "And the good news?"
Great poise, Kim.

Isabelle's calm, disembodied voice responded. "All forward ram scoops and magnetic ordnance deflector belts are testing at 100 percent capacity. All food stuff, munitions, and spare parts have arrived from the station's quartermaster."

Morden frowned, turned her chair away from her desk, and stared at the ceiling. "Great. So, we can defend ourselves, but without our Kaehey drive, we are stuck here — unless you are planning to get out and push."

The past two days had ripped by at a speed that had left Morden dizzy. Time had moved differently since her promotion, and everyone seemed to need her attention. Most of it was trivial, almost nonsensical issues any leader should be able to handle. How Captain Knight had fielded these problems without showing the slightest inkling of annoyance was beyond her. She couldn't believe how her energy seemed to evaporate as the hours flew by, one after another.

She rubbed her eyes, leaning backwards. "What the hell is the delay?"

It wasn't just physical exhaustion. She could handle that. As the master at arms on the *Ajax*, she had been known for pulling twenty-hour shifts. This was different, a psychological, almost emotional drain that left her completely devoid of energy.

Isabelle's voice broke her thoughts. "The drive units have been repaired and retuned, but Arnhem station hasn't provided replacement flow regulators. We can't go translight — that is unless the captain prefers me to restart the engines and destroy the ship. Personally, I'd err on the side of patience.

Falling behind on a timetable is bad, but my understanding is that the punishment for incinerating a defense station and ship of the line is severe."

Morden turned back to her terminal, ignoring Isabelle's sarcasm. "Is the station aware of our schedule? Command has us slotted to leave in four hours, and just restarting the engines will take half that time!"

"No information is available from the station's command or engineering section. The computer suggests the part is currently unavailable, possibly till the end of this week."

Morden clenched her fists, fighting the urge to let her table have it again. "What? Have Baudouin get the station's commander on the horn. I want to talk to him now."

The room went silent for several minutes before Isabelle responded. "Unfortunately, the communications officer wasn't able to reach the station. Scans indicate Arnhem's crew are refurbishing elements of their communications array at this time."

Morden looked up at the image of Arnhem station spinning slowly on the holoport running across the top of her office. It was one of older, smaller border stations, housing only a few hundred technicians, one last pit-stop for patrols in this region. The five small, circular sections each had two docking ports, illuminated by small, pale lights that dotted the station's super structure and looked like early morning dew on its light blue metal surface, glowing brightly against the surrounding blackness.

She had hoped to avoid going aboard. Arnhem's Commander, Major John Hainsworth, was a particularly persistent former fling who never seemed to accept that she now saw their relationship as purely professional. Apparently, Johnny couldn't move past combat school.

Morden frowned. "How long until my new officers arrive?"

"Forty minutes, assuming the last communication from the TLS transport is accurate."

Morden stood, straightening her uniform. "I expect Osterman and the honor guard to be ready for their coming-aboard ceremony by the time I return from Arnhem. Make sure my old room is finished being cleaned and re-stocked. The new executive will need it, and I don't want to waste any more time."

Morden left the room, moving quickly towards the port-side airlock. It was only one deck down from her office, near the aft galley. Her eyes lingered on the galley's entrance. She was going to miss being so close to coffee.

Morden hurried past the central lift. She had always preferred to walk, especially short distances like this. In a technical sense, the lift was faster, more efficient, but the tactile feel of her hands against the railing as she slid down the ladder felt better somehow, plus the exercise helped keep her body in shape. Before power generators, sailors had used stairwells to travel through ships. Morden couldn't help but feel connected to the pioneers who had sailed the ancient oceans using stars to chart courses to then-undiscovered lands

She slid down the ladders, landing without missing a step on the next deck. There were two, broad-shouldered marines posted by the airlock. The nearest shifted his rifle as the two men caught sight of her approach. They snapped to attention and saluted quickly.

Morden returned the gesture, then walked towards the airlock, the word "warning" running across the screen above the smooth surface of the doors. She reached out and placed her hand against the thigh-high reader just to the right of the door. "Morden, Kim, Captain. Serial number CJ79803. Going ashore."

Isabelle's voice responded. "Acknowledged, Captain departing. Acting First Officer Lieutenant Commander Jack Wilcox has command."

The doors slowly hissed open as the computer matched the pressure of the inner airlock. Morden barely noticed as the automatic warning systems blinked three times, indicating it was safe to enter the airlock.

She stepped in, tapping her fingers against her hips as the doors closed and the fifteen-second pressurization cycle began.

Morden's chest tightened as the station's old fashioned, yellow lighting peeked through the opening air lock. She pushed away the memories clawing at her mind, annoyed at her emotional response.

This is not the same place, Kim.

She crossed and uncrossed her arms as the outer door creaked open. She understood why old stations like this were still in service, why the Navy couldn't afford to waste resources, but Morden could never stand being on these old dumps.

Arnhem was one of the oldest and most claustrophobic border stations in the area. She swallowed, forcing herself to step across the station's threshold. Many of the ships she had served on had been built in the same era as this station, but for some reason they had never bothered her. She repeated the same security procedure, logging her presence on the station.

The two marines on guard inside the station, members of Arnhem's crew, didn't acknowledge her, but stood in the corner of the door frame talking, rifles leaning listlessly against the wall. She glared at them for a moment, tapping her rank pin.

They stopped talking and saluted lazily before returning to their conversation.

She shook off the last tendrils of fear that had filled her upon entering the claustrophobic space, orienting herself to the station. She started mechanically down the corridor, her steps becoming deliberately more fluid as the tension she had felt about coming aboard faded.

A tall man dressed in the khaki garrison uniform of an Army officer waved at her from the end of the hall. Johnny's dark brown leather belt, gold rank pins and drab brown buttons, each stamped with the insignia his regiment, were immaculate and perfect, just like the large number of ribbons he brandished on his chest. He had black hair and even darker eyes that complemented his handsome yet impish face. She knew him well enough to read the excitement on his face as she moved closer. His expression exuded excitement as she closed the distance between them.

John opened his arms, obviously expecting an embrace.

Morden held up her hand to block the attempt. She had expected a stunt like this when Isabelle had informed her communications were down. It was just like Johnny to try something like this to get her attention.

Morden stopped directly in front of him, crossing her arms. "*Major* Hainsworth, where are the dynamic flow regulators you owe me? The Verdun is scheduled to depart in four hours."

Johnny awkwardly lowered his hands to his side. "Commander Morden, I'm happy to see you ... and the Verdun. Please, my quarters are just down the hall. We can talk there, where it's quiet."

Morden gritted her teeth, forcing a business-like tone into her voice. "That's Captain, Major. We will talk here. I have no desire or time for pleasantries. Answer my question, or I'll mention your continued lack of discipline in my report."

Johnny's eyes left hers, fixing on the commander's rank pin, a silver rosette, still attached to her uniform. She felt her face redden. She hadn't received her new pins yet. She felt out of character, naked. How could she act the part when she didn't feel the part?

Johnny's face tightened. "Straight to business as always, I see. I have only the one dynamic flow regulator, and the Resolute requisitioned it first.

My team is manufacturing another as we speak, but it may take some time. You know how undisciplined we are."

His words hung between them, his tone icy and expression cold.

Morden uncrossed her arms. "The Resolute isn't here, and Admiral Knight's instructions make it clear the Verdun must have priority to leave on schedule. I am ordering you to have the part delivered immediately so we may get underway."

Johnny sneered, his tone sharpening to match hers. "This is my station, and you will get the part when it becomes available, no sooner. This matter is closed."

Morden clenched and unclenched her fists, the stress of the last few days seeping into her tone in waves. "No, you will get me that part now. You have time to complete the second part before the Resolute arrives. This station is a joke. Not everyone in the service ignores their duty the way you do. I expected better."

Morden stepped back, a tinge of regret washing through her.

Way to go, Captain Asshat.

Johnny saw her as a very old friend. Didn't she owe him some level of compassion? If she'd had just had one drink with him, he would have released the part. Reason and kindness would have had the same results. Johnny was an excellent, disciplined field officer. He'd been sent here because of combat injuries, not incompetence.

Why couldn't she let her guard down for just a minute?

Morden stared. She could feel the hurt and anger rising in Johnny as he stood in front of her, watching her. Suddenly, he saluted sharply and walked away without uttering another word. Morden's shoulders sagged. She felt exposed, her cheeks burning, as she tried to get hold of her emptions. She had done her duty, hadn't she? Ensured the mission was on time, her ship operational.

Morden straightened her uniform and turned to leave the station.

The pressure of the corvette's deceleration jolted Lieutenant Junior Grade Callista Urquhart hard into the back of her seat, and sent another blast of excitement and nervous energy washing over her. A braking maneuver like that could only mean they were close — very close — to reaching the *Verdun*. She could barely sort out her emotions. Being assigned to a battlecruiser for her first senior position was more than an honor. She had been expecting a destroyer, or perhaps a light cruiser at best, but certainly not a ship of the line. It had taken years of hard work to get here, but this assignment would give her the opportunity to do what she wanted more than anything else: protect people from the demons at the gate.

Urquhart looked at the small group of officers clustered around one of the corvette's two passenger bays. She had gotten up the courage to talk to several of the officers over the few weeks' journey from Second Fleet Command to Arnhem Station. They were certainly diverse, and what battles they would fight and villains they would subdue, only time would tell. She especially liked the commander, George Frost. He reminded her of her stepfather — tall, muscular, and a strong build that made him look every bit the soldier. Frost had kindly tolerated Urquhart's enthusiastic questions about their upcoming assignment — the *Verdun*, her Captain, and a dozen other topics, even though he clearly had as little knowledge as she did.

She had had equally stimulating conversations with Lieutenant Lloyd Geonor, who was likewise on his way to becoming a new department head. They'd shared some of their excitement about their new positions, despite the fact that navigators and engineers had little in common in the day-to-day events aboard ship. He had a smooth, intelligent, and sophisticated way of speaking that set her at ease. They had talked for several hours about their experience in various military actions. He had served at the Battle of Defense Station Eleven during the Quagaar Conflict, making it hard for her not to look up to him, regardless of their similar ages. She yearned so badly to be a part of stories like that, to make a difference. It didn't hurt that he was very handsome, with sandy hair and mahogany-brown eyes.

The only one of the other officers in this compartment she hadn't talked to was the commander who had taken a seat in the back corner of the bay. The woman looked hard and intimidating, despite the fact that her appearance was anything but antagonistic. She couldn't have been more than five feet six, with red hair cool blue eyes, and a fit, toned body. The closer they had come to the *Verdun*, the colder the woman's demeanor had grown. Even the senior officers, like Commander Frost, seemed to stay away. Urquhart could only guess at whatever was boiling under the woman's skin, but no matter what it was, it wasn't pleasant.

"Two minutes to docking," The disembodied voice of the pilot broke the silence of the room.

Urquhart looked out the small port window of the shuttle, straining to get a view of the battlecruiser that would be her home. She felt like a child before Christmas morning, barely maintaining the professional, disciplined composure of an officer. But all she could see was the spinning, bulbous silhouette of the station against the Arnhem star.

"This is ridiculous," Urquhart muttered to herself, tapping her foot on the deck. She wondered for a moment if the pilot was purposely teasing her by avoiding the *Verdun* as long as possible. Then she noticed that the other officers were watching her.

"Patience, junior." Commander Frost stood and walked over to her, a warm grin on his face. "It's not going anywhere without its navigator."

Urquhart returned his smile, though heat rose in her cheeks. The last thing she wanted to do was embarrass herself in front of her new shipmates.

"Besides," Lieutenant Geonor called from across the bay, his arms folded across his chest. "You'll be sick of this ship in no time. Give it a few months of patrol, and you'll be ready to … There she is!"

Lieutenant Geonor stood and pointed out the porthole. Urquhart followed his arm and felt the breath leave her lungs.

The station slid out of view, revealing the silhouette of an enormous ship.

"The Verdun." Urquhart resisted the urge to press her nose to the porthole's glass as she drank in the ship's image.

It was enormous, far bigger than she'd expected. Its long, tapered hull was capped amidships by a tall, heavily built superstructure. From the tips of the massive, triple laser cannons that thrust proudly forward from the ship's prow, to the cylindrical engine units that projected from the vessel's rear, its lines were clean, fluid, graceful. Urquhart could just barely make out the shape of the ship's twelve main gun turrets against the brightness of the Arnhem star. She raised a hand to her eyes, trying to block out the light. The *Verdun's* starboard navigational lamps blinked green, and she saw intermittent flashes that seemed to come from work crews on the ship's hull, their tenders absurdly small against the great battlecruiser.

Urquhart felt the deck shift under her as the corvette pulled alongside the *Verdun* amidships and headed aft. She blinked as darkness assaulted her eyes, the sunlight blocked by the vessel's form. Lowering her hand, Urquhart read the words *RAS Verdun* painted in black on the light blue-grey of the ship's hull, which completely filled the porthole. The deck shifted again, and the corvette pulled around the ship's transom, nosing toward one of several massive bay doors, which began to open.

"Wait until you see a carrier." Frost's voice nearly made Urquhart jump. "They're a whole lot bigger."

The TLS corvette's ramp began to creak slowly open as Morden reached the rear landing bay. The time constraint had forced her to sprint the nearly 140-yard distance from the airlock and down several decks to the bay. Morden worked to slow her breathing.

When she'd first come aboard the *Verdun*, her fears had been eased when a confident and poised Captain Knight had welcomed her aboard. She was determined to offer that same balm to her new officers.

"Just in time, ma'am." Lieutenant Commander Jack Wilcox saluted smartly, almost in time with his smoothly masculine drawl. Wilcox was the definition of a professional officer, well-built and intelligent with an infectious calm that set her at ease. His classic English bearing was accompanied by a fastidiously well-groomed appearance, topped off by the light brown hair he parted neatly. The only things that broke his stereotypically English guise were his soft green eyes. She was glad he'd be there to help her now.

The launch bay was quiet. It was only one bell into the ship's second dog watch, and most of the crew were sleeping. Even the honor guard of fifteen marines looked half asleep as they neatly formed two lines on either side of the ramp.

The exception was Major Gordon Osterman, the *Verdun*'s Senior Marine Officer, who was standing rigidly at attention. He shot her a broad smile as she looked his way. Gordon was extremely tall with the broad shoulders and strong back that defined the battle-hardened shipboard marines. Accompanied by his intelligent and piercing blue eyes, it was no wonder she had to deal with the fallout from the many women who strayed his direction. She never understood officers who chose to fraternize casually, risking the morale and discipline of the entire ship. If he weren't technically part of a different branch of the military, she might have brought him up on charges. And besides, she'd seen how tragically relationships in the service could end.

Morden hated to admit it, but despite Osterman's lack of personal discretion, she liked him. If she hadn't seen him in action, she would have taken him for a politician. Osterman was a naturally charismatic and well-liked leader. He had an easygoing sense of humor that lightened tense situations. He also was a fantastic field commander who had matched daredevil courage with calculated strategy to overcome less-than-desirable odds time after time.

Morden turned back towards the transport and the new officers who were seconds from striding down the ramp. She felt both excitement and trepidation as her mind continued to race. She took a deep breath, trying not to focus on her nerves. How long had she worked to get here?

How many peers had told her she couldn't?

The ramp slammed sharply to the deck, the sound of metal on metal breaking her thoughts. The corvette's internal air lock was open, its landing lights washing out the image of the individuals coming down the ramp. The boatswain's whistle began to shrill through the silent bay as the first of the officers reached the bottom of the ramp.

Osterman pulled his tired marines to full attention. "Attention on deck!"

Morden stepped forward, placing herself directly in front of the first person who had appeared at the top of the ramp, a woman who was just slightly taller than she was. She looked young — very young, no more than 25 — and even though she was obviously nervous, Morden could see an intense fire in her eyes. She had a slim but strong build, accentuated by long brown hair that matched her eyes. Morden wondered if any woman who looked so fragile could really handle a command position.

The woman came to a sharp stop, snapped her heels together, and saluted.

Morden returned the salute. "Why are you here?" The traditional line flowed easily from her lips.

The young woman's voice was strong and clear. "Lieutenant Junior Grade Callista Urquhart, requested and required by Naval Command to assume the role of Senior Navigator, RAS Verdun."

"Are you ready and capable to assume the role entrusted to you?"

"Yes, ma'am, I am."

Morden reached out her hand. "Then welcome aboard the finest battlecruiser in the fleet. May she be a constant companion and protector. In return, may you guide her and those under your command to swift and sure victory."

The boatswain's whistle blew again, and Isabelle's voice echoed in the room. "Lieutenant Junior Grade Callista Urquhart is logged aboard."

The young lieutenant handed Morden her file and, without missing a beat, continued walking between the rows of marines to the bay's exit.

One by one, the officers trickled down the ramp, Morden repeating the same ritual with each in turn. Lieutenant Urquhart was followed by the ship's replacement chief surgeon, Dover Cadogen, a shorter, balding, but well-built black man. Morden was impressed with the sheer tenacity and energy she could feel coming from a man so clearly past his prime.

The new Air Wing Commander, George Frost, followed Cadogan. Morden knew from the officer's grapevine that Frost had a reputation for discipline and effectiveness. Seeing him in person, she didn't doubt it at all.

Next, the new Senior Engineer, Lieutenant Lloyd Geonor, strode down the ramp, clearly excited to be on board. He lacked the physical presence of the other officers, but had a smooth and refined nature that permeated his palpable excitement.

"Lieutenant Lloyd Geonor is logged aboard," Isabelle declared to the room as Geonor walked down between the lines of Marines.

Morden turned to greet the last officer and heard—

"Commander Fiona E. Holsey, reporting as ordered."

Holsey's voice hit her like a rock, ripping into her like an arrow. Morden felt the air leave her lungs, cold sweat trickling down her back. She let her gaze rise to the top of the ramp, resting for the first time in ten years on her old friend's face.

CHAPTER 3

Morden took a deep breath, shifting uncomfortably in her chair. Sitting here didn't feel right. She knew that the last member of the command crew had just arrived for the briefing. She could feel the commander's glare burning into her as Holsey crossed the room to Morden's old seat. She couldn't bring herself to look up, even though she knew everyone was waiting for her to begin the meeting. Captain Knight had always given his senior officers time to mingle before starting a briefing.

"Gives me time to evaluate them and collect my thoughts. People need more than assignments to work well together, Commander."

It had annoyed her every time he had brought it up, but right now, it gave her time to collect her thoughts. She pretended to study the preliminary mission data on the small screen in front of her.

Morden shifted in her chair again, her uniform feeling sticky against her skin.

What am I doing here, I can't…

"And that's when he went BOOM!" Lt. Junior Grade Harry Blake slammed his fist into the table, finishing some joke he was telling Geonor, the new chief engineer, who was sitting across from him. "I never laughed so hard."

Morden was surprised to see that the normally laconic and reserved officer was taking to the replacement command staff so quickly. Morden appreciated Blake's intelligence and capability. In the few months since he had come aboard, his performance had proven he had a bright future. He was an efficient deck officer. His handsome face, short black hair and piercing hazel eyes seemed to distract the female deck hands.

Morden worked hard to avoid her executive officer's gaze, looking instead down the table towards the door opposite her. Sitting here gave her a new perspective on the room, and she fought the urge to shift in the chair again. She focused on the familiar elements of the briefing room. Sitting on her left, Major Osterman was talking softly — and suavely — to the striking new navigation officer, Lt. Urquhart.

Commander Wilcox's gaze moved across the console, brow furrowed as he studied the briefing. Lieutenants Stetler and Voth chatted with Commander Frost, the occasional burst of laughter coming from the trio. Doctor Cadogan stared into space, drumming the table's smooth surface with his fingers, obviously bored.

Maybe Captain Knight had been right about this silly fraternization. It eased some of her tension to see the old and new members of her command staff blending so well together in one of her favorite spaces on the ship.

The briefing room was small and, like most the rooms inside the *Verdun*, windowless. Its rectangular table was just large enough to fit the twenty built-in computer stations and corresponding chairs. Morden enjoyed how Spartan the space was. Even under the boisterousness and exuberance of Captain Knight, it had been simple, just business. It had always made sense to her. The *Verdun* was a warship; it didn't need the frilly posturing décor of an ambassadorial ship. This was a place for officers to meet, collaborate for an upcoming assignment, to keep their many, different jobs working synchronously. The room normally relaxed her, but right now, all she could feel was the unwavering eyes of her new executive officer.

Does she ever blink?

Morden tapped the controls in front of her, dimming the room's bright lights, activating the screens, and playing a small tone to start the meeting. The murmur died instantly as all heads turned her direction. She shifted again, trying hard to project the confidence Captain Knight had shown. She cleared her throat.

"It's time we find out what our mission is and begin to get under way. I want to take this opportunity to say that I am looking forward to working with each and every one of you."

There was a general chorus of agreement and smiles up and down the table.

"I don't have a lot of information, other than that our destination is Derek's Triangle. Otherwise, I'm in the dark. Our new executive officer, Commander Holsey, has been briefed in full, so I am turning this meeting over to her. Commander, if you please." Morden forced her mouth into what she hoped was a convincing smile as her gaze met Holsey's for the first time.

She hasn't changed.

Except for the malice that hid behind her own painted smile.

Morden fought to stay in the moment, the space seeming to shrink around her. She heard the bloodcurdling screams and smelled burning flesh, goosebumps erupting all over her. She squeezed her fingernails into her palm, pushing the thoughts from her head and focusing on the sound of Holsey's voice.

"Our mission is a milk run: find and recover a few missing civilian cargo ships." The contempt Holsey felt towards the assignment was evident, soaking through the calm, cool tone of her voice.

She went on. "We are to proceed to the Triangle and meet up with one of the colonial mercenary ships, the SS Black Fox, under one of their more experienced commanders, a Captain Paul Mostoff. With his help, we will search for signs of the missing ships and determine how and why they went missing."

There were several groans. Nothing was more tedious for a military crew than a search for a needle in a haystack.

"Forgive my ignorance, but I have never heard of Derek's Triangle," said Lieutenant Tyler Voth, the ship's master-at-arms, in his usual smooth and humorous tone. Morden had a great deal of faith in the young man. He had a conviction and courage that combined with his natural, somewhat unnecessarily goofy humor and charisma to make him a natural leader. Despite his fairly short, stocky build, he had a deeply powerful and commanding presence. It was clear that behind his green eyes, good looks, and sandy hair was a man who never stopped thinking.

Commander Frost chuckled. "I'm not surprised you haven't heard of it. The Triangle is *the* desert backwater of space."

Isabelle chimed in, automatically changing the displays in front of each officer to show a galactic map. "First explored in 80 A.Y. by the RAS Oxford, the region was named for the ship's commander, Tim Derek. Derek's Triangle is the area that lies between Frontin Space and the galactic northwest border of Gorna Territory."

Kim watched the map zoom in along the Z access, cutting through half of the depth of the Alliance before jumping out to its far-left quadrant.

"Although officially claimed by neither the Alliance nor the Frontin, it currently holds two colonies of ex-Alliance citizens who maintain a tenuous trade relationship with each other. Strategically, it is an important buffer zone between the Frontin and the Alliance."

Morden felt her stomach turn. She fought to keep her face straight as horrific memories invaded her thoughts again. She was all too aware of Holsey's gaze, which seemed to focus on her every time someone said "Frontin."

"The Triangle is sparsely populated," Isabelle continued. "Approximately thirty million people inhabit the system's two planets and various mining facilities. Originally established by Alliance corporations between the Empire Years 3490 and 3500 as a means to cheap raw materials to support the Empire's expansion. The first of its planets and by far the largest population center is the Three Rivers Colony, located on Panthos IV. Together with its smaller sister colony on Barnerious II, the people of Three Rivers have maintained a steady trade with the Alliance over the past 40 years, despite the Royal Navy's initial efforts to discourage settlement. Politically, the colonies distrust outside influence, but their weak mercenary military forces, internal pressures, and demand for manufactured goods that their limited facilities cannot produce have ultimately kept the door open for semi-friendly relations with the Alliance."

"If we don't have an official interest in the region, then why are we searching for their lost freighters?" Lieutenant Urquhart asked.

"It's quite simple, Lieutenant," Morden stated flatly. "If that region destabilizes or falls under the Frontin, it forces us to either confront them in force or increase our defenses along the border. Either option is untenable. The Milipa Empire has stepped up its military activity recently. Fighting from within the former Black Star Empire threatens to bleed over our border, and Frontin raids have increased steadily over the last ten years. The bottom line is that we don't have enough ships and personnel to defend all our borders. Maintaining a balance of power with the Milipa is taking everything we have right now—"

"The Frontin are cowards. They act and kill as a swarm." Holsey's voice cut Morden short. "If we continue to show military force in the region, it will discourage the fuckers. Typically, several heavy cruisers visit the Triangle each year as a show of force."

Morden felt a familiar heat burning her cheeks. She instinctively rubbed her shoulder. "True enough, Commander. By assisting the local governments and trying to keep the area stable, we prevent the Frontin from swarming the area."

"Makes sense." Urquhart looked up from her console and nodded.

"Sounds like a smashingly fun area. I clearly have been missing out on things." Voth chuckled to Frost, who nodded back and returned the young man's amused smile.

"But why us, ma'am?" Osterman asked." Isn't this sort of search-and-rescue mission more appropriate for a frigate?"

Morden shook her head. "The Admiralty must think the situation demands a powerful response. Seven ships have gone missing over six weeks. The SS Potsdam, the SS Hong Kong, SS Broadview, SS Oregon, SS Amazon, SS Clayton, and the SS Parnassus. These people need our help, and it is our job to find them."

"Feels more like a shakedown run." Holsey waved her hand dismissively, her voice hard. "They must not feel we are ready for a *real* assignment."

We? Or Me?

"Commander, all assignments are real assignments, big or small." Morden shot back, her hands gripping hard to her armrests as she shifted in her seat again. She took another deep breath, fighting the urge to yell back, stand up and let the frustration and anger out, match the hostility that was rolling off Holsey's every word.

"With all due respect, a twenty-four-gun battlecruiser shouldn't be wasted chasing a bunch of freighter pilots who are probably just sitting on an asteroid piss drunk and trading contraband."

Morden's gaze met Holsey's glare, rage making her pulse pound, her hands gripping her chair so hard that they hurt. "Command must feel it is important for the region's stability. You've seen up close and personal what happens when the Frontin are let loose. We can't ever afford to let that happen."

"Yes, we have. I am sure that one of the reasons we are on this milk run has to do with your experience with the Frontin." Holsey stared right back at Morden, her voice ice cold. Silence hung in the room, and Morden could see the younger officers exchanging glances, clearly confused as the two iron-willed women before them blazed a silent barrage at each other.

Lieutenant Commander Wilcox cleared his throat. "Regardless, Commander, I'm sure we will all rise to the challenges of this mission, learn from your example, and show you the quality of the men and women of the Verdun. Besides, our larger fighter capacity will make searching the asteroid fields much easier."

Morden took a deep breath, thankful for Wilcox's even temperament. It was not the first time it had been useful on an assignment. She just wished she had acted with that same good sense. She held up a hand. "Commander Wilcox is correct. This crew is the best I've served with, and, milk run or not, we will execute our orders with the highest degree of excellence."

Holsey's cheeks burned a dark red. "Ma'am, I didn't mean to suggest—"

"Think nothing of it, Commander. We all want to be in the thick of it, but this mission is vital to the continued security of our borders. I for one will make sure we succeed."

"Yes, ma'am." Holsey saluted, although Morden wasn't sure the gesture was sincere.

This isn't the place. Pick your battles, Kim.

"Isabelle, how long will it take to reach the Triangle?"

"Three weeks at 15 Keaheys, Captain."

Morden did the math in her head, calculating speed and fuel consumption. With a maximum velocity of 22.5 Keaheys, the *Verdun* could do better. "Push it to 18. That should leave us plenty of fuel. Remember these ships have been missing for long enough already, and that speed still gives us two weeks to come up with a plan of attack. Commander Frost, please work with Lt. Voth and Major Osterman to come up with ground rescue and search plans for our pilots and marines. Commanders Wilcox and Cadogan, please coordinate medical preparation and rescue drills with Lt. Blake. Commander Holsey, you are to oversee both groups and coordinate the necessary actions. I expect everyone to have their plans to me by Monday of next week. In the meantime, Lt. Urquhart, please plot the necessary course for our rendezvous with the Black Fox. Regardless of the nature of our mission, I want us to be ready for anything before leaving the Alliance. I want a full battle-readiness test, including squadron-by-squadron fighter drills. Any questions?"

"No, ma'am," the group responded loudly.

"Dismissed."

Morden watched as the various members of her staff trickled one by one out the door. Her hands loosened from her chair's arm-rests, her fingers tingling as the blood raced back into them. She sat still, quietly running through the past twenty minutes in her head. Morden had known when she'd seen Holsey come aboard that working with the woman would be difficult, but she had never imagined that she would be so openly hostile, especially in front of her new subordinates. Clearly Holsey hadn't been able to forget that mission.

Have you?

Morden had almost come unglued at those memories of the Frontin. She had struggled to keep her emotions under control through the entire meeting. That woman had pushed all the right buttons. Morden had dealt with difficult officers before. Part of her job as executive officer had been to deal with personnel conflicts. She prided herself on her ability to solve those conflicts; she was good at it.

Not good enough.

Morden stood up, straightened her uniform, and started for the exit. For the first time in her career, the hardest part of doing her job might be surviving her own shortcomings.

W*hat a long day.*
          Lt. Commander Wilcox started to unbutton his uniform very slowly.
          He stretched, then trudged across his quarters toward his music player. He had been waiting for this all day. He flipped it on, collapsing into his arm chair as the computer retrieved and activated the proper file. He relaxed, his body sinking into the soft fabric. As soon as he lifted his feet, they began to pound.

Wilcox understood that starting new missions was hectic. There were meetings to be held, drills to run, more meetings, inventories to take, tactical plans to draft — and had he mentioned meetings? But this change in command had made it ten times worse. He had not expected to deal with so much tension between his direct commanders. Organizing a crew was hard normally, but getting people on the same page when the two most senior officers were caught up in their own personal conflict made it all the more difficult.

He was dying for a shower. A private shower in his own quarters was the greatest perk of his rank — one he took advantage of to the fullest possible extent. Nothing eased his stress like some soft music and a hot shower. He focused his attention on the music, couldn't help but hum along. He had recorded the piece in a hotel room with a few friends during his last leave. He had played the horn. Although he had been eager to hear the recording ever since, Wilcox hadn't yet had the opportunity. Every time he had tried, some emergency had come up or order had been passed down.

Not this time.

Finally.

He let out a long sigh, leaning back into his chair, his eyes closing. He let himself float as the melody started gaining tempo. It was broken by the sharp, biting tone of the door chime. Wilcox almost laughed, opening his eyes and flipping off his recorder.

So close.

He buttoned his jacket back up and walked quickly to the door, opening the latch just as a second sharp tone tore through the now quiet room.

It was Commander Holsey. "Lieutenant Commander, sorry to bother you, but I'd like a word."

"Certainly, ma'am. Come right in." Wilcox tried to sound friendly. Starting on a new ship was always difficult, and as the second officer, it was his job to extend the hand of the *Verdun*.

"I wanted to apologize for my words in the briefing room. I didn't mean to suggest anything negative about the—our crew. I just wasn't expecting..." She paused. "This."

Wilcox was not sure what to say. The tension between the captain and this woman had been palpable, unusual even for a captain and executive officer at the beginning of their working relationship.

He smiled, tried to make his expression reassuring. "No offense was taken, ma'am."

She seemed to relax. "Good, I really am excited for this promotion. I've worked more than hard to get to this level." Her hands moved to rub the small of her back, and she winced. "Though I guess everyone has. I just wanted to make sure that we got off on the right foot."

"Well, then, let me say welcome aboard, ma'am. We are all excited to get this mission over with and back to the action, but this crew has been through a lot in the last six months. A 'milk run' will be good for us."

"Thank you, Mr. Wilcox." A smile creased the corners of her lips.

"Let me also reassure you," Wilcox continued, the words pouring from his mouth before he had fully considered them. "That despite our captain's reputation as a hard-ass, I have found that Morden is actually a very thoughtful and even leader. I think a woman of your clear passion will compliment her nicely. You two will make a great team."

Holsey's face tightened, and her eyes seemed to blaze, her body going stiff. This wasn't the reaction Wilcox had expected from her. He braced himself for the dressing down that seemed to be coming.

When she spoke, her voice was calm and even. "That's good to know, Commander. Thank you for your civility. I am looking forwards to working with you. Carry on."

They both stood, and she turned on her heels and walked out of the room.

Wilcox stared at the door for a moment. He was still unsure what to make of her. She's said she was excited, but she didn't act like it. Wilcox could tell that she was fighting to control her emotions. She showed none of the energy or excitement he had expected. He couldn't get a read on her, and he hated it when someone eluded his understanding. After a few seconds, he walked back to his armchair. He would take a wait-and-see approach to the new executive officer. It wasn't fair to judge someone right off the transport. God knows he'd disliked Morden at first. In fact, Holsey's intensity and demeanor reminded him of Morden when she'd been assigned to the *Verdun*.

He reactivated the music. The flowing melody filled the room again, chasing away the stress and tightness in his muscles. He closed his eyes, let out another deep sigh, and started to unbutton his jacket for the second time.

CHAPTER 4

Lt. Urquhart sat quietly in the mess hall, eyes half-shut, ignoring the wash of noise and banter from the room around her. She picked slowly at her croissant and tea. She hated mornings. There was nothing positive about leaving the comfort of her rack. The only thing that made this daily, ritualistic torment bearable was the excitement she felt at being aboard the *Verdun*. It had been almost a week since she'd arrived, and she had loved every moment of it.

She lifted her teacup to her mouth, opening her eyes as the deep aroma of the strong, dark red tea filled her nostrils. Scottish breakfast. Her favorite.

She took a deep drink of the steaming hot liquid, letting it harass her taste buds and burn its way down the back of her throat. Urquhart was a tea snob, drinking only British breakfast teas for their strong flavors — and high caffeine content. Her step-father had always kept a supply of loose-leaf tea on board in their quarters so they could enjoy the real thing, shunning the stale bags offered in the mess halls.

It was a tradition she still practiced, even though she now drank alone.

Urquhart opened her eyes, letting her gaze sweep across the embossed coat of arms above the entrance to the mess hall. She couldn't help but let her painter's eye devour the architecture of the room. The details enthralled her, the cold, hard crisscrossing ceiling buttresses smoothly painted in the traditional military grays. Warm, inviting mahogany furniture etched with crisp old-Earth style designs. The person responsible for this purely utilitarian space had taken great care to make it inviting, even beautiful. She had spent her entire life so far — at least what she could remember of it — aboard naval vessels, and she admired them. Maybe it was the artist in her, but she loved their aesthetics. The *Verdun* was no different. She was a piece of fine art, one of the most impressive Urquhart could remember. Like all capital ships, she was unique, the only one like her ever built. There were no mass-produced classes; each vessel was a creation of the human imagination, a monument to its individual designer's ability to mold steel and polymers into something powerful.

Urquhart drifted back to reality, glanced at her watch.

Crap.

Only 15 more minutes before her shift started. She was completely out of her normal routine. She hadn't exercised or painted since she'd arrived, and today seemed likely to continue that trend. The laundry list of duties she had to attend to today was ridiculous: finish the flight plan for Commander Frost, adjust the duty rotation for her team, brief her team on the deep range telemetry, and all sorts of other responsibilities befitting her status as head of the navigation department.

"Lt. Urquhart, please report to the bridge." Isabelle's disembodied voice crackled from the old speakers above the mess hall doors.

She smiled, taking one more sip of her deliciously hot tea.

So much for 15 minutes.

Urquhart was keenly aware that all ships had their own flavor, personalities that made serving aboard them unique. Isabelle was a stickler for timeliness and discipline. Urquhart desperately wanted to finish her half empty cup of tea. Mornings might be the worst thing out there, but she refused to allow them to deter her. There was no way she would get off on the wrong foot with the ship's AI. If timeliness was the key, then she would be the first one to report, no matter how early it was. She would make her mark here. No one was more dedicated to the service, and she was going to prove it to her new captain, no matter what it took.

The end was close, so very close.

He could feel it. The prey was right there in front of his guns. He could almost smell the burning flesh of his victims, feel their fear, and hear the sounds of his enemy's bulkheads collapsing, the air ripping from their mammalian lungs. Soon he would sink his fists deep into the blood of his favorite and most hated prey. The ecstasy of death and victory was his. It was palpable, it was beautiful, and he couldn't help but smile to himself softly as he felt his Tajon cruiser accelerate towards his meek opponent, closing the distance between them.

Life was good.

"Hard to port! Hard to port!" Captain Stover's voice was strained, almost hoarse.

The *SS Baron* shook as another enemy volley smashed into the rear of the ship. Fray was fighting as hard as he could to keep the ship steady. The sickly glow of the emergency lighting system bathed the bridge red and grated on his already strained nerves. The smell of burnt wires and gore filled his nostrils, making his stomach heave and his brain spin. Only the captain's voice and his training kept Fray from giving in to raw panic.

"Get us behind the asteroids. Keep them between us!!"

"Aye, sir!"

"Belise, do we have any offensive capabilities left? We need options!"

Fray heard the impact of flesh on metal as Belise, the ship's second officer, answered, panic oozing from the man's voice. "No, they fucked our missiles in the first barrage."

The ship shuddered as more enemy rockets slammed into its exposed port side. He could feel the ship's gasps of pain through his controls. The *Baron's* shaking was increasing by the minute. If they lost any more of the stabilizing thrusters…

Fray pulled back hard on the control stick, slamming the ship into sharp climb. The *Baron* jerked, leaving Fray dizzy and disoriented as the pressure of shifting inertia nearly tore the ship apart around him. The *Baron* was not maneuverable, but Fray was determined to make her dance.

He had to. All of their lives depended on it.

The engines screamed as he keyed in another command, leveling out of the climb and resisting the asteroid's gravity. He glared at the massive, slate-grey form on his display, defying it. The asteroid was pulling hard, begging the wounded ship to plummet to its death. His head was beginning to pound under the pressure as the gravity generator fought to keep inertial forces within the ship at safe levels, to hold the hull together as gravity and thrust pulled it in opposing directions.

He slammed in another command, pushing the *Baron* to full speed. He felt the ship rocket forward, and then threw the controls down to tuck her behind the safety of the nearest asteroid.

"Fray, hard to starboard. They may not see us if we get right above the crater at 21.2 degrees." The doubt in the captain's voice made Fray's hands shake as he tried to follow instructions.

If he could just get the ship behind cover, they could double back to the safety of the mining camp. But the *Baron* fought his every effort, her wounds clearly taking their toll. His panic mounted as he felt the reassuring hum of the engines give way to the belching, hissing screams of broken pressure valves and burning, sparking conduits.

He had dreamed for so long of the adventures he would have, but the reality of this adventure, fighting for his life, was overwhelming. His slightest mistake could erase his hopes, dreams, and fear forever.

Fray finally managed to pull the *Baron* next to the rocky protection of the asteroid. He felt his heartbeat slowing as the great rock filled his monitor. His scopes were clear.

Everyone on the bridge sat in silence, the relief palpable, the only sound the wailing of the alert klaxons.

Fray's heart caught in his chest as his scopes registered a contact. Like a ghost, the assailant's vessel swung up from directly below the *Baron*, their weapons flashing brightly on his monitor as its rounds tore into the ship's underside. He could see a stream of crystallized oxygen, debris, and human bodies through his camera, life flowing out of the *Baron* like water from a faucet. The enemy had guessed the captain's move.

How did those bastards do that?

Fray tried to react, tried to get the ship to respond, to move, but the controls felt wrong. Lighter, yet sluggish. She seemed trapped, stuck almost. He watched helplessly as the attacker raced past, its grotesque shape arching into a perfect 180-degree roll, bringing its main guns to bear on the *Baron*.

Fray heard the captain's voice, but it sounded distant. He was frozen, staring in disbelief at the speed and ferocity of his opponent's actions.

The enemy's main guns belched again. He could see red flame bursting from the muzzle of each massive gun then disappearing, extinguished by the vacuum of space.

He felt the deck shake hard beneath him, felt adrenaline shoot through his body as explosions tore through the bridge. He tried to breathe, tried to reach for the comforting blues and greens of his console, but his head was spinning. He could feel himself being pulled, ripped from his seat by rushing, freezing-cold air, colder than anything he'd ever felt before.

The *Baron's* bridge shuddered one more time and burst open like a ruptured pipe. Fray was vomited into space in a gasp of escaping oxygen and debris, the frozen grip of the void welcoming him to the end of his journey.

"Good morning, Ma'am." One of the two marine guards called as Urquhart finished climbing the stairs to the bridge landing.

It's way too early for that much cheer!

Urquhart tried to smile as she returned the two men's salutes. Her chest tightened. Guardrooms always made her feel uneasy, and the *Verdun's* was so similar to the *Blue Jay's* that she could almost see her father helping the doomed marines man their compact machine guns. She picked up her pace, crossing the room quickly, refusing to look at the two covered gun ports on either side of the guardroom. She turned right as soon as she entered the post, taking fewer than four steps to enter the even-smaller anteroom, where, along with an additional ominous-looking gun port, most of the ammunition and supplies for the marine guards were stored in a row of lockers built into the wall.

Urquhart took two quick lefts, entering the bridge through its large pressure door. She felt herself relax. She was grateful that at least the *Verdun's* bridge didn't match the *Blue Jay's*. It was not as large as she'd thought it would be before she'd come aboard, but there was something about its simple layout and cool, friendly grays that made her feel like she belonged there.

The lighting was low, almost as dim as the holoports, the long rectangular screens that ran the circumference of the room just below the ceiling line that functioned like windows, displaying the dark space outside the ship. She looked around to see who else was present this early. As in all Alliance vessels, the command platform with the captain's station stood in the center. The platform was raised about two feet higher than the rest of the room, allowing the captain to swivel around and overlook any of the officers manning the other five stations. The captain's chair itself had a folding computer console, currently raised out of the way, that allowed the commanding officer to interface with the ship's many functions.

Just to the left and slightly behind the platform was a smaller, lower-level station for the executive officer. It had a smaller version of the captain's command console, which Commander Holsey was bent over, studying the screen in front of her. A radio headset and microphone, stowed on a hook on the side of the chair, allowed the executive officer to maintain contact with all parts of the ship during combat and feed the captain's orders down to fire control.

Along the room's back wall was a built-in weapons locker containing several armored chest plates as well as accompanying helmets, five M7A1 pistols, and two Mk3A2 Enfield battle rifles, three shock grenades, and about five hundred rounds of ammunition per weapon. Next to the locker, about three feet from the door, was the action table, a holographic planning table about five feet long. Tied into the ship's sensors, it allowed the captain to produce a 3D representation of field operations for planning and briefing purposes. It wasn't immune to sensor errors, and its usefulness was limited by the quality of the *Verdun's* data, but it went a long way toward helping officers plan upcoming fleet and ground maneuvers.

Along the wall, opposite the door and to the left of the command platform was the ship's ops station, where the second officer, Commander Wilcox, monitored operations and responded to ship emergencies during battle. Shaped like a U, it was one of the most complex stations on the bridge. On one side was a long table, the damage control monitor, which displayed a three-dimensional image of the *Verdun*, each deck and station shown as a green grid. In the center of the U was a light board that showed the status of all the emergency air-tight pressure doors. The side of the U set into the wall featured all the sensor readouts, automatic fire suppression controls, internal security displays, and environmental system monitors, laid out in logical clusters. Headphones and a hand mike hung off the front of each station. Although the AI could control many of the station's functions, an electrical computer system, even one as sophisticated and powerful as Isabelle, could become inoperable in battle, as ships tore each other to pieces in the darkness of space.

"Good morning, Lieutenant." The voice of the communications station operator, or CSO, Chief Baudouin, brought Urquhart's gaze to the long radio station, just to the right and set against the wall. There were two consoles: one for the CSO and another to be used during fleet operations. Each console came with a bank of screens, bulky, padded microphone headset.

Urquhart waved, her eyes moving past the CSO to the pilot's den, a shallow trench directly in front of the command platform that housed the helm and all its directional controls as well as her own navigation station. She felt a small glow of pride. The navigation station was the most advanced on any bridge, connected to every sensor relay on the ship and the long-range sensor drones. Faster-than-light travel was an amazing feat, but it took incredibly careful calculations to properly manipulate the gravitational fields and thread a path through space. Although she'd admit a certain bias, Urquhart felt that navigation was one of the most difficult and rewarding jobs on the ship.

"Ah, Lieutenant, glad you're here." Holsey's voice drew Urquhart's attention. "We are just a few hours from sub-light transition at the border of the Triangle, and I wanted to make sure you have properly calibrated the drones for their combat simulations."

"Yes, ma'am. Captain Morden approved them yesterday. I only have to submit a copy of my simulation model to Commander Frost."

"Oh." Holsey seemed surprised. "Well, I would like to check it over regardless. In the future, please remember to submit copies to me before giving them to the captain."

SHIT. Was I supposed to give her a copy?

Urquhart could feel her face getting warmer. "I'm sorry ma'am. I thought you had a copy." Out of the corner of her eye, Urquhart saw the two other officers in the room exchange glances. They were clearly uncomfortable with the exchange between their new superiors.

"No. Please get me a copy. Now."

Great first impression with your new XO, Callista.

"Yes, ma'am." She nodded, then jogged to the navigation station, taking the steep steps as quickly as she could.

You're better than this!

"Ensign, you are relieved." She felt idiotic. How could she have made such an obvious misstep?

The officer stood, saluted, and left the bridge, clearly eager to be gone. She pulled up the proper file, her eyes flying over the data. Everything looked good, exactly as it should. She typed in the commands to place the plan on the Executive Officer's work station.

"Thank you, Ms. Urquhart."

The seconds ticked by, and the silence from Holsey's station began to make her uneasy. She tried to distract her nerves by finishing her report for Commander Frost, placing the drone launch coordinates in one by one and entering the gravitational survey information for the region into her computer.

What could be taking so long?

She turned around and glanced at the commander. Nothing. She couldn't tell what Holsey was thinking. The woman had the same cold, detached look that she'd worn on the corvette, her lips slightly open, her eyes moving back and forth over her screen.

Urquhart thought about speaking up, but decided against it. She still had hours of work to do on this report, and the captain had already approved the simulation rundown.

The bridge lights flashed on as the ship's internal chronometer reached the daytime setting. Like any ship, the *Verdun* still used a 24-hour clock with an 8-hour night setting to help regulate the crew's natural body rhythms.

Isabelle's voice echoed in the room as all the consoles lit up, adding their own light blue glow to the room's ambiance. "Zero-seven-hundred. Commander Holsey, the bridge is yours."

Urquhart heard the murmur of voices approaching the bridge. She turned just as the rest of the A-shift officers entered the room. The captain, followed by Lt. Commander Wilcox, Lt. Stetler, and a communication ensign that she didn't know — his name tag read Scott — trickled onto the bridge.

"Captain on deck." Isabelle's voice, cheerful and bright, filled the room.

"At ease." Morden waved her hand, stopping Urquhart from standing. "Today should be an exciting day, folks. Fighter and combat drills."

The captain's voice was about as jovial as Urquhart had ever heard it. Morden was intimidating, powerful, and clearly loved the service. It was hard not to look up to someone who was so successful at the life Urquhart had dedicated herself to since the disaster on the *Blue Jay*.

"Lt. Urquhart, you're in early this morning. Trying to get Frost his report, I see." The captain was smiling. Urquhart couldn't help but feel it wasn't her accustomed expression.

"Um, yes ma'am. Commander Holsey asked me to come to the bridge to go over the simulation calculations with her." She hesitated. "I failed to go over it with her prior to asking for your help." Urquhart hated to admit a mistake to her captain, but she wouldn't hide from it.

The captain's lips tightened into a frown, all pretense of joviality gone. "Commander, my office. Now." The tone was low and sharp.

Holsey looked just as angry as Morden. "Captain, I was just revi—"

Morden's voice cut Holsey short. "We will discuss it in private, Commander."

The two officers stared at each other for a moment, clearly unaware that all eyes were on them. Slowly but clearly, Holsey saluted her superior, letting a small but undecipherable expression move across her face. "Yes, ma'am."

Urquhart watched her two commanding officers walk out of the room, barely noticing Isabelle's voice announcing that Commander Wilcox had command of the bridge. The tension on the bridge dissipated the instant Holsey and Morden were gone.

"What did I do?" Urquhart felt her stomach tumble. She couldn't remember ever making a superior that mad before. The captain hadn't even acknowledged her.

Stetler laughed. "Wasn't you, Lieutenant. Boy, did she make a mistake!"

Wilcox nodded. "I wouldn't want to be her right now."

Urquhart barely heard the rest of the exchange, diving headlong back into her report. She shook her head. Clearly she had a lot to learn about the dynamics of command.

Chapter 5

Morden returned a salute from one of the marine guards as she exited the bridge, trying not to let the anger cross her face. She felt like she was on fire, burning up with rage. She couldn't remember ever being this angry. Holsey had gone too far. The woman was way out of line, had been out of line since she came aboard. Morden could hear Holsey's footsteps directly behind her, only the rhythm of her own legs descending the stairs kept her from wheeling around at her old friend.

How anyone had been stupid enough to put them together on the same ship was beyond her. Holsey clearly couldn't handle the job of being Morden's executive officer, couldn't keep her emotions in check. Reviewing a plan that she had approved and blatantly ignoring the chain of command was behavior unbecoming. It would be one thing if Holsey were merely inexperienced, green, but Kim had no doubts that behind the woman's behavior was the spite Holsey still felt towards her.

"That bitch did this, she forced us to ignore the regulation, ignore the danger. I blame the Lieutenant as much as the Frontin."

Morden could almost hear Holsey's voice, see her in her full-body cast at the inquest that had followed their last, disastrous mission together.

Morden could feel the anger rolling off Holsey in waves, the woman's hot breath hitting the back of her neck as they walked. Sensing the commander's anger only hardened her own emotions, heightened the anticipation of the dressing down she was about to give.

This was going to be fun.

Morden would enjoy cutting this woman down, putting her in her place. The *Verdun* was Morden's ship, and no one would subvert her authority.

Morden threw open the door to her office, waiting just long enough to hear it snap shut before wheeling around to face Holsey. This was the first time she'd been alone with her old friend since she'd come aboard. She stared at the familiar face across from her, letting silence hang in the air. Even so many years later, it felt strange to feel so much anger between them.

If only things were different.

Morden held onto the fire she was feeling. "Commander, explain yourself! It is not your place to review orders that I have already approved." Her tone was harsh, hostile, and out of her control.

Holsey's eyes seemed to bulge, her anger clearly visible. "Permission to speak freely, ma'am?" Morden was surprised by the cool, even tone of her voice.

"Granted. We're alone here. Now is the appropriate time to say what you like." Morden moved behind the desk and slid into her chair.

Holsey strode towards Morden, leaned forward, and placed her hands on the table. "My job as executive officer is to ensure that the mission is successful. You ordered me to oversee both elements of the mission and then excluded me from planning our combat drills. I was simply reviewing the data so I could ensure the preparations would progress smoothly and—"

"You were not excluded." Morden cut her sentence short. "Lieutenant Urquhart asked for my input, and I gave it. We completed the planning. There is no need for me to consult with you before making a decision."

Holsey straightened up, crossing her arms. "No, you don't have to consult me, but if you had respect for me or my duties on board, you would."

Morden leaned forward, unsure how to respond. "Oh, would I?"

"You haven't treated me as your XO, not once. We both know why."

"This has nothing to do with the past, Commander. We are talking about your actions now, in the present, on this ship."

Holsey snorted, laughed. "There you go! Now you've got it, ma'am."

Morden fought to ignore the sarcasm oozing from Holsey's voice, opened her mouth to speak, but her subordinate cut her off.

"It's my job to ensure the mission is successful, even on a bullshit run like this. If you won't include me in command decisions, then I will use any and all means to do my job regardless of protocol. Your ego isn't worth people's lives."

Morden open and closed her mouth. She had known Holsey would still feel anger toward her, but such hatred?

She shifted uncomfortably in her seat. "That was a long time ago. I made a mistake and it cost you, but I have earned my position here, and you have to trust me to lead our crew."

"Stay with me lieutenant."

Morden could almost make out Hansen's face looking down at her, Frontin barbs exploding around them. She shivered.

Holsey slammed her hands back down onto the table. "Earned it? If you'd have earned it, would we be on a mission to the edge of nowhere looking for shitty ore freighters? No." Holsey's voice rose. "We would be on the front line! Some officers slip through the cracks, get their assignments by sucking up, or by dumb luck."

Morden felt her anger crescendo rapidly. This was getting out of control.

"I—"

Holsey cut Morden short, "You got everyone killed, Ditirk, Hansen... Glen. All gone, dead for nothing. Hell, it was dumb luck that Greene, Xu, and Lefebvre were able to break us out and we all didn't die."

"That was not luck." Morden searched for the same old argument she'd told herself many times. "I left them as a rearguard to deal with situations like the one we ran into."

You don't even believe that yourself.

Holsey scoffed in disgust. "We wouldn't have needed them in the first place if you had been thinking. The fucking Frontin didn't kill our team. You did, and you didn't even get reprimanded."

Morden stood up, matching the woman's volume. "I had to go through inquests. I had admirals dissecting and second-guessing every choice I'd made. People watched my every move while I hobbled around with a shattered knee and numb shoulder. It took months of physical therapy to walk normally again."

Holsey scoffed. "I spent nine months in a recovery ward and you never even visited! I was deemed physically unfit and thrown out of the marines and had to start my career over. You got promoted."

Morden stared back at Holsey, dumbstruck. The woman's blazing accusation ringing in her ears. "Emma, I meant to visit. I—"

Holsey cut her off again, her face tightening. "I apologize for the outburst, Captain. That was uncalled for."

Silence hung between them for several moments as Morden locked eyes with her subordinate. "Commander, I don't expect you to like me. I asked you to do your job properly."

"No, you haven't let me do my job. If you had, I would be involved in command decisions. That's the issue."

Morden didn't know what to say. Had she treated Holsey like an executive officer? Holsey had been hostile and disrespectful since she had come aboard. Morden had ignored it, let the younger officer supervise the preparations for entering the Triangle. Then again, how would she have behaved if Captain Knight had assigned her to oversee a project, then excluded her from making any decisions about it?

You'd have been standing on the other side of this desk, too.

"Commander Holsey, if I haven't done enough to make you feel like a member of my crew, I apologize. My job is to run this ship, not make people feel needed. Bottom line: If I approve a plan, that's the end of it. If I decide not to include you in that planning, regardless of my reasons, that is the end of it. I do not need your approval."

Holsey nodded. "Yes, ma'am."

She sat back down, shifting in her chair as she met the commander's eyes again. "That being said, I will try to ensure that I solicit your opinions before finalizing those decisions. Dismissed."

Holsey nodded stiffly. Leaving quickly, her fists clenched tightly at her sides.

Morden's stomach turned.

She sat and stared at her computer terminal for a long time, her thoughts lost in the past. She could almost see Holsey's limp body propped against the station's wall. She'd known Holsey had been wounded but hadn't realized how her injuries had cost her.

I did what I could, didn't I? I didn't break her back!

Morden shook off the thought, turning her mind toward her conversation with Holsey. Normally, she prided herself on her adherence to the book, her military bearing, and yet she had already failed to maintain her calm twice. Emma had managed to regain professionalism, salvage her calm even through all the anger and hate. More than that, she'd had a point. Morden had ordered Holsey to oversee those plans, but when the time had come, she had cut her out. Maybe she hadn't been as welcoming as she'd thought, but who could welcome someone so hostile?

She thought back to when she'd first joined the *Verdun*. Captain Knight had welcomed her, worked with the ways their command styles clashed, and helped her grow. Morden wanted to do the same, had insisted on meeting her new officers when they had come aboard. She had wanted to make them feel welcome here. Had she failed?

The ship jolted softly, bringing her back to the present. The ship had decelerated out of translight and was slowing to a stop. It would only be a few seconds before she was called to the bridge. She stood up, straightened her jacket, and left her office, thoughts still in turmoil.

The controls felt good as Lieutenant Marcus Hillman keyed his Stallion torpedo striker into a steep dive. The craft's hull groaned as its engines kicked in hard, swinging the craft around to point its weapons toward the automated dummy drones.

Paradise.

After being locked up for weeks attending briefings, preparing flight plans, and looking at map after map of identical-looking asteroid fields, it was liberating to be in the cockpit again. Hillman loved his job more than anyone in the service—in his opinion at least. Flying was like music to his soul, and the Stallion was his instrument.

All but four of the drones began to scatter, fleeing in multiple directions. Several of Hillman's team broke formation to pursue the dispersing drones.

"Raptors, formation alpha three. John, Eliot, you have the lead. Good hunting."

His ten-man squadron split into three smaller groups. Two of the groups had three strikers aligned in tight formation, only ten feet between the lead ship and its wingmen. The final four fighters formed a diamond and flew directly in between the two other groups.

Of course, in space, left and right, up and down meant almost nothing, as a ship could fly in any direction using any object or major gravity well as an anchoring point. Any first-year cadet knew that a fighter oriented itself from the initial location of its mother ship. Hillman had always considered this a practical choice, since the fighter would need to return to the ship in order to dock. Understanding this rule allowed different fighter squadrons to standardize their navigational measurements and return quickly back to safety. In general, the home ship would orient to the relative position or axis of the nearest sun, but with the large distances traveled and the reality of combat in between systems, it was a rule a fighting ace like Hillman used regularly.

Out of the corner of his eye, Hillman saw the Raptors' smaller formations peel off and accelerate away. He could not help but feel proud of his squadron's perfectly synchronized maneuvers. One group headed down and the other shot up toward the two drones that had turned to engage the oncoming squadron. This last-minute movement would confuse the drones' targeting equipment and allow the pilots to swing back to mop up the fleeing drones after the center formation struck.

Hillman's formation flashed straight at the oncoming targets. The cool blue glow of his cockpit shifted to a dark red as his Stallion automatically transitioned into combat mode. His holodisplay, projected on the inside of his cockpit's windscreen, flashed on, showing target warnings, ammunition counts, and ship damage control readout. The KGV machine rail guns — known affectionately as "hell guns" to anyone more than a day out of basic, read hot and the torpedo tube covers were open. If it weren't for the words "simulation mode" flashing in green under his weapon readouts, Hillman would be ready to take on any Milipa, anywhere. He glanced to his right, checking the squadron command display on his window panel, which showed the conditions of the other nine members of his group. They were as ready as they would ever be.

The drones opened fire, warnings streaking across his display as simulated flak explosions were registered all around him.

"Formation A, break and attack," he spoke into his tight-beam radio set.

An instant later, he pushed his striker into a quick, sharp barrel roll before leveling off and cutting his engines, allowing the craft to coast off inertia. He had never met a drone — or any enemy ship for that matter — who would engage a drifting, seemingly out-of-control ship when other live targets were bearing down on it.

Hillman could feel his hands shaking as adrenaline flooded his system. Even though this engagement wasn't real, something about the intense flying excited him.

Just one more second.

Hillman fired, subconsciously bracing himself for the jerk of weapons fire that never came. Instead, two holographic torpedoes streaked across his screen, recording direct hits against two of the rear drones as they raced across his bow. One stopped, his computer marking it destroyed, while the other cut its throttle, simulating massive engine damage. He slammed his ship back to full speed, unleashing two more torpedoes at his target. The drone went dark as simulated death tore into it.

Hillman didn't have time to savor his kill. He turned hard towards the next set of undamaged drones. The agile striker hummed loudly as it gained speed and banked around, bringing its guns to bear. They turned rapidly, dodging his first attack, pumping fake ship-to-ship missiles toward him. Hillman could feel the Stallion's automated defensive turret spring to life as it tracked the nonexistent missile. He imagined the feel of its twin I88C machine gun kicking as each of the incoming ordnance vanished from his screen.

Hillman held down the trigger, shooting round after round toward the oncoming drones. They banked hard, maneuvering out of the hail of bullets.

Perfect.

Hillman sprang his trap, unleashing a pair of torpedoes toward the drones. The simulated warheads threaded through the drones' countermeasures. An instant later, the drones jerked hard and stuttered to a halt as the computer marked them both destroyed.

Hillman smiled, clapped his hands, and closed his eyes. He imagined the drone was an enemy fighter, he could almost see the fire burning as its atmosphere spilled into space, ending his opponent's life.

Hillman had no illusions about the life of a fighter jockey. It was kill or be killed. He would make sure it was always the enemy, not him, that would pay the price of failed politics.

That was better than textbook! Let's see those Pegasus jockeys beat that!

Hillman couldn't image a better instrument for his music than a Stallion striker, the best light fighter-bomber the Alliance had ever devised. They were small compared to the Cerberus interceptors, only fifty feet long with a modest, thirty-eight-foot wingspan.

The size never bothered Hillman. He could make this machine sing, regardless of its agility, both in space and atmospheric combat. Its quad PW 53 engines, mounted on the front wings, allowed for quick course corrections and rapid x-axis maneuvers. Of course, the Stallion had its flaws. It lacked the heavy armor and agility of the Cerberus interceptors and the speed of the Sparrowhawk pursuit fighter. Realistically, any direct ordnance strike would end Hillman's song. The vulnerability didn't bother him. He trusted his skills and the most pound-for-pound destructive capability of any attack craft in the known universe to keep him alive.

Hillman felt an affinity for the craft's design. The Stallion was meant for one thing. Close with the enemy and unleash its eight anti-ship torpedoes directly on target. Hillman enjoyed the same single-minded focus. Destroy the target and break the back of the enemy. Yes, the ship also had hell guns and various electronic warfare suites designed to destroy enemy fighters with ease, but that was not its purpose, or his. The Stallion devoured capital ships. Let the Sparrowhawks worry about fighters.

His eyes opened, returning his focus to the simulation. To his satisfaction, his wingman had followed his plan perfectly, accelerating to top speed before looping back to join the rest of the group, helping them junk their targets as he destroyed the enemy rear guard. The Raptor squadron was the best, and he was more than proud of them. They worked like a well-oiled machine. Most squadrons only flew together a few years before being reassigned, but the Raptors had been a team since the *Verdun* was commissioned. Sure, they had lost a few pilots to promotion, but, basically, it was the same team it had been 7 years ago. They had been lucky.

Commander Frost, their new air wing commander, had asked the Raptors to be the first to run through this drill. Hillman was sure they would also leave the greatest impression.

He keyed his mike. "Great job Raptors. Return to base!"

"Well done, people!" Captain Morden beamed, her satisfaction evident. "I am glad to see we haven't lost our edge."

Lt. Urquhart could barely contain her smile. She was just a few days away from her first real mission as a department leader. Finally, she could make a difference. There were so many enemies surrounding the Alliance, and, despite the bombardment of newscasts that aired back home telling everyone how much things were improving, Urquhart had seen firsthand that they weren't. Even with new ships being built at record speeds, the Milipa Navy still outnumbered the Alliance ten to one.

Morden's voice snapped her out of her cheerful reverie. "Lieutenant Urquhart, are the coordinates and navigational data ready for our rendezvous with the Black Fox?"

"Yes, ma'am." Urquhart double-checked her calculations. So many numbers and variables needed to be accounted for to allow the ship to accelerate above light speed. She punched in the final number, approving the command for acceleration to translight.

"Captain, instruments show ready," Lt. Stetler called out.

"All hands, this is Captain Morden, we are accelerating to translight. All departments report ready status."

The moments ticked by, Urquhart couldn't stop her fingers from drumming impatiently on the console. She closed her eyes tightly, trying to imagine the look her father would have had if he could see her now. She felt her throat tighten. The last time they'd spoken...

It had been an election year, the first time she'd voted. She'd supported the Democratic Socialists, and her father had stuck with the same center-right One Alliance party that he'd always voted for.

"It's bloodthirsty imperial nuts like you who are destroying this country!" She'd spat the words at him, not caring about the obvious hurt in his eyes. He hadn't actually supported the radical right-wing Imperialists, but she hadn't cared. She'd been angry, and more importantly, eighteen.

He'd walked toward her, held out a hand. "Callista, honey, you're not listening to—"

"You and yours do more to hurt us than the Milipa!" She'd stormed out of the room, leaving him standing there, an arm still stretched out toward her.

If only she'd known that later that same day—

Urquhart shook away the jagged memories that filled her mind. She'd always liked to believe that he was watching her, looking down on her from somewhere. She'd make it up to him, make him proud, show him the person she'd become.

"All sections report ready." Chief Baudouin's voice interrupted Urquhart's thoughts. "Cargo doors are properly sealed, fighter bay and drop bays are closed, and all internal systems read green."

Urquhart opened her eyes.

"Lt. Stetler, bring us to translight, eighteen Keaheys."

The young helmsman hit several commands on his console, switching the ship from sub-light engines to the Keahey drive. Urquhart felt momentarily weightless, her body being pulled in all directions at once. She blinked her eyes, the room around seemed to blur, elongate. She tightened her grip on her chair's armrests as she heard the telltale popping and shaking of the *Verdun's* gravity generators equalizing the environment as the ship broke the translight barrier. As suddenly as they'd begun, the sensations faded, and the room felt normal again.

Urquhart smiled, leaning back in her chair and listening to the sounds of the bridge. They were on their way, *finally*.

H olsey couldn't decide which she felt more, the exhaustion of the last few weeks, or her hatred for Morden. The day's efforts had left her tired down to the bone. Every muscle ached. She had taken painkillers and a sleep aid to knock her out, but it hadn't worked. Sleep still eluded her. She had been trying to sleep for hours, lying quietly on her bunk in the dark. She rolled over and opened her eyes, staring at the blank, cool gray of the ceiling. Holsey smacked the side of her bunk.

This is ridiculous.

When she'd first found out she'd been promoted to executive officer, she'd been ecstatic. It was a sign that all the hard work, the exhausting hours of physical therapy had been worth it, that she'd overcome the setback of her long recuperation. She was back on a proper, honorable path, even if it wasn't the one she'd originally wanted.

Holsey felt her chest tighten again. Everyone on this ship seemed to have bought Morden's act, though Holsey couldn't imagine how. Anything with eyes could see her ego from a mile away. Morden couldn't really be the effective leader that everyone here seemed to think she was. This was the officer who had taken Holsey's life from her. There was no easy treatment for a broken body, no miracle procedure for a broken back. Even with the most up-to-date care, most people couldn't fully recover from such a serious injury. Holsey had been a marine, one of the elite. Accepting that she'd have to serve in a more sedentary position had been beyond difficult. Sure, the Navy needed good bridge officers, people to make choices, to lead. But Holsey had never wanted to be in Navy blues. She wanted to confront the enemy head-on with a rifle in her hands, not from the safety of a warship's bridge.

Holsey swallowed, trying to put away the conflicting emotions swirling inside her. It did her no good to dwell on the past. This was just another roadblock on the way to her own command. Being this close to that woman for so long had been terrible; it had shaken her to her core. She felt trapped inside her own memory, reliving the worst seconds of her life over and over.

Every time she looked into Morden's eyes, she could feel the bones of her back being crushed against that bulkhead, smell the burning flesh as Glen's body incinerated. She looked over at the ring she kept next to her bed, tried to push his screams from her mind, but rational thinking seemed a poor match for the visceral images she fought with.

"The fucking Frontin didn't kill our team. You did."

She had been honest with Morden, and she'd meant every word she'd said. She would do everything in her power to ensure the mission's success. No one else would die because of someone's desire for promotion, someone's vanity.

"I had to go through inquests. I had admirals dissecting and second-guessing every choice I'd made. People watched my every move while I hobbled around with a shattered knee and numb shoulder. It took me months of physical therapy to walk normally again."

It had been a genuine shock that Morden had suffered. From Holsey's hospital bed, the woman's success had felt instantaneous. Holsey almost felt bad for her. They had been close once. But Morden's suffering wouldn't raise the dead.

Holsey yawned, turned over again, and wrapped herself back into her sandpaper-soft, standard-issue blankets, letting the building warmth surround her. She had to sleep. Tomorrow would be another long day, and she needed her strength. This was going to be the most difficult assignment of her life.

Chapter 6

How could this happen?

Captain Viktor Stover's eyes snapped open, taking in what remained of the bridge as the *Baron* shook again — hard — from what felt like more weapons impacts. The command deck was hazy from the acrid electrical smoke that billowed from unchecked fires. The fumes burned his eyes and choked him, making him cough uncontrollably.

His head was pounding. He raised a hand to feel blood pouring from a gash on his forehead and trickling into his eyes. How was he alive?

The bridge had been hit, and he'd watched as the front bulkhead had torn away and most of his crew had been blasted into space by the decompressing air. He'd tried to hold onto something, had heard the emergency decompression bulkhead rattling into position just as his strength had given out. He'd felt himself hurtling toward the void, then — lights out. He must have struck the bulkhead and passed out.

But for how long?

He tried to think, tried to collect his thoughts as the wailing of the emergency klaxons cut through them. They were unbearably loud. He wiped his eyes, smearing the blood from his face. The ship was shaking violently, and judging by how sick he felt, the failing artificial gravity generator was working with the ship's inertia like a pump against his stomach.

He reached above his head, grabbed the edge of the nearest object, and pulled himself up onto his knees, the vibrating of the deck fighting against his every move.

I have to get to the evacuation deck.

If he couldn't reach the escape hatch, he would blow up with his ship. A romantic notion for a warship's captain, maybe, but he had no intention of dying for agricultural cargo on this ancient freighter. He had spent his life flying cargo around the Triangle, and he planned to keep doing it for years to come. He refused to die now, uselessly. He was no hero.

Besides, he doubted he had any crewmembers left alive to abandon.

The ship shuddered again, but differently. He couldn't put his finger on it. It was too soft for the violent impact of weapons fire. Fear gripped him. The ship was beginning to rupture, tearing itself apart. He could almost see his crew's killers, sitting safely somewhere out there, laughing. Basking in their triumph as the decompression and vacuum ripped sections of the *Baron* apart.

Those bastards don't even need to get their hands dirty.

Stover reached out, steadied himself on the wall, and pulled himself to his feet. He shook off his panic, willing his body to move towards the only door on the bridge. It clearly had no power, judging by the lack of light coming off its control panel. He reached down and tore away the deck plate, the razor-sharp metal edges slicing deeply into his hand. Blood welled up around the wound.

"Son of a bitch!"

He threw the rusted plate aside and pulled on the emergency release. There was a deep groan, but nothing happened. It was jammed. He could see the rust and corrosion covering the base of the lever, untold centuries of neglect laughing at him. He shifted his position, bracing himself against the doorframe. Stover slammed his foot into the lever, and pain shot through his leg as he pressed his entire bodyweight against it. The control started to move. He bit his lip and kicked down at it. Over and over he struck at the lever, putting every ounce of his remaining resolve and strength into every blow.

"Come on, damn you!" He shouted.

The lever slammed down, and the door burst open on its hinges with a hiss of escaping air. Stover stumbled through door and into the corridor beyond. He could feel raw energy seeping into him as adrenaline flooded his blood. The deck was dancing beneath him, the pain in his head and injured hand were growing worse as he fought to keep his footing.

The air was cold and stale, the only light the dull red pulsing of the emergency lamps. The narrow hallway made the klaxon's incessant wailing almost unbearable. Viktor fought to keep his focus through the adrenal blur, blood again filling his eyes and clouding his sight. He reached out, using his hands to steady himself as he crept towards the stairwell that he knew must be close, no more than 20 paces. If he could reach it, it would be less than 30 feet to the rear escape deck and escape pods. He'd walked this route a hundred times, and yet somehow he could hardly move. His strength was slipping away.

Viktor shook his head, took a deep breath. The toxic air burned his lungs, but the pain helped him focus. He started forward again, then stopped.

What was that?

He swore he could hear footsteps as his eyes strained to pick through the darkness that filled the hall. Something was there, sprawled in the corner, moving slowly just outside the dim red light. His heart leapt.

Finally, some luck!

One of his crew must have survived, clearly injured but still living. Before Stover could say anything, he saw a bright flash and heard a small popping sound issue from the wounded crewmember's location.

He opened his mouth to call out, but instead of sound, there was an explosion of dark red blood. Viktor looked down at the stream of blood, saw a mangled, oozing wound spread over his chest.

Had he been shot?

He tried to pick out the shape of his attacker in the dark, but his awareness was evaporating into a confused world of searing pain. Everything was moving faster than he could comprehend. The captain felt as if he was bolted to the deck. He tried to move backward, but his legs give out. He barely felt the pain of his knees slamming down to the shuddering deck.

He looked up. The figure in the corner had stood and was moving lazily towards him, staying just outside the sickly red light. It was menacingly large, familiar like something out of one of Victor's dreams — or nightmares. Viktor stared at the specter, awestruck as the world around him seemed to—

There was another small pop. Viktor's body was disintegrated, a trail of thick, chunky red gore sprayed against the bulkhead the only evidence of his existence.

He could feel the smallest smile spreading across his lips. The jolt of his peaking ecstasy invigorated him as he watched the blood spray coat the wall. His eyes devoured the mangled pile of mammalian flesh in front of him. This is what he lived for, the end of the hunt, the joy of the kill. This carcass of a freighter smelled blissfully of death, death he had caused. This was glorious. Nothing could stop him or his clan. The hunger of their hearts would finally be quenched by the blood of these worthless, weak beings. He stooped down, coating his claws in the valueless remains of this animal.

This was perfect.

He closed his eyes, savoring the beginning of what would be his greatest campaign — all his eyes, that is, except the dead one.

The *Baron* spun in its death throes, electrical discharge and flame leaking from the cracks blossoming along its hull. Several of its engines were still firing in an automated and futile attempt to stop its uncontrolled spin. Deep within its heart, the damaged reactors gave out, shuddered one last time before exploding, splintering the hull. The *Baron* discharged its remaining atmosphere into space, a trail of reds and yellows against the pitch black of space. The *Baron's* burnt and shattered debris fell slowly into the gravity of the asteroid, which welcomed them to rest in the soft silt of its surface, enveloping them like a grave.

Captain Morden looked down at her command screen. "Chief Smith, please hail the Black Fox."

She tapped the screen with her stylus to show the camera view to starboard. The smaller ship was holding position only a few hundred yards from the *Verdun*. It looked to be an ancient vessel, with no visible fighter bays or any other modern equipment except for the trappings of a mercenary vessel. The hull was studded with a mishmash of older weapons, including five triple eight-inch turrets and several missile launchers. Its original, slick black paint had worn off, leaving only dull, rusted, pockmarked armor. Centuries ago, the *Black Fox* must have been a formidable destroyer. But now?

Despite the bolted-on FTL pods on the ships rear, Morden doubted that the *Fox* was even sturdy enough for translight, let alone combat.

So much for local assistance.

Morden heard the radio crackle faintly as the older chief petty officer sent the customary greeting and request for radio contact. A loud pop echoed through the room as Smith piped the response onto the bridge speaker.

"Verdun, Captain Paul Mostoff. We wish to dock immediately." The voice was deep, rough, and had a strong accent Morden had never heard before.

"This emergency has gotten worse," Mostoff continued. "We lost another freighter, the Baron. We must move fast if we are to prevent more attacks."

Morden drummed her fingers on her armrest. Something about Mostoff's voice made her uneasy. She couldn't put a name to it, but something was off. Morden wished she could see his face, read the expression on it, even though she knew it was impossible. Only a laser link between Royal Alliance ships could enable real-time, face-to-face communication.

Morden cleared her throat. "Certainly, Captain. My name is Captain Kim Morden. I am looking forward to working with you. Please prepare to receive one of our corvettes. It should reach you within fifteen minutes."

"Agreed." Mostoff's terse reply was tense, hostile even.

Morden pursed her lips, stood, and walked to the communications console. "Mr. Smith, have Major Osterman assemble his best fire team in the launch bay. Full dress uniforms and armor. I want an honor guard for our guest."

Smith nodded. "Yes, ma'am."

Urquhart's voice called out from behind Morden. "Something wrong, ma'am?"

Only in my gut.

Morden turned to look down at the younger officer in the pilot's den. "Just being cautious."

"But isn't he here to help us?"

Morden didn't respond, but strolled back toward her chair.

Commander Holsey looked up from her console. "So I wasn't the only one who felt Mostoff seemed off?"

"It certainly was not the response I was expecting." Lt. Wilcox also chimed in.

Morden cut the conversation short. "Commander Holsey, I want you to get Lieutenant Voth and secure the corridor to the fighter squadron crew room outside of bay two."

"Aye Captain." Holsey stood and started toward the door. "I suggest we also wear sidearms."

"No, that's going too far. I won't risk picking a fight."

Holsey stopped in her tracks. "I strongly disagree."

"Commander, Major Osterman will be armed. There will be one Mostoff and five of us with Voth and Wilcox in the room. If he does something…unsavory, we will be more than able to handle it."

"Captain."

Morden could feel the woman's anger bubbling below the surface. "There is more to this mission than just solving a mystery. This region must remain stable. If this Mostoff has ulterior motives, so be it. But he is our only contact in the region, and I don't want to offend him by starting off too aggressively."

Holsey locked eyes with Morden. "And if he is trying to deceive us? How many lives are you willing to trade for success?"

Morden met Holsey's eyes, willing her voice to remain even. "Commander, that old rust bucket wouldn't last thirty seconds against the Verdun. This is a battlecruiser of the line."

The bridge was silent for a moment, and Morden was keenly aware that all eyes were on her and Holsey.

Finally, Holsey grinned, though Morden doubted the expression was sincere.

"Good point," Holsey said at last. "May I at least suggest we put Shield squadron in the air, as an escort?"

Morden felt the tension in the room relax, saw everyone return their attention to their consoles.

"Good suggestion, Commander. See to it."

How much longer?

Holsey drummed her fingers on the table, her eyes locked on the door.

Nothing.

She sighed, the odors of grease, oil, and coffee mixed together, filled her nose. She let her eyes travel for the tenth time over the interior of the rear crew room. A small coffee machine by the door. A smudged, built-in refrigerator. Work coveralls hanging on a set of hooks. Alcoves filled with tools, welders' face shields, and small spare parts. Old recruitment posters showing a Milipa fighter falling in flames as a Sparrowhawk raced into star-streaked space beside a pair of Stallions. A couple issues of *Alliance Servicemember's Magazine* sitting on the table.

It wasn't the most elegant place to hold a meeting, but judging by the apparent condition of the *Black Fox*, Holsey supposed it would make Mostoff feel more at ease than just about anywhere else on the *Verdun*.

What was taking them so long?

She stood up, walked around, then sat back down again. Why was she so nervous? Morden had been right. The *Verdun's* mission wasn't only a search-and-rescue. The Frontin were evil. They couldn't risk letting the Triangle destabilize and invite the monsters to move closer to the Alliance.

Why hadn't she seen that for herself? The moment Morden had declined her suggestion to wear sidearms, she'd reacted.

Maybe try thinking next time, okay?

The door swung open, and Morden, Voth, and Wilcox appeared, followed by Major Osterman and a tall, middle-aged man.

Mostoff.

She stared at him. Holsey couldn't help but think of all those historical images of pirates she had seen as a girl. The long, disheveled black beard and hair, lean, muscled body covered with tattoos, and an unkempt uniform, if it could be called that. He wore a red shirt so dark that it was almost black, knee-high leather boots, and worn pants that seemed to be right out of a child's fantasy. The man's hard, brown eyes were cold and distant, but he exuded a confidence that filled the room.

Holsey shifted in her seat. Morden may be in the stronger position, but over-confidence had lost many battles. This man was dangerous. Looking at him glaring at the captain as he shook her hand, Holsey couldn't help but notice how feeble Morden seemed in comparison. Instinctively, Holsey rested her arm on her right hip, but felt nothing where a holster should be.

God, what I'd give for a sidearm.

The man released the captain's hand and dropped heavily into a chair nearest the door. Morden sat down on Holsey's right side, Voth and Wilcox on the other. Osterman remained standing near the wall at the man's side.

Mostoff leaned back, crossed his arms. "Captain Morden, let's get this clear. I don't want you here. The Triangle doesn't need the Alliance military any more than it needs its companies, bureaucrats, and inspectors. My administrator has told me to help you, and I will, but don't be confused. I am not your friend."

Holsey studied the man's impassive expression. She could hear some hidden emotion crackling in his deep, slurred, almost-Slavic accent.

"Captain Mostoff, you are welcome to your own political views." Morden's tone was strong and direct. the man's negativity obviously hadn't shaken her. "Nor are we interested in the internal affairs of the Triangle. We are here for one reason: Your leaders requested our help. Judging from the condition of your ship, you couldn't handle a Frontin freighter."

Movement caught Holsey's eye. She glanced at Major Osterman who had angled the weapon side of his body away from Mostoff and dropped a hand to his hip. He looked casual, dapper even, but Holsey knew it was a game, a careful plan to not call attention to himself, to keep his weapon out of Mostoff's reach should the man make any moves. Let the privateer glower at Morden. Osterman was the only real danger to Mostoff, even if the man wasn't bright enough to realize it. Holsey felt a twinge of emotion arc through her.

If things were different, that would be you, Marine.

"If I wanted your opinion on my ship's capabilities I would have asked," Mostoff responded with clear distain. "I may not be fancy like you navy bullies, but I can get the job done."

Wilcox's smooth voice cut in from Holsey's left. "Glad to hear it. Why don't we get down to it, then?"

Mostoff nodded. "As I said, I think we can handle this ourselves. There is no question. It must be the miners. Thirty years ago, they attacked my colony, as well as Barnerious II. They felt we were taking advantage of them, working them like slaves. They lost, the cowards."

Wilcox grinned and Holsey fought the urge to do the same.

What a nut!

Wilcox looked down at his screen. "If they lost, why would they dare target cargo ships? Especially since, according to your information, three of the ships were attached to the mining community."

The man laughed darkly. "They still whine. They compare us to your disgusting Alliance corporations, taking advantage of everything and everyone. But our government is not yours. We do not look the other way. Our trade with them is a fair agreement."

Morden opened her mouth to say something, but Mostoff kept talking, his voice rising. "They are inbred trash, swine. They attacked those ships to get their cargo back, sell the same ore twice, use the money to buy over-priced junk from the Alliance."

Mostoff almost spat the last word.

Why would someone so hostile towards the Alliance be chosen as our liaison?

Morden waved her hand. "We are not here to debate trade contracts or your opinions on them. If you think it's the miners, why haven't you stopped them?"

Mostoff sneered at Morden. "We have no evidence, and the colonial leaders don't want to act without it. I follow orders."

"Then why are you so sure who is to blame?"

"I am from here, I know. If you are not complete idiots, you will listen to me. There are many different factions among the mining cooperatives. Their asteroid fields are dense and difficult to navigate. Only the most experienced freighter captains can go in. It would take hundreds of ships to search the entire thing for proof. If it were easy, I would have done it by now."

"I see. What do you suggest, Captain?"

"Search the asteroid fields near the third and fifth navigation buoy. All the ships have gone missing in that general area."

Holsey leaned forward. "That's it? Go look in some asteroids?" She spoke slowly, letting a hint of derision color her voice. "What can you tell us about the colonies? Do you have specific suspects? We are not muscle for you to exploit as workers. You have to have something else."

The man locked eyes with her. "No, nothing else. I told you where to look. If Barnerious II were behind this, our spies would have caught them."

She laughed as her frustration rose. He was too focused on the miners to the exclusion of other possibilities. What was he hiding? She needed to get him uncomfortable, to break his persona.

Wilcox chimed in again. "You must have some idea of the best approach to search the asteroid fields. Maps? Homing beacons for each mining facility?"

"Maps are all old, back from the days of the Alliance companies. The miners have beacons but don't share frequencies with us. They want to stay hidden. When we run cargo, they come get us, guide us to the loading facilitates. We use colonial beacons to navigate out."

Holsey saw an opening, she curled her lips into the largest smile she could. If this bastard wanted an arrogant foe, she would oblige. "You have been searching for evidence for over a month, and that's all you've got? No wonder you crawl on your bellies for our help! You're downright incompetent!" Holsey let her voice take on an almost theatrical scorn. "You don't care about the ships! This is about getting maps to carry out some idiotic vendetta. Since you can't seem to map the asteroids yourself—" she paused for effect. "—You need *real* soldiers to do it."

Captain Mostoff's eyes bulged as he started to stand, and Holsey saw Osterman's hand move toward his weapon.

Mostoff slammed a fist on the table. "How dare you? Those are my people who died! The captain of the Baron was my friend."

Bingo.

It was the opening Holsey needed, a chance to push Mostoff and get some answers.

Morden cut in. "I apologize for my executive officer. She spoke out of turn. We just want to know what's going on. Who stands to benefit the most from the lost cargo?"

Holsey gaped at Morden, felt heat rise to her face. How could Morden not see what was going on? As long as this backwater crony felt he was in control, they were at a dead end. For all they knew, he could be involved somehow, part of a ploy to use Alliance ships to solve internal quarrels. Was Morden too incompetent to see that possibility, or did she just not care?

Mostoff eased himself into his chair. "Barnerious II, obviously. They are economically stronger. The Alliance favors them in trade deals. My colony needs that cargo."

"According to the manifest you sent, most of the crews lost were from Barnerious II. Are you suggesting they would kill their own people?" Morden pressed again.

Mostoff rolled his eyes. "I already told you, it's the miners. Barnerious II is too feckless to do something this bold, even if it did benefit them. Maybe they bought off some miners to do it. It's possible. I wouldn't put it beyond them to kill their own for money."

Morden frowned. "Have all your physical data sent to me ASAP. I will brief you on our plan when it's ready."

He scowled. "A plan? You waste time. If your ship is so powerful, you would deal with the scum now!"

Morden stood up, and gestured toward the door. "For a man so capable of handling everything yourself, you seem overly concerned with my approach. No time will be wasted. Major, escort him to the corvette."

Mostoff stood, his eyes burning right at Holsey. "You are lucky, little girl, that you are here. On my ship, I'd have killed you for that."

"If I were on your ship, I would be just as intellectually… talented as you are." Holsey returned his sneer. "I wouldn't have noticed the holes in your story."

The look in Mostoff's eyes as Major Osterman led him from the room had Holsey wishing for her sidearm again.

Holsey waited until he left earshot, then turned to Morden. "Captain, why didn't you let me press him? He is hiding something. Period."

Voth spoke for the first time since Mostoff entered the room. "He certainly looks menacing, but I agree with the commander. He clearly feels he is in control. Shocking him, making him angry, might break through the bullshit."

Morden nodded. "Very likely, but, to be frank, we don't behave like that on the Verdun. He is a representative of a foreign government. Like it or not, on this ship that means he will be treated with respect, even when he won't return the courtesy."

Holsey could feel her temper flaring again. "We can't just ignore this! He could be the person behind this whole situation. Looking weak may make us seem vulnerable. Do we even know for sure that there *are* missing ships? This could be a ploy. It wouldn't be the first time someone tried to draw the Alliance into their own power games."

Wilcox shook his head. "The captain's right. Regardless of how weak we may look, this is the strongest ship in the region. We have the power here. There is no need to flaunt it, or make our dealings with them more hostile than they need to be. Following diplomatic protocol is the right thing to do."

Holsey felt her checks warming again. Since when had Morden been a slave to the rules? "I understand protocol, but we have a mission to complete. We shouldn't allow this man to stand in our way and possibly cost us lives."

Morden raised her chin slightly. "That's not the only reason. I don't trust him either, Commander. He *is* hiding something, either intentionally or because of his blind anger towards the Alliance and the miners. I doubt he even realizes how angry he is."

"He has a sore spot," Wilcox agreed. "That friend he mentioned."

Morden continued. "If he is involved, he'll slip up, and we will be right there. If he isn't, then his familiarity with the area is valuable, regardless of his motives. Bottom line: Until we can get more information, there is no reason to burn bridges. Besides, I don't see the threat. It would take a lot of rust-buckets like that to take us down, even in a surprise attack."

Holsey was silent for a moment. She hated to admit it, but Morden was making sense. "I agree that it's unlikely, but I think caution is still in order. An attack could cost lives — Alliance lives — that shouldn't be wasted on this shithole."

Wilcox laughed. "We are the ones in control of the situation, even if this Mostoff doesn't realize it. He won't catch us flat-footed."

Morden nodded, stepping towards the door. "Exactly, Mr. Wilcox. I think he is right about one thing: We need to start with the asteroids."

Voth cocked his head to the side. "Why?"

Morden looked back. "If you were a privateer, raiding ships full of raw ore, where would you hide?"

CHAPTER 7

Morden rubbed her temples, trying to dull the ache that had been slowly building all night. Captain Mostoff had been less than helpful. There were still too many pieces of this puzzle missing. Why had they called for help? Did one group really benefit more than the others? What was it about each specific freighter that had caused it be the target of attacks? Could Mostoff be trusted?

Morden groaned, stood up, and paced back and forth across the room.

She knew what she needed to do—search the damn asteroid field. Mostoff may have been shady, but it made sense. Ignoring the political bullshit, it was the only area in the Triangle where ships could hide easily. The more she studied the asteroid fields, the more she worried. Clearly, the Triangle was far more politically unstable than intelligence had indicated. If the Frontin got a foothold here, with those asteroids to hide in…

She couldn't allow that to happen.

This mission was more important than she'd originally thought, and she wouldn't let it fail.

Her stomach growled again, bringing her mind back to the needs of her body. Her eyelids sagged, heavy. She needed to sleep, needed to eat, but hadn't been able to clear her thoughts long enough to do either. She stared at the plate of food resting on her desk. A shepherd's pie in rich, brown gravy, fresh steamed vegetables, a roll, and a dark, now ice-cold, cup of coffee.

She sat back down, forcing her hand to pick up the fork. Muscle memory took over, skewering a large glob of shepherd's pie for her third bite in the last two hours. It was good. Even cold, the gravy was excellent. The *Verdun*'s chef had clearly tried for brownie points. Unfortunately for him, Morden's current state of mind had prevented her from enjoying his labors.

She looked over at the small bookshelves built into the wall of her cabin. They'd been full when Captain Knight had occupied the room, but were now totally bare. The shelves screamed back at her, seemed to accuse her of inaction.

What would you do?

Morden lowered her fork again. She felt blind, lost in a world of political conflict outside of the realm of her military training, although that same training was crying danger. What she needed was more information.

She closed her eyes again and listened to her lungs sucking in cool air.

Think it through, just one more time.

The *Verdun* was powerful, easily the most powerful vessel in the region. The most logical place for those ships to be was the asteroid field. In that kind of dense space, a ship the size of the *Verdun* would have difficulty maneuvering and be vulnerable. Even a poor strategist could easily use that fact to his advantage against the *Verdun*. Sooner or later, the *Verdun* would have to enter there.

If they were attacked at close range, their most viable defensive option would be — Morden bolted upright, feeling a surge of excitement. It had been in front of her the entire time.

How had she missed it?

She reached for her console, opened the interface, and hastily typed in commands to the bridge. She would need to act fast to get this planned.

Seconds later, the voice of Chief Petty Officer Baudouin broke over the ship's intercom. "Commanders Frost and Wilcox to the briefing room immediately."

Morden stood up, straightened her jacket, and buttoned it back into place. She crossed the room in two strides, her dinner and coffee still sitting on her table.

Captain Mostoff shifted his bodyweight, again. He had been sitting on the bridge for hours. He wanted to hit something. Those Alliance women had been so arrogant — so *Alliance*. The readouts from the *Fox's* sensors ran across his monitor for the third time. The warship in front of him was immense. It was hard to not let its size and large number of guns distract him from his mission.

He took in a deep breath, the smell of rust and mildew hanging in the old, musty air. No matter how many times the ducts had been cleaned, the scent remained, a sign of the *Fox's* many years of use.

He smiled. The odor was familiar, comforting, so unlike the pure, clean atmosphere of the *Verdun*. It calmed him, strengthened him. Let the Alliance have their perfect air. People in the Triangle were stronger than that. Mostoff was proud of his home, his colony.

He would defend it.

The Alliance had been causing problems for too long. Like the miners, they were cowards and crooks. If it wasn't corporations price-gouging them one day for parts for the *Fox*, it was bureaucrats from their new labor government trying to regulate their rights to trade. The Alliance manipulated the lives of people they had no business harassing, hiding from justice behind the massive power of their warships and self-righteous idealism.

The villains!

Mostoff slammed his fist into his armrest. He saw all the heads on the bridge turn. He ignored their hesitant, sideways glances.

He knew they were on edge, but he didn't care. He would finish his mission regardless of the cost. Mostoff had been a Triangle captain for too long — thirty years in all. He wouldn't fail now, regardless of who stood in his way

He opened one of his shirt pockets, slid out the copy of his orders he had kept with him. Mostoff let his eyes flow over the words, rereading them one more time. He tried to imagine his commandant's face as he'd typed it out. What was written between the lines? He tried to pick out the hidden subtext of his leaders' agenda.

Mostoff refolded the paper. "Officer Marsh, please run a check on all weapons. When the time comes, we must not hesitate."

"Aye, sir," his second-in-command responded from his left, the dimly lit bridge obscuring his face.

The *Fox* was old, decaying. She had seen centuries of combat, but she was still a good ship. Mostoff would not allow this to be her final mission. It was the blood of his enemies, not his own, that would be wasted — no matter how powerful they were.

Callista was breathing hard — the muscles in her legs were burning. It felt great. It had been weeks since she had enjoyed a good run, and she was determined to savor every step. She reached the top of the Section A stairwell, the freezing air of the engine cooling system blasting her damp skin. She longed for warmer clothes than her old academy T-shirt, but nothing was going to stop her before she hit five miles.

Her physical fitness was important to her. This was the beginning of her journey, not the end. Conditioning would keep her strong for the long run. The hours of reading over navigation reports had to be worked off at a substantially accelerated rate.

"Hold up, Lieutenant." Commander Holsey's voice brought her forward motion to a halt. She jogged in place, waiting for her superior to catch up.

Callista looked around behind her to see the commander come running through a hatch on her starboard side, dressed in a similar light T-shirt and running pants.

The woman stopped beside her. "Great minds think alike. Nothing like a late-night run to make sure you sleep well. Mind if I join you?"

"Not at all, ma'am." Callista was surprised to see the woman smiling. She couldn't help smiling herself. After the incident on the bridge, she had hoped for an opportunity to interact with Holsey off duty. The woman always seemed businesslike, hostile even, at least where the captain was concerned. Callista was going to get to know the woman behind the military bravado.

Everyone needs a friend.

They started up the staircase that led toward the rear fifteen-inch turret. It was the longest run on the ship, the most intense.

Callista spoke up, trying to break the ice. "So, Commander, what do you do for fun? When you're not searching the ass end of space, I mean?"

The commander chuckled. "We're doing it now. I used to run track. Marines don't have fun. They fight."

The old inter-branch jab made the younger woman laugh. "Marine, huh? You don't seem the type. Too smart."

"I was on the smart side." The pair came to another intersection and continued up the stairs. The effort made Callista's breathing — and talking — harder.

"I paint." Callista could see Holsey start to smile again, felt a small jab of embarrassment. "I know, I know. Art isn't exactly the hard-nose stuff of soldiers, but it relaxes me."

She tried not to grimace, she hadn't meant to sound so defensive. Many officers didn't understand her passion for something as trivial as art.

Holsey laughed. "I don't know, Lieutenant. Generals used to paint, write, working as artists as well as soldiers. It's the sign of a strong mind."

I knew there was a person in there.

Urquhart looked over at Holsey. "You said, 'marine.' Why did you move over to shipboard duties, ma'am?"

Holsey's pace broke. She seemed to go cold again, the personality Callista had witnessed for a moment seemed to fade back into the stoic, businesslike officer she had gotten used to.

Callista tried to back track. "Not that it's any of my business."

"It's all right." Holsey avoided her gaze.

They ran in silence for several minutes, the only sound breaking the tension the hard fall of their boots against metal grating. The final flight of stairs was approaching quickly, and Callista could just make out the light murmur of voices coming down from the turret.

Holsey spoke flatly, betraying a hint of emotion. "I was injured badly in a Frontin raid against a listening post about eight years ago. My back was broken in five places. I had internal injuries, a concussion, and other traumas."

The pair reached the top of the stairs and cruised to the end of the corridor. Holsey began walking in circles and stretching, trying to help her muscles cool down. Callista watched the woman for a moment before doing the same. She couldn't imagine what it must have been like to try to recover from something like that. There were no scars, no outward signs of trauma that Callista could see on Holsey's body. Callista never would have guessed she had been so badly wounded.

"How did you recover so quickly?" she blurted out.

Great, Callista. I have to stop this habit of speaking before I think.

"Hard work. Discipline. I decided I wouldn't allow the kind of incompetence that led to that massacre to ever happen again. I couldn't do that from a medical bunk or behind a desk. Marines die. We give our lives willingly, but not stupidly."

Callista almost shivered. The tone in the woman's voice was intense, hard. It made her soft, small figure look sharp and fierce. A marine, finally visible under all the professional, naval reserve. Callista had always wanted to be that kind of woman, tough and unwavering, even if her bubbly sense of humor was more of an asset than most people thought.

"Commander Holsey, please report to the briefing room." The voice of the CSO on duty echoed loudly in the corridor.

Holsey smiled again. "I'm glad someone else around here knows how to stay in shape. See you later."

Callista watched as Holsey entered the gun turret. Using its elevator would be the fastest way to the bridge. There was more going on with Holsey than met the eye. She looked down at her pedometer, she still had several thousand steps left to work off after so many weeks of inactivity. She wheeled about and started running back down the corridor towards the stairs.

CHAPTER 8

Holsey ran her hand through her hair. "Are you serious?"

Morden uncrossed her arms. "Absolutely. It covers ground faster. We need answers for the questions that our *friend* Mostoff won't answer. I can't believe that there isn't some sort of political agenda at work here. I don't trust Mostoff. I don't want him operating without oversight. Putting a team on the Fox will give us eyes and ears on site." She motioned at Commander Frost.

Frost nodded. "I think we all agree that the asteroid field is the only real place to begin searching."

"Absolutely." Holsey looked down at the console in front of her, reexamining the asteroid field. It was unusually dense, full of heavy metals and other sensor obstacles. Morden was right. If Holsey were hiding stolen cargo, this is where she would do it.

She ran the details of the mission over in her head again. They would create two groups. The first would be the *Verdun*. The second would consist of forty fighters and enough accompanying support staff to allow them to operate independently. The *Verdun* would travel to the two colonies and try to shake things up enough to get the intelligence they needed. The fighter detachment, housed onboard the *Black Fox*, would begin to search the asteroid field and observe members of the *Fox's* crew to see what they could dig up.

It was a good plan. It would allow them to cover ground quickly, and, as much as she hated to admit it, the risks were acceptable. But not all threats could be assessed beforehand.

"Once we enter the asteroid field, our size would hamstring our combat capabilities," Frost continued. "If ambushed, my fighters would deploy to engage the enemy while the Verdun maneuvered into a position we could fight from."

Holsey looked back up. "Obviously, but if we detach half of our air wing, it gives any enemy ground position on the colonies a better chance to nail us while we are in orbit. The operations detachment on board the Black Fox may also be stranded without support if Mostoff acts."

Morden smiled. "Mostoff won't do anything with the Verdun orbiting his colony. He wouldn't risk provoking us to fire on his people. If his colony is our opponent, then the Verdun is a pawn for some political game. Even down forty fighters, it would take a large number of mercenary ships like the Fox to more than tickle us in open space. If Mostoff acted against our detachment, it would expose whatever he or his people are hiding, or at least point us in the right direction."

Crap! That makes sense.

Holsey's stomach turned. No matter how logical, she couldn't help but feel Morden had to be making a mistake somehow.

Wilcox, directly across the table from her, spoke for the first time. "I agree with the Captain. This move will surprise everyone. Even working together, I can't believe that these colonies have enough warships — and I use the word loosely — to attack both the Verdun and the fighter detachment simultaneously."

"True, but they could destroy the fighter detachment while it's alone. Even with sensor drones relaying data, it wouldn't be hard to catch the fighters off guard in all that junk." Holsey looked at Morden, trying to read her motives, the woman's intentions hidden under her military poise. Was this as smart a tactical move as it seemed, or another self-serving attempt to look good to her superiors?

Commander Frost shook his head. "Mostoff follows causes, regardless of how misguided. He's a patriot. He wouldn't risk the colonies to knock off forty fighters. Besides, my squadrons have an advantage over ships that size in such close quarters, and I can't see that piece of shit taking on even one of our Stallions. This plan allows us to watch Mostoff, investigate the colonies, and search the asteroids at the same time. It's a clever strategy. Hats off to you, Captain! I can see why the Verdun was tasked with this assignment."

Morden blushed, shifting in her chair as Frost beamed at her. Holsey almost laughed. She couldn't believe what she'd just seen. Had Frost's praise embarrassed Morden? Holsey was all too aware of Frost's gregariousness. He never seemed to shut up. She knew first hand that this kind of loose fraternization was an undesirable trait for a military officer. It opened them up to too much pain.

Holsey shook off the thought. "It does expose the members of the expeditionary force to extreme risks if we are wrong. We shouldn't be risking the lives of our personnel on assumptions. We just don't have enough information."

Frost waved his hand dismissively. "Risk is part of military life, Commander. Based on the best information we have, this is the right move. It gives us the best chance to succeed quickly."

Holsey felt her face flush. "I understand risk, Frost, but our job as leaders is to make sure that risk is measured, acceptable."

Morden interjected quickly. "I don't place my crew in harm's way lightly. These are acceptable risks, given the circumstances."

Holsey leaned back in her seat. "Very well. Who would head up the expeditionary force? We'd be representing the Alliance on a foreign vessel. We'd need a flag officer present."

Morden shifted her weight, looking right at Holsey. "I was thinking you could do it. You will show the appropriate caution, and your background as a marine will be invaluable if something goes wrong. Major Osterman will select his team. The rest of the contingent is up to you. Take whomever and whatever you need."

Holsey nodded her approval. "Commander Frost, I'll leave the selection of the squadrons to you. I'd like to take Lt. Voth as my second officer. He knows the crew, and, given his position as master at arms, he should have a good rapport with the marines."

"Agreed." Morden turned to face Wilcox. "Have Urquhart and Stetler prepare an emergency rendezvous point and get it to the commander before she leaves."

Frost cocked his head to the side. "Ma'am?"

"We'll be far outside of normal radio range, and any messages or communications drones we send will be operating with a lag. If anything happens, I want a known point where we can meet if we're able."

Realization hit Holsey. They would be far apart, basically unreachable. This was a lot of trust for Morden to put on her.

Like a first officer.

Wilcox drummed his fingers on the table. "I'll get them on it right away."

Morden stood. "Great, then let's get started. Have Stetler set a course for the edge of the asteroid field. Commander, I want your detachment ready to go within twenty-four hours. Dismissed."

Holsey stood up, strode towards the door. She felt better than she had since coming aboard, almost excited. This was a solid plan, even if it carried risk. Morden had given her an opportunity to be a leader, work with the marines again. She had also treated her with respect, put her in a position to safeguard the lives of the expeditionary force.

Morden's voice stopped her. "Commander, a moment."

Holsey turned and looked at the captain. It was still hard to look directly at someone who had cost her so much. "Yes, ma'am."

"I just wanted to wish you luck. I know that you don't trust me, but I trust you. You're the right person for this."

Holsey stood stiffly, not sure what to say. "Thank you, ma'am." She saluted.

Morden returned the salute. "Commander, bring our people home safe."

L ess than twenty-four hours later, Lieutenant Hillman sat in his Stallion, letting his senses join with his craft, enjoying the whine of his canopy's hydraulic motors as it finished lowering into place with a click. He could feel his heart start to race as the artificial atmosphere hit his nostrils. The internal lighting flickered as each of the indicator lights on his holodisplay turned green one by one.

Hillman keyed his mike. "Flight, Knight Rider. All systems read green."

"Understood, Knight Rider."

Hillman reached down, checking his harness. He felt the familiar jolt as the catapult arm attached itself to the underside of the striker's launch plate. The craft began to move from its customary berth to over the hatch to its vertical launch tube. He could hear the floor panel beneath screeching loudly as it moved, simultaneously turning the striker ninety degrees down into the launch tube. Hillman flipped the last few switches, locking his bird into the *Verdun's* launch control system. He could feel the pressure on his chest as his harness held him in place.

His radio crackled. "Knight Rider, launch when ready."

Hillman flipped his engines on, his heart leaping again as the motors roared to life. He bounced slightly in his seat, eyes locked on the indicator light on top of the launch tube. It flashed green.

Hillman smiled, slammed forward on both sticks, kicking down on the right foot pedal. The Stallion bucked, rocketed forward, blasted into space.

"Knight Rider, away. Raptors, form on me."

Hillman pulled hard on his left stick, space outside the striker blurring momentarily as the Stallion flipped 180 degrees on its x-axis. He pulled back on both sticks, his stomach lurching as the craft decelerated. He loved watching the rest of his squadron spill out of the ship's underside.

"Command to Raptors. Fly escort for Corvette 3A. Detachment is leaving. ETA to touchdown on the Fox is five minutes." Hillman clapped his hands together. His squadron was not only the lead squadron for this mission, but they got to escort the XO's Corvette.

The good assignments go to the best.

Hillman reached up, flipped on his squadron's laser link system. "Raptors, escort formation alpha. I have point. Let's get the boss safely to that old rust bucket."

There was a general echo of acknowledgement from his team.

He smiled, turning off the laser link and letting his next order go out over the radio. "Keep your eyes on the asteroid field. God knows what could be lurking in there. Deathwatch and Tomahawk."

Hillman never really cared for personalized call signs. The group call signs — Raptor One, Raptor Two — made sense. It kept people organized in combat. Personalized names were a distraction, especially over laser links where no one but the rest of squadron could hear them, but he never underestimated the value of intimidation. There was nothing like sinister-sounding call signs to scare the crap out of a lurking foe.

He looked down at his holodisplay, watching gleefully as Tomahawk and Deathwatch turned, training their forward guns on the asteroid field, their top two engines moving them sideways along with the rest of the convoy.

Hillman felt a glow of pride. He knew the squadrons that had been left behind were jealous, especially Alpha squadron. They were the only Stallion squadron left on the *Verdun*.

Even though escorting the Corvette was a hundred-meter milk run, it felt good to know his team would begin to search in earnest, and maybe, if they were lucky, get into some combat. The other three fighter squadrons were launching now, each ship rocketing on to his sensors one by one from the *Verdun's* twenty launch tubes — one more Striker squadron and two Sparrowhawk squadrons.

He had to admit they were forming up quickly, though not nearly as cleanly as his raptors. Hillman turned his ship towards the asteroid field, enjoying the momentary thrill of shifting inertia pushing and pulling his body before his stabilizers kicked in. He tapped his sensor controls, bringing the long-range sensor data up onto his holodisplay.

His eyes skimmed the information. The asteroid field must be made up of heavy metals or other materials that blocked sensors. There wasn't much to read.

This will be difficult.

Hillman looked out at the expanding cloud of rocks and dust in front of him. They were shifting slowly, eerily. He stared at the asteroids, and a chill moved up his spine chasing away the joy of being in the cockpit. He couldn't explain it, but he knew there was something out there, watching him. He was a hunter, and he would ensure that he and his would come out of the asteroids alive.

He watched as a group of small ships moved out from the belly of his enemy. He savored the image of his unsuspecting prey. He fought the urge to jump from cover, bear down on them, and bleed the life from every one of the filthy creatures the big ship carried. He could feel the rending of flesh and bone in his hands, smell the sweet aroma of decaying flesh and victory.

No, now wasn't the time.

He would be patient and clever. His vessel was powerful, but this quarry wasn't like his last. They weren't defenseless or stupid.

His eyes devoured the massive weapons covering its superstructure. He felt bitter, envy for its ability to deliver death and destruction. How such pathetic vermin had created such a tool was one of life's mysteries, a mystery he would solve by ripping its secrets from their dead hands. It would earn him his redemption. Victory would be his soon. The only other recourse was death.

The ships were landing now one by one on that trifling distraction of a target.

Patience, patience.

Soon, he would lure them to their end. Soon, he could bathe in their blood. Soon, their screams would fill his followers with joy.

Soon, this would all be over.

CHAPTER 9

"Touch down in three minutes." The pilot's voice broke through the dull murmur of the marine detachment inside the Corvette's passenger compartment.

Holsey reached down for the fifth time in as many minutes, letting her fingers glide over her sidearm. The cold steel of its slide felt familiar and comforting. She didn't have many opportunities aboard ship to strap her old companion to her hip. She couldn't help but feel excited. It was almost like being a marine again. Even if her navy blues didn't match the elegant steel gray of the marines' body armor, Holsey felt like she was home.

She looked around the bay, watching the twenty marines talking and laughing with each other. Osterman and Voth were kneeling next to one of the Ordnance Transportation Robots, affectionately called gun dogs, fiddling with some piece of equipment near the loading ramp.

Osterman finished talking to Voth, stood, and raised his hand to get the attention of everyone in the cabin. "People! Remember, this may not officially be a combat mission, but these colonials aren't friendlies. We could be walking into some serious shit. Be ready."

"Yes, sir!" The many voices reverberated loudly in the small space. Osterman started arranging his detachment to disembark. The eight in full dress uniforms — including their rifles — positioned themselves on either side of the ramp. The remaining marines were lining up at the back of the bay, bayonets attached.

Holsey signaled for Lieutenant Voth, who stood and started towards her. She could feel the ship's deceleration jets pushing against the floor of the *Black Fox's* landing bay.

Voth reached out, steadying himself on the wall. "Yes, ma'am."

Holsey tucked a stray strand of hair behind her ear. "If this goes south, our first order of business is to hold the transport bay. If we get control of the computer or the ship's bridge, we may be able to get the answers we need."

"Yes, ma'am, but is it possible you're overreacting?"

"Probably," Holsey continued. "If I go down, or it looks like we can't hold the bay, get as many of the marines as possible and get the hell out. Get into position."

"Yes, ma'am." Voth turned and walked quickly to the back of the bay, drawing his pistol.

Holsey stood, took her place in front of the marines. She looked up, waiting for the ramp light to turn green. She wished she were in the cockpit and could get a real look at the deck outside. Hopefully a rapid combat deployment would be enough to assert their control of the situation and prevent any hostility before it began.

The light flashed green, and the ramp dropped with a metal clang.

Holsey walked down the ramp quickly, sweeping her eyes back and forth, trying to take in as much detail as possible. She hadn't seen the armed party she had been expected, but the details of the room had her hand reaching for her holster. The room was small, even for a ship the size of the *Fox*, and very dim. What little light there was came from jury-rigged lamps patched together from industrial-style emergency bulbs, which bathed the room in an eerie, faint red light. The bay had one level and only one obvious exit, a set of double doors directly in front of the Corvette, where Captain Mostoff was standing, blocking the door. He seemed to be the only person present. There were no skiffs, no crates, no power loaders or cranes, not a single work crew. It was suspiciously deserted.

If we are attacked, there is nowhere to take cover.

Holsey couldn't make out a single control panel, but noticed a pair of small cameras in opposite corners of the ceiling. The bay's control center must be nearby, its personnel operating the doors remotely, using the cameras to monitor the room's activity.

Holsey wrinkled her nose, the musty smell of rust and mildew washing over her. It was the scent of decay and abandonment. Most Alliance stations and ships were old, sometimes many centuries older then the *Fox*, but the Alliance never would have allowed vital equipment to waste away like this. If this was the condition of one of the Triangle's best frigates, then Mostoff hadn't lied about the region's economic condition.

Mostoff opened his arms wide, a menacing smiling crossing his face. "Welcome aboard the Black Fox, Commander."

"Thank you, glad to be here." She tried to make her smile look genuine.

The old man laughed. "Please, no need for lies. I remember how you look at me. I hate you just as much as you hate me."

Holsey shook her head, glad that the lack of lighting would hide the heat she felt rising to her cheeks. "I don't hate you, Captain. I was frustrated by your unwillingness to help."

Maybe Morden was right about burning bridges.

"What my government chooses to share isn't my problem. I will only assist you as much as I am required. I am no diplomat." He glanced at the line of marines. "And neither are you, apparently."

She tried not to shiver at his ominous smile. "You're right, I'm not. My orders are to find those ships. That's my focus. What's yours?"

The old man's expression went blank. "I will see what your focus is. Until then, you and your dogs stay here, in this bay. Nowhere else. I don't trust you."

Holsey took a step forward. "Unacceptable, Captain. We can't do our jobs if we're stuck in here." She laughed, a harsh sound even to her own ears. "Don't worry. Seizing this rust-bucket is of no interest to us."

She regretted her words instantly.

Mostoff's eyes bulged, his tone dropped. "Rust-bucket? Not everything is about technology, little girl."

Great going, Emma, you idiot.

She had to get access to the ship if her team was going to get answers. Morden had been right — they needed Mostoff's cooperation.

Mostoff was still speaking, his fists clenched at his side. "I wouldn't even let one of your admirals treat me like that. This is my ship. My rules."

Holsey smiled as sweetly as she could muster. "I apologize. I only meant we can increase the efficiency of our search if we have access to other areas. But you're right." She held out her hands to either side. "This is your ship. I'll let my team know we will stay here."

Silence hung in the bay as Mostoff stared at her, his expression blank.

Major Osterman piped up from behind Holsey. "Company, at ease. Prepare to re-embark. Commander, we can work just as comfortably in the Corvette as we can in this piece of shit."

Holsey, opened her mouth to discipline the major but she was too late.

Mostoff leaned forward. "Fuck you, you arrogant bastards! You think you are in charge here? Think again."

Holsey heard several clanking noises coming one after another from above them. She looked up, and her blood froze. Cut into the walls of the upper deck were twelve or thirteen gun ports. Rifle barrels were poking out and taking aim at the Alliance contingent.

Holsey heard bolts clicking loudly behind her as the marines chambered their first rounds.

She raised her hands. "Marines, hold fast."

There was almost no sound in the room, and Holsey felt that familiar sense of time distortion that seemed to accompany combat. Her heart was beating so fast she could swear the whole room could hear it. She had to salvage this situation, make it work.

She took a deep breath. "I apologize again, Captain. Marines aren't known for their tact." She turned, fixed Osterman with what she hoped was a scathing stare.

He rolled his eyes. "Yeah, I'm sorry."

She raised an eyebrow.

"I'm sorry, *sir*," Osterman added.

Holsey turned back to Mostoff, waited for the captain to make a move. He just stood there, staring at her, his lips curving into a half smile.

"Captain." She started again, picking her words carefully. "There is no reason for this. No one is suggesting you give us access to the more sensitive areas of your ship, just the areas that we need to analyze data. The captain on the Baron was a friend, right? I know what it's like to lose people. We want the same things, you and I. Let's get the job done."

Mostoff seemed to consider her for a moment longer, nodded. "Alright. I will grant your request, but know that the only reason I spared you is to find my missing comrades. I could have killed you, and I would have enjoyed it. This is my ship. Don't forget it."

Holsey nodded, lowered her hands. "Thank you."

Mostoff turned his back on her, cocking his head to the side. "I will send someone down to assist you moving. No one leaves this bay, or any other area, without escorts. You are guests, but not free guests."

He walked out of the room without saying another word, and the gun ports clanged shut, leaving the Alliance crew alone.

Holsey heard the entire contingent sigh. She still felt uneasy. She should have listened to Morden.

Who would have ever thought that?

She heard Major Osterman's boots on the metal grating behind her, felt him place his hand on her shoulder. "I'm sorry, ma'am. I thought if I got him mad—"

Holsey turned, cutting him off. "So did I, but it clearly won't work. We need to walk carefully."

Voth came running down the ramp. "Commander, great job! I thought we were deep-fried there. I can't believe he gave in like that! Guess I still don't get diplomacy."

She laughed. "Give in? Is that what you saw? He wanted to show me who was in charge. He gave us access, but only on his terms. We have a mission to complete. Keep focused, and let's not fuck this up."

The two men nodded, turned, and walked away. She could hear the major starting to bark orders as Voth disappeared back into the ship to brief the flight crew. She sighed, allowing herself to relax for the first time, running her eyes around the room again, hoping that she'd spontaneously develop precognitive abilities or x-ray vision. She had talked them into this hornets' nest, but getting along here was going to be another matter.

Mostoff stood rigidly on the opposite side of the door, grinding his teeth. He had done his job, allowed them access to his ship. Orders were orders. He would execute them regardless of how it made his blood boil.

He listened to the sounds of footsteps and hydraulic lifts on the other side of the door. Mostoff swallowed. Having so many of those people so close was revolting.

This Commander Holsey was smart — a complete bitch, but smart. He would not have guessed that from his first encounter with her. He would have to be cautious. Like all Alliance criminals, she was rude and unpleasant and hid her agenda. He couldn't fathom any reasons for those snobs to need access to the *Fox* to complete the mission, but having the Commander's detachment spread out around the ship would make his job easier.

There was too much at stake.

Mostoff reached out, tapping the small communications pad on the side of the door.

"Mostoff to Bridge. I want a team to assist our guests. Now. Make sure they are well armed."

Morden looked up at the unfamiliar constellations of Derek's' triangle. The observation dome was empty, peaceful. It had been several months since she'd had the opportunity to visit and relax. This was the *Verdun's* only dome, a throwback to the original twenty-five Alliance capital ships. The *Verdun* was one of the newest ships in the Alliance, barely eight years old, built solely for combat in the line of battle. Big glass domes that allowed you to see stars weren't practical. They created a weakness in the ship's armor that Milipa guns could exploit. Many older ships still had dozens of domes peppering their hulls, their original telescopes and charting equipment intact. Newer ships like the *Verdun* had only one or two as a backup in case the navigation equipment failed.

Prior to sensor drones, accurate sensors, and shipboard AI matrices, it had been extremely difficult to get good, long-range navigational data. These domes had allowed people to take navigational readings or observe enemy movements in combat using more rudimentary means. But the *Verdun's* mostly remained unused, an empty room, complete with retractable shudders, sitting on the underside of the ship just aft of the launch bays.

Regardless of its purpose — or lack thereof — it was the only place on the ship where Morden could see the stars with her own eyes. She sat down against the wall, closed her eyes, and drew a slow, deep breath through her nose. She had lived among the stars for so many years, but, for some reason she had never understood, looking up at them still calmed her spirit. Even when the work bays were running at full volume, machines screeching loudly, manufacturing parts and munitions, this place was still soothing.

She smiled, memories of her father flooding back to her.

"Kim." He had said through his thick mustache. "If you weren't so hell-bent to carry on the Morden tradition of soldiering, you would be an astronomer."

"Dad, the Milipa are a real challenge! We need soldiers, not astronomers. I want to serve." She had always known war was in her blood. Her family had been in the military since before the Empire period.

"My darling girl, there is more to life than challenges and struggle! When this war is over, life will still be up here, among the stars."

She frowned slightly.

Morden knew she couldn't stay long. Someone would be calling her sooner or later, but even a little peace would help her clear her head. She needed to prepare for meeting the colonial leaders. It had been several days since the *Verdun* had separated from the *Fox*, and they'd received no word from Holsey or Mostoff since.

Don't worry. They're fine.

These communication blackouts were normal over long distances. That didn't mean Morden wouldn't worry about—

She heard the small airtight pressure door hiss loudly, its manual lock clacking loudly as it spun open. Morden jumped, opening her eyes, and bringing herself back to her feet. Lieutenant Urquhart's head popped through the hole at the top of the dome.

The young woman stiffened, her eyes flying wide. "Captain! I'm sorry, I didn't know anyone was in here."

"It's alright. Stay. There isn't a 'private' sign hanging on the door. This is a public space." Morden liked this woman. She hadn't known her long, but she could tell Urquhart had spunk and determination, the kind of hard-charging officer who didn't take herself too seriously. Morden had never socialized much with her crew as the XO, but she had a responsibility to help develop her people into first-rate servicemembers. Urquhart and her constant attempts to please screamed, 'Take me under your wing!'

"Thank you, ma'am."

Morden watched her climb down the ladder to the room's solid floor. Both women stood silently, looking into the heavens. It was nice to have some company.

Urquhart spoke again. "When I was growing up, I used to come up to these domes to hide from my dad."

"Must have been a good place to hide."

Urquhart smiled. "Yeah. There is something about being immersed in the heavens that soothes me. I can't tell you how many times I'd come here crying, upset, and leave feeling at peace. Maybe it's the starlight, or maybe we are meant to be out here. Who knows? I just feel privileged to experience it. And it always provides a lot of interesting subjects to paint."

"A painter, Lieutenant?" Morden laughed. "You sound a lot like my father."

Urquhart frowned. "That bad?"

Morden smiled. "We are fighting to preserve our way of life, especially things like painting."

"Dad wanted me to be painter, but life had other plans." Urquhart looked down. "It's funny, I always feel self-conscious when my artistic side slips out, but you're the second person on board who's made it sound valuable."

"Hold on to it. Even old blood-and-guts officers like me can use a little art."

The younger woman blushed slightly. "Commander Holsey said something similar."

Morden felt her face tighten. Even with Holsey so many miles away, hearing her name agitated her. That operation had gone badly. Morden had made mistakes, and people had died. It hadn't been the last time someone had died under her command. Captain Knight had always encouraged her to move on. Mistakes happened, but guilt could drive an officer mad.

Is that it? Am I feeling guilty?

Urquhart's voice made her turn her head. "Captain, is something wrong?"

"No, Lieutenant."

"Are you sure?" Urquhart raised an eyebrow slightly. "Is it something between you and Commander Holsey?"

Morden laughed. Was it really that obvious? She had almost forgotten the way rumors fly on board ships, especially when they concerned the captain.

Urquhart cocked her head to the side. "Did I say something wrong? I didn't mean to offend you."

"No, you just reminded me that the galaxy still spins normally."

The young officer frowned, but didn't say anything else. They just stood together, enjoying the soft starlight dancing off the dome's glass.

CHAPTER 10

Wilcox leaned back, running his hand through his hair. He blinked, looked away from the screen. He had spent hours searching through the sensor data they'd collected since entering the Triangle, but he hadn't found anything useful. No signs of debris, no unexploded ordnance, nothing that suggested an attack or combat.

Nothing at all.

For the past five days, the *Verdun's* one hundred drones, equipped with sensor packages, had been in the air constantly and collected hundreds of hours of data. They should have come up with something, anything.

How could none of it be useful?

Wilcox smacked his desk and groaned. Nothing about this made sense. Only two freighters had disappeared in the asteroid field, meaning the others had likely met their fate in open space. There should have been some physical evidence of an attack somewhere.

Debris didn't disappear or degrade in a vacuum.

Holsey was right. With the *Verdun's* resources, this should be easy. Wilcox had used the flight plan of each freighter, their last known location, and the mathematical model of how debris moved in vacuum to narrow down the search area into relatively small strips of space. A single destroyer with fewer than sixty drones and no fighters could easily patrol a search area this small. They were quickly running out of logical areas to search, assuming the freighters hadn't lied about their flight plans.

He had to be missing something.

Wilcox leaned towards his screen, reviewing the data from the beginning again. In addition to the commercial traffic, the drones had picked up four comets, three previously unmapped gravity wells, and two old mining facilities on the largest moon of Barnerious II, clearly abandoned for decades. The Triangle was teaming with life, but nothing that helped him solve this mystery.

Wilcox smiled. It wasn't as if he expected to find pirate ships sitting in the open, emblazoned with a skull-and-crossbones, but he had expected to find something. Debris, frozen atmosphere, maybe a body.

Some small detail that anyone but Wilcox would overlook.

Stetler's voice broke his concentration. "I have an idea."

Wilcox looked up, hours of frustration leaking into his voice. "You're on duty. Get back to your post."

Stetler stiffened slightly. "Sir, respectfully, this is the bridge. We are flying in a straight line. I am at my post."

Wilcox took a deep breath. "Good point."

"I know why the sensor drones haven't come up with anything." Stetler smiled. "The locals are clearing it."

Wilcox shifted in his chair, suppressing a groan "Seriously? Why in Christ's name would they call us in to conduct a search if they had already found and recovered all the debris?"

Stetler leaned past Wilcox, typing in commands. "When did I say recovered? Did you see the record from drone six? That small transport right on the edge of the star system?"

Wilcox's jaw tightened, his fingers drumming silently against his leg. "The distress call indicated the ship ran out of fuel. The crew's evacuation and recovery was clearly documented. There was no sign of foul play or anything else of significance."

"That's the one." Stetler slapped Wilcox on the back a bit too enthusiastically. "Well, take a look."

Wilcox looked back at the screen, his jaw dropping slightly as the recording ran across his screen.

How had he not noticed that before?

Stetler continued. "See it? These people are poor. Look at the Black Fox. It is one of their best, right? Mostoff is one of their reputable captains. Nothing like competition for resources to bring out the criminals."

Salvage, illegal salvage.

Idiot!

Wilcox watched as several small, unmarked ships approached the derelict transport, and secured it with tethers. At the rate they were tearing it apart, the entire ship would gone in four hours.

Stetler spoke again. "These people are desperate. Whatever was left of those ships is gone."

Wilcox nodded. "At least we know why Mostoff had so little concrete information."

He leaned back in his chair again. This was going to make things harder. All their search and rescue methodologies where built around the way life worked with in the Alliance's borders. The rules were clearly different in the Triangle.

"Call the Captain to the bridge. We have to reevaluate our approach. Good work, Lieutenant."

Lieutenant Hillman pulled back on the throttle, allowing his sensors more time to sweep the asteroids below. He studied the holographic display. The surface was nothing special — craters and ridges followed by plains covered in dust. No ships or equipment, no sign at all of any type of settlement.

Another negative.

Commander Holsey's voice shattered the silence of his cockpit. "Raptor One, Base. Your fuel reserves are reading low. Come home."

"Acknowledged, Base." He switched channels. "Raptors, finish with your current rock and get back to base."

Hillman glanced at his squadron command display. Their fuel was getting dangerously low. He cursed under his breath.

He should have noticed.

Hillman rubbed his eyes. His squadron had been in the air for fifteen hours. Stallions ran off conventional fuels. A mini fusion generator, even a small one, was heavy. Strikers needed speed, especially in atmospheric operations.

He tapped his console, keying the command to drop a search beacon for the next flight. They couldn't afford to waste time, and it would help them begin where they left off. These asteroids were even denser than the *Verdun* had indicated. In four days, the only thing he had discovered was that the universe could do with fewer rocks.

No wonder Mostoff hadn't found anything on his own.

Hillman's eyes felt swollen, sore. The striker felt far away, its controls heavy in his hands. The only upside to this process was the intensity of the flying, which at least partially made up for the monotony of the search. Correcting his course, swerving suddenly to avoid chunks of ice and rock — better than any drill for keeping his team sharp.

Hillman pulled back on his controls, kicking in his afterburners. He felt the inertia pull him as his fighter spun around hard towards the *Black Fox*.

What the hell was that?

Hillman's heart caught in his chest, the familiar feeling of adrenaline hit him. For a brief second, he had seen something.

His eyes darted back to his holodisplay, nothing was there.

Hillman slammed down on his stick, pulling his fighter around 180 degrees. The intense G's pushed him into his seat.

Nothing.

He checked on his squadron display. Raptor Six was the closest.

"Raptor Six, Raptor one. Do you have any readings from grid C-32?"

"Raptor One, Six. Negative, my screen is clear."

Hillman's eyes swept the area. "I swore I saw movement. Are you sure you don't see anything?"

"Nothing but rocks, ice, and ice-covered rocks. I can run a sweep if you want."

Hillman glanced at his squadron display again. Raptor six's fuel warning light was blinking red. He had maybe five minutes left on hard burn. Hillman looked back out. Several large asteroids were spinning slowly, casting ominously large shadows over the spot his specter had occupied.

Had he really seen something, or had it been a trick of the light?

Hillman yawned, rubbed his eyes again. "Negative, Six. Let's return to base."

"Aye, sir."

The words 'Warning: Fuel Levels Low' flashed in red across the bottom of his screen. Hillman switched on his navigation computer and locked on to the landing beacon from the *Black Fox*. He looked back at the asteroids. There was still nothing there.

He couldn't shake the feeling that he was being watched, targeted. Hunters can always tell when they are being hunted, and Hillman was a hunter.

The warning klaxon echoed loudly, followed quickly by Isabelle's voice. "Captain, several missile silos have targeted us."

Morden flipped open her console, read the data feeding onto its screen. "That answers your question, Mr. Wilcox. They know we are here. Should we let them sweat for a minute?"

"Captain?" Wilcox's voice sounded concerned.

Morden grinned in spite of the situation. "Kidding, Mr. Wilcox. Ensign Hart, please let—" She paused, pulling up the needed information. "Director Nichelle Wheeler knows why we are here."

"This is the Royal Alliance Battlecruiser Verdun sending greetings to the Three Rivers Colony." Morden could hear Hart's voice as she sent the response.

The radio crackled over the bridge speaker. "You are not supposed to be here! We have the means to defend ourselves!"

Hart looked around, and Morden met her eyes, nodded.

Morden put on her headset and keyed her microphone. "We are requesting a meeting with Director Wheeler and Director of Defense Johnathan Locknor."

The voice sounded tense. "I will pass that request on."

He was stalling.

Morden frowned. "This is an Alliance vessel, a representative of a foreign power, not a cargo vessel. Please let the administrator know I wish to talk to her *now*."

"The administrator is busy. I will put your request in as soon as I see her."

Morden starting drumming her fingers on her armrest, anger rising in her chest. "I suggest you interrupt her. My name is Captain Kim Morden, of the Royal Alliance Battlecruiser Verdun. I am not making a request. We will either be coming down as guests or with a marine platoon. It's the Administrator's choice."

The voice on the other end of the radio said nothing. Morden waited for a response, tension building in her chest.

Isabelle broke the silence. "Captain, the planet's silos have terminated their target lock."

Morden let out a breath she hadn't known she'd been holding.

Her headset crackled, and the voice returned. "I will have landing coordinates sent up to your ship. Please stand by."

"Thank you." Morden took off her headset.

Out of the corner of her eye, she saw Wilcox turn towards her. "Captain, that wasn't very diplomatic."

She looked over to face him. "No, but I don't make threats lightly. And besides, it was fun."

Wilcox frowned deeply.

I know that look.

"I see your sense of humor has returned."

She nodded. "Relax. The colony was trying to play power games. These people are all jockeying for control, even within their own colony. Our presence is a political event in God knows how many circles. I don't have time for their junk. I just decided to change their perspective. Never underestimate the proper application of the threat of force."

Wilcox leaned back. "But doesn't issuing threats politicize our presence further? Justify their prejudices?"

"Probably, but we have a mission to complete. Everything we do will be scrutinized. This way is fastest."

"I see your point. Doesn't make it right."

Morden waved her hands dismissively. "Lives are at stake."

Ensign Hart's voice cut off Wilcox's response. "Captain, we are getting the coordinates now."

"Thank you. Commander Wilcox, you have command. Lt. Urquhart, come with me. Ensign Hart, contact Sergeant Hawthorn and have him prepare a small Marine escort. Also, contact Commander Frost and tell him I want him ready to disembark in five minutes."

CHAPTER 11

First Officer Scorpus fidgeted with his hands. "Captain, this don't feel right."

Mostoff fought to keep the doubt off his face. "My friend, this is our mission. We must not fail. The Alliance has controlled our lives long enough. You know it, and I know it."

Scorpus nodded. "They are a blight on our lives. But to do this?"

Mostoff grabbed him by the shoulders, forcing a confidence he didn't feel into his voice. "The only way we escape their net is through strength. Until we can defend ourselves, we will be at their mercy. This is the fastest way."

The man still looked unsure, but nodded. "Okay, I'll set it up. I'll let you know when it's ready."

Mostoff lowered his hands. "Our people thank you."

Scorpus smiled. "For our people."

Mostoff watched the young man leave the room. For the first time since this whole thing had begun, he felt uneasy. His clarity of purpose was gone. Commander Holsey wasn't what he'd expected. After her initial insolence, her demeanor had changed. She had been respectful, willing to share information openly. Her entire team had acted with honor, not like the manipulative villains he'd expected.

Was there just a chance they were being sincere?

They had even taken the time to help refurbish some of the systems on the *Black Fox*.

Captain Mostoff pulled out his orders, read them one last time. He had to see this through, no matter how the snakes in his stomach moved.

U rquhart could barely make out the captain's voice as Morden leaned into Sergeant Hawthorn.

"Something doesn't feel right. Keep your eyes open."

Urquhart couldn't help but agree — something wasn't right. They had been sitting in silence, watching the administrator nervously flip through papers for several minutes.

Administrator Wheeler was older, at least eighty. She looked tired.

Urquhart ran her eyes quickly around the conference room, her hand resting on the butt of her pistol. The room was tastefully decorated and well-lit from large windows overlooking a calm, intensely blue lake and seemingly endless fields of flowers. Compared to the rest of the colony she had seen, this room was almost decadent. The space in front of them was empty except for the table at its center and some wooden boxes piled in the corner closest to the window.

Urquhart crossed and uncrossed her arms, shifting in her chair. Only two guards had accompanied them from the transport, Sergeant Hawthorn and Private Cotter. It had obviously been enough to intimidate the administrator — she'd brought four guards of her own to stand directly behind her.

Out of the corner of her eye, she saw Morden carefully unbuttoning the flap of her holster, her right hand loosely resting on her pistol's grip. Urquhart followed suit, careful to keep her hands out of sight.

The administrator looked up. "Captain Morden, I don't appreciate your threats. I asked for Alliance aid, not intimidation."

Morden leaned forward. "Madam Administrator, I apologize if I was too abrasive. I do not appreciate being strung along while people's lives are at stake — your people's lives. I apologize if you feel intimidated."

Wheeler frowned, held her hands to each side, an exaggerated sign of supplication. "I accept your apology, such as it is. Why did you request this meeting? You should be searching the asteroid field. As you said, lives are at stake."

Urquhart was reminded of the worst of the Imperialists back home. They always spoke from behind the same empty political façade.

I hate politics.

Morden smiled. "I have questions. Captain Mostoff was less than forthcoming."

"I'm not surprised. He is a proud man. Any woman knows that proud men are never reasonable."

Morden waved her hand, brushed off Wheeler's attempts to empathize. "Then I am sure you will be able to help me get some answers."

"Certainly, I would be happy to help." The woman forced a smile as she avoided Morden's eyes by looking out the window.

Urquhart could see the captain glance down at her tablet. "Are there any commonalities between the various ships cargos?"

"Not as far as my advisors can tell. Most of them carried raw materials. Unprocessed ores, perishable foodstuffs, and other commodities, even some textiles, but nothing special."

Morden frowned. "How about relations between the colonies and the miners? Captain Mostoff was insistent that the miners are responsible."

The administrator ran her hands through her hair. "Relations are cordial, of course. Every once in a while, we deal with petty squabbling, but what society doesn't struggle with points of contention? Folks here are simple, peaceful. We all just want to live our lives undisturbed."

Urquhart butted in, her frustration seeping into her tone. "Then what would you call the wars between the miners and yourselves?"

Wheeler smiled. "Old news. That was more than thirty years ago. Things change. There were serious disagreements about trade rights. The miners didn't want the colonies cutting into their ore market. They didn't want the competition, but in negotiations we agreed to tone down our mineral production in exchange for better prices on raw ore."

Morden looked up. "So it's also your opinion the miners aren't behind this?"

"The miners were placated by our agreement. I don't hear from them much at all. They have no single leader to deal with. They are more interested in fighting with each other. Each encampment has its own goals. Besides, they would die without the food and equipment we sell them. I doubt they would do something to risk reprisals. They have too much to lose."

Urquhart rolled her eyes. These answers were longer, but just as hollow as Captain Mostoff's. The administrator gave no evidence, no examples, no specifics. Just vague generalities. Something else was going on here. Why else was Wheeler so apprehensive?

Morden frowned slightly. "What about your neighbor? Could the Underwood Colony on Barnerious II be doing this?"

The administrator laughed. "No, they have been hurt just as badly by the loss of those freighters. The attacks are random and seem to have no purpose. Even Underwood wouldn't attack their own freighters. I talked with their leader, Mike Webb, and he was just as concerned as I was."

Morden locked eyes with the administrator. "Then who do you think is responsible?"

One of Wheeler's men leaned in, whispered in her ear. Urquhart saw the color drain from the woman's face. She stood up, quickly turning for the door. Her men pulled their sidearms and moved to stand between Wheeler and *Verdun* officers.

Urquhart looked at Morden. She hadn't seen her move, but the Captain was already on her feet, pistol drawn. She could hear the marines' bolts cycling behind her. Urquhart rose, trying to pull out her pistol, but her hands were shaking as adrenaline surged through her. She had never fired on another human before.

Morden was aiming directly at the old woman. "Administrator, don't do something we would all regret!"

Wheeler froze in her tracks and her men turned their pistols directly at Morden. "Captain, I must leave. Now. Put down your weapons, and you won't be harmed."

Morden raised one hand. "Stand fast, marines."

The administrator's men looked terrified.

Something was really wrong.

The administrator turned towards them, her eyes white with fear. "Captain, please. We must get out of here, *now*."

Morden never had the opportunity to respond. The window burst inward as gunfire whistled into the room. The stuffy decor shredded as the sporadic fire tore into the wall, spraying debris over the room.

Urquhart saw five men swing in through the open window. She dove, pulling the Captain under the table as she heard the bark of the marine's rifles.

Two of the attackers bucked, falling backward out of the window, blood spattering the floor. The other three returned fire, diving behind the pile of boxes in the corner.

One, clearly the commander, fired a fully automatic weapon, its tracers lancing through the air and into the wall. Private Cotter ducked too late and several rounds hit him squarely in the chest. The private screamed, the repeated impacts causing him to stumble and slam into the wall. Urquhart could hear him sputtering loudly as he choked on his own blood.

Morden rolled onto one knee and fired into the enemy combatants' positions. Her pistol rounds tore into the boxes, sending wooden slivers in all directions. The Administrator's men began to fire, wildly and uncontrolled, their lack of experience evident.

Morden squeezed off two more rounds into one of the attackers' exposed shoulders. "Hawthorn, get Cotter out of here."

Urquhart got up and rolled. Her shoulder smashed into the floor sending shots of pain up her arm. She saw one of the men standing, taking aim, his rifle turning towards her.

She fired.

The man jerked as his head disintegrated in a spray of blood. She glanced behind her, saw Sergeant Hawthorn dragging the now unconscious Cotter out of the door. He was still firing from the hip, pinning down the remaining attackers.

These attackers were clumsy, poorly trained, but the crates' contents were keeping them safe.

Two of the administrator's guards were hit, bullets tearing into their abdomens. One convulsed as he collapsed, the other fell like a puppet whose strings had been cut. Wheeler was yelling, still standing in the open. Urquhart saw her, stood up and ran. She dived, smashing directly into Wheeler just before the wall behind her was stuck with several rounds.

She could hear and feel the bullets whizzing overhead as she hit the floor, her body shielding the struggling Wheeler.

"Lieutenant, stay down." Morden's voice sounded far away.

Urquhart rolled onto her back, fired several quick shots. One of her .45 rounds hit home, striking the leg of one of the enemy commandoes. She pulled the trigger again, but the slide had locked back on an empty chamber.

"Fuck." She fumbled for her last magazine, but it was too late. The wounded attacker had raised his weapon. This was where she was going to die.

She saw Morden burst from cover and slam into the attacker. The captain plunged her combat knife into his chest.

The man tried to scream, but nothing came out. She pulled the knife clear, slashed quickly at his throat, blood bursting from the wound as the man's own heart pumped his life out of his body. Morden regained her footing and dove back towards the table.

Urquhart slammed her magazine home, releasing the slide as fast as her hands could work. She aimed quickly and fired.

The first few shots went wild. She corrected her aim and carefully squeezed the trigger. The shots hit home. The man collapsed, his stomach torn open.

He fought to get back up, but the blood from his wound made it too slick. Morden was already back on her feet. Her pistol barked loudly as she fired point-blank range.

The man died instantly, a pool of blood spreading out slowly from his body.

Morden turned to look at Wheeler. "Administrator, it's time for the truth."

Holsey woke with a start, energy surging through her. Someone was walking below her, inside the corvette. She rolled over, careful to keep her movements silent. The crew were all set up in the landing bay. No one should be onboard. She pushed herself up, heard the soft beep of a control keypad. Someone was trying to get into the computer.

I knew it!

Everyone, including herself, had agreed to sleep in the hanger housing the fighters. Mostoff had suggested it would be more comfortable.

It hadn't felt right.

It wasn't his style.

Holsey reached for her carbine, slid it carefully over her shoulders. If she was going to catch this bastard in the midst of whatever he was doing, she had to move quickly and quietly. The hatch in front of her had to be opened.

She reached out slowly, easing the handle carefully, gingerly, breaking the door's seal. It swung open, scraping lightly as the door caught on the uneven grating of the old TLS Corvette.

"Damn." She cursed under her breath.

She reached down, pulled open the floor hatch, carefully letting her body fall over the edge. Her feet touched the floor and she spun quickly, pulling her carbine up and aiming towards the light coming from the slightly askew cockpit hatch.

Holsey inched closer, trying not to breathe. The small confines and yellow light made her heart beat faster. She shook her head. She had to stay focused — memories had no place in combat. Whoever it was in there wouldn't get what they were after.

Holsey kicked the door open. One man was crouching over the control console, the body of the communication officers lying on the floor next to him. "I got you, you bastard. Turn around. Slowly."

The main straightened his back, then froze. Holsey recognized him immediately.

Captain Mostoff.

CHAPTER 12

Urquhart rested her head on one of her hands, trying to stop herself from shaking. Even thirty minutes after the attack on the conference room, she couldn't make her hands stay still. Morden and Urquhart were sitting alone in a small, overly warm room in the complex's center, waiting for Administrator Wheeler to be cleared by her medical staff. Private Cotter had been rushed back to the ship in critical condition. Morden hadn't wanted to let him be treated by the locals.

Urquhart avoided Morden's gaze, willing her body to remain still in her chair. Urquhart knew killing was never easy, but this hadn't felt the same as killing a Frontin or Milipa. She had killed another human being. The image of that last man's body, his eyes open, staring at nothing, the Captain standing over him, wouldn't leave her mind.

Morden touched her shoulder. "Great job, Lieutenant."

Urquhart nodded, forcing her face to remain passive. She had done her duty, saved the life of Administrator Wheeler, but that knowledge couldn't remove her victim's face from her mind.

"I am glad to see you can handle yourself in a fight."

Urquhart sat up, keeping her eyes fixed on the door. "Yes, ma'am."

Morden's voice sounded soft. "Are you okay?"

Damn.

She frowned. "I have never—"

Both women looked up as the door swung inward, hitting the wall with a loud thump. Administrator Wheeler entered alone, still looking frail. She sat down, leaned back in her chair, her eyes locked on Morden. "Thank you for saving my life."

Morden waved her hand. "Administrator, what the hell is going on?"

The woman looked up, clearly fighting back tears, "The last few months have been hard. More than hard. I was being truthful; I don't know who is behind this."

Morden rolled her eyes. "Administrator, we would like to help. Intensive scans have given us nothing. We are searching the asteroid field, but it's dense. I can't guarantee that we will find anything."

"I know that." The administrator paused, looking down. "My grandson was most likely killed in one of those attacks. Death seems to be stalking our colony."

Urquhart grimaced. "I am sorry, Administrator."

Morden leaned forward assertively. "Administrator, give us something. We can't find his killers if you don't help us."

The old woman slammed her hands against the table, almost yelling, her carefully constructed persona breaking. "I don't know who is responsible! If I did, I'd have killed them myself."

Morden ignored the outburst. "Then help me. I am not an idiot. You are hiding something."

Wheeler stood up. She paced around the room, turning her back on them, staring into an empty corner. Urquhart straightened her uniform, fidgeting in her chair as the silence hung in the room. The administrator turned suddenly, sitting back down. She lowered her head, her voice growing softer. "Both colonies are on the brink of collapse. Our inability to find these raiders has ruined my credibility. It has united several anti-government factions. Revolution is in the air."

Morden laughed. "Why would you hide that from us?"

"My decision to call you for help was unpopular, but if you can find these bastards quickly enough, the crisis would be over. Captain Mostoff is one of the most respected leaders in our mercenary fleet, a man above reproach. His orders are to help you find the attackers and plant evidence that the revolutionaries are to blame. No one expected you to come here, to Three Rivers. No one outside the government was supposed to know you were involved."

Urquhart nodded. This was an internal conflict to preserve the power in the hands of those in charge. The administrator was sneaky, using the Alliance to solve her problem while blaming her opponents for the attacks. No wonder they hadn't wanted the *Verdun* to come here. Everyone would know the Alliance had been called, and she would have to explain that decision.

Morden nodded. "I see. Regardless of what you think of the Alliance, Administrator, part of my mandate is to help maintain this region's stability. We need your government to remain intact."

"Then leave, quickly. There is nothing we can do to stop these attacks. I need you to solve this. We lost five of our best ships responding to one of these distress calls. No one knows that, not even Mostoff. By the time he got there, there was nothing left to save."

Urquhart almost laughed. "So Mostoff can be trusted?"

The administrator glanced at her. "Most of our privateers are more like vigilantes, but, without a military, someone must enforce the law. Mostoff is a good man. He is the only one who hasn't abandoned the search. He is a patriot. I would trust him with my life, though perhaps not my wallet."

Morden stood. "Administrator, thank you for your time. I will do my best to finish this up quickly."

Urquhart followed suit, walking just behind her captain as they moved to leave the room.

The Administrator grabbed her arm as she walked past. Urquhart looked down. The woman seemed even frailer than when she arrived.

"Thank you for saving my life."

Urquhart couldn't help but smile. "You're welcome, ma'am."

Lt. Hillman rubbed his eyes. It had been another ten hours without any progress. Another ten hours of running mind-numbing scans of lifeless hunks of rock and ice. He checked his squadron command display. Two of his pilots had increased their speed again.

Hillman flipped on his radio. "Raptors Three and Six, slow it down. This isn't a race."

"Raptor Three, acknowledged."

"Raptor Six, understood."

Both pilots sounded annoyed. His team was getting frustrated, and they hadn't even searched fifteen percent of the field. They were hunters, like

Hillman. They needed opponents. Examining rocks was a job for geologists, not pilots.

Hillman glanced down at his sensor display, running a search through all the sensor drones in range. He couldn't shake the feeling he was being watched, his eyes still probing every shadow.

Something was out there.

Hillman shook off the thought, increasing his speed, pulling back on the stick. His body slammed into his seat as the striker flipped over, accelerating towards the next asteroid on his list. It was a big, pockmarked bastard that filled his entire windshield.

Hillman waited till the last possible second before slamming on his brakes, forcing his craft into a tight orbit.

This is freedom.

He tapped his controls, inverting his ship so he could look down out of his cockpit to verify visually that there were no signs of life present. Getting a full survey of this monster would require his full attention. Hillman had never seen so many deep chasms and gullies. The computer was struggling to create good images of the surface. His eyes burned with the effort as the ship circled the asteroid again and again, its gravity pushing his Stallion to move faster.

Nothing.

Hillman flipped his ship back around, its sudden movement pushing against his stomach and chest. He keyed up the coordinates to the next asteroid in his grid, glancing down one more time at the behemoth beneath him.

And then he saw it.

Mostoff raised his gun.

Commander Holsey held herself still, eyes fixed on her carbine's front sight, her finger resting lightly above the trigger. She could feel the carbine's butt pressing into her shoulder. If she had to fire, she wouldn't miss.

The communications officer groaned softly.

Mostoff bared his teeth. "Commander, put down your weapon. You can't kill me on my own ship. You would never survive."

Holsey sneered at her opponent. "You are not on your ship. This is my transport. Why don't you throw down that pistol and make this easier for both of us?"

Mostoff growled. His muscles tensed to fire. Holsey didn't hesitate, sending a single warning shot into the deck plating less than an inch from his foot. The man flinched, his face darkening as he stared at her.

She stepped forward, her ears ringing from the blast. "Don't make me end you."

"All right." He hissed through gritted teeth and slowly holstered his weapon.

Holsey pulled her muzzle off target. "Captain, I never trusted you, but I never suspected you were capable of assault to steal information. You're a fucking crook."

The man was shaking visibly. "I am no crook."

"You clearly aren't seeing what I'm seeing."

Mostoff stepped forward, his hand still resting on his freshly holstered pistol "How dare you speak like that to me. This is my ship — you're a guest here. Waving a gun in my face like every other Alliance coward I've met changes nothing."

"Don't lie to me! What the fuck did you think you would accomplish here?"

He spat his response at her. "You have no idea what life is like outside the borders of your precious Alliance, little girl. Hide behind your fancy gun all you want, but don't you dare judge me."

"You want to claim the high ground? Go ahead. I got you dead to rights. Give me one reason I shouldn't grease your ass right now. It wouldn't surprise me if you were behind the whole fucking thing."

The man's eyes bulged again, his hand pulling on his pistol. "How dare you—"

"Raptor One to base."

They both froze as the communication panel crackled loudly, lighting up. "Raptor One to base. Commander Holsey, I found something. I say again, I found something."

Neither of them moved, their eyes locked on each other. Holsey couldn't read the man's expression, but it had changed.

The radio hissed to life again. "Base, get me Holsey. I think I found the…" The pilot's voice trailed off. "The SS Baron. Base, are you there?"

Mostoff's raised his hands palm out. "Commander, please answer him."

"It can wait. Why did you break in here and attack my man? What is going on?"

The man's voice cracked. "Commander…please."

She raised the carbine again. "No. You broke into my ship. The Baron isn't going anywhere."

"If there is anyone alive down there, they desperately need help. I will tell you, I won't resist, just please let me go down there. Viktor has been my friend for more than thirty years. Please let me help him. I must know what happened here."

Holsey stared into the man's eyes. She couldn't help but feel he was telling the truth. It was a different man standing in front of her — his tone, even his stature, had changed. He seemed smaller, more vulnerable, and older than she'd ever thought he was.

She lowered her carbine. "All right, but I am going with you."

CHAPTER 13

Voth pointed to the door, his voice muffled through headset in Holsey's helmet. "Sergeant Dickens, open it up."

Holsey spoke as clearly as she could. "By the book, people. Don't touch anything."

She watched the Sergeant move forward, carefully shifting the weight of the large field radio on his back as he knelt. He lit the cutting torch, letting its flame eat into the weakened surface of the ship's hull. The glow from the suddenly heated metal lit up the visors of their environmental suits, casting ominous shadows against the outer hull of the *Baron*.

Holsey opened her suit's computer interface on her left sleeve, quickly looking over the scans of the *Baron*. Whoever had attacked the vessel hadn't left much intact. The engine core had imploded, tearing the ship in half and bathing it in deadly radiation. The ship's two halves had come to rest several miles apart, sinking into the silt-covered surface of the asteroid. It was a miracle that the Stallion pilot had seen the ship's emergency beacon. Scans showed no signs of life and only weak energy signatures, but Holsey's instincts told her that the answer to this mystery was there.

She had kept the search party small and insisted on taking only experienced personnel. Wrecks like this had unforeseen dangers, and there was always the chance an attacker might have left booby traps behind. The fewer people Holsey had to keep an eye on, the better. Besides Lieutenant Voth and herself, her team consisted of Captain Mostoff and five marines — Major Osterman, Sergeant Dickens, Corporal Carter, and privates Jones and Thrace.

Holsey shouldered her carbine, fixing her eyes on the hull. The metal sagged as the torch finished its work, and the piece of the outer hull drifted down onto the deck below, pulled gently by the asteroid's weak gravity.

Holsey signaled Voth forward. "Lieutenant, on point."

The man quickly dropped a suspension unit across the opening. He ran his hands quickly over its controls, and a light on top of the unit flashed. The machine vibrated silently as it un-spooled a rope ladder into the pitch-black wreck.

Holsey flipped on the light built into her carbine's bayonet ring stud and shone it down into the hole, the pure white light illuminating a small area of debris-covered floor.

Clear.

She flipped off her light. "Teams of two. Voth and Jones, forward sections. Osterman and Carter, engine room. Captain, you're with me. Sergeant, stay here and keep the lights on."

Voth grabbed the rope and disappeared over the edge. Holsey watched the rest of her team vanish one by one into the *Baron's* hold.

Captain Mostoff pointed. "After you, Commander."

Holsey grabbed the line, slung her carbine over her shoulder, and eased over the edge. She could feel the heat from the freshly cut metal emanating through her suit as she slid past the opening. As soon as her boots touched the floor, she pivoted to her left and brought up her weapon, training its light around the room.

They were in the cargo hold, and, by the looks of it, the *Baron's* entire payload was still intact. She swung the light around the room. There was nothing unusual, though the signs of combat damage were more severe than what she had expected. The walls were streaked with carbon residue from fire, and most of the crates had broken open, spilling their contents over the deck. One of the bulkheads was missing, the asteroid field clearly visible through the opening.

Holsey saw movement out of the corner of her eye, and she looked behind her to see Mostoff drift to the deck. He swiveled around where he stood, taking in the damage to the *Baron*, his dark scowl visible through his visor.

"Captain, move so the others can drop down."

Mostoff growled back in response.

She ignored Mostoff's temper and signaled him to follow as she started towards a small door in the back of the room, following faded signs on the wall for the bridge and forward escape deck.

Holsey felt the hairs on the back of her neck prickle. The tight space and eerie silence of the vacuum pressed in on her. The wounds on her knee and back began to ache for the first time in years. The ring she kept hanging on the chain around her neck seemed to burn her skin.

Glen.

Holsey shook her head. Fear had no place in a marine, and neither did the past. She had to stay focused — distraction led to accidents. She refused to let that happen here. The key to this mission was aboard the *Baron*.

She could feel it.

Mostoff reached the door first, threw himself through it. He was moving fast, his desperation to find his friend showing in his carelessness.

Holsey caught up with Mostoff, put a hand on his shoulder. "Captain, slow down. The bastards who did this may have left traps."

Mostoff waved his hand. "I can't believe any miner is clever enough to consider planting traps. I must know which group is responsible."

"There is no way a miner did this. This ship was ripped apart. None of the cargo is missing."

He snarled. "I must know what happened."

Holsey lowered her weapon. "I understand that, but slow down. Trust me. We have to be cautious. You have my word we will make whoever did this pay."

The older man didn't respond, but ran his headlamp over the door, searching for something. The door was badly damaged, and the only access panel was burnt, covered with small dents.

They were familiar somehow.

She looked around at the corridor walls, noted their warped, cracked condition. The ship was too weak for explosives. They would have to cut their way in. Holsey dropped to her knees and pulled off her combat pack. She took out a hand torch, popped open its display, and lit it.

Mostoff groaned, slamming the door with his fist.

The flame's glow danced on the wall as she cut into the door. Sparks shot away from the metal, floating away and winking out into darkness. She had to be careful, keep her movements as efficient as possible. The torch had limited fuel, and they might need it again.

Holsey's hands worked steadily, moving the torch's intense heat over the door in a smooth line. "It's honesty time. Why were you in my ship?"

Mostoff turned away from her, his tone dark and low. "I had orders. Our administrator has lost face. So many missing ships, and my...failure to catch these bastards has left us vulnerable."

Holsey nodded. "I see."

Mostoff continued. "I was trying to steal technology, anything to bring us advantage after you left. If we could get hold of the schematics for your missile systems, we could have claimed to have outsmarted you."

Holsey lowered her torch. "You're a soldier, not a spy. How can you support that kind of dishonesty?"

Mostoff faced her again. "I am a patriot. I believe in freedom. Back home, we are known as mercenaries, the ones who do the nasty things that create the peace others enjoy. This was no different. The dissidents back home threaten our freedom. I won't allow it. I can't."

Dissidents? The situation in the Triangle must be worse than they all knew.

Holsey made a mental note to contact Morden and warn her about these dissidents as soon as she was back onboard the *Fox*. She raised the torch back to the door. "I understand."

Mostoff finally made sense to her — the anger, the nastiness, the cold heart. Killing changed people. Mostoff's nationalistic bent had made him do things he couldn't justify, ground down his reason, until all that was left was belief. As long as the cause was just, anything he did to protect it was justified. The Alliance may not manipulate people like that, throw them to the wolves to keep its hands clean, but combat still took its toll.

She had lost so many friends in the service of her own cause.

Holsey pushed the thought away and kicked the partially severed piece of metal several times, forcing it to give way. The weakened door bent inward. It broke off, drifted to the deck without a sound in the airless vacuum. Holsey sized up the opening she'd made, knew it wasn't big enough for both of them to shimmy through at once.

They would have to go in separately.

Holsey returned the torch to her pack, pulled out a flare. "I'll go first. Slide the pack behind me, then come through yourself."

She pulled the flare's ignition cord and tossed it through the opening before crawling quickly after it, carbine in front of her. She pushed herself into a kneeling position, swept her carbines' light around the room.

It looked like the ship's escape deck. Unused escape pods were visible on each side of the hall. Several of the small arms lockers were opened, and spilled weapons and emergency supplies covered the deck, which was stained with blood. The whole room seemed drenched in dry blood, the flare's sickly green light casting the dark splotches in ominous shadow. A brighter light appeared on the floor, and she looked up to see light from one of the Stallions spilling through a large, perfectly circular hole in the ceiling.

Holsey pointed at the opening's perfectly smooth edges. "Looks like they were boarded. Whoever did this caught the crew trying to escape."

Mostoff handed her the backpack. "There are no bodies?"

"No, bodies would have been blown into space when the boarding craft uncoupled from the Baron."

Mostoff stood up beside her, moving his flashlight around the room. A look of disgust and revulsion crossing his face. His light stopped on the ladder up to one of the escape crafts. A bloody hand mark streaked its rungs.

He turned off the light, lowered his head. "We need to get to the bridge. I want to look at those computers."

Holsey shook her head. "Whoever did this was extremely capable. I doubt they left the computers intact."

"It may be the only way to find out who it was. I want to wring the life out of these bastards with my bare hands."

Holsey shook her head. She keyed on her mike to the team's channel. "Sergeant, please let all teams know we have located at least one entry point. The Baron was boarded. Be on guard."

"Confirmed, Commander," the Sergeant's voice responded quickly.

Mostoff rolled his eyes. "There is no one else here, Commander."

Holsey started walking forward again. "No, but a confirmed entry point gives us an idea of where to look."

Mostoff growled, his voice low. "You waste time. The fear of death shouldn't drive a soldier."

Holsey spat a reply back at him. "Keep your advice to yourself."

Holsey placed her weapon on the landing above and climbed the ladder to the next deck. The ladder was slick, frozen blood covered its rungs. She pulled herself onto the landing, stopping in her tacks. The light from her carbine had illuminated something in the corner.

Mostoff called from below. "What are you seeing?"

Holsey shouldered her weapon, got to her feet. "I'm not sure. It's too small for a body, but it doesn't look metallic."

She starting walking forward, easing her way down the hall. She let her eyes take in the space. If that was a bomb, she would have nowhere to take cover.

She stopped in her tracks, her stomach turning.

Mostoff's light suddenly cast her in shadow from behind. She turned to look at him. His face had gone white, his eyes fixed on the object. "God, what could do something like...that?"

She turned back to the grisly sight in front of her. She had been wrong. It was a body, or what was left of one. A pair of legs and a pile of gore that once was a torso lay in the corner. Blood covered everything.

She gagged instinctively, the memory of burnt flesh and blood flooding her senses, tearing her eyes away from the remains to focus on the wall behind it, which was heavily pockmarked and scorched.

Her heart leapt into her throat. She recognized those marks. Only one kind of weapon could do that.

Mostoff was reaching for something, a small object nearly buried in the corpse. He picked it up and froze.

"Captain, what is it?"

He didn't respond, but handed her the object he had picked up. It was a badly burnt nametag. Holsey could just barely make out what was written on it.

Cpt. V. Stover.

Holsey dropped the tag, let it drift to the ground. "I'm sorry about your friend, but he gave us the answers we needed. I know what killed him."

Sergeant Samuel Dickens' mouth dropped as two destroyers ripped out of the darkness. The *Black Fox* shuddered as projectiles struck it. He watched as one projectile turned in his direction and two more streaked towards the *Baron* from the oncoming destroyer.

He picked up his mike. "Corvette 3A, attack incoming. Take off, now." The channel was dead. He tried again. Something was jamming the transmission.

Samuel turned, ran for the Corvette. If its sensors were blocked, too, the pilots couldn't see the attack. He had to get it off the ground.

The sergeant felt the all too familiar rush of combat flash through him. He barely felt his boots slam into the metal of the beleaguered ship as he avoided the deep wounds on the *Baron's* surface.

He turned his communication to laser-link, dumping its full power into the signal. It was a long shot, but maybe one of the fighters was close enough to hear him. "Mayday, mayday. Any fighters in range. Landing party is under attack."

Samuel fell against the *Baron's* outer hull as the first set of projectiles impacted the ship. He fought his way to his feet, leapt the last few paces to the transport. He keyed the entrance code on the transport, lowering its ramp slowly.

The sergeant looked behind him. As if in slow motion, he saw a torpedo coming right at the Corvette. He pulled himself up through the nearly open ramp and sprinted up the ladder into the empty machine gun turret.

He had only seconds left.

Samuel pulled the trigger, and unleashed a burst of fire from the weapon's barrel at the oncoming ordnance. He opened his mouth to yell —

It never came.

The torpedo slammed into the Corvette's hull. Samuel's body incinerated as the ship burst apart, belching flame and shrapnel out over the asteroid's dusty surface, just another scorch mark on the *Baron's* hull.

CHAPTER 14

Lt. Hillman pushed his ship up to full power, the inertia slamming his body into his seat. The engines screamed as his Stallion reached maximum acceleration. Raptor Squadron had barely picked up the distress call in time to get back to the *Fox*.

"Raptors, break and attack. Raptors Two, Three, and Four, get between the Black Fox and the destroyers. Do your best to protect her."

"Raptor One, Three. We aren't interceptors. There's not much we can do to stop incoming munitions."

Hillman rolled his eyes. "Obviously. But without the Fox, we have no place to land."

"Confirmed, One. We're on it."

Hillman reached out to his holodisplay, painting the destroyer in the squad's attack system. "Everyone else, attack the destroyer I've indicated. Commander Holsey is on the wreck it's targeting."

Scans showed that the *Black Fox* had taken serious damage. Its engines and armor were compromised. The ship's guns were still firing, but without propulsion, it wouldn't matter for long.

Hillman smiled. This is what he lived for.

He watched as his Stallions galloped into the open clearing in the asteroids where the *Fox* was engaged. Hillman opened up with his machine guns. It wouldn't cause any damage, but it would certainly get the enemy's attention. He angled his ship down, leading his team on its first strike, his finger resting on his torpedo release trigger. He watched the distance to the first destroyer shrink quickly.

Volleys of flak began exploding around him. Hillman pulled on his stick, rolling his fighter, avoiding the destroyer's fire. His proximity warning blared loudly as the destroyer launched drop pods towards the *Baron*.

Hillman squeezed the trigger, feeling his craft kick as two torpedoes rocketed towards the enemy. The destroyer banked, trying to avoid the striker's torpedoes, flak cannons firing wildly.

Hillman frowned.

The torpedoes missed, detonating just above their targets. At least they'd forced the destroyer to turn away from the *Baron's* wreckage.

Hillman turned, assessing the situation. The *Black Fox* was firing its four, eight-inch guns, but the shells were pulled off course by what looked like a fully functional magnetic ordnance deflector. He checked his readings, saw both destroyers had MODs.

Who the hell are these guys?

Was the technology needed to build one even available in the Triangle?

The *Fox* was too far away to cause any real damage. Hillman's fighters would have to deal with the destroyer, but first they had to stop those landing craft. He glanced at his squadron command board — no one was close enough.

Hillman pushed the stick forward, forcing his Stallion into a steep dive. He watched the distance to the drop pods disappear as his ship bore down on them, his eyes locked on the targeting reticle projected on the inside of his helmet's blast shield. It flashed red as multiple targets came in range.

He fired.

His machine guns barked loudly, shaking his ship as he held the trigger down. Several pods burst, flame and falling debris filling his windscreen.

The remaining pods fired their braking thrusters.

"Fuck." Hillman growled as his striker ripped past the slowing craft.

He exhaled, tugged hard on the braking thruster, pushed down on both pedals, pulling back on his stick. His vision blurred, his stomach heaving as the hard G's pressed against it. The striker flipped on the spot, 180 degrees end-to-end.

Hillman released the brake, and sent the Stallion jerking forward as his thrusters fought his own inertia. He blinked his eyes, clearing his vision and reacquiring his targets.

He fired again, his knuckles turning white as he held down the trigger. His hell guns sent waves of death at the enemy pods, all but one shredding in arcs of fire. Hillman adjusted his aim, centering the last pod in his sights.

He pulled the trigger and his hell guns kicked several times before an alarm blared from the cockpit speakers.

He glanced down at his ammo counter, saw that it read empty.

God damn it!

Hillman examined his displays, watched his fighters engaging the enemy. The computer was registering heavy flak explosions. They needed him in the fight.

He had to let the last pod go.

There was nothing he could do.

The Raptors had to take out those destroyers before they eviscerated the *Black Fox*. Everything depended on it.

"Raptor one to ground team. You have a landing pod descending fast. Estimate two minutes to touch down. Prepare to repel boarders."

The ground team would have to take care of itself.

Captain Mostoff's voice was hoarse and desperate. "Give me your pistol."

Holsey braced her weapon on the shattered crate in front of her, aiming carefully at the impact point that had just appeared on the wall. She felt dizzy. The *Baron* had shaken violently when the drop pod had made contact.

"Commander, please," Mostoff said, an edge of panic in his voice.

Major Osterman, Corporal Carter, Private Jones and Lt Voth were spread out, tucked into cover in front of them. Holsey had warned them what to expect, but not even Osterman had faced an enemy like this before. She couldn't stop her hands from shaking or the hairs on the back of her neck from stiffening.

Deep breaths, Emma.

Mostoff grabbed her shoulders. "Let me help you."

She turned her head, and their eyes met. His face was painted with the same intensity she felt. A drop pod carried fifteen to twenty combatants. Even with Mostoff's help, her team was badly outnumbered.

She didn't trust him.

She had to trust him.

Holsey pulled out her sidearm, flipped it around, and handed it grip-first to Mostoff. "I want it back when this is over."

He nodded, racking the slide quickly. She handed him her extra magazines and turned to face forward. The metal around the indentation had already begun to glow bright red. The room grew lighter, cast in a soft light by the burning metal.

Osterman shouldered his weapon. "Here they come."

Holsey could see Jones and Carter raise their weapons, Carter's RAR MK42 light machine gun resting on its bipod in front of him.

There was a flash, and the wall exploded inward, filling the room with smoke and debris. Holsey heard the whine and hum of her suit adjusting as the atmosphere from the pod blasted into the vacuum of the freighter, its artificial gravity system extending to cover the room. The weight of her rifle settled in her arms as she trained her sights into the smoke and—

Weapon's fire burst from the opening as the attackers reached the edge of their pod, the thin air making the usually explosive sound of gun fire tinny and quiet. Holsey rested her helmet on the stock of her carbine. She looked down her sights, searching for a target.

The first few grotesque beasts dropped from the ceiling and crawled carefully through the debris.

The Frontin shock troops had stopped firing. She could see one turn its head, its many black-eyes fixing on her. Its hideous, toothy mandible moved as it said something to the creatures hiding on the other side of the opening.

It smiled.

Holsey squeezed the trigger, her carbine barking as it sent several rounds into the creature's abdomen. The Frontin screamed, black gore spraying the wall as its body hit the floor with a grotesque squishing sound.

The rest of Holsey's team opened up, showering the Frontin in the doorway with deadly fire, hitting the pod's hatch from several angles. The distinct crack of Osterman's submachine gun covered the Frontin's screams.

Explosions rippled across the crates in front of her, Frontin barbs impacting all around her. She ducked, avoiding the metal splinters spraying in all directions. One of the Frontin roared, the sound tearing at her nerves.

She saw Mostoff fire several rounds at two figures darting quickly out of cover on their left. One of them lurched, its legs shattered. It stumbled slightly, but kept moving, darting back into cover.

Her team was being surrounded — fast.

Holsey took a deep breath and leaned out of cover, her eyes locating a target. She fired off several quick bursts. Her target's head fragmented, its legs scrabbling for several seconds before seizing, toppling the dead monster to the deck.

She ducked back into cover, dropping her spent magazine. "Voth, pull back to the rear entrance. Take Carter with you. We can't let them get behind us."

Voth nodded, signaling Carter. Jones got to a knee, laying down suppressive fire. Voth and Carter broke from their positions, heads low, trying to use jumbled crates from a toppled cargo loader as cover while they dashed towards the back of the room.

Holsey slapped in a new magazine and fired quick, controlled pairs in the direction of the creeping Frontin.

The Frontin went crazy and several broke from cover, charging directly at Voth and Carter. The two men were firing wildly, barbs exploding around them as they slid towards cover. Carter jerked as his shoulder exploded. He tumbled as several more barbs burst inside his torso, showering Voth with a bloody mist.

The man never had time to scream.

Major Osterman stood up, firing from the hip. The charging Frontin were cut down, split in half by his withering fire.

Holsey picked out another target. "Major, stay in cover."

Osterman dropped back behind his crate, tossing his weapon aside and pulling his pistol. "I'm out."

She slipped back behind the crates. Voth had managed to scramble to the rear, firing from a well-covered position next to the door. His shots were wild, panicked.

If he didn't calm down, he would burn through his ammunition in no time.

The Frontin's blood-curdling screams made Holsey dizzy. She shook her head, trying to focus. If they couldn't reach the door, they would all be dead in a matter of minutes.

Osterman pointed to her left, breaking the rhythm of his smooth, accurate fire for only a moment.

Mostoff screamed, and Holsey turned her head. He was dangling from one of the Frontin's claws, trying to fight with his bare hands. Its bone-white teeth glistened with slick ooze as it opened its mouth wide to crush the helmet of his environmental suit. Holsey saw the creature's face, its deep black eyes cold.

Barbs smashed into the crates in front of her, incinerating in a wave of smoke and flame. There was no way to know how many Frontin were left.

Holsey and her team were not going to make it. She wiped her visor, closed her eyes, and willed the world to slow down.

Private Jones was screaming from somewhere ahead of her, blood flowing from his mouth as fire impacted all around him.

Holsey lowered her head.

This was it. She might as well have died the last time she'd faced these bastards.

She broke from cover and sprinted towards Mostoff. Explosions followed at her heels, the Frontin's gleeful screams echoing loudly behind her. Osterman and Voth were yelling, but she couldn't tell what they were saying.

She slammed into the Frontin holding Mostoff. Even through her suit, its skin felt rough, yet slick with ooze. It stumbled, trying to regain its balance on the uneven deck.

Holsey rolled, pulling her combat knife as she regained her feet. She plunged the steel blade into the creature's brain cavity, its body shaking wildly. She gagged slightly at the noxious sight of the Frontin's thick blood as it oozed down her blade. She pulled the knife free, letting her opponent's body fall lifeless to the floor.

Something struck her, pain shooting through her back, the world blurring as she fell and hit the deck. She shook her head, letting her vision clear. Her blood froze, her eyes filled with the sickly smile of the Frontin pinning her to the ground. Its arms were raised, a long blade pointed at her heart.

Hillman jerked on his stick. "Damn it!"

Raptor Six disintegrated in front of him, the oncoming destroyer's guns scoring a direct hit. Hillman banked his Stallion hard, barely avoiding the flaming debris showering past his craft.

Lt. Hillman's consoles screamed, various alarms flashing on his dashboard. His eyes took in the damage. His defense system had failed, and his fuel was low, but he still had torpedoes and full engine power. He could do this.

He smiled.

Hillman disabled the ship's safety controls, pushing his engines past the red line. Their screaming drowned out the alarms reverberating through his cockpit. Hillman put the ship into a deep roll as the *Black Fox* fired another salvo at point break range into the attackers.

The *Fox* had fought well. It had managed to avoid most of the enemy's salvos as it maneuvered on thrusters only. His pilots had helped, using their own defensive systems to detonate much of the incoming ordnance.

Hillman wanted this kill — he just had to be close enough. The destroyer wasn't making it easy, filling the gap between them with flak and machine gun fire. He felt his craft jerk from several glancing impacts. His controls tightened under his fingers. No doubt they'd managed to hit his elevation thrusters.

Lucky bastards.

There was a bright yellow explosion to his left, the intense light forcing him to cover his eyes. He didn't need to look at his squadron command screen to know another Raptor had died. The unique atmosphere mixture of the Alliance fighters always looked the same when it burned.

His Stallion shuddered as it absorbed shrapnel from a flak explosion. He turned off his alarms — Hillman didn't need them to tell him his systems were failing. Nothing was responding to his touch.

His holographic display disappeared in a flash. He could feel an intense heat on his back that could mean only one thing.

His Stallion's fuselage was burning.

He ignored the growing temperature in the cockpit, seconds stretching on as he waited for his reticle to indicate that he was in range.

The reticle flashed, and Hillman squeezed the trigger, felt his craft recoil as its last four torpedoes blasted free of their tubes.

Hillman exhaled. "Eat it, bastards."

Chapter 15

Ensign George Masson rotated his stick, easing his Stallion between the *Black Fox* and another group of projectiles, impact warnings screaming in his cockpit. He could feel his automated defense turret firing quick bursts, reducing the shells to splintered fragments.

Masson looked at his holodisplay. "There we go!"

It was all he could do not to shout into his headset. He pulled back hard, letting his eyes take in the view. One of the destroyers was delisting, flame bursting from it amidships. He smiled, recognizing the handy work of Alliance torpedoes as they struck home, one after another. The enemy ship was burning brightly against the night of space.

His heart caught.

One of the Alliance stallions was trying to reach escape velocity, flames and explosions enveloping it. The craft's engines were already on fire. It was losing velocity.

Rapidly.

Was that Hillman? He had been the closest to that destroyer. "One, this is Three. You're on fire. Eject. Do you copy? Eject."

He tried to recalibrate his communication equipment, break through the interference of the dying destroyer. A yellow explosion tore through the darkness, blending into the belching flame from the dying destroyer. The striker's fuel cells had gone up.

George sat, helpless, motionless, his mouth slightly open, eyes fixed on the spot where Raptor One had just vanished. He felt his ship buck, the automated systems defending him from incoming fire. He hit his brakes, turned as hard as he could stand, angling his ship for the last destroyer.

He spoke quietly into his mike. "All Raptors, go after the last destroyer now. I want these fuckers dead."

On his display, Masson could see the remaining stallions turning.

These bastards would pay. He would make sure of it.

Holsey struggled, trying to shake the iron grip of the Frontin warrior. His teeth made contact with her armored gauntlet, screeching like nails on a chalkboard. Her arm seared with pain and slick, warm blood trickled down her arm. She kicked its chest as hard as she could, her legs aching with effort.

"Fuck you, bastard!"

A gunshot sounded from directly behind her. The Frontin jerked forward, collapsing onto her, blood oozing from a large hole in its armor. Holsey turned her head. Captain Mostoff had regained his feet, her pistol smoking in his hand.

She kicked again, sending its body skidding a few feet in front of her. She scrambled backwards, picking up her carbine as she moved.

Holsey grabbed Mostoff's arm, pulling him into cover as Frontin barbs whistled past.

She couldn't see the others. She hit her mike. "Marines, sound off."

Osterman's voice was barely audible over the gunfire. "Jorden and Carter are dead. I don't have a visual on Mostoff. Voth's providing cover fire, but his radio might be out. I can't raise him."

Holsey peeked around the corner. "The Captain's with me. Hold for orders."

Osterman was right — Voth had managed to crawl forward and grab the Corporal's RAR and was using it to suppress the Frontin. The ones inside the bay were hissing loudly, firing off random shots, the impacts sending shards of metal and wood spraying through the air.

Mostoff's voice caused her to turn her head. "That was my last round."

Holsey nodded. "Then keep your head down. I already gave you everything I had."

Her mind raced. Osterman couldn't have much more ammo than Mostoff. She could see him in front of her, firing, carefully picking his targets.

She slammed a fresh magazine into her carbine. There were at least eight still out there, lurking somewhere in the darkness.

Voth's rate of fire had slowed. Once his drum ran out, the remaining Frontin on board the pod would pour out. Without ammunition, her team would be overwhelmed, cut to shreds.

Holsey pulled out two grenades, yanking their pins as she stood up. She threw them as hard as she could towards the pod's entrance. She dropped back into cover, her back resting against the crate, enemy fire tearing into the area where she had been standing.

Mostoff screamed as shrapnel tore through his visor, his blood spraying out with the atmosphere of his decompressing suit. The man was writhing in pain. She threw her body over his, covering her head.

The grenades detonated, engulfing the far end of the room in a wave of smoke and flame. The Frontin on the ground screamed, their anger and frustration clear even to human ears. Holsey squinted, tried to see through the unnerving combination of human and Frontin blood that covered her visor.

These damn things need wiper blades.

Holsey pulled an emergency decompression patch from her equipment belt, applying it to the hole in Mostoff's helmet, taking only seconds to check for obvious leaks

She took a deep breath before popping out of cover. She fired quickly, lining up targets as quickly as her eyes worked. Her finger tingled as it worked the trigger over and over until her bolt locked open.

Holsey dropped back into cover, fumbling for her last magazine.

She yelled into her mike. "Major, do you have eyes on the targets?"

Osterman's voice sounded calm. "No, they aren't moving."

It was clear to Holsey now why the crew on the *Verdun* respected Osterman. She had taken him for a desk jockey and a womanizer, but he'd obviously earned his rank.

Voth's voice was barely audible, covered with static. "Ma'am, they are in cover to your left, moving along the wall toward your position." His mike must be working after all, though only barely.

She moved, letting her gaze rake past the metal of the cargo loader. Voth was right. She could see shadows crouched low, crawling slowly towards her, using a small maintenance pit for cover.

Osterman shot back quickly. "I see them. They are trying to flank us again."

She shouldered her weapon. "I don't think so. They are going after Voth. They want to pick us off one by one."

It was so quiet now. Without the gunfire and screams—

Mostoff.

Holsey hadn't noticed the man's screams stop over the sound of the fighting. She looked down at his broken body. He was breathing, but unconscious.

Holsey squeezed off a single round. "Voth, move to the front of that maintenance trench and lay down covering fire. Osterman, I want you to fall back towards my position, grab Private..." She couldn't think of his name. "The man's rifle. When they return fire on Voth, we will get them in crossfire. Move quickly."

She eased herself forward onto her stomach, inching towards the pit. She wanted to be as close to the enemy as possible. The trench was slightly beyond her position, maybe five or six feet away. She could hear the Frontin's many legs making light tapping sounds as they dragged their grotesque torsos over the debris-strewn floor.

Osterman came up behind her, leaning against the pile of unused piping she was using as cover. He gingerly set his newly acquired rifle against the pipes, steadying it as he looked down his sights into the pit.

The room had grown suspiciously quiet, the deafening noise of gunfire replaced with silence. Holsey tried not to breathe, her eyes locked on the Frontin below her.

Just a few more seconds.

Voth opened up on the Frontin, lancing fire down the pit's length. The rounds tore into the Frontin, killing one instantly and wounding several others, sowing panic. They returned fired. The rubble Voth was hiding behind shuddered with each new impact, and white-hot barbs ripped into the fragile conduits behind him.

Holsey and Osterman opened fire, carefully hitting their targets, splattering each with several deadly projectiles. The Frontin screamed as they died, the channel filling with blood and gore as the devastating fire from the Alliance rifles tore them apart.

The last remaining Frontin leaped forward, sprinting towards Voth's position. Voth stumbled as one of the rounds broke through his cover, hitting him squarely in the torso. The young man dropped his weapon, collapsed to the ground, his hands pressing into his wound.

Holsey stood up, sighted down her barrel and fired. Her round tore straight through its skull, cracking it like an egg. The creature fell, returning the room to the silence.

She lowered her weapon. "Major, check on the Captain."

Holsey ran quickly forward, slipping on the sticky blood covering the floor. She skidded to a stop directly in front of Voth, dropping to her knees, her armor clanking.

Despite his groans, she could tell instantly it was a minor wound. There was very little blood. His armor was charred and cracked, but it had done its job. She grabbed for more decompression patches from her kit.

Osterman yelled back to her. "Commander, the Captain is alive but hurt badly. His suit is losing oxygen."

She nodded, smoothing the patches into place. "Set up a homing beacon coded for medical emergency. We need help, now. You're lucky, Lieutenant, if those conduits behind you had been active, you would be dead. I'd be happy with the broken bones and contusions,"

Voth frowned. "Yeah, thrilled."

She put the last patch in place, moved Voth's hand over his wound. "Keep pressure on it."

Holsey looked up, her eyes fixed on the pitted and torn conduits. Her hands instinctively reached for the ring hanging around her neck, her fingers blocked by the steel of her chest plate.

CHAPTER 16

Wilcox gripped the edge of his chair. He could feel the *Verdun* strain under the pressure of its velocity. The deck was vibrating, the normal hum of the engines replaced with a throaty roar. Morden was pushing the ship's engines way past their safety limits, and Geonor's crew had already had to make emergency repairs on two of the heat sinks.

Holsey's coded emergency transmission burst had arrived ten hours ago, and it was all Wilcox could do to keep Morden from flying the ship apart. He had never seen her like this. She never took these kinds of risks, but she was hell-bent on reaching her stranded team.

He had been watching her pace back and forth, eyes fixed on the action table, her hands locked behind her back, for the past twenty minutes.

Wilcox spun in his chair. "You should relax. We are still hours from the asteroid field."

"I will relax when I want to." Morden waved both hands.

Wilcox hated this part of military life, the waiting. The enormous distances between planets and solar systems made long travel times a fact of life in space. Big military operations relied on strict timetables, hundreds of ships and thousands of people acting as a single entity, their anxiety ratcheting up as crews sat on their hands, praying everyone else was okay, doing their jobs. The complete lack of communication and sensors while traveling faster-than-light made even the toughest leatherneck antsy. He understood waiting, how it whittled away at morale, the pressures of impending combat. Wilcox had been in a number of ship-to-ship skirmishes, but the fear of combat had never affected him as badly as the hours of uncertainty.

Wilcox wouldn't let Morden suffer this alone.

He typed several quick commands into his console. "Captain, could you take a look at this?"

Morden whipped back towards him. "What?" she snapped.

He held out an energy bar, handing it to her. "I decided that since you won't get some chow, you would like one of the old c-rations. I just so happen to have one."

Morden crinkled her nose. "I'm fine, really. Get back to work."

He didn't budge, giving her what he hoped was a sly grin. "Regulations require officers to be of sound mind. A soldier can't fight on an empty stomach. A tense captain leads to a tense crew."

Morden glared back at him, crossing her arms in front of her. "I should have known better than to come over here. You tricked me."

Wilcox shrugged, thrusting the energy bar toward her. He prided himself on being unflappable, a rock for his captain.

She nodded slightly. "All *right*. I'll will take a short walk and get some grub. Notify me of any changes. You won't be rid of me long."

He chuckled, trying to look innocent. "I swear you will be notified of any emergencies that *won't* happen while we fly forward in straight line, with no way to see or hear outside."

She rolled her eyes. "Oh, ha, ha."

Wilcox watched her leave, waiting just long enough for Isabelle's voice to record the change in command before turning to Chief Baudouin. "If you call her before we decelerate, you'll be scrubbing the launch tubes for the foreseeable future."

Wilcox leaned back in his chair and unwrapped the decades-old food bar.

Mission accomplished.

Morden clenched her fists, stalking down the corridor towards the aft mess hall and trying not to frown. Her feet ached, her eyes dry and heavy. She had considered staying in her quarters and having the chef deliver a meal, but every time she sat down, she started dozing off.

This was not the time for sleep.

God damn Wilcox.

How the man always managed to stay even and cool was beyond her. She hadn't realized how tense she was or how her frustration could be leaking out in all directions, affecting the rest the of bridge crew. If he hadn't pointed it out...

The *Verdun* was her ship now — the crew looked to her, and she would play her part. Confident leaders inspired a confident crew. Letting the crew see her enjoy a casual meal would help relax them. As long as she could keep her damn emotions in check.

Her frown deepened unintentionally.

Morden turned down another corridor, the crewmen flowing past her quickly moving aside to let her through. The ship's vibrating deck plates made her attempts to look casual difficult.

She reached out, pushed open the mess hall doors. The overwhelming smell of food made her stomach growl painfully. Her nerves had blocked out how hungry she was. Morden picked up one of the small, metal trays resting on a stand right inside the entrance and moseyed up to the back of the line.

She forced a smile onto her face.

Morden turned the tray over in her hands. It was hot and damp, freshly washed by her kitchen staff.

One of the two young marines in front of her laughed. "No way had that happened, that old ship probably just broke down."

The other one shook his head. "Either way, the Major will take care of it. He's a tough son of a bitch."

The first one took a step forward as the line crept toward the hot bar. "Bet Holsey can hold her own. Word is she used to be a lobster like us before she switched to driving boats."

"Don't know, man, the captain doesn't like her. She must be trouble. I've seen Morden kill a Milipa with her bare hands. I shit you not."

It was Morden's turn to laugh. The two marines looked around, and the one who had just spoken turned beet red, his eyes bulging.

She waved her hand. "At ease. I'm here for grub. I like story time, too."

"Yes, ma'am," both men said in unison.

Morden continued. "Besides, you're right. Holsey and Osterman are both stubborn sons of bitches. Anyone picking a fight with them would regret it."

The two men laughed nervously. Neither were in uniform, but Morden was reasonably sure she remembered their faces. "So, anything worth eating, privates?"

"Is there ever?" The first answered. He was a big guy, rippling muscle and bald head signaling his branch. She was sure his name was Horax. He'd always seemed pretty thoughtful for a marine, storytelling aside.

She wrinkled her nose, trying to remember the other one's name. "I can hope."

The two marines handed their trays to the mess attendant. The man barely reacted, scooping some thin-looking stew into bowls. He quickly added a stale piece of bread and a big scoop of some limp green beans before handing the trays back to Horax and his companion.

Morden handed her tray over, and the mess attendant spooned the dark liquid into her bowl.

She spoke up before his hand got to the bread. "Skip the bread, please. Give me some of that … corn, I think it is. The yellow stuff. Yeah, you got it. Great."

She watched the man oblige, his face hidden behind the steamed-up glass. He filled her tray with the small, over-buttered kernels. She walked to the closest unoccupied table and sat down.

It worried her that this slop smelled so good. She couldn't remember the last time she'd eaten. The first bite of the stew sent bolts of warmth running through her body.

Damn *Wilcox*.

A young ensign she didn't recognize looked at her from a nearby table. "Captain, how's your stew?"

Morden put down her fork. "It's mess food, at night."

Several people around her laughed. Another officer from the medical division, Jackson, spoke up. "Have you heard from the detachment? I can't shake this feeling that something awful has happened."

Morden smiled as confidently as she could. She could feel all eyes staring at her. "Not since going translight. I'm not worried, though. It would take more than a handful of miners to whip our team. This is the Verdun. We are the finest ship in the fleet."

Another officer stepped forward. "The last time we responded to the beacon, we didn't like what we found. I had this same feeling then."

She recognized the voice. "Va, this isn't a war zone. There's no Milipa heavy cruiser lurking in these asteroids. We are in a dangerous line of work, but you can't take feelings to the bank. I know together we can face any challenge."

Morden couldn't blame Va. They had lost eighteen people during the Ardaugh incident. It had been the worst combat loss the *Verdun* had faced since commissioning.

Va walked in front of her, heading towards the door. "Thank you, Captain. I needed that."

Morden left the mess hall an hour later. It had felt good to eat and talk with her crew. Some were asking for reassurance like Va, and others just seemed to enjoy the personal attention of their captain. She felt lighter somehow, more focused.

Had she ignored the morale of her crew for too long? Allowed herself to indulge in her own fears? Captain Knight had always made time to keep the crew's spirits high.

Morden opened the door to her quarters, crossed the room, and dropped into her chair. She closed her eyes, letting memories flood her mind.

Five years ago, right after she had joined the crew, the *Verdun* had been on a run-of-the-mill supply mission. Morden had been on the bridge fiddling with the daily report when they'd received an urgent transmission that Admiral Knight and his carrier, the *Wolverine*, had gone missing.

Captain Knight had never flinched or frowned. That evening, she had stopped by his quarters. Morden couldn't remember every detail of the conversation, but she had vented for hours about her worries, her feeling of uneasiness at being new to the ship. The man had listened, doing his best to advise and reassure her.

When she'd stood to leave, she couldn't help but apologize.   Captain Knight had smiled. "What for?"

"Your brother is missing, possibly dead, and I'm here whining about my feelings. It's unprofessional."

He'd laughed in his disarming and annoyingly charming way. "We all have our burdens, our own emotions to deal with. In our line of work, if you don't deal with them, they can kill you."

"Then how can you just sit there quietly? Your brother could be dead, and you barely seem to care."

"I can't change what is happening out there. All I can do is complete our mission quickly and join the search. We face so many life-or-death decisions, and you can't let all of them weigh on you. I take comfort in helping my crew. When my own mind is overflowing with my personal problems, helping someone else strengthens me more than worrying about the issue."

Morden hadn't really understood that until now. By helping her crew, Captain Knight had found a strength that comforted him. It wasn't a façade — it was who he was. A real leader supported his crew, developed, nurtured, and occasionally kicked them in the butt.

DAMN WILCOX.

Morden felt the ship decelerating, the screaming of the overtaxed engines quieting to their normal hum. She opened her eyes.

Ensign Smith's voice filled her room. "Captain Morden, to the bridge please."

In the time it took Morden to reach the bridge, the *Verdun* had already begun to slip into the asteroid field. Morden's eyes were fixed on the holoports. The ship's running lights didn't seem to dent the darkness from the overlapping shadows of the asteroids. The rocks were drifting and tumbling erratically, crashing into each other with massive force. Between the dancing shadows and the constant motion, it would be hard to pick out an attacker from the chaos. She felt goosebumps prickling up along her arms. Whoever was behind this was close — she could feel it in her bones.

The *Verdun* had to stop it.

She lowered herself into her chair. "Dead slow."

Wilcox swiveled around in his chair. "Captain, sensor drones confirm the Fox is not at the emergency rendezvous point. Should we launch fighters?"

Morden drummed her fingers on her armrest. Why hadn't Mostoff and Holsey pulled back? Had they been unable to make it out?

She pushed away the dread slithering up her spine. "Not yet, but call general quarters. I want all gun crews to report to stations. We may need the ten-inchers to blast us a path."

"Yes, ma'am."

She turned to look at him. "And Mr. Wilcox? Thanks."

He ginned sheepishly. "For what?"

Morden frowned, turned back to the holoports. She watched as the *Verdun* slid past a massive asteroid towards the emergency signal.

She listened as the klaxon sounded general quarters and Isabelle recited the usual instructions.

It wouldn't be long now.

The Frontin warlord smiled his toothy, horrifying smile as he watched the *Verdun* enter the asteroid field. Even his subordinates cowered from his intensity, his hate. He stretched his claws out to their full length. He had to wait, had to control his desire for revenge a little longer. He wanted to attack now, fire on his opponent, but he wouldn't spoil the surprise.

The trap was set.

The Alliance had subverted his rise to power, prevented him from becoming one of the hive council. He would exact his revenge in an explosion of carnage so breathtaking his people would sing of it forever. His unsuspecting prey would bleed soon, die in unending agony as he ripped the life from each soul.

Their deaths would be his new mantle, his new symphony.

CHAPTER 17

Urquhart rubbed the back of her neck, kneading the tension from her muscles. She had been working nonstop for ten hours. Navigating the asteroid field was a nightmare. The *Verdun* struggled to maneuver in the tight confines of rock and ice. She was glad she didn't have to do Stetler's job, slipping the ship's bulk through narrow channels.

They were approaching the origin of Holsey's distress call.

Sensor drones had made contact with the clearing several hours before, but hadn't shown much beyond the signs of combat — debris, shell fragments, inert gasses, and pockets of frozen atmosphere.

She looked up at the holoport as the ship slid past the last of the asteroids, searching the images for the *Black Fox*.

Morden's voice echoed her thoughts. "Anyone see the Fox?"

Urquhart glanced back down at her sensor readings. "Nothing's registering, but the amount of debris floating around indicates a massive, knock-down, drag-out fight. Metallurgic analysis should be back quickly."

She looked up at the captain, trying to judge the woman's flat expression.

Stetler's chair squealed as he swiveled to face the captain. "Maybe we should hail them?"

Morden rubbed her chin. "No, not yet. This situation calls for caution. A hail would give away our location. We would lose the element of surprise."

Wilcox stood. "Stetler, bring it up on the action table. My eyes can't pull anything out of that mess."

Morden got to her feet and followed him as he walked towards the table.

Urquhart craned her neck, trying to get a glimpse of the cool blue images that flickered to life on the table. The *Verdun* was in the middle of the display, cruising towards the center of the clearing. Debris was everywhere, large chunks of metal and rock swirling past the ship's external cameras. She could make out a shattered ore freighter about the size of an Alliance destroyer, caught by the pull of a particularly large asteroid at the edge of the field and falling slowly towards its surface.

Wilcox pointed to something Urquhart couldn't make out. "Do you see that?"

Morden nodded. "Guns. That ship is covered with weapons."

Urquhart stood slowly and walked towards the table.

Isabelle's image appeared next to them. "Commander Wilcox is correct. Although the amount of interference is immense, I have located ten intact emplacements. Most still show signs of unexploded ordnance. I'm not detecting any radiation signatures. Infrared scans show no heat, and motion sensors show no movement on board. She is dead, ma'am."

Urquhart noticed something. "Look there, on the bottom right. That looks like one of the missing ships."

Morden tapped a few controls on the table's edge, refocusing its view on the wrecked vessel. "Isabelle, reposition Drone Thirty-Three to grid Seven-B. Get me a better view of that wreck."

One of the six visible drones darted toward the asteroid. The details of the wreck magnified, its details resolving as the drone drew closer, the scarred and twisted hull identified by the faint lettering on its shattered bow, *SS Baron*.

The small drone continued upward, feeding fresh images to the table as it curved around the asteroid. Urquhart's breath caught.

The *Fox*!

A small panel appeared in the image directly next to the *Fox*, displaying the sensor data of the ship's condition. The ship was delisting, spinning slowly in space on the dark side of the *Baron's* asteroid. The drone's readings came back quickly as Isabelle redirected the drone. No emergency beacons, no power readings, no signs of life at all.

The image made the hairs on the back of Urquhart's neck stand up. The ship was just floating in the open, weapons armed, in between several large asteroids.

This felt like a trap.

The captain looked up, turned back towards the command chair. "Launch defensive fighters. Ensign Smith, prepare to hail that ship."

Urquhart turned and hurried back down to her station. She could feel the familiar thumps as the Cerberus fighters dropped from the ship's underbelly.

Her heart raced. This would be the first time she'd navigated a ship during combat. It was hard not to focus on the number of people whose lives relied on her.

Isabelle turned towards the captain, her voice flat. "All stations report battle ready. All emergency bulkheads report green. All fire suppression systems green. All defensive squadrons away."

Wilcox's voice followed a second later. "Captain, my boards agree. All systems combat ready."

Morden spoke quietly. "Ensign, hail the Black Fox."

Urquhart exhaled softly, trying not to hold her breath, listening to Smith's voice. "Black Fox, Black Fox. This is the RAS Verdun. Please respond."

Silence followed.

Urquhart clenched and unclenched her fist, fighting to keep her hands still. The ship should have responded by now. Something awful had happened here. She couldn't explain it, but she knew it, somehow.

Morden's voice almost made her jump. "Resend the message please and boost the transmission this time. Our fighters might be hiding."

The ensign repeated the hail, the radio crackling loudly from Morden's station.

"Verdun, Raptor Three. It's great to see you. Request permission to dock. All fighters danger-low on fuel."

Urquhart's board lit up as several drones registered the engine flares of the fighters.

Isabelle spoke again. "Transponder code verified."

Morden nodded, putting on her headset. "Raptor Three, Verdun. Come on home. Where is the rest of the detachment?"

Several seconds passed before the fighter responded. "The Black Fox lost life support after the attack, and the crew used a few skiffs to get to the surface. Commander Holsey's team managed to seal enough of the Baron to use it as a life raft. There are wounded down there who need immediate evacuation."

"Sergeant, bring your squadron home. Smith, have Commander Cadogan assemble an emergency medical team. I want them in Landing Bay One in ten minutes. We will be taking on wounded."

Urquhart stood without thinking. "Permission to leave the bridge. One of the command staff should be there to greet them."

Morden smiled, nodding. "I was going to send Wilcox. Do you have any objections to letting our young friend go in your place, Jack?"

Wilcox shook his head, leaned back in his chair. "No objection here."

Morden gestured towards the door. "Permission granted."

Commander Frost ran back across the deck, the muscles in his thighs burning. "Come on, Rogers, lock that bird down. We got another one coming in thirty seconds."

The detachment had been landing for the past twenty minutes, but there was still a lot of work to do with three squadrons in the air.

Frost had been listening to his crew chiefs chattering back and forth over his headset. This team was not well drilled. Not that it surprised him. Battlecruiser commanders often ignored their air wings. Their power was in their big guns, while their fighter compliment was a secondary concern.

Frost had commanded carrier air wings for too long to accept lax standards. He was determined to make the *Verdun's* birds top notch.

The first damage reports were coming in. Raptor squadron had been seriously beaten up. Three destroyed, and most showed serious damage. Fortunately, only one pilot had been killed, while the others had managed to eject from their craft.

Frost looked down at his clipboard. The repair crews would need to pull double shifts for a few days to get the Stallions back in space. His fighters would be playing a major role as long as the *Verdun* was in tight quarters like this asteroid field.

Frost heard laughter. He turned, saw Lieutenant Blake talking to the sergeant from Raptor squadron in the corner, the man's headset dangling lazily around his neck.

Frost wasn't sure what to make of Blake. He was charismatic, smart, and a natural leader, but carried himself with the swagger and pomp of a naval desk jockey. He certainly wasn't a run-of-the-mill senior deck officer.

Frost sighed. The young man had potential, but he needed to be sharpened. "Blake, get your ass over here. Bring the sergeant with you."

The two men walked over.

Frost waved away their beginnings of a salute. "Sergeant Masson, what happened?"

The man frowned. "Those bastards attacked the Fox while we were all separated in the field. Only we Raptors made it back in time. The Lieutenant managed to fight 'em off, killed one of those bloody things. The other ran when it saw its buddy go up."   Frost nodded. "I want a full report ASAP. Blake, clear the sky, then get the repair crews going. I want double shifts from now till all our birds are ship-shape. I don't want those shitheads to catch us with our craft on the deck. We still have a lot of areas to search."

Blake glanced at the sergeant. "Sir, shouldn't we let them rest first? We lost at least three Stallions and one man."

The commander shook his head. "Blake, you're the deck chief. You kick the ground crew in the butt, and let the pilots rest. That's how it works. The ground crews have been sitting on their hands enough. Get these birds fixed up. I want a preliminary time estimate five minutes after the last squadron is down."

Blake gave him a forced smile. "Yes, sir."

Frost watched the two men move towards the central control tower. Colonel Pintar had obviously run this deck too loosely. He would fix that.

Starting with Blake.

Urquhart flattened herself against the wall, trying to keep out of the way. Medical teams were rushing by, whipping stretchers around corners at an alarming rate.

Maybe she had made a mistake coming down here. Urquhart barely recognized anyone, even excluding the large number of wounded from the *Fox*. She frowned. Maybe she hadn't been on board long enough to do something like this.

She watched Commander Cadogan rip down the ramp at the head of a gurney.

His face was grim and taut as he ran, yelling directions at his orderlies. The bed's occupant, Captain Mostoff, looked barely alive, his face as white as the sheets of the gurney. He was a far cry from the intimidating, angry, larger-than-life man she'd met. He must really be in the woods to cause such a calm person as Cadogan to be so loud.

Urquhart caught a break between medical personnel and dashed over to the transport. She was certain the captain wanted to know which of the *Verdun's* crew was hurt, and she'd be damn sure she got that information.

Commander Holsey's voice reached her ears moments before the woman appeared on the ramp. "Lieutenant, you seem lost."

Urquhart tried not to seem shocked. The woman looked awful. Her armor was drenched in dried blood and grime. The detachment had seen combat, and not just the ship-to-ship variety.

She looked up. "Not really. Just trying to stay out of the way."

Holsey smiled, waving her arm towards the ship. "Give me a hand. I need to get Voth to the med deck." The woman turned her head back to the transport, her voice getting louder. "The idiot is refusing a stretcher."

Urquhart nodded, stared up towards the top of the ramp. "I am glad you're okay, ma'am."

Voth laughed. "Oh, I see the guy with gaping wounds doesn't get a hello."

He sat at the top of the ramp looking pale and tired, his midsection covered in a bandage soaked through with blood.

Urquhart blushed, reaching down to grab him under his arms, Holsey pulling him up by his feet, his weight balanced between them.

Holsey grunted. "Stop griping, you baby. This flesh wound is the only way you could hope to get a woman, any woman, to touch you. Maybe you asked the Frontin to hit us just so you could finally get some action."

Voth snorted indignantly.

Urquhart almost stumbled.

What did she say?

She tried to keep her voice steady as the word crossed her lips. "Frontin?"

Holsey caught her eye, nodded. "As soon as we reach the med bay, I want you to return to the bridge and have the captain call a briefing."

Urquhart shivered slightly. "Yes, ma'am."

The Frontin.

She thought she had been prepared for that possibility, but she'd been wrong. The Frontin were ruthless killers. They murdered and raped people for sport as they pillaged entire systems. She had seen one of those systems as a child, and it wasn't something she wanted to remember.

Holsey stopped just shy of the ship's central lift. "Don't worry, I've looked over the scans of the 'destroyers' we faced. The Verdun is more than a match for them."

Urquhart stepped into the elevator, forcing her thoughts back to the situation at hand. The lift door opened, and the two women shifted Voth's weight against the wall. The lift started descending toward the ship's center. Medical bays were always in the core of a vessel. It isolated them from incoming fire and made defending them easier in a boarding action. Anyone who was wounded in the line of duty deserved the best protection. The marines assigned to defend the medical bay would hold it until the last man, giving the medical personnel time to evacuate.

Not that any of that had helped her father. The downside of security protocol was the distance from response teams to outlying areas like the bridge.

Had that distance killed him?

Urquhart shifted Voth's weight, stepping off the lift.

He grimaced as they started down the hall. "Ladies, I know my weight is enormous, but my ribs are killing me."

Urquhart rolled her eyes. "I can't believe you're crying over a few cracked ribs. I thought you were a tough guy and didn't need a stretcher."

Voth's attempt at a laugh became a moan. "Your bedside manner is as impressive as Holsey's."

They reached the door to the infirmary, and Holsey led the way inside. "Just means she's smart, or you're a wimp."

Voth grimaced again, his face getting even paler as they passed him off to an orderly who rushed up to meet them. Holsey started describing the man's injuries to the orderly. Urquhart slipped away quietly, hurrying back down the corridor towards the elevator, her mind buzzing.

The Frontin.

She had wanted to face down the enemies of the Alliance, protect innocents from the monsters at the gates. How many times had she fantasized about this? How many nights had she imagined leading a strike against a Frontin raiding party?

Callista, be careful what you wish for.

CHAPTER 18

Holsey lowered herself into her chair next to Morden, her feet pulsing as soon as she leaned back. She took a deep breath, letting the feel of the fresh uniform resting against her skin rejuvenate her. The smell of the Frontin blood had been turning her stomach for days while they'd been stuck on the *Baron* waiting for the *Verdun*.

Morden looked up from the head of the table. "The Frontin are here. We don't know how many, and we don't know what they're after. We need to crack this now. The clock is ticking."

Holsey could feel the tension as Morden said the word 'Frontin' out loud. She ran her gaze around the room. Frost was sitting stiff-faced and cross-armed opposite from her. Geonor and Stetler, both looking oddly pale, were to his right.

Urquhart, Osterman, and Blake were to Holsey's right. Urquhart was sitting rigidly in her chair, face blank, eyes locked on the captain. Blake's arms were resting in front of him, fingers drumming lightly on the table. Osterman looked tired, dark circles visible under his eyes.

Morden was the only one who looked calm and collected.

Commander Frost spoke up first. "Shouldn't we be focused on what we need to do, not worrying about what motivates bugs?"

Morden shrugged. "Where do we go? We know the bastards are hiding somewhere in this damn asteroid field, but no more than that. If we can figure out what they are after, it'll narrow our search."

Wilcox leaned forward. "Captain, with all due respect, if this is the best they have, we can take them easily. I say we start sweeping this asteroid—"

Urquhart interrupted. "We can't shoot what we can't see."

Morden raised her hand, stopping the fledgling argument. "There is more to this than cargo. This system borders billions of Alliance citizens. We can't afford to miss a single Frontin ship."

 Holsey nodded. "She's right. There is no way a Frontin raiding party would be here to knock around some freighters. It's not their style. The Baron's cargo was intact, all the vital equipment in place. I'd bet my command bars that the freighters are the tip of the iceberg here."

Osterman rubbed his chin. "I agree — the Frontin are rarely this overt."

Frost gave a dismissive flick of his wrist. "Obviously, but our air wing has already been bloodied. We have one pilot, a squad leader, dead, ten fighters down for repairs, and two that won't fly again without new parts. We already have enough work to keep us busy around the clock for five days. I understand we can't give the Frontin the initiative, but we can't go letting those smaller ships pick off my fighters one by one. It's doubtful they can overwhelm the Verdun, but we may lose good people trying to flush them out."

Morden smiled. "Possibly, but the bottom line is we can't hit a target we can't find."

Blake sat up. "They're nearby. We should use the drones to run them to ground. Frontin equipment emit pretty distinctive emissions."

Lt. Stetler piped up. "It won't work. Too much interference among these rocks. Without the Fox, using the fighters will be slow going, too. The Verdun is just too big to maneuver easily, and we risk expending munitions trying to protect the ship from collisions."

Wilcox sounded unusually serious. "Assuming we are capable of dealing with anything out there. This isn't just dangerous. We might stumble into a hornet's nest. They could easily hide a hive ship in there. There is no way in hell we could take one down unassisted. I think our best course of action is to get the Fox operational again and follow the original plan."

Holsey caught Morden's eye and nodded.

Morden cleared the hair from her eyes. "Agreed. We smoke them out. Our priority now is getting the Fox online."

Geonor looked up from his console. "I've been going over the data from the teams we sent over to the Fox. We can patch her up in three days, but without dry dock time, her engines won't run much better than 12 percent of normal capacity. On the bright side, their life support generators won't need much work, and the ship's structural integrity should be easily maintained."

Holsey activated her own screen. "What kind of personnel will you need?"

He shrugged. "At least a quarter of my staff."

Morden nodded. "Get it set up. I want the first teams ready to go by 0700 tomorrow. Major, put together a few squads of marines to go along, just in case."

Holsey crossed her arms, leaned back in her chair, frowning. Something was still missing. Morden's encounter with the local government, why the Frontin incursion seemed to be in tandem with the miners. None of it added up. Why were they here? Why would they hide when they were so close to killing their prey, and the locals had no means of stopping them? Frontin were fearless killers, they didn't retreat until their leader was dead or their forces were decimated. Even outnumbered, they were more likely to fight to the last bug than flee.

What were they missing?

She understood why the Frontin might use old mining vessels to keep their presence hidden but —

Idiot.

Holsey cut off the conversation she had ignored. "That damned ship. The answers are right in front of us. Permission to take a team to investigate the enemy wreck."

The room went silent.

Wilcox's eyes flew wide. "If any of the Frontin are still alive, the advantage would be theirs. They know the turf and don't need oxygen. The entire ship may be rigged to detonate. There is too much interference to get any readings off that hulk."

Frost looked directly at her. "We already lost one transport crew. This will expose another to serious risk."

Geonor nodded in agreement. "That ship is incredibly unstable, and it's gradually falling towards the asteroid. There's just too much structural damage. I already had Isabelle send over a sensor drone. It was destroyed within minutes when one of the outer decks collapsed. I don't recommend sending a team."

Morden sat quietly for a moment, her eyes locked on her screen. "Holsey's right — we're missing something. I won't search endlessly through these damn rocks. The stakes are too high. The information we can gather from that ship's computer is worth the risk. I won't let the Frontin call the shots and destabilize the Triangle. In the meantime, get a report put together for command."

Wilcox turned towards Morden. "Captain, I strongly disagree, I —"

"The decision is made. We need to dig up whatever we can. I'll risk a trap, but I won't sit here and do nothing. Besides they would've scuttled her if any of them had been left alive."

Holsey smiled. "Thank you, Captain. I'll have a team together in two hours."

Morden shook her head. "No. I want Wilcox and Urquhart to go."

Urquhart jerked. "Wait, why me?" The young woman smiled. "Not that I don't want to, of course!"

Holsey cheeks burned. "I have more experience with the Frontin. I'm the most qualified to lead this mission."

Morden put up her hand. "I agree, but you need to rest. You just got back from five days of extreme stress. As I have been annoyingly reminded recently, rest keeps people sharp. I need you sharp, Commander. As for you, Lieutenant, if we find navigational data, you will be the one using it. It makes sense to let you see it firsthand."

Holsey rubbed the back of her neck. Fatigue pulled at her eyelids, but her heart felt lighter. Even if Holsey couldn't shake off her desire to board that derelict ship, Morden had trusted her enough to follow her recommendation. Maybe they could really work together again.

Osterman patted Urquhart's shoulder, sounding suave. "Don't worry, I'll watch your back."

Holsey almost laughed. The man's reputation for charm was well deserved.

Morden shook her head again. "No, Major, you need rest as well. Select ten of your best marines to go along."

Osterman's face contorted angrily. "There's plenty of time to rest when I'm dead."

Morden turned back to her screen. "Get started selecting the squad. I'll need you at your best if we have to tangle with a large ground force."

The man looked furious, his whole body tense, but he nodded his agreement.

"Geonor." Morden turned to face the engineer. "Please assign two engineers to accompany the boarding party. I want the Black Fox underway in four days. Frost, that's your deadline for the fighters as well."

Frost's eyes widened slightly. "Not possible. We need at least five."

"Four days. If you need help, get some of Geonor's people to assist." Morden raised her hand at the look on Geonor's face. "I know you and your team already have a lot lined up, but do what you can. Fighters are a priority."

Geonor nodded. "Yes, ma'am."

Morden stood. "Anything else? No? Great. Let's get to it."

M orden quickened her pace. It had been almost an hour since she'd received the message that Mostoff was awake. He had been injured protecting members of her crew, and she had to thank him, face to face.

She heard Urquhart's voice behind her. "Captain, I'd like to talk to you."

Morden turned around. The young woman was running down the hall, dodging other crewmembers.

"Watch out!" one of them yelled back at her.

Morden nodded, waving her arm in the direction of the med bay. She didn't want to delay the conversation with Mostoff too long.

Urquhart caught up with her, panting. "I wanted to apologize for my behavior."

Morden looked at her. "For what?"

Urquhart's eyes were fixed on the floor in front of her. "For balking at going over to the wrecked destroyer."

"I understand. It's hard not to be scared by those things. Very few officers jump at the chance to hunt Frontin. Rangers, maybe, but anything beats hiking around rusty old forts all day."

They started down the steep spiral stairs adjacent to the main elevators. Morden hated using elevators. It never seemed like a great idea to rely on a machine to move between decks. Power outages happened during combat, trapping personnel in transit.

"Maybe, but I don't want to be the kind of person who hides from danger. I didn't comport myself like a member of the Royal Navy."

Urquhart had never sounded so negative. Morden fought to keep her eyes locked on the stairs in front of her. Staring would only make her feel more self-conscious.

"We all get scared sometimes. The first time I faced the Frontin, most of my team was killed. I barely made it out. I still feel uncomfortable in tight spaces or when I breathe the old air of those rust-bucket supply stations like the one where it happened."

"Captain, my father — stepfather — was killed defending the bridge of the Blue Jay against one of the splinter groups from the Black Star Empire. I joined the service to help keep creatures like that at bay. You offered me that opportunity, and I blinked."

Morden stopped just shy of the bottom step and turned to look up at the young woman. Urquhart was young, not much over 25, but Morden couldn't help but be struck by her intensity. Her fists clenched tightly to her side, lips pursed into a thin line, gaze fixed on her own.

"Callista, you didn't blink. No one can remain unafraid all the time. Being an Alliance officer means we have to put ourselves in harm's way for our citizens. That doesn't mean we aren't just as afraid. It's a dangerous, sometimes short-lived job. The difference between a bad officer and a good one is the ability to overcome that fear and do the job."

Urquhart looked away.

Morden couldn't help but wonder what she was thinking. "What matters is how you react when the shooting starts and things go to hell. If you can look yourself in the mirror and know you protected the people at your side, you can hold your head high. I watched you save the administrator, fire on humans without a moment's hesitation."

Urquhart looked up, nodding.

Morden reached out, rested one hand on her shoulder. "Believe me, nothing is harder than firing on another human being."

The young woman's eyes darkened, her brow furrowing slightly. "Thank you, ma'am. I'm sorry I wasted your time, I know how busy you are."

Morden tried to smile reassuringly. "It's my job to take care of my crew. It's just as important as my other duties. Without officers like you, I'm not worth much. I'm here if you need to talk, as long as we aren't in the middle of lobbing shells."

Urquhart smiled faintly, the dark look on her face lifting as she turned and walked away.

Morden watched her as she made her way back down the corridor. Clearly, Urquhart's experience in Wheeler's office had been hard on her. Morden clenched and unclenched her fists, trying to drain away the anger welling up inside her. How could she be so stupid? Urquhart was young, new to the job. Why hadn't she taken the time to check in on her?

No wonder Holsey thought she didn't care about her people. Morden took a deep breath, straightening her jacket. She didn't have time for doubts now.

She would just have to do better.

M orden passed the sleeping Lieutenant Voth on her way to one of the rear isolation rooms at the back of the infirmary. The room was small, filled to the brim with state-of-the-art medical equipment — scanners, skin bonding equipment, and sterilization fields.

Commander Cadogan was standing by the entrance, reading from a small pad.

Morden called out, pointing her thumb back at Voth. "How's he doing?"

Cadogan looked up, dark circles staining the area under his eyes. "Stable, but he's taken a beating. Deep lacerations to his face, neck, arms, and chest. Several small fractures. A significant number of Frontin barbs were buried throughout his legs. I am worried about infection."

Morden nodded. "And the other wounded personnel from the Fox?"

Cadogan tucked his pad under his arm. "Some bad burns and respiration issues, the normal number of shrapnel victims and chemical burns, but most are easily treatable. I expect to discharge all but four of them tomorrow."

Morden reached out, placed her hand on the isolation room's palm reader. "Great. I am going to talk to Mostoff." She raised her hand, cutting off the doctor before he could object. "I will not be long."

Morden could feel a familiar warmth as the device scanned her hand. The door latch opened, breaking the seal with a sharp squealing sound.

Morden opened the door and walked in, her gaze falling on Mostoff, who lay covered in bandages on his bed, a brace circling his neck. He looked awful, scowling slightly as he turned his gaze to meet hers.

Morden put on what she hoped was an encouraging smile. "How are you feeling? Our medical staff seems to think you will recover."

He shifted on the bed, winced. "I feel how I look — half alive, but I am grateful to be that."

Morden fought back a laugh. "I wanted to thank you for your efforts on the Baron. I know you don't trust us, but you saved my people. Commander Holsey's report was clear."

The man's mouth turned downward. "I hate the Alliance for the suffering it has caused my people. I will never trust them, but I do trust my own eyes. Your crew acts with honor. I owe them my life as much as they owe me theirs."

Morden rested her hands on the side of his bed. "And I owe you thanks, one leader to another."

The man cocked his head as much as his neck brace would allow. "No, Morden. I owe you. You have rescued my crew, are repairing my ship, and have risked your own to help us stop those creatures. I, like you, believe in my cause whole-heartedly. Without my crew and my ship, my life means nothing. If all the people of the Alliance were like your Commander Holsey, I think we would finally be able to trust you."

"I don't know much about what goes on here, but I hope the two of us can mend some of that mistrust."

Mostoff gave a weak smile. "If you had said that when we met, I would have laughed in your face. Maybe there is some hope for our peoples."

Morden reached out and touched the man's arm, squeezing it gently. "There is always hope, Captain."

She turned and left the room, resisting the urge to throw her fist into the air. Since arriving in the Triangle, she had received nothing but resistance from the locals. This felt like a victory. The *Verdun's* actions here might really rehabilitate the Alliance's image in the region. This mission's importance had grown quickly. Defeating these monsters would do more to secure their borders than simply bloodying the noses of the Frontin.

It was cold. He could barely feel his extremities. His hands and chest ached with every small movement. His lungs burned with the effort of breathing. He tried to open his eyes, but they were too heavy.

He refused to die this way, frozen by the vacuum of space. He had to hit the controls, bring his heat back again before he froze to death.

There was no other choice.

He forced his eyes open. The frost on his visor blocked his view of the console in front of him. He reached up, scratching off some of the frost, improving his vision slightly. He could see his breath filling the small pod like fog. He reached out and hit the small glowing control in front of him. The lights slowly turned on, and he could feel the warmth of the heater starting to seep into his skin. He shook his body slightly, letting the heat thaw away the numbness.

It was wonderful.

He knew he only had a few minutes before he had to power down. The close proximity to the engines gave him some protection from detection, but not much.

Hillman rolled over in his escape pod, letting his eyes close again. This damn ship had to get where it was going soon. His oxygen was getting low. Until then, all he could was wait patiently. He couldn't walk on the ship's hull when it was accelerating.

Hillman turned off the heat, letting the power drop back down to minimum. He was the best, a Raptor. It would take more than a destroyed fighter and a long trip in a survival pod to stop him.

CHAPTER 19

Lt. Urquhart took a deep breath, claustrophobic in her heavy armor. She could feel the transport's maneuvering thrusters firing, tipping the craft downward to match the freighter's position in space. Her heart was racing, beating in her ears so loudly that she wondered if the marines next to her could hear it.

She couldn't shake the fear.

"Two minutes." The pilot called.

The marines locked their bolts, separating into two rows on either side of the bay. Two marines at the front of the line slapped the magazines of their submachine guns into position. The team's technicians looked out of place, small service pistols strapped to their legs, weighed down by their bulky equipment packs and pouches.

Urquhart racked her own bolt, pulling the rifle to her chest. The dim lights of the transport didn't help her stomach. Its soft yellow light made her skin crawl.

She looked around, trying to ignore her uneasiness. Commander Wilcox was directly across from her, his face passive and quiet. He seemed to be listening intently to the conversations passing back and forth between his team.

He met her eyes. "Lieutenant, can I do something for you?"

She felt her face burning. "No. I didn't mean to stare."

Wilcox laughed. "It's not the staring. A brigand like myself is used to stares. You seem nervous."

"No, sir. Just distracted."

He nodded. "Alright. Run me through our mission parameters."

She smiled. The opportunity to bury her emotions in the back of her mind where they belonged appealed to her. "Yes sir. After securing our landing area, we will detach one marine from each squad to defend the transport. Frontin can survive conditions we can't, and we don't want to leave our only escape route unprotected."

He motioned her to continue.

Urquhart shifted the weight of her armor, sweating under her pressure fatigues. "I will take my team to the ship's bridge and try to hack into the computer. You are going to take yours and explore the brig, looking for any prisoners or remains of victims that may help give us clues."

He slapped his knees. "Exactly. In and out, quick and easy."

The pilot cut in. "Fifteen seconds."

Urquhart felt the ship jerk as the ship's landing thrusters kick in. The marines' chatter died out. Wilcox stood, drew his pistol, and moved to the front of the line. She followed suit, locking down her helmet's visor, fixing her carbine into the crux of her shoulder. She saw the marines exchange glances. It wasn't exactly standard procedures for the naval officer to go in first.

The ship jolted hard on the uneven deck, nearly knocking her off her feet.

Sergeant Harkin stepped towards Wilcox, held out a hand. "Sir, I think you need to get behind us —"

"Marines, move out." Wilcox shouted as the door slammed down, echoing in the darkness.

Urquhart activated her night vision, bathing the room in a dim green light, moving carefully in behind the marines. She swept the floor in front of her, trying to not stumble. The movement settled her stomach, and muscle memory from years of training took over.

The room was large, with high, vaulted ceilings, almost gothic in style. She shined her light up, trying to see in between the many openings — perfect hiding places for Frontin.

Her heart started pounding again.

Wilcox's voice echoed loudly in her ears. "Clear."

Her eyes swept the ceiling one more time. "Clear."

Wilcox tuned left down the corridor. "Private Dunham and Corporal Roah, guard the ship. Alpha team, move out."

Urquhart had to follow Wilcox's example quickly. She didn't want to look weak in front of marines. She took a deep breath, lifting her carbine slowly. "Beta team, let's go."

They moved down the hallway carefully. It was long, without doors, and empty, except for debris and a pall of smoke that hung in the thin air.

The next corridor was indistinguishable from the first. It had the same old gothic architecture that characterized Empire-era stations, but the smooth, curving walls, pale green panels, and dark brown color were like nothing she'd ever seen, alien.

Something wasn't right.

Cold sweat trickled down her neck. She fought to keep her breathing steady.

Sergeant Harkin came up beside her. "Is everything alright with your oxygen, ma'am?"

She ignored the comment, signaling the team forward. "Sergeant, keep your eyes open."

Her radio crackled to life, making her jump. Her hands tightened around her rifle. She listened intently for Wilcox's voice.

Nothing. Only a faint crackling sound that made the hairs on her neck stand up.

She cursed her nerves under her breath. They were less than fifteen yards from what scans had indicated was the bridge. "Harkin, Orvil, guard the door. Morris, Franklin guard the perimeter. The rest of you with me."

They entered the room, and two of the marines stopped, falling to a kneeling position and swinging their guns around, aiming back down the hall covering their rear. Urquhart stepped forward, scanned the room. It was much smaller than the bridge of an Alliance warship. She could see only four stations. The two consoles in front were smashed beyond recognition, charred and melted, wiring protruding through their broken panels.

The last two stations weren't in much better shape. The first, an Alliance-style command chair, was separated from its stand, a large I-beam resting directly across it. Its panels were dark. The second was more or less intact. Its top was split, but some of its controls were glowing faintly.

She shouldered her rifle. "Chief Aldero, see what can be recovered."

Urquhart dropped to one knee, pulled her pack off, and searched for her mobile data device. If they could get a clean connection to the computer, she was going to download as much data as possible. They could decode it later.

She pulled out the small tablet, fighting her shaking hands as she plugged it into the panel's data port.

CALM DOWN.

The radio crackled again. "Beta team, Wilcox."

At the same time, Aldero spoke. "Lieutenant, this computer is smashed. We aren't going to get anything here."

She nodded. "All right, chief. Beta team, prepare to move out." She clicked her mike. "Alpha, Beta, go ahead."

After a second, the radio crackled again, and Wilcox responded. "Lieutenant, get back to the ship. We found something, fall back."

Something in the man's voice made Urquhart's chest constrict. "Copy."

Why were they pulling out? Had the other squad run into trouble? The tone in Wilcox's voice had done nothing to ease her tensions. Her squad moved carefully back towards the shuttle. She fought the urge to run as she turned off her night vision, the bright landing lights of the transport washing away the cold green of the infrared.

Urquhart repressed a sigh as they crossed into the relative safety of the bay. Her heartbeat slowed. Tension gave way to growing irritation that she hadn't found anything. But she had done her duty, kept her cool.

She lowered her rifle, pushed her way through the group of marines circled just in front of the transport. "Why are you standing around, where is Wil —"

And then she saw it.

Morden's stomach turned. The body in front of her was sickening, like some nightmare come to life. It had belonged to a human male, but he was wearing Frontin hive armor. This made no sense. How could someone work side by side with these monsters?

Since first contact with humans, the Frontin had killed billions of people, playing with them like toys, hunting and enslaving men, women, and children, using them as victims for their own glorification and advancement in some sick political system she didn't want to understand. How anyone could help them was unfathomable.

Morden was alone in one of the small medical examination rooms. She couldn't collect her thoughts. The room was icy cold, but she was rooted to the spot, couldn't make herself move away from the corpse before her.

From day one, this mission had not been what she'd expected. Although she would never have admitted it, she had felt the same way Holsey did — this mission was meant to be routine, almost a shakedown. The Admiral had wanted to see how she performed under pressure.

But not this much pressure.

She stared at the grotesque image in front of her. Captain Knight had always said every mission is an important mission. Maybe he had been right. This region was an important strategic border, but until she'd seen this abomination, she hadn't really understood how important it was.

The pieces of this puzzle were starting to fall together.

The Triangle was falling apart. The political leaders were losing power to the radicals in the region. The miners were cut off from trade, relegated to their mines and becoming more and more desperate. The pressured colonial leaders were raising the miners' quotas under the threat of reprisal.

Mostoff had been right, in part. The miners must have turned to the Frontin. What wasn't clear was why the Frontin would help.

The worst part was they had gotten nothing from the ship's computers. The system had been wiped clean in the brig, and, according to Urquhart, the bridge was smashed beyond repair. The *Verdun's* fighters had done their job, smashed the attacker and saved the *Fox*. Unfortunately, their efficiency prevented them from using the enemy hulk to answer their questions.

"Fuck me. That's a Frontin uniform."

Morden jumped at the sudden noise, turned to see Holsey step into the room. "I know."

Holsey reached out, steadying herself on the wall. "If the miners are involved, the bugs could be hidden right in front of us, and we would never know."

Morden nodded, looking back at the body. "Geonor believes these ships are hybrids, a marriage between old Alliance tech and Frontin systems. We won't be able to distinguish them from other traffic until they are right on top of us. I asked Isabelle to examine the readings from the first attack, see what she can come up with, but it's a long shot at best."

"I suggest we pull out of the field and call for reinforcements. If we had more ships, we could box these bastards in."

Morden shook her head. "No. If we pull out, they may escape, or worse. I won't give these abominations any quarter. Once a communication drone reaches the Alliance, it would be a month before another vessel reached us."

Holsey's voice tensed. "Those destroyers, weak as they are, can fly circles around us in this area. You can't seriously suggest we try to catch them on their own ground."

Morden looked back at Holsey. "These aren't the Milipa. As long as we keep applying pressure, the Frontin will slip up, give into their hive mentality, regardless of their leaders, and try to take us all at once. I'm sure they are watching. If we try to pull out, they will know. I doubt we could get to the edge of the asteroid field before they'd jump us."

Holsey's brow furrowed. "I agree that we can't leave them unattended, and I agree that it's unlikely they are not watching. But fighting an unknown number of enemies on their terms is *very* dangerous. Even strategic rejects like the Frontin."

Morden nodded, collecting her thoughts. "I can't let something like this stand. If just one of those bastards escapes and informs their clan that this area is weak, we could be looking at a full-scale attack."

She had to get Holsey on board. This was the only way. The Frontin knew they were here. Wilcox had reported almost no bodies, meaning most of that crew had probably escaped. If the Alliance showed weakness, retreated now, the Frontin would run them down before they could escape the asteroid field.

Morden remembered her first lecture on Frontin tactics. Never back down or run unless it's the last alternative. This was no exception. It was the standing order on the Frontin, attack unless completely outmatched.

Morden smiled softly. "I know it's a serious risk, but you and I both know how those animals are. The standing orders state we can't back down. How many died repelling the last hive attack eighty years ago? Half a million?"

Holsey looked back at the body, her tone softening. "Something doesn't feel right. I just can't shake the feeling that we are dealing with more than a bunch of piecemeal destroyers."

Morden couldn't help but see her old friend for the first time since she had arrived. Holsey's warmth seemed to be leaking out past all the anger.

She put her arms behind her back. "I am certain this is the right course of action. If we can find these bastards, we can take them."

Holsey turned to leave. "I hope you're right, but it is going to take a miracle for us to find wherever they are staging themselves, and I don't believe in miracles."

CHAPTER 20

Lt. Hillman willed his eyes open. Wavy ice patterns covered the entirety of his windshield. He had been sleeping again, his body stiffening as his cockpit temperature fell to dangerous levels. There wasn't room to move. The escape pod wasn't much more than a long, body-shaped tube with life support, communications, and monitors.

His fingers burned as he turned the heat back on. The pod's battery beeped loudly in the still air. Hillman picked up his canteen, let the last of his water trickle down his throat.

Not good, Hillman, not good.

The low battery warning went off again. Despite his best efforts to extend its life, his pod was out of juice. Without power, the oxygen supply would freeze, and he would suffocate, assuming he didn't die of hypothermia first. Hillman's survival suit had enough internal heat and oxygen for six hours. His only hope was to pop the hatch and try to walk along the ship's hull to an external entry port.

It was a long shot at best.

If the destroyer was moving too fast, he would be crushed by the ship's inertia during maneuvers. Worse than that, he had attached just below the rear engine assembly. It was unlikely that a hatch would be located anywhere nearby.

Hillman had some explosives, a sidearm, fifty rounds, two grenades, and a small length of rope. If he had to blast his way into the ship, it would give him away.

The console beeped again.

Regardless of his chances, he didn't have much longer before he had to act. He had five, maybe six hours left at most before the battery was dead.

You're a Raptor, Hillman. This is nothing.

Hillman stretched his body, working each limb carefully in the cramped space. He cranked his heat to full, setting the sequence to blow the hatch. He was going to enjoy the warmth while it lasted.

It might be the last time he could.

L ieutenant Geonor rubbed the sweat from his brow, pulling himself into a sitting position, listening carefully.

The *Black Fox's* engines roared to life.

Geonor smiled, enjoying the cheers from the people around him. The frustration of the last few days had been worth it. This ship was old and rusted. In fact, in the few days Geonor had been aboard, he hadn't found a single patch of clean metal. He had never seen so many jury-rigged components.

The *Fox's* engines were badly damaged. If they'd been at home, he would have recommended scrapping the engine and installing a replacement. Unfortunately, that had not been an option. His teams had been forced to replace most of the internal wiring, rebuild its ignition system, machine seven flow converters, and weld patches all over the exhaust system.

Geonor pulled himself to his feet, muscles screaming the whole way. Like the rest of the ship, the engine room wasn't much to look at. Opposite the engine access hatches was a small reactor surrounded on all sides by seated work stations. The ceiling was covered with antiquated piping inlaid with dim control panels for regulating the flow of their contents, accessible from a small catwalk around the top of the room.

Geonor closed the access panel, carefully watching the status monitors for any unusual activity.

Everything looked okay.

He could finally let Holsey know the *Fox* was ready to move. She had been hounding him for the last few hours. Geonor was never one to panic, but the tension on the *Verdun* was beginning to affect him. No one liked the idea of sitting still, waiting for the Frontin to attack.

Geonor picked up his radio. "Verdun, Geonor. Engines on the Black Fox are back up."

A voice he didn't recognize responded almost immediately. "Geonor, Verdun, copy. Return to the ship immediately."

Geonor had always considered getting to know the many individuals in support positions to be the hardest part of taking up a new post. It had taken most of a year for him to recognize the voices of the communications staff on his last assignment, the Halcyon project. Geonor turned to face his team. "Pack it up, let's go home. Great job, people!"

Officer Gillian, the *Black Fox's* engineer, walked over. The man was too tall, with dark brooding eyes and short-cropped hair. His only notable feature was a large scar trailing down his arm. So far, he'd been laconic, speaking only to bark orders to his men and insults to the Alliance personnel.

Geonor tried not to grimace at his approach. He had done his best to remain polite, but even he had his limits.

Gillian crossed his arms, stopping in front of Geonor and just a few inches too close. "Finally getting out of my engine room, Alliance?"

Geonor ignore the man's sharp tone. "It's all yours."

"Good." The man didn't move, his eyes locked on the *Verdun's* team, watching them pack up their equipment.

Geonor rolled his eyes. "Anything else?"

Gillian took a deep breath. "I wanted to...thank you."

Geonor tried not to sound stunned. "You're welcome."

The older man looked at him. "I know I made your time here harder. You must understand I have never received help from the Alliance that didn't come with a price tag. I misjudged you. I'm sorry."

Geonor didn't reply for a moment, taken aback by Gillian's sudden change of attitude. He found his voice. "I understand. I joined the Navy to escape a manufacturing planet."

He remembered all too well the squalor of the dimly lit factories that covered his home world, the feeling of being trapped with no way out. He had seen so many people maimed in accidents, watched their spirits broken.

The man nodded, smiling for the first time, reaching out his hand. Geonor took hold, shaking it firmly. If this mission brought the Alliance and the Triangle closer, the Frontin might actually serve a useful purpose, for once.

This was one of the small victories that gave his job meaning.

Commander Holsey sat at her station, reading the data that was beginning to stream in from the fighters as the *Verdun* and *Black Fox* left the clearing. It was easy to see how the *Black Fox* had been caught off guard. This field was so dense that a smaller ship could hide in one of the millions of larger craters.

She switched to the second squadron's input, saw the same disappointing lack of readings from the heavy, mineral-rich asteroids. She forced her eyes across the screen, trying to ignore her misgivings with Morden's plan. The captain was right. They had to deal with this threat now. If even one Frontin got past them —

The *Verdun* had to take the fight to them.

They didn't have time to sit around — there was too much at risk.

At least Morden had the insight to keep the gun crews in their turrets. If those bastards tried to jump them, they would regret it instantly.

Urquhart's bubbly voice broke her concentration. "Commander, why so serious?"

Holsey looked up. "Shouldn't you be guiding the ship?"

The lieutenant shrugged, an infectious smile covering her face. "Ma'am, my shift hasn't started yet. Someone needs to break that frown. It's tense enough in here."

How anyone could stay that sickeningly chipper so often was beyond Holsey. "I don't remember regulations requiring a bridge officer to smile."

Urquhart laughed. "Who was talking regulations? It just makes life more pleasant. Have you ever had to navigate an asteroid field with angry eyes staring at the back of your head?"

Holsey rolled her eyes, putting on her best half smile. "Please get to work — *now.*"

"Yes, ma'am." Another big smile.

I shouldn't encourage her.

Holsey shook her head, turned back to her readings. The *Verdun* pitched and rolled as Stetler dodged another larger asteroid. She focused on keeping herself loose, moving with the ship, trying and failing to convince herself that the knot in her stomach was just motion sickness.

There was too much at stake.

Chief Yugola, one of the turret's loaders, laughed. "Come on, loosen up."
Lieutenant Merry Smyth threw up her hands. "You're gambling on duty. What the hell did you expect me to say?"

The chief was short, overweight, and balding. Merry hated his lack of professionalism, but it was hard to come down on him. No one could handle a loader like him. She remembered the first time she saw him work the loader—five seconds to fill all three lifts. Her best time was ten seconds.

He looked up from his hand. "We're playing cards, not gambling."

Shipman Cutler nodded, taking another swig from a mug she was sure held more than coffee. "There ain't nothing going on. Just blowing time. The old girl's all loaded up."

Smyth shook her head. "You two are the sorriest excuse for gun rats I've ever seen."

She tried not to smile, knowing full well that wasn't true.

The chief groaned. "All right, we will get back to work — after this hand."

Smyth nodded, starting up the turret's large spiral stairwell. She had to get back to the targeting controls. If they got a chance to blow an asteroid to dust, she wanted to be the one to give the order.

Being in charge of one of the *Verdun's* main gun turrets was exhilarating. The three massive barrels could propel a 15-inch shell at more than four thousand feet a second, delivering powerful, two-thousand pound warheads with great precision — timed HE shells for area fire, or penetrator rounds for more precise hits at closer ranges. Granted, many engagements took place outside those ranges, but Smyth had always loved the idea of smashing enemy vessels into slag.

Smyth's eyes checked the readouts on the various monitors on the wall, watching her subordinates tracking the different asteroids around them. If they wanted to react quickly to the threat of collision, they needed to stay alert. Aiming the guns with the fire control system took a few seconds to acquire target lock, and that was if they started the process early. A single delay could cost them time they couldn't afford. Smyth glanced over their shoulders at one of the sensor displays, counted the status of the drones feeding it data. Thank goodness the drones were flying. When they weren't blown apart in combat — which the enemy almost always did — they allowed the target control system to work faster, triangulate the signal for greater precision. And if all of that failed — well, they could always fall back on good, old fashioned optical gun sights and aim down the barrel. Any gun rat officer knew that, at the end of the day, her crew used skill to hit their opponents. Fancy equipment was for the Army.

Smyth reached the top of the stairs, taking in the three men working there, Chaves, Va, and Higgens. They were seated, monitoring the targeting and fire-control computers. Four more men were leaning on the other side of the transparent barrier that separated the control room from the loading room. Once the fire-control center received the order to fire from the bridge and sent it down to the turret, the ceiling lighting would shift from normal to green. Until then, they would just monitor the various targets, do routine maintenance, run drills, and — her favorite — inventory shells.

This room was much different from the floor below. Instead of the large, hydraulic lifts and winches, it had state-of-the-art computer readouts. In place of the rows of shells, the massive breeches of the three barrels extended into room. Against the wall near the small door was a built-in weapons locker and inset storage for their ear protection.

Big guns made big noise.

Smyth loved her job. Turret Two was *Verdun's* sword. During a battle, they operated almost independently of the ship, her 20-person crew sending death to the enemy. If enemies boarded the ship, it was her job to hold this gun, without marine assistance, or blow it up. If it was up to her, Turret Two would keep firing, even if the ship was breaking into pieces.

Va spoke as soon as he saw her, his eyes full of energy. "Good timing. I bet we will go green. That pig is getting close."

Smyth leaned over the monitor. The turret was tracking a very large asteroid closing in on the *Verdun's* port side. She felt the ship rock, but it didn't clear them from the rock's path. Va was right. They would have clearance soon.

She grabbed his shoulder. "Get me a firing solution. Let's be ready."

The young man jumped from his seat. "Yes, ma'am."

The three men went to work, typing coordinates into the targeting computer. Smyth's heart leapt as the deck rotated, the gun swiveling towards its target. The room filled with the hum of the turret's massive hydraulics.

Smith hit her headset. "Turret Two operators, ear protection now. Be ready to fire on my mark."

There was a surge of excitement, as everyone dashed for the wall, each pulling his or her own personal ear protection and helmets from the wall, shoving them without ceremony onto their heads.

Chief Farnsworth waved from the other side of the glass. "Fire room reports ready. Guns sealed. All panels are green."

A light humming noise filled her head, the telltale sign that the magnetic rails were charged and at full power.

"Target lock onto the asteroid." Va called out.

Yugola voice called out. "Munitions loaded and ready. Penetrator charges."

Smyth looked up at the go bulbs, waiting. "Any second, boys."

During a battle, they would have been free to fire at will, unless a specific target was designated. The bridge didn't always see targets in the same light as a gun rat. They would try other options before losing munitions, but she was sure they would give the go ahead this time.

The *Verdun* bucked again, the ship tilting forward. Clearly there was more than one big rock out there causing problems. The ceiling lighting turned green, giving the room a surreal glow.

Her team pulsed with energy.

Lieutenant Niret came over the intercom. "Turret Two, Fire Control. Salvo authorized on asteroid marked on your targeting computer."

She glanced at the computer screen confirming they were locked on the right asteroid.

"Fire!"

The three barrels barked loudly one after another. The room filled with intense heat, and she heard the hiss of the breech sealing against the vacuum of space for reloading. A moment later, the unique smell of the guns' heated rails hit everyone as the empty chambers opened.

She watched the monitors, saw their payload slam into the giant rock's center. She smiled as the asteroid sprayed debris and ice in all directions. The asteroid was smaller, but still drifting towards them.

One more salvo, with penetrator charges, should do it.

Smyth barked into her head set. "Reload. B-8 Penetrator."

She walked over to the railing, looked down. She loved watching each step of gun loading. The two-thousand pound shells rising from the munitions elevator and sliding onto the lifts. The floor in the firing room would have already been retracted, allowing access to the lift. Each of the three gunners slid the conveyor tables into place.

The lift screamed upwards, stopping just long enough to let the team slide the massive round onto the loading ramp. The firing crew operated the rammer, pushing each of the three rounds into the firing chamber before latching the hatches shut.

Farnsworth yelled again. "Fire room ready."

Smyth smiled. "Fire!"

The gun barked again, sending screaming death at the rock spinning slowly towards the *Verdun*. Smyth watched the three rounds slam into its surface, bursting it into millions of tiny pieces.

Life was good.

U rquhart's light-hearted voice broke the tension. "That was close."

Holsey looked back at her combat screen, double-checking that the gun crews had done their job. Klaxons where still screaming on the bridge, but she cancelled them quickly. That had been close. The asteroid field was definitely denser here.

This was dangerous. They couldn't maneuver quickly enough.

Even the fighters would need to choose their courses carefully in this mess. All the Frontin had to do was wait until the ship had burned through most of her ammunition, then pounce, ripping the *Verdun* apart like a pack of wolves.

What else could they do? They couldn't run because it would show weakness, but this wasn't any better. There had to be another option. What was she missing?

Stetler cried out. "Asteroid to larboard. I doubt we can dodge it."

Holsey nodded. "Stetler, do what you can. Isabelle, prepare the ship for collision." She keyed her headset. "Target control, Bridge. All guns green. Fire when ready."

The ship started to pitch again, rolling to port, its thrusters pushing it away from the massive ship killer. Isabelle restarted the klaxons. Holsey gripped her armrest, trying to keep her body centered.

She could feel the forward turrets fire again, the deck plating shaking as the guns kicked. The asteroid disintegrated into small, harmless chunks, which curved around the field generated by the *Verdun*'s magnetic ordnance deflector. She sighed quietly.

No, she was sure they couldn't do this forever.

CHAPTER 21

L t. Hillman's legs and joints ached as he forced himself to his feet, pulling himself over the side of the escape craft. The destroyer had come to a stop, holding station at the edge of a large patch of clear space among the asteroids. There were at least three other destroyers hanging silently in the dark nearby. Hillman could just make out a large, T-shaped station at the opposite edge of the field, dark except for a few running lights. It had to be one of the mining stations, though it certainly looked abandoned.

He bent over, grabbed his survival pack, and lifted it onto the deck, grateful for the lack of gravity. Even with the heat from his survival suit, his muscles felt cold, pain lacing through his nerves with every movement. This had to be the central base of the attackers. He had to warn the *Verdun*, let them know where he was. They couldn't be too far away. His emergency transponder should be able to reach them even with all the interference, let them know where he was.

Them and everyone else in the asteroids.

There was no way to know which frequencies these destroyers monitored. He tried to clear his head.

Hillman pulled out his combat knife, used it to pry the emergency transponder loose, and shoved it roughly into his pack. He had one chance. If he put it close enough to the engine core, it might seem like background noise to someone not looking too closely.

The people who put this ship together were certainly not engineers. The thing looked like it had been thrown together.

Although they had managed to shoot him down.

Something was familiar about the way these ships fought, their weapons, but he couldn't put his finger on it.

Hillman pulled out his pistol, aiming carefully at the pod's control console. He fired five quick shots, the sound of the gunfire and bursts of glass lost in the vacuum of space. The damn coffin may be out of power, but he wouldn't let these fucks get their hands on it.

He threw the pack over his shoulders and started walking, trying to avoid any of the odd bits of metal. He couldn't risk using his light except in small bursts for fear of being seen. The ship's hull was rough, and scars from weapons fire and asteroid strikes were everywhere.

At least you didn't get away Scot-free, you bastards.

The forward sensor cluster would be the best place to start — the sensitive infrared readers, radar dishes, and receivers required regular maintenance. Even warships like the *Verdun* had entry hatches in that area, although they were heavily defended.

Hillman stopped, trying to get his bearings. He couldn't make out any obvious sensor equipment, but there was an antenna maybe a hundred feet to his left. It would be slow going — the ship had almost no hull lighting, and the vessel's mishmash construction and protruding sections made the footing uneven.

He stepped over another set of pipes, changing direction towards the antenna. At least he could confirm these ships were not originally meant for war. The hulls of warships were covered with smooth armor plating, except for the raised weapon platforms, sensor stacks, and other combat equipment. These pipes were obviously part of the engine cooling system, their intense heat still apparent through the makeshift steel plates welded over them.

Hillman recognized the builders' attempts to cut corners by running these semi-insulated steel pipes outside the hull as a cost-effective cooling system. Super-heated engine runoff cooled quickly when exposed to the subzero temperatures of space.

The walk was slower than he had expected, his muscles screaming with each step. He wanted to avoid resting too often. He couldn't shake the ridiculous thought that someone inside would hear his footsteps. He looked around quickly, trying to ignore the sound of his heart beating. The pod had been painfully cramped, but he had felt safe, secure.

Out here, he was exposed, surrounded by hostiles and the unforgiving vacuum of space.

Hillman's legs grew heavier with each step, his lower back screaming as he clambered over another set of pipes from the ship's coolant system. The warmth of his exertion added to the suit's emergency heating system, turning the suit's environment from ice cold to overwhelmingly hot in moments. The antenna was more than 25 feet away. Fighting to ignore his discomfort, he dropped to one knee, carefully examining the area for signs of movement.

Nothing.

He couldn't see any means of entry. Even with the aid of his helmet's infrared scanners and visual magnification, he couldn't see any openings, hatches, or hull breaches. There were pits and scarring, clear evidence of missile damage, but either the crew had sealed them or the rounds hadn't punched through the armor enough to reach the ship's interior. Regardless, there was no obvious way in here.

So much for that great idea.

He had to rest. He let himself down and rested his back against a small rise in the ship's armor. Things were not looking good. Even if he could get inside, he was drained. Sweat was dripping down his body. He closed his eyes and leaned back, wishing he could feel the ice-cold metal through his survival suit. Hell, he'd settle for turning the suit's heaters off, but it wasn't designed to be adjusted. Just to keep him from dying in the extreme cold of space. As wrong as it might be, at least he could comfort himself in the kill he had achieved. He could almost see his torpedoes smashing through the other destroyer, tearing it open, air and fire streaking into space.

Those bastards had killed several of his team, and lord knows how many on the landing party. He could die easy knowing his fish had avenged them.

Hillman bolted up. He had been going about this the wrong way.

This piece-of-shit ship was damaged. He shouldn't be looking for hatches, but air leaks. In a warship, each area had air-tight doors to prevent decompression during combat and subsequent field repairs. Most freighters only had them in vital areas to save costs. Without that protection, even the best patch would leak. All he had to do was locate one and blow it. The crew would assume that it hadn't been sealed properly and had simply decompressed.

He stood back up, ignoring the pain shooting through his limbs. He turned off his infrared sensors and pulled out his binoculars. He scanned the area looking for anything that might be escaping atmosphere.

His heart leapt.

He could just make out a small vapor trail thirty yards down the ship's starboard side, near an impact crater. It wasn't much — hardly more than a micro fracture — but it should work.

He moved his stiff legs as quickly as he could, forcing them to bend and straighten. The adrenaline and excitement helped keep him moving. By the time he reached the vapor, his lungs were burning. He cut the icy column of mist with his hand. The leak was indeed coming from an impact crater from what looked like an unexploded rocket. If the warhead was intact, he could activate the time delayed detonation sequence and let it do the work. No one would have any reason to suspect his presence. Explosions from undetonated ordnance were part of combat. It wasn't unheard of for them to go off weeks later if the hull wasn't properly surveyed.

Luck was clearly on his side.

He skidded to a halt directly in front of the rocket, pulled out his combat knife, and carefully started unscrewing the casing. The panel cover broke loose and he cast it aside, watching it float away in the low gravity environment around the ship. He eased out the emergency controls, snapping them into position. The machine lit up, its small screen flickering as it displayed various command options. He scanned the list quickly, his heart fluttering with excitement.

There.

Hillman gave the command for a timed detonation, entering two minutes and looked around for a place to duck down. It had to be far enough back to protect him from the blast and yet close enough that he could reach it before the rocket exploded.

Time was also a factor after it blew. He had to get into the ship and hide before an emergency repair team arrived. His eyes caught a small rise twenty yards behind him, another set of poorly armored cooling ducts. Even with his aching muscles, it wouldn't take long to reach.

It wasn't the best cover, but it should work.

Hillman started the sequence and threw himself to his feet. He ran, the seconds feeling like hours as he sprinted across the metal hull. He stumbled, picked himself up, and kept running. He jumped over the pipes and settled himself as low as he could get, forcing his body to parallel with the pipe. He wanted to leave as little of himself exposed as possible. The last thing he needed was a ripped suit.

The timer ticked down fifty seconds.

He pushed his body further under the pipe, its heat starting to seep through his already unbearably hot suit. Forty seconds.

Hillman unclipped his holster, pulling out his pistol. Thirty seconds.

He flipped off the safety. Twenty seconds…

He took a deep breath, his heart pounding in his ears. Ten seconds…

The rocket lit off, the heat and pressure washing over him as the surface beneath him jerked. Shrapnel and massive bits of hull were shooting off in all directions around him, some of them striking and bouncing off the armor plating before drifting away into space.

"Go now!" he yelled at himself.

The lieutenant sprang up and ran, hoping the time it took to cross to the opening would be enough for the decompression to subside. He lowered himself feet-first into the newly formed cavity, twisting his body, barely avoiding burning piping and shattered metal as he floated down towards the deck below. His knees buckled as he was yanked the last few feet to the floor, the ship's artificial gravity taking the place of vacuum.

He looked around. The hallway he'd dropped into was narrow with green lighting. It had only one visible exit to what he guessed was a small maintenance hatch, maybe three yards away.

He crossed the distance slowly, fighting the urge to run, to shoot the hatch off its hinges. Stealth was still important for this plan to work.

Hillman holstered his sidearm, reached down, and twisted the handle. The hatch opened with a pop audible though his helmet as decompression ripped the oxygen out of the maintenance way and into space.

Hillman bent down, grabbed the wall and pushed himself into the opening feet first. He reached behind him, tugging the door shut with a satisfying snap. The sound of sucking atmosphere died, replaced by the wail of alert klaxons. It only took seconds for him to hear the sound of heavy boots racing down the corridor he had just left. The destroyer's crew had responded far faster than he had expected.

Maybe they weren't as amateur as he had hoped.

Hillman crawled as quickly as he could. Darkness surrounded him as he moved farther from the light leaking in from the hallway's entrance. He stopped at the first T-junction, stretching his wrists. He had to rest soon. The adrenaline was wearing off, intensifying his discomfort, his survival pack growing heavier by the second. His shoulders, wrist, and elbow ached from supporting the weight of his body and survival suit.

He took a deep breath, starting down the left-hand passageway. The crawlway rose slightly, curving back in the direction he had come. It was moving up and above the hallway he had entered the ship from. He could barely make out the sound of low, snarling voices from below.

He pulled off his helmet and lowered his head down, pressing his ear to the cold metal.

Two individuals below were speaking clearly, their suits' speakers giving their voices a tinny quality, to a third who was barking back orders in a language Hillman didn't recognize. He could just make out a small grate ahead. He set his helmet down, moving cautiously towards the opening. He reached the grate, then carefully peered through the metal and down into the dimly lit hallway.

His blood froze.

Two of the voices were from human men, and the third was from a—

Good God, no.

Towering over the men was a Frontin.

What the hell am I going to do?

The two men were kneeling down in front of the Frontin in EV suits. The taller one was holding a small piece of rocket fragment. Hillman could see they had already put up a plastic air shield, temporarily blocking the escaping air and allowing the area to refill with atmosphere.

The shorter man looked up. "Lord. I know this seems suspicious, but it's nothing. I'll have it patched quickly. It will not prevent your—"

The Frontin growled loudly, turning its back to Hillman. It reached out, pinning the man to the wall. The human screamed, kicking and flailing as the Frontin reached for something at his side.

The taller man stood up, panic riding on every syllable. "We haven't had the opportunity to search the hull yet for unexploded ordnance. This was an accident. See for yourself, my lord."

He handed the small rocket fragment over to the Frontin. It turned its head and looked at the second man, speaking only inches from his face, saying something Hillman couldn't make out. Hillman inched back from the grate, his desire to run growing each time the Frontin spoke, its predatory, raspy growl setting off his most basic animal instincts.

Finally, it dropped the shorter man, kicking him as it stepped towards the exit, the tapping of its many legs on the deck easily audible over the gasping chokes of the miner.

The taller man waited for the Frontin to leave the corridor before helping the other man up. "Are you crazy? You trying to commit suicide?"

The man's voice was hoarse, and he gasped as he spoke. "No."

"Then give them the damn evidence first. You know failure means death to them! Didn't you see them rip the Captain of the *Urgnia* apart? He was one of their own!"

The shorter man nodded, his voice barely a rasp. "Let's just get this damn thing done, okay?"

Hillman un-holstered his pistol, scooting back down the crawlway. A forty-five wouldn't go far against a ship crawling with Frontin, but it would have to do. His hands shook slightly as he tried to focus. Regardless of the cost, he had to contact the *Verdun*. It didn't matter if he was caught or killed.

This couldn't be allowed to happen.

The most logical choice was the engineering deck. Venting near the main engines would prevent the Frontin from picking up his beacon, but getting that far across the ship without being caught would be nearly impossible.

But it was better than waiting here to be found.

Hillman willed himself to start moving again. He could still do this. The pain in his elbows and the numbness in his muscles didn't matter. He had a job to do, and he would get it done.

He was still a Raptor, still the best.

Morden sat in her office, the pitching and rolling of the *Verdun* breaking her concentration. She had buried herself in the ridiculous piles of paperwork that came with command. Requisitions forms, power consumption reports, material reports, medical updates, and all forms of minutia. It wasn't her favorite part of the job, and she wasn't one of those paper-pushing officers who earned promotion through keeping her I's dotted and T's crossed, but it did keep her mind off the tedium of the search.

Not that she'd ever avoided paperwork. Order was an integral part of running a city in space. The *Verdun* had a crew of thirty-five hundred sailors plus two Marine battalions, another sixteen hundred personnel. It was her job to keep them fully fed, properly cared for, and in tip-top fighting condition.

She took that job seriously.

The door chime rang.

"Come in."

She breathed a small sigh of relief. She could use a few minutes' rest from the excitement of the requisition form Frost had submitted.

Commander Wilcox walked in, followed closely by Holsey, their expressions serious, grim even. Maybe sticking to paperwork would have been better.

The ship bucked again as the two officers stopped in front of her desk.

Holsey spoke first. "Mr. Wilcox and I have concerns we would like to discuss about our current course of action."

Morden nodded, pointing to the chairs in front of her. "I thought we were in agreement. Backing down would open a Frontin buffet in this region and would seriously damage our border security."

Holsey sat down, crossing her arms. "I agree, but I am still concerned."

Wilcox cut in, his tone terser then she expected. "There is a huge amount of tension onboard, as I'm sure you have noticed. Although the Commander agrees with you, I'm worried the crew will break under the pressure."

Holsey nodded, taking back over. "I'm also worried about how quickly we are expending shells. I don't want to walk into a hornet's nest on empty."

Morden nodded, leaned backwards. "I agree it's alarming how fast we're using ammunition. My last report indicated that our workshops are manufacturing new munitions now."

Wilcox grabbed the top of Holsey's chair as the ship banked again. "What's being done to deal with the crew's stress? No one can deal with this much tension forever."

Morden paused for a moment, not used to Wilcox being this confrontational. "These are some of the Navy's finest —"

Wilcox leaned forward, cutting her off. "With all due respect, that's bullshit. Even the best crew can get fatigued. If we keep on blindly running through this damn asteroid field, we will waste ammunition and exhaust our crew. We should pull out of the field, assume a defensive posture, and contain the enemy in this area until reinforcements can arrive. These bastards shouldn't be allowed to control our decisions."

Morden was stunned, she had never seen Wilcox so upset.

Holsey spoke first. "Commander Wilcox, that's enough! Another outburst like that, and I will ask you to leave the room."

Wilcox turned towards Holsey. "No, it isn't. This is our job, to call our captain out when we feel something's wrong. I have always backed her up in front of the crew. Just ten minutes ago, you agreed. Crashing into an asteroid won't protect the Alliance."

Wilcox tried to keep going, but Morden cut in. "Enough, both of you. Commander, we can't allow the Frontin to gain a foothold. I won't sacrifice the millions of lives that hang in the balance here in the Triangle. Our communication drone won't reach the Alliance communications network for weeks, and weeks more for reinforcements to arrive. Who's to say the Frontin won't have overwhelmed us by then?"

Wilcox didn't say anything, so Morden continued. "I know our chances are slim, and I know we will have to do something to help ease the tension, but our job is to hold the line, regardless of our own safety."

Holsey's eyes fixed on Wilcox. Morden was glad their intensity wasn't aiming at her for once. She wanted to pinch herself — Wilcox angry and Holsey on her side?

Wilcox looked normal, except that his usual smile was missing.

Morden spoke up before Holsey could speak again. "I hear what you're saying. It might take a miracle to find them in here, but they won't hide forever. The Frontin lack self-control. They will strike sooner or later."

Holsey turned back towards Morden. "All right. The crew is showing signs of stress. I have had reports from most departments of arguments and officers snapping at each other. I had to break up a spat that almost boiled over in the mess an hour ago. Most of the people aboard have never fought Frontin before, and the ones who have never faced them in large numbers. We need to be proactive."

Morden rubbed her chin. "All right. What did you two have in mind?"

Isabelle's melodic voice sounded over the intercom. "Officer of the watch requests all senior officers to command. I say again, all senior officers to the bridge."

Hillman leaned back against the bulkhead, body aching, eyes burning, the rhythmic sound of the engines making him groggy, adding that much more weight to his eyelids. He pushed the transceiver in between a pair of pipes above his head, its steady pulses of light indicating that it was functioning.

His instincts told him he should move as far away from this spot as possible, but he couldn't budge. His eyes closed. He could feel his head dropping on to his shoulder.

Hillman didn't want to wait here to die, cramped inside a lightless crawlway, but he had to rest. Whatever happened now, he had done his job.

CHAPTER 22

Morden's heart leapt. "Confirm that, Chief!" No one spoke as Chief Baudouin rechecked Isabelle's readings through her communication board. Everyone's eyes were locked on the communications station. Morden forced herself to breathe in, her hands drumming on her armrests.

"Codes confirmed. We are receiving a homing beacon from one of our missing Stallions."

Holsey clapped her hands. "Distance? Lock in on it."

Baudouin nodded. "Relaying data to navigation. The signal seems to be nearby, judging by its strength." She paused studying her screen. "I think there's a message embedded in the signal. I'll try to decode it."

Morden glanced over at Lieutenant Urquhart, who was already crouched over her screen, tracing the transmission carefully back through the asteroid field. "The signal is about 250 miles away, with a z axis of 22 degrees."

Stetler looked up at Morden. "Ma'am, that's less than an hour from here if we can maintain this speed."

Morden drummed her fingers on the arm of her chair, staring at the communication chief.

Come on, come on.

Baudouin looked up. "The message indicates that the pilot stowed away aboard one of the enemy vessels."

Morden held the chief's gaze, the same mixture of excitement and tension written on the woman's features.

They'd found the bastards.

Morden looked over at Holsey, who nodded. "Set a course."

There was a general chorus of cheers from the bridge crew. The waiting was over.

Morden keyed the intercom. "This is Captain Morden to all hands. We have received an emergency signal from one of our missing Stallions. Hopefully, the signal is coming from the location of the main Frontin forces. All hands to general quarters, recall all fighters for refueling and rearming."

L t. Voth hit the side of his medical bed. "God *damn* it."
The mood onboard had changed, ripples of fear and excitement replacing the tension. He crossed and uncrossed his arms. Voth was the mother fucking Master at Arms! He should be in fire control, giving orders, helping Major Osterman coordinate the defense of the ship.

But he was here, resting, nursing a few broken ribs. "Damn."

He could feel the eyes of the other patients, but he didn't care. This was idiotic, intolerable. Was he really so weak?

The echoing of combat boots in the corridor outside made him cringe more. He recognized that sound. No one else on board created a battle rattle like marines weighed down by full body armor. If the marines were preparing to defend the ship, then they really had found the Frontin.

Voth kicked the bed. "Son of a bitch!"

He couldn't just lie here like an invalid as the crew fought for their lives. No amount of fear or pain was worth this feeling. He turned over, the pain in his side surging, his vision blurring slightly. Voth flipped his legs over the edge of the bed, gingerly tested their strength.

They held.

He couldn't help but notice the tug of his sutures against his skin, the pressure on his ribs making his eyes water. He took one step towards one of weapons lockers by the exit.

A voice behind him made him turn. "*What* are you doing?"

The young nurse he had been flirting with all day was approaching quickly, intent on getting him back into bed.

Voth straightened his back. "Nothing that concerns you, Ensign."

The woman put her hands on his shoulders. "You are not cleared for duty. Go back to bed."

Voth pushed her hands aside, his ribs protesting the movement. "I don't care. I will not sit here twittering my thumbs while the ship is in combat. A chest plate will fit over this damn dress as well as any uniform."

The nurse looked at him, opening and closing her mouth several times. He locked eyes with her, hoping the resolve he felt overshadowed the pain. No one in the Alliance had any illusion what fighting the Frontin meant. They were animals, headhunters. If the opportunity arose, they would board the ship, take prisoners, and kill as many as possible regardless of whether they were in the infirmary or not.

For the Frontin, mercy didn't exist — they loved to kill too much.

The nurse finally nodded, reaching over and putting her arm across his shoulder. They walked silently across the room to the weapons locker. He punched in his code, waited a few seconds for the reader to authenticate his handprint.

The young woman reached in, pulled out a chest plate, and helped him strap it on. The heavy steel armor sent waves of agony through his body, its weight pressing hard against his ribs. He threaded a pistol belt around his waist, pushed a sidearm into the holster at his side, filling magazine pouches with as many spares as they would hold.

He turned, easing his way toward the hallway on his own. He felt his face twisting with pain, but it didn't matter to him how much it hurt. He had to do this. If those bastards made it onboard, he would help the marines hold the infirmary.

Or die trying.

Surviving wasn't worth knowing he had left others to die in his place.

As he left the room, he heard her call after him. "Take care of yourself, sir. We'll keep your bed just how you like it."

Lt. Smyth strained to hold the glee out of her voice. "Chief Hagthow, make sure our backup generator checks out."

These were the moments the gun rats lived for, the chance to unleash their salvos against an enemy with teeth. Smyth wouldn't describe herself as a person dying for promotion, but everyone knew distinction in battle put you on the fast track.

Va was laughing loudly. The loaders were barely able to stand still, and she could even hear the voices of the munitions teams below over the deafening groan of the hydraulic ammunition winch. She fought the urge to pace in front of her console, forcing herself to stay planted in her position in the turret's center.

The noise of the situation was intoxicating — the clanking of metal, the screech and scent of the freshly oiled chains, her men yelling back and forth across the deck.

She glanced over at Ensign Va, observing with pride the way his team ran the targeting computer and manual targeting equipment through their pre-combat checks. The back of the final barrel was sealed with a satisfying clang.

They were ready.

The lights dimmed and switched from white to red. Smyth checked her sidearm. "Here we go, boys. Ear and eye protection and sidearms. Let's send these monsters straight to hell."

Her gun was going to make these shitheads think twice about fucking with the Alliance.

Morden rubbed the back of her neck as she entered the bridge. The last hour had passed slowly as she'd walked the ship, visiting different posts. Military tradition. It was important to let people see her confidence, her resolve. Wilcox had been right — tension onboard was high, and her own apprehension was distracting her.

Holsey and Wilcox were standing over the action table, studying the readout carefully. She crossed the distance quickly, taking in the images the long-range sensor drones had taken.

The beacon was coming from one of the destroyers on the far side of a clearing in the asteroids several times larger than the one the *Fox* had been attacked in. Probably man-made, judging by its perfectly circular shape and the mining station on its far edge. The station seemed derelict — no heat signatures or energy readings of any kind.

These were all good things.

The *Verdun* would have plenty of room to maneuver, and given the isolated location of this base and small number of ships visible, the miners working with the Frontin were likely a splinter group and not connected with the others.

It seemed impossible that anyone would work with the Frontin.

The drone had brought back images of seven hybrid destroyers, all clustered close together in a tight combat formation in front of the station. One of the ships showed serious damage, all had active engine cores, and, according to the readings, plenty of active weaponry. Seven of those ships were unlikely to stop the *Verdun*, but even one could easily overwhelm the *Fox*.

Morden leaned over the table. "Isabelle, call Captain Mostoff to the bridge."

Holsey looked up at her. "The man is still in a wheelchair. He should rest."

Morden nodded. "He should, but he'll want to be a part of this. The Fox is his ship, and I have no authority over him. He has earned the right to be here."

Holsey went back to studying the display. "Yes, he has."

Morden followed suit, looking for anything that might be lurking in the darkness. Nothing was there, every image was clean. They had caught the enemy with their pants down, and these bastards had no idea what was in store for them.

The bridge doors swung open, and Morden looked up. A nurse was wheeling Captain Mostoff onto the bridge.

Mostoff fixed his eyes on her. "Do we have them? Are you sure?"

Wilcox smiled. "Yes, the imaging system identified them as a perfect match to the ships you engaged."

Mostoff frowned. "What is your plan, Morden?"

Morden became very aware of Wilcox and Holsey watching her. "I want to use the Fox as a decoy, protected by twenty of our defensive fighters."

Mostoff remained quiet, eyes fixed on the holotable as it began to run images of her battle plan.

She pointed to the left side of the clearing. "The Fox will enter here, going slowly enough to make it seem like you stumbled onto them accidentally. They should respond quickly, at which point you will accelerate away from the destroyers to exit the clearing here."

The exit point turned yellow, a small red circle highlighting the spot as the holographic representation of the *Fox* exited the asteroid field.

She continued. "The Verdun will wait for the destroyers to cross our path, then accelerate to flanking speed. We will hit them from the side, cutting straight through their formation."

Wilcox looked up. "Without launching our fighters first?"

Morden pointed back towards the table. "Exactly. Cutting that close to those ships would leave them exposed. I don't want to risk our fighters like that. Once we have completed our first pass, we will launch all fighters. The remaining Cerberus interceptors will form a defensive barrier, while the Sparrowhawks and Stallions go after the scattered destroyers with the Fox. This will allow us enough time to come about hard and re-engage."

Holsey's tone was low. "Captain —"

Morden shook her head, stopping her. "By which time we should have any remaining enemies wedged in between the two groups. We will either finish them off, or force any human elements among the enemy forces to surrender. I'd like to take at least one ship captive." She pointed towards the destroyer from which the rescue beacon was transmitting. "That one."

Mostoff smiled broadly. "A bold plan. You are a fighter, Alliance."

Morden reset the table. "I am glad you approve."

Holsey sounded exasperated. "It's too risky. I agree flying that close risks too many fighters, but without at least the Cerberus wings, we risk taking some serious hits. I suggest we pre-launch the fighters. They can hide near the Fox's exit zone."

Wilcox nodded his head. "I disagree. Pre-launching the fighters would prevent us from using them to keep the destroyers from running. They would be out of range. In an asteroid field this dense, they would be hard to chase."

Morden placed both hands on the table and leaned forward. "Exactly. If we launch before our initial attack, the fighters won't be able to keep up once we accelerate to full speed. Otherwise we would have to slow to allow the Cerberus fighters to keep up, which would blunt our element of surprise. Additionally, the more engines running, the more likely we are to give ourselves away. We have no way of knowing how accurate the Frontin sensors are. The destroyers we don't pulverize in our initial salvos would have time to escape into the asteroid field. We will launch the fighters right on top of them as we pass, when they are still disoriented and before they can activate their anti-fighter defenses. When dealing with the Frontin, the answer is always maximum force right from the get-go.

Holsey's tone was still low, her arms crossed tightly in front of her. "Leaving them no choice but to fight or die. I just worry about the casualties we risk flying right down their throats without fighter cover."

Morden pushed her hair out of her eyes. "So do I, but I can't risk them escaping. The Cerberus fighters can hit them with their maximum payload with as little resistance as possible from the enemy. It is a bit risky, but if it works right, we won't need that fighter cover long."

Mostoff signaled for his nurse. "Agreed. I will return to the Fox. We will be ready when you call."

Holsey looked over at him. "Not so fast, Mostoff. There is no room for error here. There is a delay from our sensor drones to us. If you jump the gun and attack too early, we may not reach you in time. Even with our fighter screen, they would blow you from the sky."

He didn't respond, the idea of following an Alliance officer no doubt extremely hard for him. Despite the man's attitude and behavior, it was clear he seemed to have an intense, albeit archaic, sense of honor. She didn't doubt he would do his part.

Morden smiled at her officers. "Commander Holsey, inform the department heads of our battle plan, including Osterman. I want his teams ready if they try to board us. Wilcox, make sure the fire, communication, and decompression response teams are armed."

"Yes, ma'am," they said in unison. The two officers left the table, each focused on their individual tasks. Wilcox jogged off the bridge.

Holsey stopped and turned around quickly. "I still don't like the idea of going in without our fighter wing in the air."

Morden shot her a look. Holsey nodded and left the bridge. Morden hoped she was right. This plan wasn't clean and by the book. She was way outside her comfort zone, but she knew the consequences if the Frontin escaped the sector. Their reinforcements were much closer than any help the Alliance could muster.

The pressure of her task was closing in around her. They had to be stopped. The *Verdun* was the only rear guard of the Alliance.

She was the only rear guard of the Alliance.

Major Osterman deployed his squad just outside the laser cannon control room, their bayonets fixed. He couldn't shake the feeling that they would need them. A marine's life was never shorter than during a boarding action. Everyone in the Alliance understood the stakes. Warships couldn't be allowed to fall into enemy hands. The Navy's technology, especially their laser cannons, kept the Alliance alive. It was their ticket to victory.   Marines' lives paid for that advantage.

Osterman looked down the hall. "Isabelle, activate the Internal Cover System, authorization code 022156."

The deck started to shift as Isabelle complied with the Major's request. Directly in front of his fire team, five two-and-a-half-foot sections of the decks rose, forming a half circle in front of the laser cannon room's entrance. The Internal Cover System gave the marines an advantage, funneling the enemy down the halls to strategic hard points.

Sergeant Kilwalski leaned against one of the barriers. "Isn't it a bit early to call up the ICS? We don't even have a bug problem yet."

Osterman hoisted his weapon onto his shoulder. "Not yet, but I want to be ready. I would hate for us to lose hydraulics and have to watch one of those fucking spiders rip your pretty face off, Kilwalski."

The sergeant smiled. "Come on! I'm way too pretty for one of those bastards to get me. It wouldn't sit right with, ya know, God!"

Everyone laughed, except Osterman.

He hoped Kilwalski was right. The last thing he needed to do to lock down the hallway was close the pressure doors, but he would wait until the shooting started. Getting the ICS ready gave him time to get his team in position, time to coordinate the other marine fire teams on board.

Osterman walked forward, pointing to one of the defensive walls. "Tanner, Navie, fix that light machine gun here, facing towards the elevators. And, Corporal, for God's sake, make sure you load the soft tips this time."

Navie locked eyes with his. "What are we in for?"

Kilwalski laughed again. "The hell you say? You've never seen Frontin up close?"

Osterman glanced around at his men. Several others had turned, shaking their heads, their gazes fixing on him. Osterman felt a wave of annoyance at himself. It hadn't occurred to him that most of his team hadn't engaged the Frontin. Then again, the damned spiders didn't show up often.

Kilwalski folded his arms across his chest, leaning back against the wall. "It's no fucking picnic — those shit-for-brain bugs are tough. No fear. Big guns."

Osterman nodded. "The drones are the easiest targets. They tend to be slightly smaller and usually pretty dumb. The biggest trick, with any Frontin really, is not to fall back unless it's absolutely necessary. They see your back, and it whips them up into a frenzy."

Kilwalski cut in. "Especially drones. They always remind me of cartoon baddies, lots of yelling and growling and roaring, but unfocused and stupid. Hence the name, drones."

Osterman nodded. "Intelligence believes that Frontin get smarter as they get older. Their life span is huge, so a drone is like fighting a ten-year-old. Think of them as entry-level unseasoned, green soldiers."

"Soldiers." Summers rolled his eyes. "The Frontin ain't got no military. It's not like we are facing shock troops. They have their armor and shotties, but I got mine." The young man stroked his gun, nodding his head. "Intelligence spends too much time trying to figure 'em out."

Kilwalski shot him a look. "Stow it, Summers. They may not have a military, but they do seem to have castes, clans, and there certainly seems to be some sort of rank or hierarchy at work. How else can you explain their warriors?"

Osterman rubbed his face. "Warriors are the real threat. They are much bigger. Their armor is marked with pictographs showing their victories. Most carry large swords and pistols, for lack of a better term. They fight smarter." He tried to sound matter-of-fact. "I'd compare them to officers, but even though Frontin might follow a plan, the reality on the ground is more like a free-for-all. The drones generally flock to warriors. Killing them will confuse the drones temporarily."

Kilwalski uncrossed his arms, pointing. "Don't be mistaken. Even unorganized, these guys are a real threat. I've seen a warrior take out a squad in two seconds flat."

The color drained out of Navie's face.

Osterman forced on a smile. "At least you can comfort yourself in the knowledge we won't be facing a slew of Leaders. Those bastards are tough, or so I've heard. I've never met them. Some are very smart. Intelligence believes getting to that 'rank' is measured in more than just body counts. Luckily, they rarely leave their ships. They're like generals — they come up with plans and watch the results. They look a lot like the warriors, except bigger."

Summers laughed. "A smart Frontin. Now this I have to see."

Kilwalski's eyes bulged. "The likelihood that they will get down to us is next to nothing. Lots of guns between here and the ship's hull. Let's get back to it, people."

Osterman watched Kilwalski cross over to Summers, whose smile disappeared quickly. If the Frontin did get on board, his teams would need to be dug in well.

He turned his attention to preparing the rest of the *Verdun's* defenses, barely noticing the ship start to bank and accelerate or the combat klaxons blaring on.

Sergeant Masson finished his preflight check, the loud rumbling of the fighter's engine steadying his shaking hands. Nothing about this moment was right. He had dreamed of commanding his own squadron, but not like this. To replace a pilot like Hillman, his mentor, felt wrong.

He activated his mike. "Raptors, Raptor One. Sound off."

"Raptor One, Two. All boards green."

As he listened to the radio traffic from his pilots, his thoughts shot back to his last image of Hillman, his Stallion disintegrating into a blinding ball of yellow flame. He could do nothing to help Hillman. Now it was Masson's responsibility to keep the remaining raptors safe.

No more of Hillman's men would die in this asteroid field.

He felt the familiar surge of adrenaline hit him as his fighter was pulled out of its docking bay towards the launch ramps. His cockpit snapped shut, locking out the sound of the ship's klaxons. Masson pulled on his helmet, latching it down tightly. He felt the momentary sense of weightlessness as his ship was lowered into its vertical launch position. The loud scream of metal disappeared quickly as his fighter locked into place.

"Raptor Seven reports ready, sir."

The *Verdun* had four catapult decks, and his squadron would be one of the four in the first wave. The Raptors would distinguish themselves now with as much courage as they had when Hillman was alive.

Seargeant Masson closed his eyes. It wouldn't be long now.

S omehow, they had found his base.

The Frontin commander stared at the screen, stunned. The Alliance leader had avoided his first trap. He had expected them to fall back to the edge of the field, expected them to try to control where they were attacked, but they hadn't. They had found him.

He growled low, watched his prey approach, debating his actions. He hadn't even had time to deploy his ships throughout the asteroid field for the ambush. He'd thought the Alliance ship would hesitate longer, but its commander had charged ahead.

Like a warrior.

He closed his eyes.

Yes. This would work perfectly. Better than his original plan. He couldn't help but smile. The gods had favored him, given him a better way.

He opened his eyes and looked at the images of the meek little destroyers on his screen. He could warn them, but that would give away his newfound advantage, the final surprise.

No, those ships were expendable.

He had waited too long to risk failure.

This was it, his chance. The time of his redemption. He let himself slip back towards his blood rage. His nostrils yearned to smell burning flesh again. He longed for the shrill screams of these creatures, the same filthy creatures that had taken away his rightful place as hive leader. Now they would clear the way for his ascension.

With their blood.

CHAPTER 23

Mostoff flipped open his armrest controls, watched his active radar display. The *Black Fox* slipped into the clearing as slowly as he dared. The *Fox's* supports shook badly, even at this speed. Accelerating wouldn't be easy. The bridge was silent, the crew barely seemed to be breathing. These hybrid ships had hurt them so badly before, and none of his crew expected this to be easy as the Alliance officers predicted.

Officer Krilic looked pale, his voice cracking. "They've spotted us."

Mostoff willed his voice to be even and calm. "All batteries, fire at will."

The ship turned painfully slowly, the room shaking as the acceleration stressed the damaged metal.

The thirty Alliance fighters moved to screen the *Fox*, their weapons pointed at the oncoming destroyers. Even though he couldn't see the green-brown bastards accelerating, he couldn't remove the image from his mind. Their long, thin frames, bristling with rough armor and thin rocket ports — all swiveling quickly towards his ship.

Mostoff slammed his fists down, screaming. "Why are my guns still silent? Get me more speed now."

The *Fox* jolted, its first salvo of missiles shooting towards the destroyers, the recoil causing the ancient ship's superstructure to groan. Mostoff started to feel lighter, adrenaline pumping through his body. None of his birds would score hits, these bastards were too well armed.

The automated impact alarm blared.

The *Black Fox* shuddered, straining against its own inertia and age as the pilot tried to outmaneuver the oncoming ordnance. Mostoff's whole body hurt as he braced himself for impact, his legs pulsing with pain.

The ship rocked, his wheelchair bucked hard against its brakes, his body pressing against the restraints. "Damage report!"

Krilic's voice sounded weak. "None. The missile was destroyed prior to impact. The computer is confused. It's tracking hundreds of torpedoes in the air."

Mostoff growled. "Get this ship moving, or we're dead."

The moments ticked by, and Mostoff prayed. The *Fox* had survived so many battles, and he wouldn't let it die now.

He felt the ship dive, the gravity drive straining against the inertia. The ship shook, his vision blurring as the room jerked violently.

That was no near miss.

Mostoff could feel the *Fox* losing speed, the vibration in her super structure churning his stomach.

Another impact tore through the ship. The world seemed to blink out for a second, pain searing through him. He tried to stand, but his legs refused to move. He shook his head, realized he was on the cold metal floor.

He couldn't remember falling. His mind spun as he tried to remember what was happening. The *Black Fox* shook again, another torpedo tearing into her. Mostoff rolled over, his arms strained to pull himself back into his chair. His body ached with the effort, and the pressure in his legs made him want to call out, scream the pain away.

He wouldn't let himself.

The *Fox* pulled up hard again. The hull clanged as a torpedo skipped off it. Mostoff hated that sound. The fish scraped loudly against the *Fox's* side before propelling itself away, drifting uselessly into space, the detonator failing to ignite. Dave, his helmsman, looked frantic. Mostoff yearned to stand, grasp the man's shoulder to steady him, but the pain was too intense.

This is hopeless.

No. He refused to think like that. Mostoff gritted his teeth, watching the radar pings of the continuous flow of missiles streaking towards his ship. He had never seen anything like it. Morden had been right — had he found this place, tried to fight these murderers alone, without the fighter screen…

"More speed, give me flank speed. We have to get out of here."

His helmsman turned towards him. "We'll break up."

Mostoff spat back at him. "Did I ask for opinions? Flank speed."

The ship convulsed, he couldn't tell if it was from an impact or the last of the power being poured into the engines. The deck was vibrating so hard he felt like he was spinning. He was sure he was bleeding again, the pain in his legs was so fierce.

Mostoff felt his chest burning, his lungs heavy and weak. The heat and smoke being pumped into the room made his head spin.

Wait, smoke?

He tried to think. His mind was so hazy. Smoke from the atmosphere processor could only mean one thing—

Krilic cried out. "We're on fire."

M orden's knuckles turned white as she braced herself for acceleration. "Stetler, flank speed."

Stetler's voice was calm. "Aye, aye. Engines to full."

The *Black Fox* was in trouble. Morden had been watching the situation evolve on her screen. It wasn't clear how badly she'd been damaged, but the ship's engine output was falling. Morden was relying on what she could see on the holoports and the small amount of data the ship's sensors were relaying to her console. The sheer number of missile and torpedo explosions prevented laser links from the sensor drones closer to the *Fox*.

Damn it.

Those destroyers were faster than she had anticipated. At least they had taken the bait, firing with everything they had.

"All defensive batteries to full. Gun crews engage targets at will. All fighters to stand by condition. Bring all backup generators to full. Load forward torpedo tubes. Medical and repair teams be prepared." Morden glanced down at her command console, saw the distance to the enemy decreasing quickly. "We will be at point-blank range in forty seconds."

Morden heard the *Verdun's* combat capability spring to life, the hum of the Magnetic Ordnance Deflector, the far-off grumble of the hydraulics of rotating gun turrets, the thump as torpedoes locked into their tubes. She looked back at her command screen, willing the ship to move faster.

"We are in range, Captain," Wilcox called from behind her.

Morden quickly selected targets with her stylus. "Give all guns permission to fire. Torpedoes, fire all salvos. Stetler, execute a left, 180-degree turn on my mark."

Morden felt the main guns fire, the entire ship reverberating with the sound of the discharge. She felt adrenaline surge through her, reminded herself to breathe. Things were going as planned. Morden was a soldier — no amount of fear would make her back down.

The *Fox* didn't have a magnetic ordnance shield, and judging from the images she was seeing on the holoports, it needed one right now, explosion plumes visible all around the old ship. The MOD, powerful magnetic bands running along the outside of the ship, was the last line of defense the *Verdun* had against any ordnance, missiles, or torpedoes that survived the Cerberus interceptors and defensive guns. Any incoming ordnance would run into this magnetic field, slow down, or be deflected away, depending on the amount of kinetic energy behind it. Propelled rounds would be forced away, curving around the hull, either failing to detonate or hitting the armor at an angle, nullifying the impact of any penetrator rounds. The downside was that the more ordnance that hit or detonated near the hull, the more gaps appeared in the field. Once damaged, there was no replacing the MOD without splashdown or time in drydock

Morden watched as the destroyers' guns started pouring fire at the *Verdun*, taking some of the pressure off the wounded *Fox*.

There we go.

The holoports flickered, catching the interference from the massive intensity of the explosions as the incoming ordnance impacted the wall of fire the *Verdun's* defensive turrets were dumping out.

The captain watched the distance close between the *Verdun* and her targets. The destroyers were fighting to turn their vulnerable sides away from the Alliance warship.

She glanced at the readings of the *Black Fox*, strings of text and numbers streaming across a drop box on her command screen. She enlarged it, interpreting the data. The ship was still slowing and signs of serious structural damage were visible, but Isabelle's analysis indicated that the mercenary ship should be more than capable of escaping on her own.

Still, Morden couldn't help but worry. They had been hit harder than she'd thought. All she could do now was hope Isabelle's analysis was correct and the *Fox* would hold out while the *Verdun* engaged the enemy.

She shrank the box, bringing views of the battle back onto her screen. The *Verdun* was almost on top of the destroyer formation. Salvos from her guns, indicated by dots on the screen, were streaking toward the targets. The lead destroyer shuddered, falling out of formation, no longer able to keep up. It was bleeding oxygen, flames spurting from several deep cracks forming along its hull. The ship was tumbling, its thrusters clearly no longer able to correct its course.

A second destroyer slowed for a moment as several torpedo markers disappeared into its forward decks. The images showed armor cracking, shedding debris and frozen vapor in the ship's wake.

Yes, damn it.

This was exactly what needed to happen, break the bastards fast. As a collected formation, they were dangerous — individually, they were fodder.

This was too easy.

Isabelle's voice rose above the ship's klaxons. "All hands, brace for impact, we are danger-close to approaching ships. All hands, brace for impact."

The *Verdun* started to cross directly between the destroyers. The enemy weapon locks set off warnings on Morden's screen as the enemy guns swung towards her ship's superstructure.

Morden could hear the roar of detonating rounds as they curved around the *Verdun* harmlessly. The few seconds it took to cross paths with the destroyers came and went in a blink of an eye. Impact klaxons wailed loudly as several salvos hit, detonating against the hull.

She tapped the screen, bringing up the information from Wilcox's damage control station. Their armor had held, and there were only a few reports of minor injuries coming through the data feed. She exhaled and returned to the camera view of the battle.

Another destroyer had fallen out of formation, banking to the left. Its engines fired sporadically, fighting to prevent itself from delisting. The ship's power readings were dropping as the *Verdun's* rear guns fired. She watched the dying ship try to get out of the way, its side thrusters firing, spinning it like a top. The salvo slammed home, shredding the destroyer, flame and debris spewing out in rings as each half of the vessel continued spinning, trapped in their own inertia.

The Alliance ship bucked as several pieces of debris struck her.

Morden's screen raced as injury reports flowed in, but she didn't want to wait. "Damage report?"

Wilcox yelled over the alarms. "Two defensive turrets are out, and my sensors indicate that we have patches of compromised armor just behind the rear struts, and —"

Isabelle cut him off. "All fighter loading arms are down."

Holsey cried out. "Shit. We should launch the fighters that are already in the tubes, now!"

Morden cursed under her breath. Without the loaders, they could only launch a portion of their fighter compliment. The damage was relatively light, but this would hurt their offensive capabilities. The destroyers were adjusting their tactics much faster than she'd anticipated.

They needed to end this battle fast.

One pass had inflicted heavy damage on the two destroyers and reduced one to slag, so why were they still so organized? She had expected them to try to escape — flee towards the safety of the asteroids or dissolve into panic.

"Stetler, come about. Let Mr. Frost know he may launch when ready."

Morden could feel the ship swing up, it's nose climbing fast, the internal gravity working overtime to compensate for the extreme speeds and tight maneuvers. The destroyers were circling back around in tight formation. They were stacked up directly in front of the *Verdun*, slowing to allow the damaged destroyers to crawl into the protected center of the formation.

This was her chance. She could take them out all at once, now.

Morden glanced at her screens. The *Fox* was still drifting slowly, trying to escape. If the destroyers continued to adapt their tactics this quickly, they might overcome their lack of firepower with maneuverability, causing the *Verdun* more damage. If they went after the *Fox*, there was nothing she could do. They — she — would have to watch that ship die.

Morden activated her head set. "Morden to fire control, prepare to fire laser cannons."

Holsey's voice was hoarse. "Are you sure? Once we fire —"

"I am aware of what happens when the lasers fire. I want to clear my sky."

The laser cannons would obliterate a formation of ships like this, but there was a downside to that kind of firepower. Once she fired, the *Verdun* would be vulnerable for several minutes as the enormous power drain left her on battery power only. It would also be fifteen minutes before the laser cannons could recharge and come online again. Standard operating procedure discouraged their use when outside of large formations.

Maybe Holsey has a point.

Morden questioned herself for a moment.

They could still do this conventionally, but at what cost? The destroyers had learned from their mistake, holding fire until they could get closer to their target. Without the ability to launch fighters, the *Verdun* would be even more vulnerable to anything that survived the laser cannons. But if they got in another lucky shot or broke for the *Fox*...

She wouldn't take chances dragging this out.

Morden could feel the first few fighters kicking off from the *Verdun*.

Isabelle spoke. "We are now at optimal laser cannon range."

Holsey's voice was intense. "I strongly object to this, Captain."

Morden swallowed. "Fire."

Holsey's next outcry was drowned out by the sound of the laser cannons firing.

CHAPTER 24

Sergeant Masson felt G-forces pushing down against his chest as his Stallion blasted out into space. Even with inertial dampeners, the intensity of launching while the *Verdun* was rocketing through space at flank speed left his body tingling.

The Sergeant yanked back on his stick and swung his fighter's nose up, pointing him to the nearest destroyers. They were trying to come about, tightening their formation.

Masson highlighted one of the center ships on his command console. "Raptors, Raptor One. Accelerate to attack speed, and form up on my six. Target the wounded destroyers in the formation's center. Trigger's free. Let's light 'em up."

He glanced at his holoscreens, which only registered one other fighter squadron in the air, one group of the ship's interceptors. The *Verdun* wasn't where he'd expected. She was halfway through a 180-degree turn, her thrusters pushing hard to bring the ship head to tail from its previous position. Morden was being aggressive.

Very aggressive.

The Raptors screamed towards their target, maneuvering quickly to avoid the machine gun fire filling the space in front of them. Masson was furiously working his controls, staying one step ahead of the enemy's fire. These miners didn't seem to know how to lead a target — he and his squadron would take advantage of their lack of training.

The darkness outside his cockpit burst into brilliant shades of red and his headset fizzled into static. His Stallion shook, leaving him dizzy, as three continuous beams shot past him.

The *Verdun* had fired her laser cannons.

Masson was mesmerized as the hot streams of energy struck the lead destroyer amidships, punching straight through the target. The destroyer hung there for a moment before its forward section splintered and the entire ship began to explode. Flame and atmosphere spurted into space, its form disintegrating into pieces. Debris from the blast tore into the other enemy ships as they desperately tried to avoid the three super-heated beams.

One of the damaged destroyers took the brunt of one of the beams on her bow. The laser liquefied the makeshift armor, slicing a deep crevasse into the ship. The destroyer jolted to a stop, its momentum halted as if it had run headlong into a wall. It shook, escape pods billowing out of its side, puffs of smoke and vapor marking the path of each small craft against the blackness. The destroyer vaporized, the shockwave lashing out in all directions as the reactor went critical.

Masson couldn't help but admire the Captain's decision — two more of the destroyers were dead. The final two undamaged destroyers were panicked, separating from each other and their hobbled sister. The captain had gambled, choosing to forgo launching her fighter cover in order to catch the enemy formation off guard. Had the gunners been slightly more careful, they might have eliminated another one. Under normal circumstances, the *Verdun's* fighters would have defended her while she restored main power.

His Raptors would just have to clear the air a bit.

He checked his screen. His team was only thirty seconds away from the damaged destroyer. The ship was drifting so far from its formation that they could finish it off without even worrying about flak fire from the remaining enemy vessels.

Masson transferred power to the engines, painting his target on his newly installed command screen for the rest of his squadron to see. "Raptors, hit that ship now."

He looked out his windscreen. The destroyer was growing bigger as his ship barreled down on it. His target lock alarm sang as he waited for the last possible second. He squeezed the trigger, unleashing two torpedoes. They hit right on target, making the destroyer shudder as they detonated.

Masson flipped over on his x-axis, slammed the deceleration jets. The intensity of the turn made him feel slightly sick. The destroyer came back into view, and he watched as successive waves of explosions encompassed the target. The last of his team were pouring it on, torpedo after torpedo mangling the ship's meager defenses. It was spilling atmosphere and metal fragments into space like blood. It was a beautiful sight, red and orange plumes of fire against the now nearly lightless *Verdun* in the background.

That's for you, Lieutenant Hillman.

The mauled destroyer was still intact, but it was crippled, drifting helplessly towards the edge of the asteroid field. His sensors showed minimal radiation from its power plant and only one intact gun battery. Its days as a warship were over.

Masson pushed his engines back to full power, maneuvering back towards the *Verdun.* "Great shooting, Raptors. Return to base, let's help keep the other two destroyers off till she regains full power."

The two destroyers seemed to have regained their wits, both turning back towards the *Verdun.* Masson couldn't help but think how minuscule they looked next to the massive battlecruiser. The destroyers were firing, their missiles filling the void like clouds of mosquitoes. The *Verdun's* defensive emplacements were responding, their effectiveness and speed only diminished by their reliance on backup generators for power.

Masson ignored the rockets strike against the *Verdun's* forward armor from the nearest destroyer. The ten Cerberus interceptors were almost into position to protect her bow, but their relatively low speed had allowed the enemy to tear into the *Verdun.* The sensor drones indicated damage to the port side ordnance shield.

The *Verdun's* main turrets were firing slowly, their massive shells streaking towards the destroyers. The two ships seemed to have reached their maximum acceleration, maneuvering quickly, banking hard to avoid fire. The destroyers were losing accuracy, but from their angle of attack, Masson was sure they were more interested in avoiding fire until they closed to point blank range.

The sergeant pulled into the gap between the destroyers and the *Verdun,* holding down the trigger on his machine guns, blasting away at the missiles filling the sky in front of him. He pulled up, swinging his fighter up and over the Alliance battle cruiser, avoiding the flak detonating around him.

He keyed on his laser link securing his radio. "All fighters loosen up. Heavy flak."

Eliot's yelling cut him off. "Fuck! Sarge, the station is —"

Masson's cockpit lit up as Elliot's Stallion vanished in a cloud of burning oxygen and shrapnel.

Masson's head spun. His fighters were caught in a crossfire, flak and machine gun fire ripping at them from multiple angles. He pulled back on his controls, throwing his Stallion into as steep a climb as he could manage without blacking out from the intense G's. The wail of his fighter's master alarm filled his cockpit, warning of damage to several systems.

He coughed, the smell of burnt wiring filling his cockpit.

He glanced at the command screen. Several fighters had incinerated along with Eliot in the intense burst of incoming fire. He flipped his craft over, inverting himself to get a view of the station. There weren't any surviving drones near enough to get clear readings.

His jaw dropped.

The station that had seemed abandoned was lit up like a charismas tree, hidden gun batteries uncovering themselves all over its massive hull. A gigantic door was starting to open. How had the drones missed that?

Directly in front of him, Raptor Four vanished, leaving nothing but metal bits and vapor. Masson's cockpit clanked as the remains of Raptor Four bounced harmlessly off the glass, the sound echoing in his ears.

He didn't need to look at his consoles to know most of his team had died in seconds. His own fighter was dying, smoke forcing him to activate his suit's oxygen mask. The Stallion's engines were losing power, the stick more and more sluggish in his hands. There was nowhere to run to, nowhere to land.

Masson glanced down at his radar display. The *Verdun* was being hammered, its rear armor absorbing a massive attack from the station.

There was no time left for indecision.

He pulled his ship around. "All remaining Raptors, cover the Verdun's aft section."

Masson punched his thrusters to full, disabling the alarms. He switched to his machine gun and held down the trigger, filling the air in front of him with hot steel. Large anti-ship shells disintegrated all around him as he screened the *Verdun*.

The *Verdun* had managed to swing its defensive weapons to the rear. Even hampered by the energy blackout, the turrets cut large swaths into the incoming cloud of ordnance.

But it wasn't enough to stop the ship's rear armor from absorbing strike after strike from the station's weapons.

Masson cut his thrust, easing his beleaguered Stallion closer to the incoming fire, tricking his automated defense turrets to target the oncoming salvos.

His body shook violently as another bright explosion bloomed to his left, the last of his team burning up in a haze of gunfire. He steadied his rocking ship, trying to keep all his guns on plane. Stallions were not designed to fight like this. Masson's hand was cramping with the effort of trying to hold the ship steady and keep his weapons firing constantly.

His sensors indicated the *Verdun* was starting to come back on line, the rate of fire from her defensive weapons increasing quickly. Her aft armor was seriously weakened, and Masson's equipment indicated no functional magnetic coils left for the rear MOD

Masson looked back towards the station. Its door was fully open now, and a Frontin Jon frigate and three Nitva heavy cruisers were emerging out of the bay.

They opened fire.

He never had time to react — the last thing he felt before the enemy guns ripped his ship into pieces was his weapons running dry and his ammunition alarm screeching loudly. The Stallion's debris spread out in waves as the enemy ships rushed towards the *Verdun*.

Hillman pushed himself off the cold deck plating. His chest ached from where it had struck the floor. He took a deep breath, trying to get as much air as he could. The ship had lost integrity, atmosphere rushing past him on its way to the nearest hull breach. The destroyer had been hit by something big, very big.

He had hidden just above the escape deck, waiting for his opportunity to stow away aboard a pod. This was his chance. He could slip down, steal a pod, and hope to God his people picked him up. But Hillman hadn't seen anyone trying to reach the escape pods. Maybe the ship wasn't so damaged after all, or the damage was limited to his section only. Or maybe the crew had been killed.

The fear he had felt inching up his spine was evaporating, replaced by a desire to stay. This had to be an attack from the *Verdun*. If the crew was dead, he had time. He could make his way to the bridge, possibly contact the *Verdun* for help. He might even be able to gain access to a Frontin computer. It was easier to call for help than hope to God someone would see him.

That had to be worth the risk.

The ceiling lights were flickering, smoke swirling in tendrils through the thin air. He slid out his pistol, thumbed off the safety and waited for several moments, listening for any sound. The only thing he heard was the slow whining of the ship's emergency klaxons.

Hillman dropped from his hiding spot, walking quickly towards the door. He peered around the corner, pistol ready. He worked his way through the hallway, moving as best as he could toward the upper decks. He didn't know exactly where the bridge was, but it had to be somewhere in front of the emergency bulkhead that had dropped into place. Traditionally, merchant ships built their bridges next to the escape deck.

He followed the airshafts back to his original entry point. All he had to do was crawl down to the next deck, bypass the area on this deck that was closed off, and come back up to this level. The bulkheads couldn't be fully intact. Even if the air were breathable, he could feel it rushing past on its way into space.

It only took a few minutes to reckon his way to the bridge using the few wall markings visible. The temperature inside the ship was unbearably hot, and he felt sweat pooling under his survival suit. Hillman pressed his ear against the bridge door. Someone was moving inside the room. His heart pounded, and he tightened the grip on his pistol.

He could just make out fragmented pieces of an argument through the door.

"Lord, I can't contact the lower decks," one voice said, the sound muffled through the hatch. "The fires must have killed everyone."

A second, deep, inhuman voice responded. "I won't miss a fight, not like this. I can taste victory!"

That had to be the Frontin. No human could sound like that.

A third voice cut in. "We have partial engines back, but no weapons."

The first voice sounded scared. "We should abandon ship. There's nothing we can do. Once our batteries run dry, we will be defenseless."

The Frontin screamed loudly, the unmistakable slam of its fist on metal echoing loudly. Hillman took a deep breath, keyed open the door, and aimed his pistol into the opening. He swept his eyes across the room quickly. It was small, most of the computer consoles were out, and the room was dark except for the cold flicker of the damaged emergency lighting. The Frontin stood in the middle of the room, right in front of a command chair, his two human companions on opposite ends of the room. One was bent down trying to rewire some circuits in the right wall, the other was sitting at what looked like a helm.

All three started to turn. Hillman fired. He hit the Frontin dead center with two shots. It screamed and crumpled backwards, gripping its wounds.

Hillman fired at the officer at the helm, hitting him in the side of the head, showering the helm with skull fragments and blood. He tried to swing around and aim at the third man, his shots going wide before his slide locked back, his chamber empty.

The man had shaken off his shock and drew his weapon. Hillman ran several paces, diving behind the nearest smashed console, the sound of ricochets echoing loudly in his ear as the man returned fire.

The Lieutenant peered around the corner. The Frontin had risen, pulling its scatter gun from its hip. Hillman slapped a new magazine into place and released the slide. He ducked back behind the console just as the Frontin gun went off, its deafening roar making his ears ring. The top of the console disintegrated, metal shavings and debris raining around him and stinging his skin.

He leaned out to his left, aiming as quickly as he could at the creature's many shins. He swore he could hear its malevolent laugh as he heard it pump another shell into the chamber. Hillman pulled the trigger, firing all ten rounds into the Frontin's legs.

The Frontin Leader fired as it fell, screaming as blood and pieces of exoskeleton spattered the deck. Hillman could feel the Frontin barbs brushing past his skin, tearing his suit and glancing off his armor, his opponent's aim thrown off by its fall. Its huge black body shook the deck, its scattergun skipping away with a loud clatter.

Hillman scrambled back behind the console, the final human's shots going wide of him. He loaded his last magazine, waiting for a break in the man's panicked fire. It only took seconds for the shots to cease, replaced by muttered curses and the metallic clacking of a magazine hitting the floor.

Hillman stood and fired at the man. His first shot went wide, cutting into the paneling behind the miner. He corrected his aim and squeezed the trigger again. This shot hit the man in the side, covering the grating below in hot blood. The miner screamed, his hands fumbling with a spare magazine.

Hillman never gave the miner the chance, firing several more rounds into him, ending his life.

The Frontin growled, his speech soft. "You are what kills me. I am ashamed."

Hillman holstered his nearly empty pistol. "Shut up, fucker."

He walked over to the Frontin's scattergun and hoisted it up with both hands. He rested its end on the deck, using his body weight to pump a new round into the massive weapon's chamber.

The Frontin made a laughing sound. "Human, you haven't won. I was fated to die here, my seer told me. You and your ship have fallen into our trap."

Hillman rested the massive barrel against the Frontin's grotesque face. "Trap?"

"Threats won't persuade me. Death will clutch me to her."

Hillman frowned, pushed the weapon down harder. "What trap?"

"Believe what you want. Think what you will. Believe we would stoop to work with humans for this pitiful corner of nothing. You bags of bones are as stupid as you are ugly."

Hillman watched the Frontin curl its face into a smile, forcing him to look directly into its many eyes. He shuddered, felt the worst chill of his life envelope him as he saw its expression. The green-gray blood from its shattered legs was pooling around its feet. It smelled of rotting flesh and burnt ozone.

Hillman's stomach turned, and he fought to repress his nausea.

The Frontin waved his arms. "These pathetic creatures whine for freedom. We gave them means, taught them how to build weapons, but they aren't hunters. They aren't strong. We don't help the weak, don't care about causes. No. We knew it would bring you. My clan leader will take your ship, unlock its secrets, and unlock the galaxy to our control using your sticky blood as the key."

The Frontin's laughter filled the room as Hillman pulled the trigger. The Frontin's head disintegrated in a wave of gore, the weapon's recoil throwing the Alliance officer to the ground.

CHAPTER 25

Morden closed her eyes and opened them, making sure she wasn't seeing things. The station had unleashed two Nitva heavy cruisers and a Jon. She hadn't expected to see another capital ship in the region, even if it was only a frigate.

She'd known this fight had been too easy.

Holsey's voice made her turn. "They have us dead in their sights."

Her eyes were flashing with that anger Morden had come to know so well.

Morden waved her hand and looked forward again. "Simmer down. They were here regardless. We can deal with this."

The tension in the room was high. The *Verdun* was taking damage. Urquhart and Stetler were rigid, eyes locked on the image of the Jon on the holoport. Holsey had to know arguing with her now would only further undermine the crew's morale and get people killed. They had to seem confident, unified.

Wilcox's smooth voice cut in. "We are still in good shape. At least we aren't stuck in the middle of two enemy formations."

Holsey didn't respond. The woman's anger had started as they had watched Raptor squadron being torn to pieces. Morden was just as upset — she had known some of those pilots for years — but now wasn't the time to let her guilt win out.

Morden looked at her console. "Time until we have full power?"

The battlecruiser rocked as another salvo of shells hit her rear quarter. The rear defenses were being overwhelmed, the MOD had given out, and several of the point defense stations had been destroyed. The engines, stabilizers, and armor had all taken beatings, but the ship's combat capability was still intact.

"Ten seconds, Ma'am," Wilcox said

From the corner of her eye she could see his damage control boards flashing brightly, the LED lights glowing with each new impact.

Morden winced as the ship jolted again, her safety harness biting into her skin. The next ten seconds couldn't pass by fast enough. She was going to fuck these guys up. They were going to regret being born.

The Jon had clarified everything. Nothing had felt right. These destroyers were designed to wreak havoc on the locals, stir up the area, get them fighting amongst themselves, but they had always seemed to lack an actual goal.

But there was a goal — even if they didn't know what it was. A Frontin capital ship hadn't been seen in the last century. Clearly, their actions here were part of some larger strategy.

The thrumming of the *Verdun's* engines roaring back to life announced the ship's power systems coming fully online. The deck kicked, pushing Morden back into her seat, and Isabelle's form fizzled back into view. Morden could feel the vibrations of the fighter deck launching the ten Cerberus interceptors and the forty Stallions that had been waiting in the launch tubes — not a lot to work with, but they'd have to do until the loading arms were back online.

Isabelle's sweet accent seemed to ease the tension in the room. "Captain, our engines have taken damage. Only two of our rear defensive turrets are at a hundred percent. Both thirteen-inch rear turrets have lost hydraulics, and our aft MOD is completely offline."

Morden took a moment to look at her screen, trying to formulate a plan. "Urquhart, plot us a course right down the destroyers' throats. We need to turn this into a one-sided fight. Stetler, keep our starboard side to the station and the cruisers. Chief, tell Frost he has ten minutes to get our fighter loading arms back online. When we get the remaining Stallions in the air, have them go after that damn station and silence those guns.

"Aye, captain," the pair of junior officers said in unison.

Morden could feel the *Verdun* start to change course, lining her bow up with the destroyers. The Alliance guns were blaring again, their rhythmic fire finally forcing the enemy ships to focus as much on flying as firing.

Holsey's voice was stern. "We should pull back, force them to come after us."

Morden looked back at her. "If we run, they will have the advantage in the asteroids. They won't just let us go."

Holsey pursed her lips. "But our fighters would have the advantage over them. They could use hit-and-run tactics until we get clear of this field."

Morden shook her head. "Enough. Either fall in line, or get off the bridge. We are a ship of the line. We don't run at the first sign of trouble."

Holsey sat down, her eyes smoldering. "Captain, it is my duty to point out alternatives for you."

Morden turned her eyes to her command screen. "Commander, thank you for executing your duty to the fullest. Now, let's get these bastards."

The ship banked, dodging another wave of inaccurate projectiles from the Jon. The main batteries barked again, the shells plowing into the bow of the nearest destroyer, knocking it backwards, fire bursting from its open wound.

S myth yelled into her headset. "Pour it on! Reload!"

Turret Two was firing as fast as her teams could load, heat filling the gun compartment, the crew's rate of fire keeping the automatic plasma ejector hard at work. Radio chatter filled the room as her three ensigns coordinated the three barrels, trying to keep them firing in tandem. She glanced into the gunroom. All three barrels had lowered into loading position, the two-person gun crews slamming another projectile into each breech.

The barrels swung back up into firing position, and Smyth adjusted the coordinates on her targeting control pad, feeding the information back to her fire chiefs. The weapons automatically shifted, and the entire turret traversed quickly to point towards the closest destroyer.

Va's voice came over her headset, seconds before Smyth's screens turned green. "All guns are green."

Smyth yelled at the top of her lungs. "Fire!"

The room exploded with sound as the three barrels cleared their throats together. Smyth locked her eyes on the screen.

The first round missed, but the other two smacked into the destroyer's mid-section, the fierce flash of their detonation blinding her camera view for several seconds.

When the blaze cleared, the destroyer was vibrating, its engines visibly strained. She could see its thrusters desperately trying to right itself after the grave hit. Several shells whizzed by it narrowly as the other forward batteries fired.

Smyth loaded more coordinates into the system. "Reload. Get this girl singing, boys!"

This was her kill. Just like the Jon would be. Nothing would stop her. Not with her team at her side.

L t. Hillman felt a slight nudge as he fired the destroyer's engines, pushing it closer to the station. He was still sick to his stomach, still light-headed from the thinning atmosphere of this crippled ship. At least he could breathe properly now the bridge was sealed and he was no longer at risk from lack of oxygen.

But his relief from asphyxiation wasn't the only thing on his mind. He had watched the station tear apart a squadron of Stallions, watched the Jon appear, the sickening laughter of the Frontin echoing through his mind.

The *Verdun* had launched more of her fighters, and the Stallions were angling towards the station. They would have a hell of time taking it on, having to cross such a large distance under fire, especially with the two heavy cruisers and the Jon blocking the approach.

His Raptors were out there, somewhere. Hillman couldn't watch any more fighters' burn up, not when he should be with them.

He had an opportunity, and he was going to take it. This destroyer couldn't fight or maneuver well, but it would be identified as a friendly by the firing computers of the Frontin. If he could get in close enough, he could detonate its reactor and incinerate the station and any of the ships nearby.

Assuming the sheer act of moving didn't blow the wreck up.

Hillman keyed in the sequence that would set the generator to overload. He had to be careful. The reactor needed to run poorly, but not look like someone was making it go critical. If the Frontin noticed something unusual, they would destroy the ship themselves.

It would take his wounded vessel at least ten minutes to make its way through the clearing. Hillman had to work fast, make every moment count. The controls were hard to use — bulky, heavy, and poorly organized, the obvious side-effect of a marriage between two incompatible technologies. To make things worse, he wasn't an engineer. The bridge was seriously damaged, and what was functioning had been jury-rigged to get it that way.

If he survived this, it would be more than bragging when he said he could fly any gutted piece of crap.

Of course, to survive he would have to figure out how the hell to get off this death trap before it exploded.

One thing at a time, Hillman.

Right now, it only mattered that he reached his target.

Captain Mostoff sucked in his first breath of fresh air, the smoke from the fire finally vented. His body hurt, his legs burned. Blood trickled down his leg from torn sutures. He leaned back in his chair, trying to understand what was happening. In his wildest and darkest nightmares, he wouldn't have guessed this was possible, not even from the miners.

A Frontin frigate, a capital ship, here in the Triangle. The entire merchant fleets of both colonies couldn't take it down.

Why had the beasts come here?

Mostoff closed his eyes. Everything had changed. All the petty squabbling between colonies, their power play over the miners, the constant jockeying for position, all the anger he had held onto for so long, meant nothing.

This was the stuff of nightmares.

He scowled. What would cause these people to call the Frontin? His mind fell back to his list of achievements, personal victories. Arrests, detainments, successful interrogations, the string of increasingly harsh demands and deadlines the colonies had decreed and he had enforced with gusto.

And you never thought they'd strike back?

His head spun so fast he could barely sort out the mix of guilt and hatred clashing in his heart. The conflicting feelings burrowed into his sense of reality like a splinter tearing its way into his mind. He felt weak and, for the first time in his life, lost.

Frontin in the Triangle, in force. Only a week ago, he had felt Morden was the biggest danger in the Triangle, the greatest threat to his way of life.

The wounded *Fox* shook as it fired its thrusters to decelerate, escaping to the relative safety of the asteroids. As long as the Alliance ship had the enemy engaged, he had time to run, time to warn the rest of the Triangle of the danger.

Run?

Mostoff opened his eyes. Regret was useless and panic killed. Warning people couldn't save them. If this frigate escaped, no amount of warning would help. He was a captain, and he wouldn't let any enemy or any self-doubt shake his resolve.

He opened his command screen, taking in the damage reports as they scrolled by. Mostoff focused on his readouts, trying to ignore the pain shooting through his legs. There was some serious structural damage to all decks, two engines cores had burnt out, and his surgeon reported twelve dead and many more wounded.

With that kind of damage, his ship wasn't out of danger, even sitting still. There was a lot of work to do. He couldn't let his self-indulgent reflections distract him from his duty. The *Fox* had survived worse battles, and he wouldn't give up on her yet.

At least his weapons were still online.

The computer indicated fires were burning on several decks. Unlike the Alliance, he had no automated fire suppression systems. A fire could gut the ship, detonate weapons magazines, or burn through his oxygen reserves.

He felt useless in this chair. Normally he led firefighters or assisted the damage control teams personally. He had set the correct actions in motion, but he would just have to trust his crew to get it done without him.

Mostoff looked over his tactical display. The *Verdun* was in over her head, surrounded on all sides but fighting valiantly. He could only read one intact destroyer besides the one limping slowly towards its base.

He couldn't do this — let others defend his home while he sat back and licked his wounds. The *Fox* could still maneuver, still fight.

Mostoff snarled. "Officer Krilic, contact our escorts. Release them. Let them return to the Verdun. Dave, set a course to run along the outer edge of this clearing. Get me near that base."

Krilic's voice cracked. "But without escorts, we don't stand a chance in hell of —"

Mostoff cut him off. "Krilic, we will not let the Alliance fight our battles without us. We have never needed escorts before! This is no different."

"This is not like before! This is a battle station supported by a capital ship." Krillic's voice held a note of panic. "They will tear us apart."

Mostoff looked into the younger man's eyes, and he was surprised to see the same pain and doubt he had been wrestling with. The wounds of the Triangle were deeper than he realized.

He softened his voice. "We can't just run. If the Alliance loses here today, then we are lost. From behind, that base is vulnerable. It is focused on the Verdun. We need the Alliance's weapons to defeat the Frontin. It is the right thing to do."

The man stared back at him silently for a moment before nodding his head. Krilic turned slowly, helping the shaking helm officer key in commands. They had fought beside him for a long time. Mostoff could feel that bond between them.

Mostoff's heart began to race, fresh adrenaline rushing into his nervous system. The pain of his wounds quieted, washing over him in short bursts only. He had to focus, had to use all his experience now to help bring victory. He switched his damage control feed off, brought back his active radar display. The *Verdun* had eliminated the last of the destroyers. The remaining enemies were accelerating, trying to catch up with the battlecruiser before it turned.

The station was firing massive shells and rockets toward the *Verdun* and her fighters. His tactical display indicated a smattering of anti-fighter emplacements surrounding its six largest batteries. Even from short range, it would be difficult to destroy, but not impossible. He couldn't stop that frigate, but he could silence that station.

Or die trying.

CHAPTER 26

Morden kept her voice even. "Finish that ship off!"

The main guns shook the deck as they fired their salvos towards the final destroyer.

The beleaguered ship fired her engines, struggled to pull up, its commander no doubt trying to move its aft out of the way of the incoming shells. He failed, and several rounds slammed directly into the ship's engines, blasting waves of debris in all directions. The ship started to tumble uncontrollably, its final remaining engines pushing forward without their counterparts to stabilize them.

The stress of the spin was too great for the weakened ship. Piece by piece, its own power ripped it apart. Its debris would keep spinning in space until the pieces impacted the nearby asteroids, leaving hundreds of buried and burnt monuments to the Frontin's treachery in the Triangle.

Halfway there!

Morden tried not to think about the cost in lives. Casualty reports were still coming in. Several of the manned defensive turrets had been destroyed, and one of the main guns reported a fire burning.

She repositioned her camera, switching the feed to the holoports. The Jon and heavy cruisers were trying to close the distance and match the *Verdun's* maneuvers. The Stallions still hadn't been able to get close enough to the base to do any real damage. Between the flak from the Frontin ships and the base itself, the fighters were keeping their distance.

The Frontin had marshalled their forces more carefully than she would have thought possible. The Alliance vessel shook as another shell slipped past her fighter screen and detonated on her mangled rear armor.

There was a still a hell of a fight left.

Even at full strength, a Jon frigate wouldn't normally be a match for an Alliance battlecruiser, but the *Verdun* was vulnerable. If Morden wasn't careful...

She entered in a new course. "Stetler, bring us around. Holsey, I want our defensive fighters to form up in front of us. Main batteries target the leftmost heavy cruiser."

Wilcox called out. "We can't take much fire from behind, and with two of our guns out, we can't stop them from flanking us. We should avoid them, stay back, wait till the laser cannons recharge."

"I agree," Stetler said. "With the asteroids acting as a wall, we should be able to hold our position, use our main guns to hold them off."

Morden knew it was sound advice, by the book. Her instincts told her it was wrong. She pulled up the status monitor of the fighter squadrons in the air. The heavy cruisers had managed to pick off three more planes, and they still had not gotten anywhere near the base. The one remaining damaged destroyer was creeping around, within minutes of the base.

She shook her head. "No. Our fighters are cut off and under fire. I won't abandon them."

Holsey agreed. "We need to break them up, get back the initiative, keep those damn Frontin off balance. Target set for the left heavy cruiser. Aye, captain."

Morden looked up again, watching the enemy frigate move towards them. "Urquhart, plot the course to run us over the top of the cruiser. We can break down and away. I want to minimize fire to our aft sections."

"Yes, ma'am."

Morden braced herself against her chair as the *Verdun's* engines fired. "Commander Holsey is right. We can't let them set the rules. It's three versus one if you don't count the station and four to one if you do. Wilcox, I want all free damage-control teams standing by. Isabelle, prepare the ship for impact."

The pressure pushing on Morden's chest grew, the safety restraint pressing into her skin as the ship turned. Seconds ticked by as she watched the distance to her target shrink, the combined speed of her battlecruiser and the Frontin hastening the moment of contact. Even through the armor, Morden could hear the hydraulic groaning from the turrets turning as one.

Morden leaned forward. "Stetler bring our nose up. All guns, fire!"

At the last second, the battlecruiser started to rise. She could feel the turrets discharging their salvos in unison. The *Verdun* shuddered as enemy munitions curved around the hull, detonating above and to the side of the ship as the Magnetic Ordnance Deflector parried most of their attacker's blows.

The three ships had only been on top of each other for the span of few heart beats, but the cost was real.

Morden examined the sensor reading from the enemy cruiser. It had taken some serious hits but was still flying, no real drop in power output from its reactor, no loss of speed, and, as far as she could tell, no hull breaches. It had taken four direct hits to its superstructure and its portside batteries seemed to be dead, but it was hard to tell.

She input fresh attack vectors into the screen. "Bring us around. I want that cruiser gone. Tell the Cerberus fighters to tuck in close. We need their help to screen us in tight quarters. Wilcox, damage report."

Wilcox sounded distracted. "Superficial. Isabelle registered impacts to our dorsal section, but most of it was absorbed by the armor. We did lose our dorsal sensor stack, and I am reading more gaps in our MOD. There are some minor hydraulics issues with a couple defensive emplacements. Repair teams have already been dispatched."

The deck trembled as more shells burst around the battlecruiser. She clicked on her monitors to backtrack their trajectories — all the way to the station. It had opened up on them with surprising accuracy, even from long range. The sound of exploding shells as the MOD forced them to curl around the hull was deafening.

For the first time, Morden started to doubt they could win this.

If the MOD failed, the torpedoes and missiles that were being deflected would hit home with deadly effect. The *Verdun*'s nose was pointing directly at the wounded heavy cruiser. They had to do some serious damage on this pass. Time was not on their side.

Morden's body was forced forward, her eyes losing focus as the Alliance and Frontin ships crossed again. Shells, torpedoes, and machine guns fired, filling the narrow gap between the ships. The bridge lit up, the holoports bathing the room in the reds, blues, and greens of exploding ordnance.

The emergency lighting flickered on.

Her ears rang, her vision blurry. She could hear someone nearby howling in pain. She tried to focus, tried to clear her eyes, blink past the sensory overload from the holoports. The smell of electrical smoke filled the room, the air scrubbers fighting to filter out the fumes.

Had the deflector failed? It had felt like the inner armor had been penetrated. She looked quickly around the room, assessing the damage. The holographic table was sparking, many of the overhead lights had burst, but otherwise the bridge was intact.

In the corner, Commander Wilcox was cursing, his hand pressed against his shoulder, blood flowing down his arm and through his clenched fingers.

She undid her belt, walked towards him. "Stetler, get us some distance from those ships. Chief, call a medic to the bridge!"

Wilcox groaned as she pressed against the wound. "I'm fine. It's a scratch." He turned to his console. "Fires are reported all over the ship. We are showing serious signs of weakening structural integrity. Otherwise, we're okay. At least we fried that heavy cruiser."

Morden looked up at the rear holoports. The first heavy cruiser had gone dark, its inertia pulling it towards one of the large asteroids on the clearing's edge. If the cruiser couldn't restore power, it wouldn't take long for it to crush itself against the surface of that rock.

Chief Baudouin yelled. "Captain, we have reports of Frontin raiders on board. Communications center reports boarding parties on several decks."

Morden clenched her fists. "They must have launched them when they were right on top of us."

"Marines are already engaging, but it's unclear how many Frontin are on board," Holsey called out.

Morden picked up Wilcox's headset. "Fuck. Chief, give me ship-wide." She slipped the headset over her head, keying it on. "Captain Morden to all hands. We have Frontin on board. All departments are ordered to hold their sections. Do not move between sections without marine escort. Good luck, Morden out."

Isabelle repeated the message. Morden could hear the Marines in the guard room slam the blast doors to the bridge shut. Two of them entered the room in full armor, taking up positions behind the slowly rising internal cover systems.

Morden pulled off her headset. "Isabelle, activate all internal defense systems, and get robots to defensive positions around Laser Control. Holsey, get our weapons locker open and issue sidearms. Stetler, bring us back around. Let's not let them know we've been hurt."

Morden had forgotten she was holding Wilcox's arm. She looked at him. His eyes were set, focused on his work, not his wound. She let go of his arm, nodded to him, and stood up, crossing to the now-open weapons locker. She pulled out a chest plate and fastened it in place, the old wound in her shoulder protesting the weight. Holsey was passing out weapons to the other officers one at a time, moving between their posts.

Stetler sounded frazzled. "We lost several fighters on that pass. Delta Squadron reports additional hits on the crippled cruiser, blowouts on several decks, visible flames, and almost no power readings. Do we target her again?"

Morden strapped on her sidearm. "No. Have torpedo tubes fire on that ship from a distance. Keep long distance fire on her until she hits that asteroid. Run us past the other cruiser. Frontin always go for the wounded, they will expect us to do the same. I want them distracted. We don't want any more company for dinner."

The emergency lighting gave the room an eerie glow. Morden's heart pounded like it was trying to escape her chest. The Frontin were on board. The last time they had faced her, she had nearly died along with most her team. Their screams were almost audible to her: the images of their bodies breaking, Hansen's smile just before he died.

It was happening again.

She shook her head, fought to clear her thoughts. She didn't have time for this. Her crew needed her here, now, in the present.

If they could take out the last undamaged cruiser, the laser cannons could finish the Jon. There were no guarantees — they would have to keep the Frontin off guard. The *Verdun* might still be able to win a slugging match, but with the Frontin on board, the ship's technology was at risk.

At least you prepared for boarding.

Morden glanced down at the laser cannon's timer on the tactical display. Eight minutes and thirty-three seconds until the lasers were recharged. "Stetler, take us in."

Hillman was almost there. Another minute on this trajectory, and he would be in range. He drummed his fingers on the control panel. The *Verdun* was taking serious fire, though the Frontin had been bloodied. He had watched the ships cross paths, exchanging fire. The battlecruiser was going for another pass at the heavily damaged cruiser, long-range fire from the station forcing it to evade more than its wounds allowed.

He tore his eyes from the screen. He had to stop watching. He had to focus. Sweat ran down his face, the salt burning his eyes. His stolen destroyer had lost life support, and the reactor's cooling system was offline, making the bridge unbearably hot. The thought of making himself hotter by bolting down the hallway to the escape hatch was not appealing.

On the bright side, he had managed to reactivate the pressure doors for that section, so there would be at least some atmosphere left. That was assuming the hatch he had seen in the schematics was actually there and not down on one of the lower decks.

He hadn't seen an escape pod in the hall as he'd walked by, but he hadn't been looking. Regardless, it was his only chance. There was no way he could make it all the way to the main escape deck. He was exhausted, his body drained by days of extreme cold and abuse. The adrenaline from his firefight had worn off, leaving his limbs heavy and dull.

Once he blew this fucker, he could rest in the pod, wait out the battle until the *Verdun* collected survivors. He just had to stay focused for a little bit longer.

Assuming the *Verdun* survived.

The destroyer jerked suddenly, klaxons screaming loudly as weapons fire tore into his crippled hulk.

Hillman looked down at his sensors, his jaw dropping. "Oh no. Idiots!"

The *Black Fox* had just emerged from the side of the asteroid field and was assaulting the base's guns and his own ship with everything they had. The destroyer wouldn't last long. He could already hear the metal beginning to succumb. Hillman checked the containment program he had put in place. It was destabilizing. His time was out. Close enough or not, this was where he got off.

Hillman turned, pushed open the door and ran through it, focusing all his attention on pumping his legs. He almost fell as the ship convulsed violently. Suddenly, he felt lighter. The internal gravity was failing with the ship's engines.

He turned to his left, barely righting himself before he hit the wall. He slowed slightly, trying to find the hatch through the failing emergency lighting. Smoke filled the entire ship as the destroyer burned from multiple missile strikes.

His heart slammed in his chest. He couldn't see the escape pod's hatch. There were no screens, no doors, nothing to give away its position. He fell, his legs giving way, his knees slamming the deck. He was almost thankful for the lower gravity as the exhaustion and smoke took its toll. He let the Frontin scatter gun drop, bracing himself with his hands.

This was it. This was how he was going to die. Blown apart by the people he was trying to save on a cobbled-together slag heap.

Hillman almost laughed, leaning back against the wall.

The wall gave way, dumping him head over heels into a small corridor just below the main hall. He shook his head, blood from a new cut adding to the burning smoke clouding his eyes. The room was small, with a single control panel against one wall below a small window. Most of the room was covered in paneling, and it was empty except for a console, a small chair, and a heavy door.

It took him several seconds to realize that this was the escape pod. It was probably never meant to be seen or accessed by the crew. This was a captain's personal pod. Clearly, the Frontin had never intended to go down with a human crew.

Hillman pushed himself to his feet, pain streaking through his head where it had hit the floor. He had only a handful of seconds left. He kicked the door closed, twisting the latch as hard as he could. He could hear the pod pressurizing, a good sign that its seals were intact. He stumbled towards the control console, reaching for the large glowing symbol he hoped was the eject button.

Hillman rammed his fist into the button, felt the pod eject, just as he heard the roar of an explosion on the other side of the hatch. Hillman fell to the floor, his head slamming into the grating, and the entire world went black.

Mostoff cheered, pain streaking through his legs as the first of his missiles tore into the station. The time the *Fox* had spent picking its way through the asteroids had been worth it. They were right on top of their target. The floor was vibrating, the *Fox's* damaged bracers lurching as they compensated for the recoil of its guns. The energy of the fight had washed away Mostoff's doubts, returned his clarity of purpose. The destroyer was a bonus, a feather for the *Fox's* cap.

This wouldn't take long.

Several of the base's gun batteries had been destroyed, and the *Fox* could disappear into asteroid field. The station was trying hard to bring around its guns, but didn't have the angle.

Missile after missile from the *Fox* pelted it, gutting the asteroid housing the station.

Mostoff chose more targets for his gun crews, his gaze locked on the images of the disintegrating target. One of the flak turrets detonated, the pressure from the exploding ordnance magazine blasting shrapnel through the station's hangar door, air leaking out into space from the numerous holes.

 He knew it was wrong, but he felt satisfied. Even though it had been his peoples' actions that had caused this, these fuckers had killed so many, including Viktor, and it felt good to return it in kind. If their landing bay was compromised, no one within would be able to escape. Their secret base would collapse around them. The scum on board the station would pay for their transgression in blood.

Krilic's yelp startled him. "The destroyer—we got her!"

Mostoff switched camera views. The destroyer was collapsing in on itself, flame and debris leaking in all directions, a massive shock wave spreading out from it.

Mostoff's knuckles turned white. "Full reverse, now!"

The wave hit the station, ripping it into pieces, rock and metal pulling apart violently. He couldn't help but watch the station incinerate. When he had first seen it open fire, it had seemed insurmountable. Now it shattered like glass, falling apart in broken shards, leaving nothing more than fire and twisted metal.

His eyes bulged. The *Black Fox* was still too close to the explosion. The wave was getting closer. The only had thirty, forty seconds at most until it tore through them.

The engines kicked and vibrated as the *Fox* tried to maneuver away from the blast. The *Fox* wasn't accelerating fast enough, her ancient systems too old and too damaged to move her quickly. All Mostoff could do was watch the wave eat up the space between them, watch as his crew fought to gain every inch of distance from the blast.

He felt helpless, the seconds until impact disappearing.

The wave crashed into the *Fox*, and Mostoff felt his body lifting from its chair and falling towards the deck, but he never felt himself hit the cold metal floor.

CHAPTER 27

Voth stumbled as the battlecruiser shifted, changing course. His breath caught in his lungs, his vision blurring, his broken rib colliding against the barricade. The medical deck was eerily silent, the only sound the cries of patients. He checked his pistol for the third time, pulling back the slide and visually confirming the chambered round.

Damn it.

He should be in fire control keeping the turrets coordinated, not here, though he did recognize the importance of protecting the wounded. Anyone who was injured in the service of the Alliance deserved to rest — safely. If he had to be stuck toting a pistol somewhere, at least it was here.

He looked around at the twenty marines positioned along the corridor, the place that Osterman and Voth had chosen to establish defensive positions. It was long and narrow, ending in a large T-junction ahead of them that formed a natural choke point.

The right side of the junction led down to the emergency stairwell, and the left led to the outer decks. Captain Holsted and Lieutenant Barker had carefully positioned their marines.

Voth had specifically chosen these two to hold this area, knew both men were exceptionally calm leaders, men with ice water for blood. The key to holding this corridor was suppressive fire, at least according to the previous master at arms. There was nowhere to run, their backs were against a wall. They had to hold this corridor until the wounded could be evacuated or help arrived.

Their RAR-42 light machine gun was up in the center of the corridor, nestled behind one of the ICS segments. Sergeants Haines and Dolber were covering the emplacement, tucked in near the front of the series of barricades. Nearby, Corporal Bilward and Private Stoker had their eight-gauge automatic shotguns. From that angle, they could shower the space in bursts of deadly shot. The rest of the defense team, except for Voth, were spread out evenly between the larger support weapons. It was a strong position, but he understood now the nightmarish stories about fighting Frontin.

He hoped his group would be enough. They hadn't had time to make another ammo run before the boarding alert had come from the bridge, and if they were cut off from supplies later...

Voth set his pistol on top of the barricade, trying to keep the tremble out of his voice. "Captain Holsted, has checkpoint fourteen radioed?"

The gruff old man ran his hand over the stubble of his chin, eyes set on the end of the hall. "Not yet."

The captain's voice doubled through his microphone. Voth watched him closely, trying to see what he was fixated on. He couldn't help feeling his skin tingle at the boom of the first scatter guns and the telltale crack of Enfield rifles from somewhere at the edge of his hearing.

The Frontin were coming, soon.

The lights had begun to fade on and off, the ship's power grid fluctuating under the intensity of the enemy's barrage. Voth hated this part, the buildup, the anticipation. Just once, he wanted a fight that wasn't proceeded by a long buildup and moody, low lighting. The tension tore at his stomach, his skin slick with clammy sweat that dripped beneath his armor, the act of waiting gnawing at him as the enemy moved silently nearby, preparing to kill them all.

Out of the corner of Voth's eye, he saw Holsted tense, motioning for his squad to get down, Barker's men following suit. Voth strained his eyes, peering into the dim, curving corridor before him. He picked his sidearm back up, flipped off the safety, counted the magazines in his belt for the third time.

Lieutenant Baker's voice came over the radio. "Fix bayonets. Prepare to repel enemy."

Voth tightened and relaxed his fingers around the grip of his pistol. Voth couldn't see anyone or anything. The hall was empty.

The friendly, cool gray halls of his home seemed foreign, dangerous.

Wait.

He could hear something dragging. It was distant, very light, but unmistakable, like a snake slithering through dry grass. It was getting closer.

He lifted his weapon, aimed down the corridor, his ribs screaming as the pistol's weight transferred to his shoulders.

He coughed quietly, bracing his arm against the barricade like a bench. Pain wouldn't stop him. He wasn't going to sit by and let others fight in his place.

The dragging stopped.

Scattergun blasts lit up the end of the hall, and the first Frontin underling pounced into view. It screamed, its scattergun firing wildly, rotten yellow teeth visible in the low light.

The Marine riflemen fired down the corridor in staccato bursts of carefully aimed shots. The first drone twitched and jerked as bullets riddled its exoskeleton, its putrid blood coating the lift doors.

Four more broke out into the open, firing wildly down at the marine contingent, each of their ten black legs beating loudly against the metal. One of the riflemen behind Voth screamed, his chest bursting as a Frontin barb hit him squarely in the shoulder.

Voth could see countless more black behemoths streaming toward him, adding their soul-crushing cries to the deafening scene.

He took aim and squeezed his trigger, the small bang of his sidearm joining the sharp crack of the rifles. His first few groups hit home, causing the closest attacker to stumble slightly before jumping on to the ceiling, its massive claws gripping into the metal.

Two of the other drones tried to join, but Stoker's rapid eight-gauge blasts cleared the ceiling, blood and carapace covering the Frontin still on the ground. The group roared, stopping as they let off successive bursts of fire.

The RAR bellowed, sweeping a stream of bullets back and forth across the ranks of the fucking bugs. Several of the combatants crumbled, torn apart by the light machine gun's wrath. Voth fired at the legs of one of the charging bastards, its speed bringing him too close for comfort. The beast shook, falling to the ground, several of its legs shattered. Sargent Dolber's Heinlein submachine gun finished it off, its dead body still thrashing violently.

He emptied the rest of his magazine into its twitching carcass, just to be sure. It was already becoming harder to see, the smoke from the Frontin's firearms and the shotgun shells filling the air.

Voth slapped in a fresh magazine, moved his free hand to key his radio mike. "Voth to marine control, Frontin engaged outside the infirmary."

He adjusted his aim back to the hall's entrance in time to see several rounds blasting through one of the beasts' chests. Pain shot through his stomach as he released the slide forward.

No. This wouldn't be an easy fight.

M orden's mind raced, a fresh burst of adrenaline flooding her blood stream.

In less than five minutes, the tide of the battle had changed twice. She had not expected Mostoff to risk his ship to engage the Frontin base and destroyer. The first Nitva had broken up, vanishing in a flash against the asteroid's surface. It had opened up possibilities, swinging the momentum to the *Verdun's* favor. The next course of action had been clear: take out the Jon and then mop up the last wounded cruiser.

But as quickly as the battle had turned for the Alliance, it had swung back against them. The *Black Fox* was now adrift, hanging on the edge of the asteroid field, its engines firing sporadically. It had managed to attack the station, only to be wrecked by the explosion of the last destroyer. It made no sense — Frontin didn't commit suicide, but the destroyer had gone up from the inside, the blast indicating a core overload.

Morden's mind painted a grim image of the upcoming events. The remaining heavy cruiser would turn and go straight for the *Fox*. She was easy prey. Morden would be forced to put the *Verdun* in between them. They would have to fight on the Frontin's terms to protect Mostoff.

Holsey's voice cut through her shock. "Orders?"

Morden leaned forward. "Helm, put us between the Frontin ships and the Fox. Chief, get me Mostoff. *Now.*"

She could almost feel Holsey's tension from behind her, but Holsey didn't object.

Wilcox groaned in his chair, causing her to turn. He looked pale, weak. "Computer reports at least fifty-four percent of our magnetic ordnance shield is disabled or non-responsive. AI has taken over most defense turrets, and we have reports of raiders all over the ship. Three check points haven't reported in, and the infirmary is under attack."

Holsey's voice sounded almost breathless. "Laser Control?"

"Osterman hasn't reported any activity," Wilcox answered.

At least that wasn't screwed up — yet.

The ship shuddered as it flew past the Frontin ships. The main guns fired again, many shots going wild, the high speed making target acquisition more difficult. Fortunately, it made it harder for the enemy to target them back, too.

The ship started to brake, banking around and putting itself directly in between the rapidly turning heavy cruiser. The cruiser's main gun fired, the shells from its barrage evaporating in the withering fire from the defensive fighters that held tightly to the *Verdun*.

With the station gone, the Frontin's weapons were no longer overwhelming the fighters' defenses.

Baudouin called out. "We are receiving a mayday."

There was a crackle as the chief switched the signal to speakers, then Mostoff's strained voice filled the room. "Mayday, mayday. Black Fox to Verdun."

Morden activated her head set. "We read you, Captain. We've taken up a defensive position between you and the Frontin. Get your engines back online quickly and get out of here. We have sustained damage and will have difficulty standing our ground."

He responded quickly. "It will take some time. Nothing is working well. Our power grid is down. We've barely restored communications. Leave us. We will die with honor for the Triangle. Just make sure those things don't escape."

"I won't abandon an ally. Get your engines online, and get out of here."

Mostoff didn't respond.

The *Verdun* launched another salvo of warheads at the heavy cruiser, but it was turning rapidly, already at an angle, and its ordnance shield threw the shells wild. The Jon was further away, turning slowly just outside of optimal targeting range. Every reading indicated that the Frontin capital ship was undamaged.

"Flight deck reports our offensive fighters are low on ammunition," Baudouin called out. "Commander Frost requests permission to bring them down to re-arm."

The Stallions were not nearly as good at dealing with enemy fire, but would come in handy attacking the cruiser. The next few minutes could make or break this fight. Morden felt another flash of anger as she studied the battle. She had fallen into this trap.

This ought to have been an easy fight.

The heavy cruiser was coming on fast, pushing the limits of what the computer readout indicated it was capable of. The ship's angle indicated it would try to streak past the *Verdun*, to blast the *Fox* to dust. It would likely unload on them as it passed. Morden could see several possible courses the computer had fed to her station. She selected several Cerberus squadrons, repositioning them to protect the most likely course of the Nitva.

Staying almost stationary, the wounded battlecruiser would have a difficult time defending itself at close range.

Morden leaned back in her chair, trying to determine what the cruiser would do. "Chief, let the flight deck know they can bring in the Stallions. Holsey, have all gun crews prepare armor penetrating shells for the heavy cruiser as it passes. Have them track the optimal firing trajectory. I want to pulverize that bastard, bring it down to the Jon and us."

Holsey was talking quickly into her head set, coordinating with the fire control room. Without the rumbling of the engine, the ship felt quiet for the first time. The one positive of the *Verdun's* stationary position was that it maximized the defensive weapons' ability to block fire.

Less motion to compensate for.

Morden looked up at the heavy cruiser's image in the holoport. "Stetler, six seconds before contact. Fire all thrusters towards them. I want to move us just enough to throw off their barrage. Let's see if they're paying attention."

The heavy cruiser streaked towards them, its shells detonating short of the hull as the defensive fighters and anti-ordnance fire took them out. The wall of white fire grew closer as the cruiser neared. The seconds seemed to slow as Morden watched, her hands tightening on her armrest, the sounds of explosion becoming louder with each tick of the clock.

Morden raised her hand instinctively, even knowing the gun crews couldn't see her. "Weapons hold. Prepare to fire on my command."

The distance fell quickly, her gaze locked to her screen's counter.

Six thousand yards. Morden's heart thrummed. She could almost see Holsey's face as the commander audibly sucked in air behind her, tensing for the split seconds of destruction coming. "*Fire!* Stetler, now!" Her arm swung down hard, slapping into her chair.

The battlecruiser banked and all of her weapons fired simultaneously, rocking the massive ship, the force of its own guns pushing against the maneuvering thrusters. Morden felt almost sick as her chair vibrated, its belt cutting into her stomach and chest. She tensed, waiting for the enemy's reprisal.

It didn't come.

Her screens cleared as the momentary fizzle caused by the guns passed. Morden's heart dropped. The cruiser had braked hard at the last moment, the *Verdun's* tracking system showing munitions strikes against the asteroids at the edge of the field, the Alliance ship's massive fire power shattering and burning rocks in an impressive but fruitless display of destruction.

The collision warnings blared loudly. They had moved directly into the cruiser's path.

Isabelle's calm voice filled the bridge, an icy contrast to the chaotic events unfolding in front of Morden. "Captain, the ship has launched another wave of boarding craft. I am tracking at least thirty with additional heat plumes indicated on the cruiser. The sensor drones' infrared scanners indicate upwards of four hundred Frontin on board."

Morden grimaced, realizing the enormity of Isabelle's words. There was a Frontin Leader out here. There was no other way to explain boarding the *Verdun* instead of taking a weak target like the *Fox*. Frontin never turned down an easy kill — except for when a leader wanted his war trophies. A Nitva only had a crew of six hundred at most. For it to send so many of its crew out during a battle could mean only one thing.

They were in the Triangle to capture an Alliance vessel, her vessel. The *Verdun* would not be the prize of these animals.

Morden wouldn't allow it

She gripped her armrest hard, her nails digging into it. Her voice was harsh, her words sharp. "All fighters, engage landing craft. All weapons, fire at will."

Morden felt several of the landing craft slam into the hull, her screen full of targets. She could feel the bridge's defensive turrets swing back and forth, blasting away at the landing craft.

The Jon had finished turning, its engines burning brighter now as it approached the *Verdun*. The cruiser was turning away, its skeleton crew pulling out of the action, another dozen landing craft leaking out behind it.

Turret three fired, its salvo of shells tearing into the ship's dorsal side at nearly point-blank range, visibly shredding its armor. The ship began to fall towards the *Verdun*, its shattered engines and hull spewing burning atmosphere and radiation in all directions.

Morden watched in horror. "Evasive action! Get us out of her way... now!"

Isabelle's voice was as calm and even as ever. "Fifteen seconds to impact."

The *Verdun's* engines roared back to life as Stetler fought to get the massive warship out of the way of its dying enemy. The cruiser was coming apart, breaking under its own inertia.

Morden couldn't help but watch the defensive fighters scatter in the holoport, giving the remaining boarding craft a clear path.

Isabelle's voice went ship-wide. "All crew, 10 seconds to impact. Automatic lock down procedures in effect to the rear quarter. Air-tight doors closing. All hands in sealed sections, prepare for decompression survival protocol."

Turrets One, Two, and Four fired in unison, their high explosive shells slamming into the delisting ship. It hung still, its inertia cut by the impact of so many shells. The devastated hulk burst apart, the strain of its death throes rupturing its armor and lacerating its hull into metal scrap.

Morden let out a breath. The cheers from the bridge crew made her stop and look around. Even Holsey's expression was easing as their enemy shook apart. She had been so lost in the tension she had almost forgotten her fellow officers.

The *Verdun* shuddered as the shock wave hit, the fractured bits of the enemy ship striking the battlecruiser's armor. Morden felt a tremor under her feet, her body weightless for a moment.

Something was wrong.

"Cascading power failure, attempting to re—" Isabelle's voice cut off midsentence.

Before Morden could utter a command, the ship went dark, the noise from the engines falling silent. Every familiar sound of Morden's home disappeared. Even the emergency lighting sputtered for a moment before failing.

Morden couldn't move, her gut twisting. Her ship, one of the great jewels of the Royal Navy, was floating dead in space, its attacker prepared to finish its lethal task.

CHAPTER 28

Ensign Va shivered, his hands reaching for his pistol, eyes fixed on the turret's sealed entrance.

The cheers and jubilation of the turret crew had died seconds before the lights had gone out. Moments later, clicking and growling sounds had become audible through the door, followed by heavy banging. So many of the boarding craft had been blown into scrap, hit by the blast wave of the incinerating Nitva heavy cruiser. It hadn't occurred to him that any of the few remaining craft would hit nearby.

How had they overwhelmed the marines outside the turret so quickly?

The gun's first floor was pitch black, the customary sounds of activity having faded to silence, the vibrant, friendly colors of the consoles replaced with the greens and whites of his night vision visor. Va closed his eyes, blinking back the sweat. It had happened so fast, they hadn't even activated the internal cover system before the power had failed.

Their entire twenty-person crew was in cover behind desks, chairs, door frames, and any other sturdy piece of equipment they could throw against the ground.

Smyth spoke up from somewhere in the dark, her voice tense. "We hold this gun no matter what. It can't and won't fall into the hands of the enemy."

Va put his hand onto Shipman Higgins' shoulder, tried to steady the young man. They all knew their duty. No one signed up to be a gun rat without knowing the risks. Running a turret took guts and skill. It was a fast track to promotion, but it could also be a death sentence. Standing orders dictated gun crews were to defend their stations at all costs. Failing that, they would destroy their turret before allowing an enemy to capture it.

Arming a few explosives and a five-minute fuse had been the final task for many gun rats.

The sounds outside stopped, and many of the younger crewmembers sighed in relief, but not Va. This wasn't the first time he'd fought the Frontin. They didn't just give up while their leader lived. They could smell fear.

This turret was drenched in it.

Va lowered his pistol and turned to the Lieutenant, who had stood up in front of him.

She cleared her throat. "Alright, people. Get my emergency power generator going! This fight isn't —"

Smyth never finished her sentence, her body breaking as it was thrown back in a wave of shrapnel and flame. She struck the wall, falling to the ground in a wrecked heap.

The door was gone, its frame warped and cracked under the pressure and heat of a thermite explosive.

Va didn't wait, firing several controlled shots into the gaping opening. The answering howls from the other side told him he hadn't missed.

"Fire at will. Give these bastards hell!" He barely recognized his own voice. It was strong and clear, not at all how he felt.

The stunned gun rats fired, rifles and shotguns filling the entrance with projectiles. The screams and howls of dying Frontin reached them, their bodies just out of sight of the Alliance personnel.

Va saw Higgins and Michener shudder, Frontin barbs exploding in their bodies. The attackers were firing back, their massive weapons destroying the humans' poor excuses for cover. They were pinned down as badly as the Frontin in the corridor outside.

They had to hold that door.

If those things get in here...

He didn't want to think about it. His team wouldn't last long without the ICS. Chaves stood up, moving himself past the edge of the table, his big SMG showering the entrance with bullets.

Va yelled at him. "Chaves, stay down!"

Too late.

Chaves spun, his shoulder and face disintegrating as barbs bit into him. He collapsed, jerking violently, what was left of his throat desperately trying to scream, only a raw gurgling sound escaping it.

Va ducked down and slapped in a new magazine, his skin crawling. He saw several more men, Jordon and Lillian, get hit, the table they were hiding behind bursting into shards. Blood splattered the grating in front of Va, the wounded officers' screams lost in the deafening fight. Chief Yugola tried to drag Lillian into cover, but the enemy's fire was too intense. The older man took several grazing shots, his armor dented as the blows ricocheted off.

Va leaned out carefully, his eyes locked on the shadows outside the room. He squeezed the trigger, letting bullet after bullet strike across the door's threshold.

He yelled. "Fire, now, Goodard, Sheen — get ready to pull Lillian back."

Chief Hagathow tensed, ducking behind cover and yelling a warning. Va turned his head, saw a grenade sliding across the floor. He threw himself towards the gun's loading doors, diving behind their steel protection, rolling onto his back. Millar, Goodard, and Sheen all tried to do the same, falling short as barbs tore into them, dropping them in a wave of gore and blood.

The grenade detonated, shrapnel and flame blasting in all directions. Va pressed himself against the loading doors, secondary explosions bathing the deck in fire.

Chief Hagathow was caught by the flames, his flesh burning and smoking. The man screamed, jerking out of cover as he tried to pound out the flames with his hands. Va reached for the back of his armor, attempting to drag him into cover. A Frontin scattergun caught him directly in his chest, bursting it like a balloon, showering the remaining terrified defenders in blood, the stalwart chief's burning remains nearly hitting Va as he collapsed.

Va picked up Hagathow's rifle, pointing it at the smoke-concealed door. He fired at the Frontin, who were now pouring into the control room. Their shadows left ghastly patterns on the wall, the boom of their scattergun's splitting the air.

Defender after defender vanished in a hail of barbs and blood-cuddling roars from the energized Frontin. Va knew they had lost. The Frontin had broken through, breaking the spirits of the Alliance personnel while they were disorganized and confused.

It was about buying time now.

Va fired as quickly as his finger could pull the trigger, Cutler and Javier following suit. The combined firepower of their rifles cut down warrior after warrior as they fought to move forward into the shattered room. The Frontin pulled back, taken aback by the ferocity of the fire. He couldn't see anyone else, couldn't hear any other rifles joining in.

The gravity of the situation hit him. They were all that was left. The gun had to be destroyed — they couldn't allow the Frontin to gain access to it or its equipment.

Va would see that duty out to the end.

"Cutler, Javier fall back into the gun room. Covering fire!"

Cutler pushed himself to his knees, fighting to control his fire, cutting down the shaken attackers.

Va turned, ran through the entrance to the gun chamber. He tried to turn around, his foot slipping on the blood-soaked floor, pain running up his back as his knees broke his fall. He steadied himself on the wall, bringing his rifle to his shoulder, adding his fire to that of his comrades.

Javier had followed him through the door, managing to avoid falling on the slick surface. Va's rifle locked back empty as Cutler turned to run. Va yanked his pistol free, firing poorly aimed shots downrange, trying to cover the man's retreat. One of the Frontin launched itself over the deck and through the Alliance fire, kicking Cutler directly in the back.

The man jerked forward, his jaw pounding into the ground with a thump. Faster than Va could react, the Frontin drove a long blade into the man's back.

Javier fired, hitting the Frontin in the shoulder. "Blow this fucking gun, Va!"

Va turned, working the manual dials that would blow the gun, desperately trying to ignore Javier shouting as he tried to hold off the Frontin.

Va looked back at the plethora of targets streaking towards them. Javier screamed, a Frontin barb catching his shoulder, sending his rifle clattering to the floor. He fell, somehow managed to keep himself pointed towards the open door. Javier unholstered his sidearm and started firing again.

Va admired the man's tenacity in the face of death. His hands shook as they sprinted through the detonation sequence.

Come on, come on.

Blood splattered the controls in front of Va. He turned in time to see Javier's body blow apart. Va fired the last few rounds of his pistol into the chest of a leaping Frontin, its green gore mixing with Javier's red. He drew his bayonet and slammed it into the beast's skull.

It was a weird feeling, knowing he was going die. Va could feel his heart pounding, the blood rushing through his veins. If this was how his life would end, he was determined to make it count. He pulled the blade free, planting his feet squarely with his shoulders, and took on the next attacker.

It went for his face, but he rolled his body to the left, stabbing down at its neck. Va spun, kicking it free of his blade, just in time to avoid a scattergun blast that hit the injured Frontin instead.

Some acts of valor are recorded for all time, and some happen in the dark places of the battlefield, where no one can see them. Va's act of defiance was the latter — he knew no one would talk about or reward his act of defiance, but he owed Lieutenant Smyth and his friends the effort.

He tried to free his bayonet again, but couldn't. Va let go, pulling his combat knife free, knowing its size would make killing one of these things nearly impossible. A glint of metal caught his eye. It looked like Smyth's submachine gun. Va grabbed it, firing as he brought it to his shoulder, just in time to shred the nearest attacker.

He had to move quickly. The renewed sound of gun fire had caused the Frontin to pull back, but their hesitation wouldn't last.

He backed up, firing as he reached for the terminal. The bulletproof glass next to him shattered, a pitch-black Frontin slamming through it, grabbing him from behind. Va struggled, kicking his assailant, driving his knife into its hand. The warrior screamed, shaking him hard, tossing him against the console.

Va hit the floor, shock and pain stabbing through him as he struck the ground. The beast placed its feet on his chest, smiling, its few good eyes looking menacingly down at him. Va couldn't move his body, just glare.

"Fuck you, you bastard."

The Frontin put his scatter gun on Va's head and fired, never noticing the young man's arm reach up and start the self-destruct timer.

Holsey stared at her blank console. Things had gone so wrong. The *Verdun* was floating dead in space. She could hear screaming and gunfire reverberating through the ship, and she had no idea what to do.

In all her time as an officer, she had never not known what to do.

Morden's voice cut through her confusion. "Wilcox, get me a damage report. Pronto."

He responded immediately. "Reports from engineering suggest that a section of the cruiser impacted the drone bay, seriously damaging our power distribution. Before my terminal lost power, I read a massive decompression of that area and possible secondary explosions."

Morden nodded. "Can we raise the Fox?"

Baudouin responded. "Yes, ma'am. The radio is still functional on battery power."

Morden's jaw clenched. "Good, raise her. Commander Wilcox, take several Marines and head down to the evacuation deck. Get as many people off the Verdun and out of the line of fire as possible. Hopefully you can take refuge in the Fox while the Jon is busy trying to take us."

Holsey recognized that look. It had been the same one that had confronted her that day on the station. She wanted to argue, wanted to throw something back at the woman's arrogant resolve, but how could she? So much of what had happened was blind chance, an aberration of bad luck and timing. There was nothing left to do. They couldn't let the Frontin take the ship, let them shift the balance of power and wreak havoc across known space.

Wilcox's voice was angry. "I will not run. I am staying if anyone else is."

He was staring directly at Morden, their gazes locked across the smoke-filled room, his hand still clutching the slowly seeping wound on his shoulder.

Morden softened her voice. "Mr. Wilcox, you're wounded. I will stay behind with most of the marines to ensure *our* crew get clear."

He shook his head defiantly. "Ma'am, I will not run and watch while you go down with the ship. What if you're captured? Your knowledge can't fall into their hands any more than the ship can. I should be the one to cover your retreat. Holsey is the XO. She should be in command of the evacuation. This is my —"

Morden closed the gap between them, placing her hand on his good shoulder. "Jack, you're hurt. Realistically you won't be able to fight these guys. I understand how you feel, but this is the best option. I am the captain and this is my ship. I've made my decision. The discussion is over."

The room was quiet, everyone watching the exchange. Holsey had never pegged Morden as the type to go down with the ship. Maybe the woman in front of her was different from her old friend.

Holsey found her tongue again. "He's right. You should take command of the evacuation, and I should stay behind and blow up the ship. If you're captured, you may reveal details under torture that—"

Morden laughed. "Commander, I haven't been a captain long enough to know anything of value! Now get to it."

"Yes, ma'am." Holsey saluted, and most of the people in the room followed suit.

Wilcox's eyes were still burning. She understood his anger. Being ordered to run while your comrades had to sacrifice themselves to save the rest, to be forced to be the survivor and not the hero…

She was glad she didn't have to face that fate.

Morden returned the salute. "Lieutenant Arnot, take two of your marines and go with Wilcox to the evacuation deck. Get hold of Major Osterman and let him know what is going on. His team will need to coordinate holding key areas of the ship."

Arnot nodded. "Yes, ma'am"

Morden continued. "Stetler, Holsey, I want you to head to medical and break them out. The last report said they were under heavy attack. Holsey, once the situation is resolved, take command of the evacuation and make sure we don't lose that bay. Urquhart, you're with me. Everyone else, go with Wilcox. Make us proud."

"Aye, Captain," the voices all responded at once.

The bridge bucked violently and Holsey almost fell, her legs like jelly under the vibrations. Her head was cloudy, and she felt nauseated as the internal gravity struggled to maintain potency on battery power. She raised her head, trying to see what had happened. Several consoles were burning, making the air thicker and acrider than it already was.

Had someone blown the outer doors?

A marine corporal spoke. "What was that?"

"Must be more boarding craft impacting nearby," Baudouin chimed in, the slight shake in her voice betraying her fear.

Holsey coughed. "No, that was too big an explosion for a boarder."

Morden stood up, her voice low. "That was one of the main turrets — one of the guns has been destroyed."

Good God.

Holsey understood that gun crews would destroy a gun rather than letting it fall into an enemy's hands, but she had never felt it before, never imagined it would happen under her command.

"You all have assignments." Morden continued. "Get to it."

She stood, signaling to Stetler. Wilcox hadn't moved, his eyes burning hotter than coals. The young commander dropped his injured arm and loosed his sidearm. The command crew started to disperse, some of them exchanging quiet handshakes. Wilcox turned sharply away from Morden, catching Arnot's eye.

Morden turned, talking to what must be Mostoff through Baudouin's head set. Holsey was trying to sort out her feelings, wrestle the conflicting emotions back down where they belonged. Something about this didn't sit right with her. This isn't the way things should have played out. She took a deep breath.

Holsey was still a leatherneck at heart. She would do her duty to the bitter end, regardless of how it felt.

She turned on her heels, grabbed Stetler by the arm, and marched out the door. Each step she took solidified her resolve, the woman who had haunted so many years, the woman who had destroyed her life and who'd once been her best friend, left behind on the smoldering bridge of the *Verdun*.

The Frontin commander roared. His skin was burning, his good eyes stung. That animal had hurt him, ripped part of his prize from him. These Alliance scum kept wounding him, kept beating him. It had felt so good to disintegrate his enemy's skull, spilling its life blood over the ground. The ape had destroyed one of the big guns, turning the sweet taste of its blood to ash. That gun emplacement would not be able to help him achieve his destiny, his perfect prize blemished.

If he could kill the man again, he would tear the flesh from his skeleton, crush the bones of his extremities, and let him bleed to death. The man would understand fear.

Had the Frontin Lord not left the turret just before it had blown, he'd have died.

The commander roared again.

He pushed himself up from the smoldering debris. No, the gods had spared him, chosen to keep him alive. Revenge was his victory. It didn't matter how many insignificant victories the Alliance won — they would soon be on their knees.

This ship would be his, and, just like the defiant mammal who had almost killed him, they would die.

The Frontin pulled the last of his limbs free, kicking the smoking body of one of his drones aside. He smiled at the pain streaking through his limbs. He stretched his burnt and charred arms to their fullest, focusing on the sensation. It strengthened his resolve. Pain was how the gods communicated. He had always known that.

The Frontin Lord reached down, freed his scatter gun, and headed towards the distant sound of gunfire. One way or the other, he would taste the blood of his enemies, know release from this torment. Nothing would stop him.

The gods had spoken.

Chapter 29

Major Osterman took a deep breath. The air was already beginning to smell stale. Losing power in a fight like this was dangerous. Without air scrubbers, the fires on board would eat up the ship's store of atmosphere, leaving behind noxious gases. The final communication from the bridge had indicated that the ship was being assaulted in several key areas. He had felt at least one of the fifteen's blow. Shit had clearly hit the fan. Not that it bothered him — fights never seemed to go the way they were planned.

He closed his eyes, shutting out the rest of the ship. He had a job to do. It was only a matter of time before he was caught in the same fighting that had the rest of the crew occupied. He checked his rifle, pulling back his bolt slightly, the dull-looking bullet visible in the chamber. It was ready. He popped his safety off and pushed the bolt back into place.

When the Frontin did hit them, he would make them pay for every marine that died on this ship.

Kilwalski's voice was barely above a whisper. "Movement ahead."

Everyone raised their weapons, and the light machine guns swung toward the source of the noise. Osterman held up his hand, silencing his marines, keeping them still and focused.

They had limited ammunition. He didn't want to waste it in a chaotic manner or expend it too quickly. The Frontin were tough and relentless, with no fear of death. They fought under a blood fever, their hunter instincts driving them to kill. It made them terrifying and unrelenting, not to mention deadly, but that strength was also their weakness. They were not known for their professional skills as soldiers.

They were on his terms now. He was a marine, a trained, professional killer. His team was a disciplined group of warriors, and these Frontin would soon know the difference that made.

Corporal Xigler's voice crackled in his ear. "Major, I'm coming in hot."

Xigler was one of Lieutenant Arnot's marines, assigned to the bridge.

Osterman signaled his men. "I read you, marine. Prepare to engage targets. As soon as Xigler clears your line of fire, go weapons hot."

The young man flew around the corner, wrestling with his sidearm. He was trying to load a fresh magazine while at a full sprint. The terrifying sound of the Frontin pursuers was clear now, their multiple, large clawed legs tapping ominously close behind the young man. It sounded like a small group, no more than three. Of course, three Frontin could do serious damage.

The wall exploded to the side of Xigler, metal shards scattering in every direction, the massive power of the scatterguns scarring the *Verdun*.

Osterman saw the first one turn the corner, its sickening slimy carapace flashing into view. He fired, the crack of his rifle unleashing an explosion of sound and activity from his team. His first shot hit the Frontin in the leg. It stumbled, slamming into the wall.

Private Summers' eight-gauge shotgun boomed to his left, its nickel-plated double-aught buckshot flattening the wounded Frontin in a shower of black blood.

The second beast flew from behind the corner, trying to slow itself down with its claws. It fell victim to the second bark from Summers' shotgun, the rounds passing straight through its body. It fell, writhing on the ground. Its eyes burned brightly, its bleached white teeth bared with hate and pain. It tried to raise its arm, aiming its massive hand cannon at the entrenched marines.

Crack, crack, crack.

Osterman and several other marines fired in succession, their rounds bursting through its blotchy, hardened skin. Its head and face shattered, its screams silenced. The major readjusted his rifle, sliding it back against his shoulder, waiting for the next bug to emerge for the slaughter.

Minutes passed, and nothing showed. The entire marine contingent relaxed slightly. There must have been only two.

Xigler took a knee, saluting smartly. "Sir, Captain Morden's compliments. She has ordered the Verdun to be evacuated. You are to coordinate the marines to hold the necessary areas. Those being evacuated will meet up on the Black Fox and head out of the asteroid field."

The major opened his mouth. Abandon the *Verdun*? He'd never imagined that would be Morden's decision, adrift or not. Morden was a marine at heart. She didn't run from a fight.

Sergeant Kilwalski spoke first. "What the fuck is happening up there?"

The corporal shrugged his shoulders. "Everything's down, and the Frontin Jon is still nearby. Without weapons, there isn't much we can do."

Osterman nodded. "I haven't felt any shells hitting the ship for a while."

"Just boarding parties, major."

Osterman's next thought was broken by Frontin battle cries and Alliance guns. The light machine gun screamed above the rest in quick, deadly bursts. Xigler threw himself down, his back against the nearest cover he could find, still fumbling with his magazine.

Osterman peered down the hallway, keeping his head just above the level of the ICS barricade, his eyes absorbing the grisly scene.

There were already five more Frontin corpses littering the hallway, more sweeping round the corner in tight groups, some leaping for the wall and ceiling. He could feel the impacts of their weapons against the defensive emplacements, hear the telltale buzzing of barbs overhead as the creatures fired wildly. Too many shadows to count danced off the wall at the opposite end of the hallway.

This was it. The Frontin were going to hit them hard and try to take Laser Control.

There was no time to organize other marines around the ship — he would have to trust his platoon leaders to handle their own affairs. If Morden followed their standing procedures, his best troops were already holding critical areas, and they would all have a five-minute warning to reach escape craft before she blew the ship.

He lifted his rifle and started firing at each Frontin as it tried to cross the threshold.

Osterman yelled to his team. "We hold them here. No one gets past us! For the Alliance!"

There was a general chorus of cheers from the marines, causing the Frontin to roar, enraged by their prey's defiance. Each time one of their number fell, they grew louder. Osterman picked another target trying to sneak slowly down the hall, hiding behind the increasingly large number of dead bodies.

He pulled the trigger, and the top of its head burst.

The Frontin were trying to return fire, their powerful rounds bursting all around Osterman and his marines. He popped in a fresh magazine, working the bolt. Even the Frontin couldn't sustain losses like this forever.

Several grenades rained down in front of the barricades, and the small explosives detonated almost on contact. Osterman's ears rang, the heat washing over his face in a wave. The RAR machine gun stopped singing its song as the crew knocked it off its tripod, diving clear of the explosion.

The Frontin charged, filling the hallway with drones, smashing their fallen comrades as they went, eyes wild, teeth bared. Osterman pushed himself back to his knees, aiming his rifle carefully, trying to slow them down as his men shook off the impact of the grenades. He grazed one, its angry cry the only sign of injury. He corrected quickly, squeezing the trigger again, felling several in a row, just shy of pouncing distance.

Osterman fired again, and his trigger clicked on an empty chamber.

He cursed himself for not noticing the bolt lock back. Kilwalski was up, firing inaccurate but deadly bursts of forty-five down the hallway from his SMG. The charging Frontin, packed in the hallway like sardines, fell in droves. Those still alive fired at him, trying to regain their momentum. Kilwalski ducked, the bugs' poor accuracy his only savior. The metal around his position sparked and groaned under the impacts of their scatterguns.

The Sergeant stood his ground as they tried to push forward. Privates Fore and Burk were up and firing their rifles with quick, accurate shots, their heavy rounds popping the black masses of flesh and bone at the end of the hall.

The light machine gun crew, Private Tanner and Corporal Navie, struggled to right the weapon. The rest of his squad had regained their footing, the intensity of their fire stemming the enemy's charge.

Osterman didn't see the grenade the Frontin used to cover their retreat. It landed past the barrier, skidding under the machine gun. Navie grabbed it, cocking his arm to throw.

It detonated. The flame and shrapnel killed Navie instantly, and Tanner screamed as the explosion encompassed him.

Osterman jumped to his feet, running over to his wounded comrade. The details of the battle melting away as his mind focused on one burst of speed. He ignored the heat from the flaming wreckage and stinging bits of metal from barbs striking the barrier.

He threw himself over the young private, smothering the flames with his body. He slipped a shot of morphine from his chest pocket, injecting it into the man's leg. Tanner's screams echoed loudly, exciting the Frontin. He grabbed Tanner's shoulders and pulled him next to the gun chamber's door.

Osterman turned and lifted his rifle in one smooth motion. He squeezed the trigger, firing off his remaining rounds. Another few Frontin dropped dead on the blood-soaked deck, instantly replaced by others.

This wasn't a random boarding party that had encountered them — this was a deliberate attack. The Frontin knew what Osterman and his troops were guarding, and they were committing huge numbers to the assault, were probably diverting drones from other areas.

Escape might not be an option. These Frontin wouldn't let them get out. He was sure of it. This fight could only end one way — with their death or his.

L ieutenant Commander Wilcox threw himself into the cramped passenger seat of the escape shuttle, locking the safety harness closed. He shouldn't be leaving the *Verdun*. He didn't care if Morden had the authority to make him do it. It wasn't the right call.

He was already injured. If anyone should stay behind and blow up the ship, it should be him. Wilcox had been onboard the *Verdun* since the day she was commissioned. It was his place.

Ensign Lynch called over the radio. "We are transitioning to space in three, two, one."

The small shuttle shot free of the evacuation deck, turning sharply away, fighting its own inertia as it went. Wilcox's shoulder protested painfully, the G-forces pushing on his arm. His collar bone had to be broken. He could feel it shifting each time he moved.

He was a bit light-headed, and try as he might, the bleeding wouldn't stop. If his muscles could talk, they would have cried for joy when he sat down.

Wilcox glanced out the holoport, its images flickering to life as it processed the information from the few active exterior cameras on the craft.

The Frontin Jon was sitting directly in front of the *Verdun*, two long tethers digging into her bow, holding the battlecruiser in place. It was a sickening sight, his sleek, noble home ensnared by the ugly Jon. Even with its battle scars and smoldering forward gun turret, the *Verdun* looked beautiful. The Frontin ship was jagged and uneven, black with bumpy, segmented armor covering its long, thick ovular hull.

With a tether like that, thousands of Frontin could board. Morden had been right, they needed to abandon ship.

The bastards will get my goddamned trumpet.

The ship bucked again, and his eyes watered as his shoulder strap pushed against his injury. The pod's low blue lighting was a refreshing change from the darkness and sickly yellow emergency lighting on the *Verdun*.

Wilcox scowled, remembering again where he *should* be.

The Jon opened fire, its anti-ship weapons trying to pick off the escape craft darting away from the battlecruiser's hull. Each flak explosion rocked the ship slightly, sending a new jolt of agony down his side.

He peered forward again. He couldn't see out of the pilot's cockpit, but he could just make out the tactical display. The first wave of escape craft was moving quickly towards the *Fox*, using the debris of the cruiser and the defensive fighters to screen their movements.

He had almost forgotten the Cerberus fighters were still in the air.

They were almost out of range of the Frontin's guns, for all that was worth. Wilcox had never imagined running like a coward. No, he reassured himself, he hadn't chosen to run, he'd been ordered to run. Logically, he understood the reasons. Someone had to take care of the crew, and without an arm, it was hard to hold a rifle.

He was injured. He despised admitting weakness like this. Otherwise, he was in perfect physical health. To be taken out of the fight by a stray bit of metal.

It ate at him.

Wilcox took a deep breath. He had to calm down. Mostoff would need his help to figure out how to accommodate so many people on his tiny ship. They would fill every inch of free space on the *Fox*. More importantly, his people's stay on the colonies would be difficult. It was sure to be a politically charged situation, and they'd need a command officer to handle things.

Lynch's voice sounded off through his earpiece. "Prepare for deceleration. We are touching down in twenty seconds."

Wilcox tried to shift his weight so his shoulder and collar bone wouldn't hurt as badly this time. He had to be at his best, make sure his crew were taken care of.

The pod was slowing, its rapid braking made him feel dizzy and weak, the pain and loss of blood creating havoc in his system. The escape craft lurched as it touched down with a thump.

Wilcox stood and tried to look confident. Even in a wheelchair, Mostoff had presence. He wouldn't let the situation or the man intimidate him. Wilcox had to get to the bridge, start directing the shuttles and fighter squadrons. Every one of those damn boats had to make it to the *Fox* safely.

The survivors would get home. He could at least see to that.

The ramp began to lower.

Survivors. That's what they were now, shipwrecked survivors. How many times during his career had he rescued survivors, the people wearing ashen and downtrodden faces, the image of defeat showing on their faces? Now it was his turn to be saved, but he refused to show defeat here. He walked, forcing his shoulders back despite his injury. Pain was just an impulse, and he would control it.

Maybe this was how it started. Was this what defeat was—a stoic acceptance of fate? Was this defiance how all those people started?

Wilcox left the pod, his heart sinking further with each step. He coughed — the smell of electrical fires and smoke burned his throat and stung his eyes. The *Verdun* had been pasted, but the reality that it had been a lucky shot was confirmed by the condition of the *Black Fox*. The old ship was in shambles. Scorch marks and debris covered the deck, wiring and cabling hung from the ceiling, sparking and popping, and the majority of the wall panels were missing.

Several of Wilcox's crew had followed him off the pod, examining the torn-up bay with looks of exasperation and loss. It was like being trapped in a nightmare.

This bay would have made a great haunted house. The bulky, antiquated Empire-Era technology reminded him of the ghost stories he'd read as a child. He could almost see the book's cover picture, the *EE Dominion* haunting the space lanes with its dead crew of traitors.

He turned, waving his personnel off the pod. No one from the *Fox* was present. "Arnot, get these people moving. Get anyone from engineering and start cleaning this place up. We will need the space."

Arnot nodded. "Aye, sir." He seemed unfocused, like he had come out of a dream. Wilcox knew enough to recognize someone slipping into battle fatigue. His people needed him to be a leader now. It may not be when or where he wanted, but he wouldn't fail them.

"Captain Gilbrant?" Wilcox coughed again, the thick, smokey air burning his throat.

Gilbrant, a big, mustachioed man, turned, his armor dull in the dim lights. "Assemble any marines on board and start organizing rescue parties," Wilcox continued. "The people on the Fox may need our help as much as we need theirs. Your medics are the only ones we have until the infirmary staff get evacuated from the Verdun."

Wilcox turned, looking at the pod.

The pilot spoke for him, reading his mind. "Jettison this pod and get more coming in, aye, sir!"

Wilcox nodded, ignoring his annoyance. He hated being interrupted. "We need to get the Fox flying quickly. Have Lieutenant Geonor get me a report on weapons and engines as soon as he hits the deck. Commander Frost should be landing presently. Let him know I expect him to take command of getting people off these shuttles and assigned duties ASAP. We can't afford idle hands. I am going to the bridge to take remote command of the evacuations. I want regular reports by runner every ten minutes. Questions?"

"No, Commander!" They broke up, all running to take care of their duties.

Work kept a military mind busy. It was all they had right now. Between work or fear or despair, he would choose work every time. Death might be stalking them everywhere they went, but he would ensure his people didn't have time to worry until it was too late.

He would get them out of this.

Wilcox turned around, fighting back the tingling hairs on his neck, his own fear pushing at his calm. He couldn't help but feel angry about being knocked from this fight, but he would never surrender to defeat, no matter how hard it wanted to knock at his door.

CHAPTER 30

Urquhart's stomach turned again as she watched the captain. Morden hadn't moved or spoken in several minutes, but had just sat at her station monitoring progress of the evacuation. The faint ticking sound emanating from the blinking overhead emergency light was the only noise in the room. Another burst of gunfire sounded from the guardroom outside.

She checked her pistol for the fourth time, the sleek metal slide still snugly in place over her chambered round. Urquhart's imagination was running wild with the sounds of combat. She remembered all too well how bloody holding a ship could be.

She had hoped it was an experience she would never repeat. Urquhart took a deep breath, running her hands through her hair to settle her nerves.

Right now, the bridge was out of the Frontin's way, but eventually the creatures would attack it. They needed to blow up the ship quickly.

"Captain…" Urquhart's voice sounded weak, even to her own ears, sending a bolt of irritation running through her.

Morden stood up, straightening her uniform under her chest plate. "Get me the Fox."

She walked over to the damage control board, and Urquhart could see her entering commands and studying the results.

Urquhart had never even seen video of an Alliance ship self-destruct. There were some stories her dad had told her from the war, destroyer captains scuttling their own vessels. She turned, moving toward communications, her limbs heavy, weak.

Fear was a funny thing.

She stared at the different screens and controls for a minute, trying to remember how to operate the damned thing. She hadn't worked a communications board in years. She found the cluster of controls that worked the external radio, picked out the channel dial, and turned it a couple of times, trying to guess which one the *Fox* would be tuned into. She stopped, drummed her fingers on the armrest of her chair. She'd never been much good at this. Her eyes caught a button on her screen with the words "Multiple Simulcast" written on it. She pushed it, remembering with a small jolt of energy. The simulcast would transmit across several general channels at once, ensuring the *Fox* would pick them up.

She picked up the headset, slipped it into place. She looked for the push-to-talk button on the console, clicked it on. "Verdun to SS Black Fox, come in please."

The silence that followed made her heart beat faster. Were they any better off than the drifting Alliance battlecruiser? Had the *Verdun's* escape pods been destroyed?

Urquhart adjusted the gain dial, straining her ears to listen for a reply among the static. She had a greater respect for the communications team. Making this stupid thing work with all the interference from the asteroids wasn't easy.

She repeated the hail, twice this time, but the familiar sound of static was all that greeted her. Urquhart kicked the station, hoped her face wasn't going red. She wouldn't admit to Morden that she couldn't get this damn thing to work, but she couldn't just keep fiddling with it blindly.

Once the Frontin reached the guard post, their only way out would be the starboard escape pods, if they were still intact.

She finally heard a muffled response. "This is Black Fox, Wilcox here."

Urquhart boosted the gain again, trying to enunciate her words clearly. "Ma'am, I have Black Fox, actual. Wilcox."

Morden grabbed her own head set. "Wilcox, where is the Jon?"

Wilcox still sounded tense. "Directly in front of you, attaching tethers. On the bright side, a core overload will light the bastard up at that range."

Morden nodded. "And the Fox?"

Wilcox chuckled. "A shattered bit of ship, ma'am. We have communications and minimal engine power. That's it. Geonor believes that we can limp back to the colonies with the fighters as escort, but…"

"But what, Commander?"

Wilcox started again. "The ship is almost completely out of ammunition and fuel cells. We had to convert our fighters' cells to power back up, meaning they will have to fly in shifts and be abandoned one by one to keep the Fox moving."

Urquhart sucked in air. This wasn't a pretty scenario for the captain. Losing a ship and its entire fighter complement would most likely earn her a court martial — assuming they would even survive.

How could the captain remain so calm?

Urquhart doubted she would be able to if the situation were reversed.

"Wilcox, as soon as the majority of the crew are aboard, get moving," Morden was saying. "If you can find one of the mining camps, they should have fuel, and, if you're lucky, a long-range communications relay. If not, get our people home."

"Yes, Captain."

Morden looked over at Urquhart, the smallest smile on her lips. "Jack, are you sure about the Jon's location?"

Wilcox's intonation was unreadable, his emotions unclear. "My arm's broken, not my eyes. I will enjoy watching it burn when the Verdun goes up—"

The deck shuddered, the muffled boom of a distant explosion. A loud, electric pop interrupted Wilcox, dissolved into deafening static. Urquhart yanked off her headset.

"What the hell?"

"Can you get him back?" Morden came to stand behind her.

Urquhart looked over the screen in front of her, saw the words "System Error" flashing across it.

"They must have hit the antenna or the communications center." She turned around, was surprised to see a slight smile on the captain's face. Morden didn't seem bothered at all that the ship had just lost its radio.

They were about to send the *Verdun* to her grave, the worst duty Urquhart could imagine. She had been so excited to become a member of a battlecruiser's crew. She had never imagined this. Her own body seemed distant, as if she were watching someone else's actions. How could Morden be so happy, so calm and collected?

Morden looked around the room. "Do we have any of the portable radio sets here?"

Urquhart furrowed her brow. "No, ma'am. The last group to leave took the backpack and the remaining helmet pack sets with them." What was Morden getting at?

"Damn." Morden drew her pistol. "We'll have to do this the old-fashioned way. Let's move out."

Urquhart stood. "Ma'am?"

The Captain smiled again. "The ship isn't lost yet."

Voth dove to his left, the pain of his broken rib unbearable as he hit the floor. The Frontin's blade barely missed his body, its owner colliding with the wall. Voth popped to his knees and fired at point blank range, the last few rounds of his magazine splashing the deck with his attacker's blood. He crawled back into cover, his chest aching. Maybe his nurse had been right.

He ought to have stayed in bed.

Voth fumbled with his last magazine, trying to keep his head down. The Frontin hadn't stopped coming, wave after wave breaking against their defenses. The marines had been magnificent, but their ammunition was starting to run low. The MG was down to less than two hundred rounds, and the eight-gauges were dry.

Captain Holsted tired voice crackled over his headset. "Team One, dig in. Team Two, fall back to ammunition locker C3. Dolber, Simpton, and Arnor, reinforce the forward firing positions."

The three men jumped up, moving forward directly in front of him. The RAR machine gun was sweeping fire back and forth, covering the end of the hall. Corporal Dolber lurched and fell backwards, a gaping hole in his chest, his screams lost in an explosion of barbs.

The Frontin rounds slapped off the walls as they saw a chance to kill, rounds whizzing above Voth. He fired several shots downrange, trying to give the exposed men time to reach cover.

Arnor and Simpton tried to grab their comrade, pull him into cover with them, but the fire was too intense. Simpton was dead before he hit the ground, his face gone, the air escaping his lungs in a silent scream. Arnor took a hit to the shin, his leg crumbling beneath him, blood spraying from a torn artery.

He would be dead in minutes.

Voth picked his targets carefully. He had to make his last rounds count. "Captain, we have to fall back," he yelled.

The infirmary was almost evacuated. If they didn't move soon, the remaining Frontin would overwhelm them as soon as their ammunition ran dry. Each time he had thought they had killed enough to wipe out the combatants nearby, another wave tore into them.

On cue, the Frontin charged again, screaming in unison as they mounted the forward position. Voth watched man after man die, Privates Yolvan and Gustoff falling as the Frontin weapons cut them apart, a bloody mist filling the air. Sergeant Haines managed to stab one through the throat with his bayonet, before the Frontin Warrior returned the favor, burying its sword in his side.

An Alliance grenade went off, thrown from somewhere out of his range of vision. The three uninjured Frontin were peppered with shrapnel, gaping lacerations ripping across their dark forms. Their screams of pain echoed in the back of Voth's skull. The private beside him fired several shots, finishing them off.

He peered out of cover. The end of the hall still had the ominous slithering sound that seemed to accompany the screaming warriors. That attack had been the costliest yet. He doubted the machine gun ammunition would last through another wave like that, and without the suppressive fire of the shotguns, the situation would be beyond lost.

Lieutenant Barker broke from cover, retreating toward Voth's position, the last few of his men right behind him. They all were firing from the hip, trying to keep suppressive fire on the end of the hall.

The corridor exploded with excited, blood curdling howls. The Frontin flew around the corner full-force, trying to catch the fleeing marines. Everyone opened fire, trying to trade their limited ammunition for their companions' lives. Warrior after warrior collapsed under the Alliance troops' concentrated barrage.

But luck wasn't on the humans' side, and their light machine gun ran dry, its sudden silence worse than the screams of the attacking Frontin.

"Grenades!" Holsted yelled.

Corporal Dairen obliged. "Last one!"

Its detonation plastered the walls with Frontin carapace, the first row of the massive killers disappearing in the blink of the eye. Voth could see at least fifteen more of the huge black monsters filling the corridor, their legs beating furiously over the slick deck.

Several pushed off the deck, latching to the walls and ceiling in a desperate attempt to be the first to slaughter Baker's retreating squad.

Voth screamed into his headset. "Cover fire, cover fire!"

The Frontin were almost on top of them. Lieutenant Barker skidded to a halt, dropped to one knee, and turned to face the Frontin. He fired rapid groups into the Frontin, buying time for the rest of his men to escape.

Captain Holsted's team did their best to cover the man, tearing into the attackers with rapid fire from their rifles. Voth's pistol ran dry as he squeezed off one final round into the chest of a warrior almost on top of Barker. The lieutenant stabbed another and kicked it free of his bayonet, but another Frontin pounced over him, landing directly behind him.

Baker dropped, trying to avoid its blade, but he wasn't fast enough. It hit him in the side, and his body crumpled as the Frontin threw him aside, freeing its blade.

It turned, looking down at the injured Arnor. Voth wouldn't let this happen. He refused to cower and die one by one as the ammunition ran out.

He stood up, pulling his knife. He ran forward, screaming at the top of his lungs, barbs bursting on either side of him. He crashed into the nearest of the black monsters. It slid, lost its footing, and tumbled over one of the barricades. He didn't let it get back up. Voth lunged over the wall, sinking his knife into its skull, the blade breaking off as the creature's death spasms threw him free.

Voth grabbed Arnor's rifle and fired its last rounds into another one of the bastards. He knew he only had seconds left before they were on him. The rifle was dry. He would be down to his bayonet.

Voth stood up, finishing off one of the injured warriors. "Let's dance, fuckers."

He squared his stance, brandishing the long bayonet in front of him. The first Frontin spread its arms and opened its mouth to roar. Voth stared dumbfounded, the creature falling backwards as if it had hit an invisible wall.

He looked back. Private Arnor had propped himself against the ICS, firing his pistol at the charging Frontin. Captain Holsted was only a few yards behind him coming forward fast, the remaining members of both squads in tow. Voth turned back towards the enemy, yelling loudly as he dashed toward the startled Frontin.

Commander Holsey would have given her arm for a mirror. She peered around the corner, trying to get an idea of the enemy's position, but saw nothing. She could feel them, the damp, moldy, fetid smell of their bodies burnt into her memory.

The same scent infested the hall ahead.

This was taking too long. She had been trying to cross the ship's interior for the better part of an hour. Her team still had several decks to go.

The entire ship was crawling with Frontin raiders, small boarding ships protruding from empty escape craft ports or sticking out of jagged holes in the *Verdun's* armor. They had managed to take several key junctions, forcing the marine squads to fall back all over the ship, frustration and fear painted on the faces of the displaced soldiers.

Holsey signaled her ragtag unit. They would have to push forward…

The group fanned out on either side of the hall, staying as close to the walls as possible. She followed, moving quickly, trying to stay as low as possible. Her eyes burnt with the effort of focusing through the dim light.

One of the marines in front yelled. "Contact left!"

Holsey squeezed the trigger, her shotgun filling the small space with its heavy shot. More Frontin broke from the doorways where they were crouching, and others rushed toward them from the adjoining hallway.

The marines dispersed, everyone dashing for the best available cover. One marine, a gnarled sergeant, lurched back, twisting as his body absorbed the Frontin's fire. Another just fell, toppling to the deck, his head leaking thick gore from where his ears used to be.

Holsey ducked into a doorframe, shielding herself from the barbs filling the corridor. Several other soldiers took cover with her. She caught the eye of the nearest one, a tall, lanky looking woman, a large scar across her left cheek.

She mouthed the word "grenade" at the private.

The woman shook her head, pointing at the empty bandolier across her chest.

They would have to do this the hard way.

Holsey had lost sight of Stetler. Hopefully he had the good sense to stay back and keep the wounded safe. She dropped to a knee, leaned out, and fired several rapid shots into her exposed enemy.

One of the Frontin stumbled but kept running, ignoring the blood gushing from its side. Several others fell, hit by the sporadic shots of Holsey's squad. Four more uninjured warriors were still charging them, eyes flashing with rage.

Fire ripped down the hall in each direction, barbs and bullets bouncing off the walls and ceiling. Several light fixtures burst, sending more smoke billowing into the air. Holsey could see the forward marines starting to fall back, firing quickly as several more Frontin burst from the doors on either side of the hall.

Holsey started to yell orders, trying to rally her troops. She turned, realizing what was about to happen seconds before it did. She grabbed the young private closest to her by the back of her armor, flattening them both against the ground. The door next to them tore from its hinges, three more Frontin fighting each other to be the first through the door.

The other marine, a young corporal, tried to get out of the way, but thick arms grabbed him from behind. He kicked, slamming the butt of his rifle into the creature's face. The corporal fell, landing on his knees with a horrifying cracking sound.

He screamed, rocking forward on his shattered patellae.

Holsey fired, emptying the few rounds left in her magazine into the doorway. Two of the Frontin screamed, bullets punching into their torsos and heads, their bodies taking time to realize they were dead. The third roared, pushing its dying comrades out of the way and thrusting a sword at the injured corporal.

The man tried to bring his gun up to block the blow, but his legs buckled, saving his life, the blade passing just over his collapsing body.

The private pulled her trigger, an unsatisfying click greeting Holsey's ears. Her weapon was out of ammunition. Time seemed to slow down, the monster walking toward them, menacing its enormous blade at them, its thin mouth pulling back to growl.

Holsey felt trapped with death on all sides, just like on the station.

She threw herself at her attacker, shoulder down. She smashed into its center, knocking it to the ground. The scraping of its blade against her armor plating sent jolts up Holsey's spine. She rolled to her left, narrowly avoiding its follow-up blow, and pulled her combat knife free.

It tried to stand, but Holsey was ready. She threw herself onto its back. The warrior struggled, its many arms swinging at her, trying to dislodge her. She stabbed down into its neck, and it shrieked, grabbing hold of her wrist. Holsey tensed, preparing herself for the impact of his throw, but it never came. The creature tensed and then went limp, sinking to its knees, gasping.

The young private was in front of it, her bayonet deep in the creature's chest. Holsey stood, picking up its long sword. She gaped at it. It was an older Alliance sword, the Royal Marine crest on its ricasso unmistakable. Rage exploded in her chest and she swung the blade at the Frontin. The sword passed through its neck, parting its head from its body in a clean stroke.

Holsey turned, not waiting for its horrifying body to crumple to the deck. "Good job, Private..."

The woman smiled. "Gunn, ma'am."

Holsey's next step came up short, sharp pain shooting through her right leg. She winced. "Great job, Gunn."

The hall was still alive with combat, yelling and gunfire torturing the air beyond the doorway. Frontin were crossing the entrance, firing at her scattered team. They looked smaller somehow, less intimidating. She had feared meeting Frontin face-to-face again for so many years, but these bastards hadn't killed her then, and they wouldn't now. They had taken her life from her, but she could return that favor.

Holsey tucked the sword under her arm and slapped a magazine into her pistol. Taking the blade back into one hand, she signaled Private Gunn to move out. The two women emerged behind the advancing monsters, firing at point blank range.

Captain Morden's heart thrummed her chest, energy pushing through her limbs. She could still win this fight. Fate had given her the way out, handed her the kill. The small light was still on, still clear and green. The power had gone out so suddenly that she had missed it, hadn't realized how close they were to victory.

Once the Jon had been melted into slag, her marines and crew could easily stop a bunch of frightened animals. She could almost hear Admiral Horline's lecture on the Frontin at the academy.

"Kill the Frontin leader, and you take the fight out of 'em."

Ten years ago, she couldn't use that advice. But she could now.

Morden took a deep breath and looked down one more time, making sure she hadn't imagined it. The light was still there. Energy surged into her limbs. The damage control boards registered all three of the laser cannons undamaged, their energy buffers at maximum power.

They were ready to fire.

CHAPTER 31

Morden eased her way through another hatchway, the light from her headlamp disappearing as she pressed herself through the narrow opening. She and Urquhart had been moving slowly through side ducts, maintenance hatchways, and crawl spaces. The ship was more overrun than she had realized. The Frontin were everywhere. The few remaining marine units were doing their best to keep the hordes of drones at bay.

It sickened her to see these fucking creatures on her ship.

She shook her head, focused on her goal. If they scrapped that damn Jon, they could even the odds, teach these boarding parties a lesson one at a time. The two women were halfway there, only feet from the starboard side landing bay. It was the only way to reach the access crawlway to Laser Control.

It wasn't going to be fun.

Urquhart, to her credit, had kept silent, her normally bubbly personality suppressed behind her steady breathing. Morden liked the girl's ability to make light of situations, to smile when she should be furious.

She wished she had that skill.

"Be ready to run," Morden whispered. "The landing bay will probably have visitors."

Urquhart chuckled. "Running — that will feel good after our exciting adventure in crawling."

Morden continued, ignoring the sarcasm. "I'll jump first and cover you while you cross the bay and open up the room. The faster, the better. I don't want to expose us to any more fire than absolutely necessary."

She could see the grating up ahead, the bay's soft, yellow light spilling into the musty, pitch-black tunnel. She switched off her night vision. The green image disappeared, replaced by the dim, eerie emergency lighting. Morden blinked as her eyes adjusted to the gloom.

She yanked her pistol out of its holster, flipping off the safety. Her heart was beating faster, adrenaline filling her system in anticipation of combat.

Morden peered down at the bay, trying to see or hear anything below them. The room looked abandoned, stacks of boxes and metal crates visible in one of the corners opposite her. The floors were strewn with junk, the various unbolted workstations laying on their sides. The launch doors were closed, the large blast doors still locked in place. She studied the left side carefully, searching each of the dark fighter berths that ran up the wall. Nothing.

Maybe they would be lucky.

Morden pulled open the grate, turned it sideways, and pushed it back toward her partner. Then she took a breath and jumped the eight feet to the deck, rolling as her feet contacted the floor. Her knee popped, the old battle wound reacting to the impact.

She tried to ignore the pain lancing through the strained knee, gingerly putting weight on it. She swung around to look at the corners she hadn't been able to see from the tunnel above.

Motherfucker.

Five Frontin were crouching by the room's entrance. She didn't wait for Urquhart, but opened fire. If she could cut them down before they realized she was here, she and Urquhart could take their time. Round after round split the cold air. The startled arachnids jumped, legs curled under their torsos, attempting to escape the onslaught. One of them shuddered and collapsed with a thud, cut down by Morden's rounds.

Urquhart jumped down beside her and bounced to her feet. She fired slowly, aiming carefully, the report of her pistol mixing with Morden's. The Frontin were shrieking, falling back under the withering fire. They weren't armed, their weapons in a heap by the door.

What the hell are they doing?

Morden dropped the empty magazine out of her pistol, pointed toward the crawlway hatch on the opposite side of the room. "Open it up."

But one of the Frontin was already turning and bolting towards the door, all its grotesque legs pumping quickly as it covered the short distance.

Morden's heart sank. If it got outside, attracted reinforcements, she and Urquhart would be fighting the entire way to Laser Control.

Morden ran, her knee pulsing with pain as her legs pumped. She pressed in a new magazine, jumped into the air, extending her good leg. She kicked the sprinting Frontin in its side, her momentum toppling both of them. She rolled, pressed the pistol to its head.

She fired twice, blood washing over her hands.

Morden's vision blurred. Her knee ached, and pain shot up her back. Her neck snapped forward as another Frontin's arm wrapped around her, lifting her into the air.

The warrior shook her, and her Colt slipped from her hand, bouncing off the wall. Her armor groaned as the creature pushed her into the bulkhead. It tore her helmet off, crushing it in its claws. It spread its jaw into a toothy grin. She felt sick from the reek of its breath washing over her face. Morden kicked hard with both feet, her knee popping again, her feet connecting with its jaw.

She fought the urge to scream, the agony in her leg surging as she hit the floor, overwhelming the pain of her other scrapes and bruises. She propped herself up on her elbows, scrambling quickly towards her pistol.

The Frontin's horrifying red eyes were locked on her, burning with anger, its mouth open, blood leaking from its shattered face. The warrior tensed, preparing to leap, spread all four arms, bared its claws.

Then it convulsed, its body collapsing as a handful of well-placed shots mangled its torso.

Urquhart moved in front of Morden, firing quickly, all pretenses of marksmanship gone. Morden hadn't seen the final Frontin break from cover, but now it was almost on top of them, already airborne.

Urquhart stood her ground, catching its shoulder with the magazine's last rounds. It fell to the deck, lashing out with its claws. She drew her knife and threw it, the blade sinking to the hilt between the wriggling drone's top set of eyes. The Frontin stopped moving, blood seeping slowly down the knife's hilt.

She grabbed Morden by the shoulders and pulled her to her feet. "Not quite as much fun as crawling, but it'll do!"

"I thought I told you to get that hatch open."

Urquhart cocked her head to the side, the corners of her mouth tugging with a slight grin. "I thought you meant open up on the enemy."

Morden leaned on the younger woman for support, her knee screaming each time she put weight on it. If anyone were nearby, they wouldn't have missed the sounds of combat. They moved towards the room's far side, stopping just shy of the blinking maintenance entrance hatch.

At least I don't have to jury-rig the power!

Morden leaned against her subordinate for support, opened the control pad cover. She spread her fingers, allowing the scanner to read her palm, then typed in her access code.

Morden's heart was pounding, adrenaline still pumping through her. Urquhart jumped as the servos activated, spinning loudly as the door unlocked. She grabbed the handle and pulled the hatch open, the air inside escaping with a soft hiss.

She heard a bang on the bay's main door. The Frontin were here.

The two women moved through the hatch, Morden's swollen knee slowing them down. She felt Urquhart ease her down as she pulled the door shut behind them.

Darkness shut in around them. Morden put her hand against her knees, letting the sweat run down her face in the cool air. Her body relaxed, her burning muscles and bruised shoulder calming to a dull ache.

She stretched out her knee, pain stabbing up her leg.

Idiot, you can't save the dead.

Her desire to kill each and every one of these bastards was reckless. These weren't the same Frontin. If Urquhart hadn't been so alert, she would be dead and the *Verdun* lost. She was a captain, not a marine. There was more at stake here.

Urquhart holstered her Colt, knelt next to Morden. She pulled a shot and bandage from her aid kit, injecting a dose into Morden before she could object. Morden grimaced, the intense pain of the auto-injector offsetting the ache in her knee slightly.

Morden grabbed the gauze and started wrapping her bleeding knee. "Damn it! I need to be alert. We aren't done yet."

Urquhart smiled. "Oops, my mistake. I thought you needed to walk."

Morden tried not to move as Urquhart tightened the bandage. "The last time I needed to stay alert, morphine wasn't my first choice."

Urquhart laughed. "That's why I used the fentanyl."

Morden pushed herself up, heat spreading through her cheeks. "Then we better get moving."

Morden tested her knee, dropping the remaining bandages onto the ground. The pain had started to numb. She had forgotten about the fentanyl.

Kim, you're the fucking new guy.

Morden stared into the pitch-black crawlway, cursing the loss of her helmet's night vision device. She flipped on her wrist light, the dark beaten back by the harsh white beam. It wasn't tactically sound choice to use a light, but she had enough problems without trying to navigate blindly. Morden took a step, limping, the pain hanging on despite the narcotic. Her eyes caught the deck number. There was still a long way to go. She forced herself to take another step. One way or the other, the Frontin wouldn't beat her this time.

The Frontin commander's claws ripped into the door, pain still dancing across his scorched skin. The metal felt weak and fragile in his hands, and he tore the door in half, throwing the pieces behind him.

The room beyond was quiet, the broken remains of his drones stoking his anger. Five of his best dead, scattered across the deck. The glorious smell of death was everywhere, but without the intoxicating scent of human flesh.

They had been slaughtered, but no one was here to pay for it. He roared as he paced slowly around the room, letting his few good eyes examine every inch of the space. The lasers would wait. Some of these humans were strong, less beaten than he thought.

He stopped in his tracks, his blood-rage easing. He'd almost missed it — the sweet aroma of human blood coming from the small door on the opposite end of the room.

Osterman ducked as another grenade exploded directly in front of the marines' position, heat washing over him. He checked his ammunition — two magazines, plus his sidearm. Most of his team had sustained some kind of injury. Tanner had lost consciousness, his head resting limply on his shoulder.

Gunshots broke the air as two more Frontin threw themselves at the entrenched marines, testing the defenses again. They fell quickly from Fore and Burks' expertly placed projectiles, their bodies disappearing in the bloody mess of corpses covering the end of corridor. For now, the enemy seemed stymied, their ferocity beaten back by the calm training of his team.

Osterman couldn't shake the thought that the Frontin knew they were close to breaking their opponents.

He racked his bolt. "Ammo check."

"One full mag, plus a little."

"Same here, Major."

"I'm on my last now."

Kilwalski, who was resting near the rear of the defenses, answered last. "Down to sixty rounds for the big boy, two magazines for the Heinlein, plus my sidearm."

Osterman tossed a piece of metal back at him. "Now I know why everyone else is out, Kilwalski."

Sixty rounds for the machine gun would last less than a minute. The next charge the Frontin made would end in cold steel.

Why were they still here? Morden should have blown the ship by now. Osterman shivered. If she were dead, if the bridge had been taken before she'd had time to activate the destruct sequence ...

He had to spike the lasers himself. Osterman looked at the faces of his men. They were dirty, tired. They wouldn't last long in hand-to-hand combat.

Osterman signaled Fore forward, trying to maximize their field of fire.

His men fired again as the corridor filled with Frontin. They were charging forward, impeded by the great mass of their own dead at their feet.

They are almost as stubborn as you are.

Osterman took aim and fired, cursing himself as his first shot went wide. He corrected his aim and squeezed the trigger, his Enfield cracking, ending his target's life in a green mist.

The machine gun had already died, its thunderous roar replaced by the less reassuring sound of small arms. Summers fired quickly, his shotgun vaporizing several attackers advancing on Fore.

Kilwalski pulled his SMG from his shoulder, adding bursts of forty-five to the steady fire from the other marines. The Frontin started to break under the Alliance barrage.

Fore twisted, a surprisingly accurate shot punching into his chest, killing him before he hit the floor. The smell of blood reinvigorated the attackers, deep howls echoing down the hallway. Osterman slid over slightly, dropping his rifle onto the wall to steady it. He fired as quickly as he could aim, trying to keep them at distance, where the humans' superior marksmanship could make up for their diminished numbers.

Osterman saw one jerk backwards and crash to the floor, disappearing under the feet of his shrieking comrades. Another one split in half, its greasy black interior showering down the deck in front of it as fire hit it from several directions. A third snapped, looking stunned before collapsing in a bloody heap, its eyes rolling back into its grotesque skull. The attackers kept flowing forward methodically, steadily absorbing the wall of well-aimed fire from the marines.

One of the marines in front of Osterman wrenched hard, his face unrecognizable, barbs tearing into his flesh. The man shrieked, toppling into cover, skull bleeding, shoulder shattered, leaking like a punctured hose. Burke and Shane started crawling forward, trying to reach him.

Kilwalski shouted. "Cover fire! Cover fire."

Osterman fired as quickly as he could line up shots, knowing full well his rifle was almost dry. Rounds ripped down the hall, shearing metal and bone, his rifle's recoil bruising his tired shoulder.

His eyes burned as the fumes from the Frontin's archaic weapons built up in the stagnant air. Osterman blinked, attempting to keep his vision clear as he focused on his front sight.

Barbs were exploding around Burke and Shane, skipping off the metal surface as they tried to inch forward. Osterman realized it was too late. The wounded marine was too far forward, already too pale. He was bleeding out, his gasps for air inaudible over the harrowing din.

Osterman tapped his radio. This was costing them too much ammunition. He wouldn't sacrifice the living to save the dead.

Shane glanced back as Osterman shouted for them to fall back. They never got the opportunity. The nearest Frontin leapt in between the two marines. They turned, piercing its chest with their bayonets. They couldn't see the small, light-gray grenade barely visible in its claws.

The major dropped into cover, his voice lost in the blast. The multiple explosions sucked the air out of his lungs, flame incinerating soldiers and atmosphere, leaving the sickly scent of burning flesh in the air. Screams and ricocheting shrapnel replaced the roaring sounds of combat.

Osterman pushed himself to his knees, pain arching through his legs, his muscles burning as he pulled himself up. He looked down, saw blood running freely from a new gash on his thigh.

He looked up, barely able to see past the thick smoke and flames. Shan and Burk were dead, their twisted, mangled bodies draped over the ICS barricade.

Son of a bitch.

Osterman rested his shaking hands on the wall in front of him. Another Frontin was crossing the barricade, its thick hand arching down towards the faceless marine, his mouth moving with its last defiant utterances. His team was watching him silently, each one realizing what he already knew.

The battle was over.

The major met the sunken eyes of his platoon, the sickly light making their faces look hollow. His throat felt dry. "We are going to spike the lasers. Sergeant, take Summers, Hammond, and Barker, and fall back into Laser Control."

Kilwalski nodded, still firing his SMG in small bursts. "Yes, sir."

"Yustremski, Lee, and I will hold here until that door opens." The words caught in his throat, as the gravity of what he was about to order struck him. "We are getting the hell out of here."

Corporals Yustremski and Lee turned back to the wall without speaking. Osterman took a magazine off Tanner, slapped it into place. He released the bolt and lined up his sights on the first target. He squeezed the trigger.

The Frontin fell, its head split by the rifle's round.

Sergeant Kilwalski's team was moving behind him. He could hear their armor scraping against the floor as they crawled, keeping low to avoid the Frontin barbs cutting the air. Two more Frontin lunged past the barricade screaming, jagged knives drawn.

Osterman took a deep breath, firing two shots at the first and dropping it. He swung his rifle at the second target, his cheek pressed to his stock. He fired again.

It screamed, body crumpling just shy of the wall. Another Frontin shrieked, scrambling into view, eyes wild, arms flailing frantically and knocking debris from its path.

Shots from Lee's rifle knocked it back, causing it to stumble enough for Osterman to place another bullet through its chest.

Osterman saw another few Frontin fall. This was almost unreal. These monsters had unwavering focus. His team had killed more than he could count, but they just kept coming. Stumbling over their comrades' shattered remains with no more care than if they were running over a rock-strewn slope.

One of the drones leaped in the air, landing right in front of him. He pulled the trigger, felt the trigger click.

Empty.

He swung the rifle like a bat, knocking his opponent's legs out from under it

He cursed under his breath as he beat the writhing creature on the ground. "Worst. Day. Ever."

Osterman shot to his feet, thrust his bayonet into his attacker.

He withdrew his blade, dropped back into cover, and set the rifle aside. He pulled his pistol, clicked off the safety. Yustremski stopped firing, her mouth open in a silent scream. Osterman's gaze followed her limp body to the ground.

He caught movement and rolled to his left, his lacerated thigh seizing up, his assailant's knife passing over him as it jumped the barricade.

Osterman fired from his back, sending four slugs into the overextended Frontin.

Lee grabbed him by the shoulders, pulling him to his feet. The corporal helped support him as he struggled to run to the now open door.

Osterman hadn't seen or heard it open. Thank God Lee had. He reached for his earpiece, but it was gone, along with his helmet. The two men dodged past the last barricade, throwing themselves towards the open door.

Lee's leg exploded as a scattergun blast hit him just above the knee. The pair collapsed just a few feet shy of the door. Lee screamed, reaching for his missing leg.

Osterman turned over, emptying his pistol at the oncoming enemy. He pushed himself up, warm blood running down his leg, muscles burning. He reached for Lee, trying to get hold of the writhing man. Osterman felt something strike him in the back. His felt himself falling. Everything seemed far away, distant, Lee's screams muffled.

Osterman felt his eyes closing. He pushed himself against the wall, trying to get his body into a sitting position, but he felt numb. The pain in his leg and back were gone. The urge to shut his eyes was too much. He let them close, the world washing away into blackness.

Kilwalski worked the doors shut, activating the emergency seal. The sounds of the Frontin roars as they reached the outer blast door were terrifying. His marines were broken, breathing hard, eyes empty. Seeing the major fall had taken their spirits.

He had to keep them focused. "Get that door sealed. Summers, check the weapons locker. I am going to choke these fucks on their prize."

The small band of tired marines jumped back to their feet. Kilwalski slung his SMG, willing his heart to slow. He had been a shipboard marine for thirty years. He'd always thought he'd die on a worthless rock, not aboard ship.

Summers drew his gaze, shaking his head and holding up a bandolier with ten magazines in it. He hadn't really expected to find much. When the gun crew had evacuated, they'd all been armed.

He smiled reassuringly. "Pass it out, and boot up the emergency generator. This gun needs to be molten in five."

Kilwalski turned away, seating himself at the gun's controls. His hands shook as he turned the first dial, setting the destruct sequence for three minutes.

CHAPTER 32

Voth ran after the retreating Frontin. They were stunned, confused, and didn't seem to know how to deal with an enemy charging them. The nearest Frontin brought his weapon up a second too late. Voth impaled the drone, his bayonet's tip breaking into its abdomen with a cracking sound. The warrior screamed, fighting to get loose. Voth dodged the blows, kicking its chest to free his weapon.

Before the Frontin could move again, he thrust his bayonet into its throat, blood flowing down the cold steel blade.

A second Frontin lurched at him and Voth wheeled to his left, bringing his bayonet in front of him. The Frontin slammed against it at a full sprint and blood sprayed in a mist onto Voth's hands. The creature's momentum slammed Voth into the wall, the butt of his rifle hitting his chest plate.

He could feel freshly set ribs crack again, pain arcing down his side. Voth locked his hand to his rifle, trying to keep the wounded Frontin from reaching for his throat.

Private Sipton appeared airborne behind the flailing warrior, stabbing down between its neck and body. It stopped fighting, eyes rolling back into its head as the two Alliance troops threw its carcass aside. Voth dropped to one knee, breathing hard.

The few remaining enemies were caught in the open, falling under the ferocious onslaught. The marines poured on fire at point-blank range, combining their gunfire with bayonet points.

Voth groaned as he stood. He stumbled towards the end of the hall, bringing his rifle up to meet the masses he expected to find hiding around the corner.

The Frontin weren't there.

He focused on his rifle's sights, waiting for even the slightest sign of movement. Voth looked back. Captain Holsted and his men stood, breathless and scattered around the shattered corridor.

There was still intense gunfire up ahead. Someone was assaulting the Frontin boarding craft from the other side. Voth took a moment to realize what had happed. Another squad was coming to break them out. Vigor flooded through his limbs. He had been prepared to die, but now ...

Even so, he could barely stand. The pain in his chest was excruciating, but he had to help the other marines. He refused to let the Frontin win this, and he certainly wouldn't abandon a team brave enough to attack a Frontin boarding ship to fight alone.

Voth used his rifle as crutch. "Holsted, push forward. Let's hit 'em from the other side."

The men pulled themselves into some semblance of readiness, distributing the remaining ammunition between them. If Voth survived this, he decided, he would rewrite the damn standing combat orders with Osterman. The ammunition lockers were too far from the defense stations, and they didn't contain enough supplies for a sustained firefight.

The sounds of combat ahead died off. Voth felt his body shake as several loud explosions ripped through the deck. Voth turned as quickly he could, anchoring himself to the nearest wall. He raised his weapon, the weight of the front-heavy rifle making him dizzy, his arms shaking at the pain in his ribcage.

Suddenly, the feeling of suction, of air blasting down the hallway, hit him. Voth gasped, his lungs fighting to take in the thinning atmosphere.

Explosive decompression.

He felt himself lifting from his feet, hours of decompression drills flashing through his mind. As quickly as it had started, the decompression stopped, and the unmistakable sound of Frontin claws replaced the din of suction.

The marines opened fire as a horde of Frontin warriors charged around the corner, their weapons raised, firing point-blank into the marines. Corporal Haines and Bilward died instantly, their bodies shaking with repeated impacts.

There was no cover available for the Marines. Private Cook twisted so violently he vomited blood as he fell, his ribs and organs crushed by the force of the Frontin scatterguns.

The drones were panicked, running headlong into the remnants of the marine squad. Holsted's men met them head-on, steel to bone, the yelling and blood curdling howls of the drones filling the small space.

Things were moving fast. Voth lost track of his own movements as instinct and training took over, his bayonet slicing and punching into the oncoming enemy with deadly effect. It took only moments, but all eight Frontin were dead — along with three more marines. The few surviving marines were battered. Voth let his rifle fall, leaned against the wall, pain running through every muscle in his body.

Voth's ear piece came alive. "This is Four-Four to Alliance units ahead. Coming in. Hold your fire."

He clicked on his mike. "M-One to Four-Four. Acknowledged."

Four was the platoon responsible for defending the front section of the ship. Why were they so far aft?

Voth got his answer in the person of Commander Holsey, who rounded the corner with a group of twenty or so marines in tow. The men and women with her were clearly from several different units from all over the ship. The evacuation and sheer tenacity of the Frontin attack must have forced the marines to disperse, just like his own. Voth let himself slide to the deck, relief washing through him at the sight of the commander's familiar face

She stopped in front of him. "Why are you still here? Captain Holsted, how close are we from getting this ship evacuated?"

Voth pursed his lips. "Nice to see you, too."

She looked away. "I'm not the one on the floor."

He laughed. "Your ribs are still in one piece."

Holsted walked over to stand next to Holsey. "The medical section has almost fully evacuated. Thanks for the assist, ma'am."

Holsey nodded. "It's time to get the rest of our personnel off this ship."

Voth tried to push himself back up. "What? How can we take back the ship from the Fox? I won't abandon the Verdun."

Holsey turned back to him. "I've had enough of your stubborn heroics. You're leaving now. The captain's scuttling the ship. The Frontin won this one. We are going to deny them the prize."

Voth felt sick. "Holsted, move our team out. We are evacuating, now."

Holsted turned around, pulling his men to their feet. Voth grabbed his rifle, forcing himself to stand. He walked behind the others, his ribs aching so badly it made his eyes water. He kept his gaze forward, ignoring the broken bodies all around them.

He had never considered losing the ship. Voth had just watched so many people die to save her. He had never considered his comrades were trading their lives for failure.

Even if they did stop the Frontin here, what could possibly be worth losing the *Verdun?*

Commander Holsey looked down at her watch. Her breath caught in her chest. It had been over forty minutes since she'd left the bridge. Shouldn't Morden have called for the final evacuation by now? Why hadn't she?

Holsey keyed her headset. "Bridge, this is Holsey... Bridge, what's your status." Holsey waited, but no one replied, the seconds ticking by in agonizing silence.

Had enemy fire destroyed the bridge entirely? Had the bridge been taken? Were they under attack and fighting for their lives?

They had to deny the Frontin the ship. If the bridge were compromised...

She shifted uncomfortably. She had hated Morden for so long, but the idea that she would just die and leave the job undone ... Morden was an egotistical bitch, but Holsey couldn't just let her die like this.

Morden had a lot to answer for, but they were both fighters, both Alliance officers. Holsey had a responsibility to the ship and crew, including Morden. She made up her mind in seconds.

"Voth, take command here." She turned, and without giving the man time to respond, she jogged back down the hall.

Alone.

This was a bad decision, as foolhardy as anything Morden had ever done in the past. By all rights, Holsey was disobeying a direct order. Even if the *Verdun's* destruction took the Frontin Jon with it, getting the crew to the *Fox* and keeping them alive on that dump would be tough. It would be Holsey's job if the captain was killed.

It didn't matter. Something inside her told her she needed to stay on the *Verdun*. The captain still hadn't started the five-minute countdown. That might be up to her now as well.

No. She pulled her sidearm free again. It didn't make sense. She was certain this was where she was supposed to be. It was both unsettling and calming to take her own destiny into her own hands.

Holsey had to stop herself from laughing out loud.

Destiny, fate.

She had never believed in any of that malarkey. It didn't matter why, but she felt she needed to be here. All that mattered was her duty. She was the executive officer of the *Verdun* and she would make that mean something.

Even if she was the only one who would ever know.

Morden moved as quickly as she could, the lingering pain in her knee forgotten. The sounds carrying up from the decks below kept changing as they passed through different sections of the ship. Some roared with the sounds of combat and the screams of the dying, while others echoed with ominous silence. She wanted to join the fight, throw herself into the enemy swirling beneath her, but she couldn't.

She had to turn defeat into victory, but passing pockets of her crew fighting and dying didn't sit right with her. There was no way of knowing how many marines and crewmembers were fighting for their lives just on the other side of the metal — or how many wouldn't win that fight, sacrificing themselves so she could survive. Morden wished it were the other way around, wished that she were the one against the wall, fighting tooth and nail while her crew moved safely through the ducts.

The maintenance shaft sloped gently up, finally ending in a small ladder to the next deck. Morden lowered herself down and felt her boots touch the deck below.

Her knee was aching dully again as she started crawling, avoiding electric cabling and cooling pipes running along the walls. The grating beneath her bit into her hands, jagged holes punched through it here and there, the metal distorted and bent up into lots of sharp barbs, the acrid smell of explosives and blood wafting up from below.

Bullet holes.

"This junction has been torn up," Urquhart whispered from behind her. "Where are we?"

Morden moved her hand carefully over a power transfer unit. "Right outside Laser Control."

Osterman's fire team would be below them. The thought was unsettling. She had never considered that the guns might have already been overrun.

Morden drew her pistol. "Be ready. The room should be clear but —"

Urquhart's soft lilt interrupted her. "That'd be a switch. I don't know what I would do with that roll of the dice."

She almost laughed, the pain in her knee causing her to bite her lip instead. Her stomach knotted up, and cold sweat ran down her back. Urquhart seemed completely unfazed by the growing tension. No wonder she had moved up the ranks so fast.

Morden slowed her pace. The last thing she wanted was to alert the Frontin that someone was above them. The duct broke into two passages. The first continued forward, rising towards a ladder to the deck above. The second branch turned right, terminating at a raised access panel. Morden strained her eyes, picking out the words LASER CANNON POWER CONTROL and FIRE STATIONS — BARRELS ONE AND TWO illuminated above the panel. She turned right, ignoring the passageway to the gun room for the third barrel.

Two barrels were better than one.

Morden stopped, resting her weight onto her heels as she opened the control panel cover.

She sighed. The command pad was glowing, still operational. Fortune had smiled on them when Alliance designers had given these panels their own battery backups. She typed in her code, her hands steadier than her heart, the keys beeping softly as they depressed under the pressure of her fingers.

The panel opened, and Morden tensed, the sound echoing much more loudly than she'd wanted. The door swung forward on its hinges. Morden pushed herself backwards as several light beams lit her up from the deck below. She moved back, keeping her body away from the opening, listening to the sounds below. The voices sounded human, the footsteps devoid of claws.

She took a deep breath, wishing they had set up check point passwords. "Osterman, it's Morden."

"Sergeant Kilwalski here. Glad to hear your voice, Captain. We are spiking the guns now."

Morden's heart dropped. Kilwalski was Osterman's sergeant. "Hold that. My team's coming down. Where's Osterman?"

The gruff man's voice sounded oddly soft. "He fell, ma'am."

Morden fought back a surge of regret at the thought of Osterman dead, his body tangled somewhere in the mess beneath that shattered duct. They had served together for more than five years. It was Osterman who'd been the first one to make her feel accepted when she'd come aboard, angry and haunted by her own mistakes. She could almost hear his suave voice and laughter.

"Once a marine, always a marine."

Morden dropped towards the deck, leaving her emotions behind her. Her knee made an unsettling popping sound as she rolled, a dull stab of pain running up her leg. The four disheveled marines reached for her. A dull scraping and knocking sound filled the room. The Frontin were right outside the pressure doors. The men around her looked defeated, their eyes dull and tired, their bodies covered in minor wounds.

Urquhart landed next to her, swaying slightly as she hit the deck. She grabbed the nearest marine to steady herself. The room looked untouched, the fire control boards and targeting stations against the far wall of the room were dark, but undamaged. She looked at the guns, each of their massive first reinforces and cascabels were resting comfortably within the firing channels running along each wall of the room. Steam was still rising slowly from both heat vents as moisture condensed on the still-heated barrels.

Morden pointed to the controls. "Urquhart, get to work. Sergeant, I want your men to get the generators restarted, fast."

Kilwalski crossed his arms. "Ma'am, with respect, I think it's best we destroy them before those fuckers rip in here."

Morden nodded. "If the Jon wasn't sitting directly in front of these barrels, I would agree."

His eyes widened. "You mean—?"

The captain turned towards the door. "I mean to blast that motherfucker back to the stinking slime it came from."

The group broke up without another word and started working. Morden's eyes locked on the door, the sounds of their enemy's roars muffled by the metal. She wanted to sit down, her knee pulsing with pain again.

Morden was going to complete this mission, even if it meant spending the rest of time as a plaque in the Hall of the Fallen — right next to Major Gordon Osterman.

Holsey put her back against the cold wall, slowed her breathing. The inner door to the bridge was ajar, warm light from several consoles spilling out into the guard room. Morden had restored the generators. The self-destruct protocol should be available.

Why hadn't she started the countdown?

There was no sign of damage, no scoring or shrapnel marks inside the guard room, although both of the heavy machine guns looked dry. The room smelled of smoke, but nothing else—no Frontin or weapons discharge.

The people defending the guard post had left, which meant they were not being actively attacked. Holsey's heart sank. Morden wouldn't have just abandoned ship, would she?

She moved carefully, inching closer to the door, straining to hear any movement on the bridge. She tapped her headset twice, listening for any response to the classic marine tactic for signaling when the radio was compromised. Holsey moved quickly, pushing through the doors, her gaze sweeping the room.

The captain wasn't here. No one was. Where the hell was Morden? This was her post, the best place from which to scuttle the ship.

Holsey punched the nearest console, a jolt of rage rising inside her. She had fought her way through the ship, done her job, risked her life to come back here just to find that Morden had run to safety as her own crew struggled and died to buy her time.

Holsey wanted to scream. She had let her guard down, allowed the woman's words and false sincerity to convince her things had changed.

She paced around the room, trying to decide on a course of action. Her mind turned to all the men and women bleeding on the deck all over the ship for this cowardly bitch. Holsey wanted to hit her, hurt her.

She slammed her fists against the damage control station, the butt of her pistol smashing loudly through several buttons. Holsey let herself fall into the seat, felt her eyes burning, tears welling in them.

She rolled her head, trying to get a hold of her spinning emotions. Holsey was a marine. She hadn't cried for Glenn, and she wouldn't cry now. Her gaze ran back over the console.

She stopped, jolting from her chair as realization hit her, eyes resting on the laser cannon indicators. Morden hadn't run — the crazy bitch was trying to save the ship.

Her heart pounded in her chest. They still had a chance to win this battle. Maybe the whole thing hadn't been in vain.

She started for the door. These Frontin had hurt them, killed so many of Holsey's comrades. It was time to break their necks.

CHAPTER 33

Lieutenant Urquhart worked to lock onto the Jon. Time was running short. She could hear the enemy burning through the door, the smell from the hot, disintegrating metal growing stronger with each second.

She took a deep breath, turning the final dial. The hydraulic motors kicked on, moving the barrels to optimum position. This would be so much more certain if they could maneuver. The frigate was directly in front of them, but it's thin profile and the limited arc of the laser cannon made targeting tricky. There was not going to be a second chance.

Urquhart stood, turning back towards the door. "Target locked."

Whatever happened, she was going to stay at the controls. She had to fire as soon as the guns were ready. Without power, they couldn't lower the inner blast doors, and it wouldn't take the Frontin long to burn through the hatch.

Urquhart ran her gaze around the room. Morden was barking orders at the young corporal working with her on the final generator.

The other three marines were concealed as best they could given the lack of cover. Sergeant Kilwalski was kneeling next to the left gun channel, where his Heinlein would get the best field of fire on the door. It left him exposed, but the angle and generally poor marksmanship of Frontin drones would make him hard to hit. The man also had a satchel with their remaining grenades to help him deal with close encounters.

The two riflemen were tucked in farther back and to the left, hidden behind an old scissor lift that had tipped over in front of the firing console. Urquhart's hands shook as she worked. It was hard not to notice how scared, haunted even, these people looked. Marines were life takers and heart breakers, the toughest the Alliance had, but to face death like this...

Urquhart remembered the first time she had realized death was part of this life. Her step-father had been seriously wounded, his arms broken and his skull cracked. She remembered crying, holding his motionless hand in hers. He looked smaller than normal, weak and frail under the infirmary's bright lighting.

He had smiled up at her from the medical bed, wiping the tears away. "Sweetheart, we all make sacrifices when we serve others. How will things ever get better if we don't fight for each other?"

Every time she faced one of these life-or-death situations, his bright green eyes looked up at her, comforted her, and solidified her purpose. He had been determined to make the universe better, and that determination had taken his life.

The door shook violently, bulging inwards as something outside rammed it. Urquhart pulled her pistol, moving closer to the riflemen. Her responsibility was to fire, but she couldn't do that if she were dead. The firing platform was exposed.

The door shook again and fell open, the metal sheered from its tracks as several of the monstrous creatures tried to throw themselves into the room through the damaged hatch.

The marine next to her fired, hitting one squarely in the head, toppling it backwards into the hall. The two sides of the door broke apart, clanging against the floor.

Urquhart gagged as the smell of blood and burning flesh from the corridor outside washed over the room.

Two Frontin rushed through, both cut down by bursts of gunfire just inside the door. Shrieks of anger and pain echoed loudly through the room as a third Frontin charged through the opening, jumping as soon as it crossed the threshold. It landed next to the far wall. Its small pistol-like weapon sounded like a pop gun compared to the massive scatterguns of the others.

A second threw itself at the scissor lift, landing right behind the toppled machine. It slipped, dropping its weapon in front of Urquhart. She fired three rounds in quick succession, hitting it in the chest and face. It tensed, tumbling forward over the bars of the lift. The rate of fire from Kilwalski was increasing, his SMG chattering continuously.

Fire tore at them from the right as another Frontin managed to escape several shots from Morden. She had put herself in front of the corporal, screening the man as he worked furiously on the generator. The marine next to Urquhart fell backwards, clutching her chest, a spray of dark red blood leaking from between her fingers. The young woman was dead before she hit the floor, her rifle skipping across the deck. The remaining rifleman swiveled, firing several shots at the charging beast.

"Reloading." Kilwalski's voice was barely audible over the din.

A second later, one of his grenades detonated directly in front of the door, sending shrapnel in all directions. Urquhart turned to cover her eyes, aiming her pistol towards the door. She had to trust the marine next to her to finish off the target. Urquhart fired, emptying the weapon at the enemy as fast as she could work the trigger, adding her fire to Kilwalski's.

Urquhart pressed the magazine release, pulled her last spare magazine, and slapped it into the pistol. Ten rounds weren't much, but she would make them count. Sometimes, ten rounds were the difference between defeat and victory.

The images of her father's last stand flashed into her mind, his stoic face as he'd kept her behind him, facing the fire of the Quagaar separatists who'd stormed the bridge of the *Blue Jay*.

Urquhart depressed the trigger at one of the Frontin crouching to jump. It bucked, the round cracking its skull, showering the drones behind it in slick black brain matter and sickly blood.

Nine.

The Quagaar were one of many splinter groups of the old Black Star Empire. They had seemed mysterious to her as a young girl. Their jet-blue armor and surprising military discipline made them terrifying. Urquhart remembered the panic, wondering why they had been attacked. The *Blue Jay* had been part of a peace envoy to the Black Star Empire, escorting medical supplies. The mission was supposed to have been safe.

No one should have died there. The same fear she could see in the marines with her now had been written on the faces of the *Blue Jay's* bridge crew.

Eight, seven.

She fired two more calculated shots at the warriors bursting through the door. They collapsed, their bodies destroyed by the cross fire from the Alliance troops. Kilwalski's SMG was spitting fire at the door again

Urquhart had been in awe as her father had fought fiercely against the unknown foe. He'd stood his ground as member after member of their bridge crew had died, cut down by the guns of the enemy. She remembered feeling helpless, cowering behind a console, watching them all fight to save the carrier.

Six, five, four.

One of the drones propelled itself into the air toward Morden, who had knelt down to help get the generator working. The Frontin twitched, collapsing to the deck in a pile of broken gore as Urquhart's bullets caught it in midair.

Urquhart hadn't seen what had hit her step-father, but had watched him fall to his knees, gasping for air, his eyes glazing over. His pistol had fallen right next to her. She had picked it up off the deck, its grip still warm from his hands, and fired at the remaining attackers. The rush of anger and the adrenalin of combat had been foreign, scary.

Three.

One of the injured Frontin pushed itself to its feet. Her round broke through its back.

Urquhart had been shaking when the marines had broken through, cutting down or bayoneting the remaining attackers. She couldn't remember much after that. The *Blue Jay* escaped back to Alliance space, the funeral of so many fallen heroes that mission's only legacy.

She brought her attention back to the present. No one was coming to save her this time. Had her stepdad felt this calm as his death had approached? There was no way to know. Urquhart wished she could see his face now, feel his arms scoop her up.

Two.

She sent another round tearing into a surging enemy. The room teemed with energy as the sounds of the laser cannon's charging sequence peaked, a beeping sound issuing from the firing console. The generator was online. The guns were ready. Without thinking, she turned and ran, holstering her almost empty weapon.

She covered her head, avoiding the shards of Frontin barbs detonating around her.

Urquhart felt herself jerk forward as something hit her shoulder. She caught herself on her hands and knees, expecting to see a Frontin standing over her. Pain shot through her shoulder and something warm was trickling down her arm. She looked at her shoulder. It was mangled, blood seeping out from her shattered armor, the beating of her heart forcing her own blood from her wound. The world spun around her. She blinked, trying to focus.

The firing computer

Urquhart had to activate the cannons. She pushed herself up, crawling the last few feet to the firing computer.

The captain was yelling something, but she couldn't make it out. It didn't matter. She knew what to do. Urquhart reached up, pain blurring her vision. She pulled down the lever. The emergency bulkhead and blast doors came down one after the other, shutting out the Frontin. The sounds of bone and carapace being crushed filled her unfocused senses as a charging drone was caught beneath it.

Callista Urquhart placed her hand on the recognition reader, steadying herself on her elbow. The computer beeped softly, verifying her biometrics. In one motion, she lifted the firing control cover and pushed the button.

The *Verdun's* top two laser cannons discharged, bright red energy lighting up the darkness of space, hitting the Jon head on. The frigate shuddered violently as the intensity and heat of the blast reverberated through it. The thick black armor burned and cracked, the metal screaming under the pressure and shearing off like fish scales. Its inner decks burst open, atmosphere burning into jets of flame as the incandescent beams tore through it. The ship's decompression accelerated. Explosions bloomed from both sides of the vessel as its munitions stores lit off, smoke leaking from the ship's broken, cracking sides.

The beam stopped, and the two ships hung for moment, clean and quiet against the surrounding space. Then the Jon exploded, the area in between the two ships filling with burning debris and atmosphere, the few remaining boarding craft incinerating into nothing. The *Verdun* bucked under the intense shock wave, the Jon dissolving into slag off its bow. As the explosions died down and the flames burned out in space, the *Verdun* was left hanging in space, alone.

CHAPTER 34

Morden watched the Jon breaking up on the holoport, secondary explosions consuming the fearsome warship. The room burst into cheers, the three remaining marines elated by the victory.

Morden sagged, her body suddenly weak, the tension of the afternoon washing over her in waves. Her muscles screamed for rest. Her knee felt like it was about to buckle, the pain sharp. Her eyes wanted to close, but there wasn't time to rest. The ship was still infested, and they had to move fast to take it back.

Morden's gaze moved over the room. "Sergeant, see to the lieutenant."

Urquhart looked pale and gaunt, her eyes half shut, her back resting against the fire control panel. Kilwalski walked over to her, knelt next to her, placing his SMG on the floor, and unhooking his first aid kit from his belt. Blood was flowing freely from a deep gash in her shoulder.

Private Shane climbed up onto the scissor lift, rifle triumphantly raised over his head, and Summers cheered him on. Morden felt the urge to quiet things down, maintain discipline, but they'd fought hard and deserved their moment of celebration regardless of her misgivings.

Morden knew almost instantly she would regret that decision for the rest of her life as her eyes inched upward, catching sight of the open access hatch. Her heart slammed against her chest. It was already too late to yell as a massive, black Frontin expelled itself from the unsecured opening with a blood-curdling howl.

Shane didn't even have time to look up. The Frontin landed directly on top of him, and Morden's stomach turned as the sound of the Private's back and legs shattering and cracking under the weight of the Frontin echoed in the room.

Morden fumbled for her pistol. The Frontin turned and blindly swung the massive broadsword it was carrying in a wide arc around it, catching the recoiling Summers across the chest. Blood spattered down his shattered armor, pouring from the bone-deep wound.

The young man stumbled, dumbfounded, clutching his chest. He didn't scream, just struggled desperately to pull his sidearm. His knees gave out, and he toppled over.

Morden aimed and fired at the beast, hitting one of its arms.

It ignored the wounds, kicking the marine in his chest. The man flew across the room, crashing headlong into the opposite wall, his broken body slumping into a bloody, silent heap.

The Frontin lord whirled around, firing a disciplined burst at Kilwalski. The sergeant tried to hold his ground as barbs burst around him, firing his nearly depleted SMG. The Frontin's fire grazed his thigh, barbs bursting through his armor and skin. The man rolled, avoiding most of the projectiles, but slipped and fell into the gun channel, the sound of metal on bone telling Morden he was either unconscious or worse.

The Frontin warrior's grotesque armor was marked with the faded images of hundreds of battles, of humanoids she didn't recognize. The realization hit her with a jolt.

This was their leader, its enormous size and greater intelligence obvious. It was focused and collected, not lost in blood rage. He had timed his attack perfectly, taking advantage of their distraction.

Morden fired as best she could. Despite its enormous size, her angle was bad. Her shots went wide, hitting the lift and the wall behind it. The warrior pivoted its head, cocking it slightly to the side, its jet-black eyes coming to rest on her. A long, thin scar covered half its face, several of its eyes missing.

The Frontin commander drew its thin mouth up at the corners, baring its teeth in a smile.

Morden's heart stopped, her body instantly covered in a thin film of cold sweat. She stumbled, sending another pair of rounds flying haphazardly in the wrong direction.

It was the one. The same leader who had attacked that station ten years ago.

It had stopped moving, caught in the same moment of recognition. "You...Alliance. You robbed me of victory again."

The creature's broken English and deep, ghostly voice made her shiver. It jumped off the scissor lift, dashing at Morden, its ten legs beating furiously in the air.

She emptied her magazine at it. Her knee buckled under her, throwing her shots wide, the pain easing again as shock and adrenaline blurred her senses. It landed, crossing the small distance to her. It raised its blade above its head, slashing down at her. She dove to the left, barely avoiding the weapon, the clang of metal against metal slamming just behind her.

Morden dropped her pistol. There was no time to reload. She pulled out her combat knife and ducked as the Frontin overextended itself trying to swing at her, its inertia caused its attack to miss. She slashed down at its outstretched hand.

The leader screamed as the blade passed through his hand, black blood splattering its pockmarked armor. The sword fell from its grasp, clattering loudly as it hit the floor.

Morden tried to keep the initiative, her senses sharpened as the adrenalin spike evened out. She used her good leg to kick one of its legs, causing it to drop. She stabbed the knife into its torso. Her blade punctured the creature's armor as she put her whole weight into the blow.

The Frontin thrashed out with its arms, tossing her backwards, her knife still lodged in its side. Morden hit the floor, her head pounding as she tried to steady herself. She looked up, her mind filled with the angry screams of the Frontin leader. It pulled her knife free, tossed it aside. It turned towards her, rushing carelessly at its prey.

It was getting angry, reckless.

Good.

Morden knew she had only seconds. She felt woozy and confused, tried to shake off the impact. Morden dropped, pushing herself towards the door, scrambling forward, her knee screaming.

The Frontin commander hit the back wall, narrowly missing her. She heard the blast doors starting to creep open. Her chest tightened. Even if she beat this fuck, its drones would kill her.

She tried to regain her feet, the cold metal floor chilling her hands as she pushed herself up.

Her opponent didn't wait — he was too focused and too fast. The Frontin's hands closed around her torso, pressing hard against her armor. Morden felt weightless as her head spun and the floor moved away from her.

She tried to kick him, but all she felt was air as her desperate blows hit nothing.

It turned her over carefully, slowly, keeping her away from its body. She could feel its breath against her skin, flashbacks of their last confrontation lancing through her mind.

It was happening again.

It held her so tightly she had to fight for each breath.

The commander fixed its good eyes on her. "You…you have stolen my triumph. Again!" Its voice lowered into a groan. "But at least this time, I will have the pleasure of killing you."

Its long scar seemed to bulge as it stretched its mouth into a blood chilling smile, the pulsing of the emergency lights behind it casting shadows across its grotesque face.

This was it.

Morden knew what was coming. The warrior wanted to watch her die. She felt light-headed, her lungs still fighting for more air through its powerful grip. Thick, black blisters covered the length of his forearms, as if he had been burned.

Morden put her fists together and brought them down hard on the disgusting wounds. The blisters popped, fluid splattering over her hands as she hit the raw flesh beneath with repeated blows.

The leader grimaced, tightened its grip.

The Frontin wasn't going to let go. His hate was more powerful than the pain she was causing him. He wanted to kill her intimately, with his bare hands, crush the life from her inch by inch. Morden thrashed, strained every muscle, pain coursing through her, her consciousness drifting into the fog of suffocation.

Her ribs felt like they were going to cave in, her lungs fighting to expand against the Frontin's iron grip. The world started to fade, the dim lighting growing fuzzy as her last strength waned. The Frontin had started to laugh, the same horrid tone that had haunted her for so long.

"Zero."

Morden swore she could hear Urquhart's weak and muffled voice somewhere behind the veil of her suffocating mind.

Two shots rang through the room. She felt herself falling. Her legs slammed into the metal grating, collapsing under her, air rushing back into her lungs. She coughed. The world started to clear. The Frontin's shoulder was shattered, black blood oozing from a hole in its armor. Urquhart was kneeling, bracing herself against the console, pistol falling from her hands.

The lieutenant shook, sagged against her support, barely conscious. The Frontin commander turned, towering over her, ripping its handgun free of its holster. Morden tried to get up, but the pain was too strong. She reached out, grabbed one of its legs to knock it off balance. The beast turned, lifted the pistol, and aimed at her head.

She closed her eyes, tensed.

Several shots tore through the air. She gasped, expecting the rush of pain, of darkness.

It didn't come.

She opened her eyes, saw the Frontin sway and fall beside her, its sickening breath coming in shallow gasps.

Morden opened her eyes, confusion filling her. She watched the Frontin's torso expand and collapse. Then the gasping stopped, and its dark eyes glazed over, a look of hatred and surprise covering its features. Its mouth fell open, muscles relaxed.

The warlord pulled a final, rattling breath, and was still.

Morden lifted her head, looking around her. Standing in the open doorway was Commander Holsey and a battered, bloodied, but breathing, Major Osterman. Both officers' rifles were still raised in the air.

CHAPTER 35

Morden breathed a sharp sigh of relief, leaning back in her desk chair as the low thrumming of the engines resonated softly through the deck plating again. The ship had been too quiet. Even the sound of the diligent repair crews, who'd been working non-stop to patch up the engines and power distribution systems, hadn't made enough sound to create the customary warm noise of activity aboard the ship. Morden had never realized how comforting the subtle sounds of the *Verdun's* system were. Without them, the ship felt colder, lonelier.

And it was harder to ignore the screaming silence of the six hundred fifty-two dead.

She tuned back to Lieutenant Geonor, who was in the middle of giving a briefing.

"We are making good progress," he was saying, "considering the extent of the damage and general exhaustion of the remaining crew."

The remaining crew.

There was no blame in Geonor's voice, but Morden swallowed down another pang of regret. Her emotional resolve wavered as guilt, her constant companion over the past two weeks, washed over her again. Besides Osterman and Sergeant Kilwalski, the entire group protecting the cannon had perished, a story that was still circulating among the crew. Morden had lost people under her command, but never on a scale like this.

So many dead and wounded.

Morden was thankful that at least the injured were going to recover. Lieutenant Urquhart had lost a lot of blood and had a nasty wound, but was already up and about. Wilcox was in the same boat. His shoulder would heal, the broken bone having been successfully fused. The tendon damage would take longer to heal, and he wouldn't be at 100 percent for months.

Voth and Osterman were a different matter. It would be months of bed rest and physical therapy before their various injuries healed. Osterman had survived with a collapsed lung, broken ribs, and multiple lacerations. Morden couldn't believe his stamina. How he had survived that much blood loss she would never know.

She tried to keep her face passive, the corners of her mouth turning downward. She should be stuck in the medical wing healing, not them. Her injuries were superficial. The dislocated knee would need a brace, and her ulna had needed to be fused, but she'd heal.

It wasn't right. So many lives had been lost because of her command. Those closest to her had taken the physical brunt of her decisions. Had she not chosen to fire the laser cannons when she had, maybe…

Focus.

Morden tried to concentrate on Geonor's voice, but heard instead Captain Aldine's words, saw him standing over her in the infirmary of the *Ajax* after that first terrible fight against the Frontin ten years ago.

"Death is part of the job, part of life. They put on the uniform, same as you. Make the best decision you can, but even our best won't be good enough to save them all."

She shook her head, taking another deep breath. There was no point in second-guessing decisions. What-ifs and maybes only led to unanswerable questions, and her heart already had enough of those to last a lifetime.

Morden looked down at her tablet, the image of the Triangle filling its screen. She fidgeted in her chair. There was still much to do before they could get underway and leave this place. She looked back at her chief engineer, aware for the first time that he had stopped speaking, his face wearing a sympathetic look. She frowned, hoping he hadn't been staring too long.

Morden made a show of putting her pad down. "We're on the clock."

The man nodded. "Engines are up, but barely functional. Realistically, we need to go in for major repair time, either by splashing down or getting serviced at an orbital shipyard, whichever we can get to first. I can't promise more than forty percent capacity until then."

Morden began to speak, but the engineer put up his hand. "I know. I'll keep working on it, but with so much damage to the power distribution system from the detonation of the gun turret—"

"There's significant structural damage, obviously." Morden leaned forward, interrupting Geonor. "It also limits our combat capability until we can install a replacement."

"Yes, ma'am. Not to mention the drone bay. The secondary explosions there caused extensive damage to the life support flow regulators for the upper decks and the robot control systems. Between that and all the small arms damage to the lower decks, my section will have a lot to get done."

Morden nodded. The bastard who'd led the Frontin had been uncharacteristically effective for one of his species. His attack had cut the ship in two, blocking people's escape routes and causing damage to key systems.

Geonor continued. "I would like to try to address at least part of the damage to the ordnance deflector, assuming I can do anything at all. Initial visual examinations by the air wing are inconclusive. Until the AI comes back up—"

Morden crossed her arms, interrupting him again. "You told me I'd have Isabelle back today."

Geonor's face tightened. "I did, but her circuitry suffered more feedback damage than I thought. We may have her up by tomorrow night. Maybe."

Morden ran her hand through her hair, thinking. "Discontinue the fighter checks. The MOD is secondary, unless you are planning to get us in a firefight in the near future. Inform Frost I want those squadrons to join the search of the area."

He made a note on his pad. "Aye, ma'am. My understanding is that the sweep will be done this afternoon."

Morden picked back up her tablet. "Faster is better. If any of those bastards are out there, I want them drawn and quartered. By oh-seven-hundred tomorrow, I want an estimate on the fighter repairs and munitions replacement needs. Coordinate with Lieutenant Blake, please."

He stood to leave. "Yes, ma'am."

"I know you've done what you can, Lloyd, and you are doing a fine job. Better than I expected. I want us to still look like a ship-of-the-line when we limp home. We've sacrificed too much."

"Consider it done. My team will stay focused. I could use help with some of the incidental problems. Light fixtures, control boxes, and other aesthetic damage."

She nodded. "Take whomever can be spared. Staying busy will help keep people's minds distracted from ... other matters. I'll have the department heads report any available crew members to you."

The overhead chime rang.

Great, the one thing I didn't miss.

"We have the Corvette on approach." Lieutenant Stetler's voice, weak but clear, crackled over the speakers. "Looks like Commanders Wilcox and Holsey are back from Three Rivers."

Morden picked up the hand mike on her desk, keyed it. "All right. Inform me when they are down."

Her stomach turned a little. She was not ready to deal with her XO.

"Yes, Captain," Stetler continued. "Commander Frost requests you meet him in Landing Bay Two."

The crackling of the intercom faded as she stood up.

Geonor smiled. "0700 tomorrow?"

Morden nodded.

The walk down to the landing bay was excruciating. The farther down into the ship's lower sections Morden got, the worse the battle damage was. Burnt and scored metal plating, the smell of ozone from blown-out conduits stinging her nose—she knew it was irrational, but each pockmark pulled at her.

Good God, look at her.

Had Captain Knight felt like this after a battle? How would she silence the voices of the dead?

She turned into the last corridor, nearly knocking headlong into Doctor Cadogan and several medical personnel with a stretcher.

Her heart sank, frustration drenching her tone. "Doctor, don't you have patients to attend to?"

"Frost paged me down. He didn't really elaborate."

Morden nodded, following the medical team towards the flight deck. There was a muffled sound coming from the other side of the door.

Screaming.

Her blood chilled.

Why hadn't they called an alert? The marine sweeps must have been wrong. Some of the Frontin had survived, and they were making a play for the landing bay.

More lives were being traded for the Triangle.

She signaled for the doctor to get behind her as she dashed to the nearest weapons locker. She wouldn't trade even one more soul for her own. Not one. Morden reached out, keying the open sequence on the locker.

The bay door opened, and Morden's mouth dropped. The men in the bay were jumping up and down, cheering. It wasn't screaming. They were celebrating. The pilots and deck crew were yelling themselves hoarse. They were mobbing in front of a wrecked escape craft from one of the destroyers.

Morden straightened her uniform. She glanced back at Cadogan, who had the same bemused and confused look she imagined was plastered over her own face. She walked forward, pushing past the mob of ecstatic crewpeople one at a time.

The room quieted as more and more of the deck crew caught sight of her. Commander Frost was at the front of the circle, talking enthusiastically to a ragged man sitting with his back against the pod. He was thin, his tattered flight suit covered with grime. The man looked familiar, but she didn't recognize him.

Frost's team had done it, managed to catch one of the Frontin's human accomplices. So far, they'd all committed suicide before their pods could be retrieved.

Morden's voice made both Frost and the man look up. "Good work, Commander. I'll handle the interrogation personally. I'll get the answers we need."

Frost laughed. "We don't interrogate goddamn heroes on my deck, ma'am. He's got more than answers for you."

The young man struggled to his feet, saluting weakly.

Morden's jaw dropped, her heart skipping several beats. She recognized those eyes. The man standing in front of her was a ragged, tired, undernourished, filthy-but-breathing Lieutenant Hillman.

He reached out with an old fashioned, dented computer pad in his hand. It was the same kind of device used to record official ship logs.

The next twenty or so minutes flew by as Hillman recounted his tale. Her heart felt lighter for the first time since the guns had quieted. Six hundred fifty-one felt better than six hundred fifty-two somehow.

Hillman smiled weakly. "When I woke up, I found that pad in the escape craft. It's mostly functional. Don't know what it says, of course. I don't speak Frontin. I figured Izzy could translate."

Morden turned the pad off. "I'm sure Naval Intelligence will find this interesting. Cadogan, get our hero to medical and check him out. He deserves the royal treatment. Lieutenant, you have done the Alliance and this ship proud. I'm going to pin a damn medal on your chest."

Morden helped lift the wounded man onto the stretcher, then watched Cadogan and the others take him from the bay to a renewed explosion of cheers.

CHAPTER 36

Captain Mostoff blinked, looking around the brightly lit halls of the *Verdun*. The first time he had come aboard, the ship's ample space, clean lines, and fresh air had seemed foreign, intimidating. A massive warship from the corrupt, militarized enemy he despised. He could handle that. Hate and fear were convenient, familiar safety blankets. Inside their folds, he could comfort himself with his own self-righteous, dogmatic truths. As it turned out, that's all his ideas about the Alliance crew had turned out to be — simple prejudice.

He should be feeling uneasy, tense, but he wasn't. Even the nagging pain of his wounds wasn't bothering him. The old man frowned. He felt *safe* here. These halls were no longer foreign or dangerous. The men and women on this ship had risked — and given — their lives for his.

For longer than he could remember, the Royal Alliance had been a demon stalking him, his only solace coming from his military defeats of the backward miners. Now those victories tasted like ash, knowing they had led those people to such a level of desperate fear that they had turned to the Frontin. He'd been so stuck in his own immobile views and political agenda that he had lost sight of the humanity of his enemies. The miners just wanted the same thing that he accused the Alliance of suppressing. Freedom of choice.

Mostoff was the nightmare the miners feared. Would his people have turned to the Frontin to destroy the Alliance?

The men and women on this ship had risked their lives for his way of life.

Many had done more than risk them.

Mostoff grimaced. *That* was the problem. The enemy wasn't clear anymore. Everything in his experience screamed that this place was dangerous, full of corrupt bureaucrats brandishing guns and bent on stripping him of his independence. He prided himself on being a single-minded man of focus, a man of singular devotion and drive, a man meant to live free.

"Captain, let me help."

Mostoff looked up, Wilcox's voice breaking his train of thought. He had forgotten the two young commanders were walking beside him. The kind smile from Wilcox intensified his emotional turmoil. He should have looked at Holsey. At least her uptight frown might have settled him.

He pulled his hands off his chair's controls, allowing Wilcox to push his wheelchair. He tightened his grip on the armrest, a twinge of regret running through him. He had become weak, forced to let someone help him. Less than a month ago, he never would have permitted this.

They were almost to the conference room at the end of the hall. No, Mostoff never would have allowed himself to be helped by a scum-sucking member of the Alliance. Showing weakness to an enemy is like begging for death. He wouldn't have even allowed his own crew to succor his pain. It would make him seem vulnerable, and vulnerability wasn't permissible in the Triangle.

Scum-sucking Alliance.

Even that phrase didn't feel right anymore. When he had met Wilcox, his kindness had seemed false and had made Mostoff abhor him. His fastidious grooming and smooth accent dripped with decadent weakness. Hating someone like that had felt right. This was the image the old Triangle had grown up with. The rich, corporate bully protected by his fancy technology and big guns. It was the epitome of everything that kept his people buried in squalor.

The problem was that the young Alliance officer was genuine and brave. His self-confidence wasn't arrogance at all, but came from a deep well of courage. Mostoff respected him. The man had been injured fighting for the Triangle. The bastard he had seen in front of him had been a demon of his imagination, not the real man.

Nothing seemed right any more. His easy black-and-white world had been wiped out and replaced by murky grays. The blanket of hate and rage had been shredded by battle. He had fought side by side with these people against terror itself. They had lived, not because of his strength or his stubborn focus, but by their honest sacrifices.

Mostoff took a deep breath as he watched Wilcox open the doors. The only thing he could take comfort in was the same dread for this meeting with Morden that had accompanied his first. Knowing that the axe had fallen from above him didn't make this right. This crew had earned better.

Mostoff was pushed through the door, immediately taken aback by the smile on Morden's face. He had never seen her look happy. The woman glanced at her officers, her face reacquiring the intense expression he was accustomed to.

Morden looked back at him. "Good morning, Captain. How's the leg?"

Mostoff tried to force a smile. "The pain is less than it was."

She smiled again. "That's good to hear. So, where are we going to set down to begin repairs? I imagine the Administrator will want to keep us off of Barnerious II, given her feelings about that colony."

The sincerity of her smile made Mostoff's heart catch, knowing what his orders required him to say. "No. The administrator will allow you to remain in the Triangle only until your engines are repaired. Then you must go. They refused to provide supplies. They asked me to inform you—"

Holsey's voice cut him off. "That's putting it mildly, Captain. Administrator Wheeler seemed more focused on casting blame on us than listening. She wants us gone, wants to shove this whole incident into a clean box and hide it under the bed."

Wilcox sat down next to him. "It was like being in the middle of those political ads from the Imperialist Party. Wheeler was setting up her campaign, going on about the dangerous Alliance threat. I felt like a terrorist on trial. I can't believe how narrow-minded those people are."

The man's honesty cut Mostoff deeply, but he was right. Wheeler was using this incident to control people at home, manipulate the situation. As far as the Triangle governments were concerned, the Frontin were gone. They cared more about their own power than the people Mostoff served. Was there truly freedom in the Triangle? Had they really become the very thing he had fought against? Was the negative image of the Alliance he'd lived with for so long just another tool for Wheeler and others like her to assert their control?

Mostoff couldn't stop his face from contorting into a frown.

Morden leaned back. "I never expected them to accept my offer to open negotiations for protection, but to just ignore the facts ... If the Frontin are entering a more active phase, then everyone in the sector is at risk, not just the Alliance."

Mostoff looked at the table. "To her, the Frontin seem far away, not a real, tangible threat. The colony has been unstable for a while. The Alliance is the scapegoat we all know and loathe."

Morden's voice rose. "That's idiotic. You've seen the Frontin. There must be something we can do to persuade —"

"Yes, but it's reality." He met her gaze. "Wheeler is taking the easy way out. The fear of being consumed by the Alliance is something we have known all our lives. Hating you was easy, far easier than standing up to those monsters. I already tried to convince them, but they won't hear me."

Holsey slammed the table. "Idiots! Fucking morons! Mostoff, if the Frontin come, they will kill everyone, destroy everything."

Mostoff roared. "I *know* that. But my people don't. They didn't see. They can't understand what those creatures can do, how they hunt us. They are apparitions to my people, legends. The Alliance is a real, measurable threat."

Wilcox cut in. "You have to do something. Your people could be slaughtered."

"I already told you, they won't listen. I am one voice among many. They won't accept the idea that we are in danger."

Wilcox responded. "Joining the Alliance is your only hope. You rant about freedom. We are a democracy."

Holsey threw up her hands. "These people don't need suffrage. They need protection."

Wilcox turned towards her. "With all due respect, suffrage is exactly what they need. We can't change the way these people think by parading warships through their system."

Holsey crossed her arms. "If they won't accept protection, then fuck 'em. Bottom line — we can't give the Frontin a foothold here. It's too dangerous for everyone, including them."

Wilcox rolled his eyes. "These people don't understand. They are ignorant of what's out there."

Holsey glared. "Then we have to make them understand. Mostoff figured it out, and when we met him, I thought he was the most pig-headed son-of-a-bitch alive!" Holsey stopped, looking over at him. "Sorry, but it was probably mutual."

Mostoff nodded, couldn't help but smile despite the situation.

Wilcox's voice rose, frustration seeping into it. "Look what it took to change his mind. I would prefer not to repeat the experience."

Mostoff stopped listening. Morden was staring at him, eyes steady, unwavering. It was uncomfortable having a warrior like her sizing him up. What was she thinking? He had known this would be hard, but what else could he do? Nothing these people did could change the way things were.

Morden cleared her throat loudly, silencing the debate between her officers. "Captain Mostoff, if you feel there is nothing to be done here, then we will leave for home within the hour."

Holsey's face flushed. "Are you nuts? We can't just leave the area and give the Frontin free rein."

Wilcox nodded. "I agree. This is insane. Without an Alliance presence, there will be nothing to stop them, nothing to even slow them down. I may not agree with Holsey's approach but—"

Morden held up her hand. "I wasn't asking for opinions. We are sworn to protect our own, not disrupt governments or shield people against their will. Holsey, what were our orders?"

"To find the freighter, stabilize the region, and—"

Morden placed her hands on the table. "And nothing. We have completed our mission. We can't save people from themselves. We will give them the data Lieutenant Hillman recovered."

Wilcox's eyes widened. "Hillman's alive?"

Morden nodded. "Yes. We can't dig these people out of their own ignorance. Change has to come from within. There is too much history between our peoples. The Verdun will return home for repairs."

Holsey nodded, her tone softening. "True. We can't even call for back up from here without long-range communication drones."

Morden typed something into her terminal. "Exactly. Our duty is clear. Respect the sovereignty of these people and return home. Let the diplomats sort it out. We will have enough questions to answer without causing an international incident."

Mostoff had never thought they would just leave. He had expected them to come up with solutions. Morden had always had an idea before.

Captain Mostoff let his jaw fall. "You can't just leave, Morden."

"Captain, there is nothing else I can do."

His heart fell. "But so many of your people have died here. You can't just let their sacrifice be for nothing."

Morden's composure fell. For a moment, no one said nothing, Mostoff's words hanging in the air.

Mostoff held her gaze, understood. He'd been a captain for a long time, knew the doubt and anguish of losing his own.

Morden regained her composure, and her smile returned, but didn't reach her eyes. "It wasn't. The situation we came here to deal with has been resolved. I'm sure someone else will resolve the Triangle's issues, just not us. It's time to accept that. Mostoff, you are a leader. You are still in a stronger position to help your people than we are. Find someone who will listen. I promise that I will do what I can to help when we get home."

"I understand." It was the only thing he could think to say.

She was right, even if he didn't want to admit it. It didn't matter how, but he had to change his people's minds, the way this experience had changed his. He couldn't pretend things were still the same.

It wasn't possible anymore, not for him.

Morden leaned back into her chair. "I hope so. I appreciate your help, Captain. I misjudged you. You are a good man."

Mostoff shook his head. "Morden, it is I who should thank you. You saved my people. You saved me, lifted my blindness. I know you will face many questions from your commanders. But I want *you* to know you did something good here. You saved thousands of lives and changed one old man's mind. My leaders may not appreciate what happened, but I do. My crew does. Thank you."

Morden's expression was unreadable. She nodded. "Mr. Wilcox, please escort the captain back to his transport. Make preparations to leave."

Wilcox stood up, grabbing hold of Mostoff's wheelchair. For the second time in his life, Mostoff allowed himself to be helped, his mind just as crowded as when he'd arrived. At least he had a small twinge of purpose again. It may take the rest of his life, but he wouldn't allow the Triangle to die, wouldn't let his freedom be taken by monsters — be they Frontin or his own foolish leaders.

Morden sat back in her chair, waiting until the door closed before speaking. "Commander, we need to find a safe port for repairs. I want to avoid any area the Milipa could see us."

Holsey looked at her. "Agreed. We don't want them getting the idea half-functional wrecks are patrolling the border."

"Or seize that opportunity to raid us and capture our technology," Wilcox added.

Morden nodded. "I have no desire to turn the cold war into a shooting war."

Morden's heart ached. So many had died here. Mostoff was right. There was going to be a lot to answer for, a lot for her own conscience to grapple with.

Holsey spoke softly. "They are still out there."

Morden looked up, realized that Holsey had guessed what she'd been thinking about.

"We may have slowed them down," Holsey was saying. "Stopped them for the moment, but—"

Morden interrupted. "If even one survived, they will see this area as open season. Without a real military presence, these people will be fodder. It's only a matter of time."

The two women held each other's eyes, the same horrifying image running through their minds. This wasn't the end. The Triangle was too rich a feeding ground, too tempting, and too vulnerable.

Holsey rubbed her neck. "We could always—"

Morden shook her head. "Find us a place to lick our wounds, Commander. We need to use the time we have to get ready. If the Frontin attack in force, our wounded girl won't be able to do much to stop them."

Holsey nodded and left the room. Morden sat there, running things through her head. There was no other alternative. They had to return to port. It was the *right* decision. She was going to get the ship home, back to safety. Naval Command would have to make a decision whether the area was worth the resources to defend or not.

Morden shivered.

What if Command abandoned those people? She couldn't escape the feeling that the Frontin were still out there, watching them from the darkness.

This event had been a living nightmare. She could only hope the people in the Triangle had not inherited one of their own.

Morden wouldn't let that happen. Someone at Command would listen. She stood, straightened her uniform. It was time to leave this place.

M ostoff and Wilcox moved quickly down the corridor. Mostoff could feel the tension rolling off the young man. He knew Morden was right, but Wilcox was a man of principle. Leaving the Triangle in danger wouldn't be easy for him to accept.

"Captain Mostoff, I want you to know I don't blame you," Wilcox stated flatly. "I just want things to be different. I wish I could make people understand."

Mostoff tried to sound sympathetic. "I am sorry it bothers you so much."

"The captain is right. We are not a diplomatic ship. I just feel like I'm being asked to run, abandon a problem that is partially our fault."

The two continued down the hall in silence. He couldn't ignore the anger coming from Wilcox. The commander's unflappable spirit had been darkened, and Mostoff couldn't help but wonder if he wasn't the only changed man. Had he done something to upset Wilcox?

The commander pushed him up the Corvette's ramp, then turned to leave.

Mostoff swiveled the chair around. "Mr. Wilcox. Don't leave like this. You helped me preserve my ship during the battle. I owe you."

The man turned around slowly, a tired expression on his face. "Sir, you owe me nothing. I followed my orders."

Mostoff locked his chair into place. "Then what is bothering you? Your exemplary behavior under fire helped show me who your people really are. You should be proud."

He shook his head. "I did nothing. I was ordered to run, leave my post when my crew needed me. This stupid injury—" he shrugged his shoulder, grimacing slightly "—caused Morden to send me away."

Mostoff was taken aback. "You kept your crew safe and saved mine. There is no shame or cowardice in following orders, and certainly none in saving lives. I wish my leaders had the same good sense."

"Would you feel that way if it had been you? If you'd left your crew when they'd needed you most?"

The young man waited for a response, but Mostoff had none. They both knew the answer.

Wilcox continued. "That's what I thought. I should have been here with those who died, facing that same fire. I've fought many battles in space, but never face-to-face with my enemy. I'm good at a desk, but not very useful with a rifle in my hands. Morden knew that and sent me away."

Mostoff shook his head, trying to sound reassuring. "I've watched her. She relies on you."

Wilcox threw his uninjured arm in the air. "Maybe for some things, but not this time, and I can't go back and prove to her that she was wrong."

Mostoff nodded. "I have felt the need to prove myself under fire before, and it never went well." He thought back to the adventures and stupid decisions of a young man eager to show others his mettle. He shook his head, inwardly wondering how he'd survived. "Your captain knows your heart is brave, just as I do. Know that for one man in the Triangle, you have already proven yourself worthy. I'd take you in to battle at my side without hesitation."

Wilcox smiled at him, some of his normal warmth suffusing his expression. "I appreciate that, sir."

The two men stared at each other, eyes locked as the landing craft's ramp began to raise. Mostoff felt certain he would never see Wilcox again. The ramp shut, cutting off the sight of the brightly lit Alliance landing bay.

Mostoff worked his hand controls, moving his wheelchair towards a seat. He doubted he had helped Wilcox much. He knew all too well how internal conflicts could eat at someone. Everyone had to face their demons, real and imagined. There was so much out there to face.

The galaxy had become a bigger place.

Wilcox watched the landing craft throttle up, turning slowly to exit the bay. Mostoff was right. Morden trusted him with her life. This had been a fluke accident. He would get his chance to prove himself to her, to meet the enemy at close quarters. He would have his shot to avenge his fallen comrades. He was an officer of the line. Combat was part of his life. He would see it again, and when he did, he would show everyone he was made for it.

That was a certainty.

CHAPTER 37

Dear Mr. and Mrs. Va,

It is with a heavy heart that I inform you that your son, Ensign James C. Va,
was killed in action.

Morden stopped typing, guilt tearing at her heart.

Killed in action.

So many men and women gone forever because of her decisions. These
weren't nameless faces. Many of these people had been with her for years.
Writing these letters made it harder for her to forget her part in their deaths.

This wasn't going to be the last time she lost someone under her
command. She understood that.

Nevertheless, she couldn't stop dwelling on her decisions. She had let
herself down. Even worse, she had let Admiral Knight down. He had shown
such confidence in her, and now she would face an inquiry at best. At worst,
she would lose her command.

Her throat tightened at that thought. How would she explain what had
happened here? How could she justify herself? Morden tried to type again,
focused on taking comfort from honoring the dead.

How do you survive without a safety net? It was easy to point your
finger up, blame the one at the top. Top-level command had been her dream,
but the reality seemed to be so much different than she had expected.
Morden wanted to be able to say that whatever happened from now on, she
was going to be the best leader possible.

But how could she guarantee it?

The door chime rang, bringing relief from the emotional pool she was drowning in.

She cleared her throat. "Come in."

Commander Holsey entered, wearing her normal gloomy expression. Morden's heart dropped again. Emma would try to pin the disaster on her when command started asking questions. She was sure of it. Some of Morden's decisions had turned out to be wrong ones, but she was sure Holsey would paint a damning, one-sided narrative. Morden wanted to hate her for being so unfair, wanted to lash out, but given their history, how could she?

Morden met Holsey's negativity with a smile. "Commander, please come in." She tried to sound friendly and confident.

Holsey stood stiffly, looking down at the floor. "I think perhaps you should choose our destination instead of me."

Morden let the smile fall from her face. "You have my complete confidence. You were correct when you suggested I should allow you more leeway. I'm sorry my learning curve was so steep."

The woman still looked uncomfortable. "Then perhaps you could give me some guidelines, besides avoiding the Milipa border."

Morden leaned forward. "Holsey, level with me. You don't need me to micro-manage you."

The woman pointed. "May I sit?"

Morden was surprised at the question. "Certainly, I didn't mean for you to stand. I apologize about the mess. I haven't really settled in."

Holsey lowered herself into a free desk chair, crossed her legs. "Captain, may I speak freely?"

Here it comes.

Morden tried not to tense. "Always, Commander. A lack of directness has never been one of your shortcomings, even before the Verdun."

"I am concerned about when we get back to the Alliance." She started slowly, but gained momentum as she spoke. "There were some questionable decisions and with the length of time it will take us to get back, we will be under even more scrutiny."

Morden sighed. "Yes, there will be. We ... I lost a lot of good people here. There will most certainly be questions, possibly an inquiry, but that's not your concern, Commander. I will take responsibility for my decisions. You have nothing to fear."

Holsey nodded again, a subtle look Morden couldn't read slipping onto her face. She fought back her irritation at still not knowing her crew. The number of times Captain Knight had looked at her and just known what she was thinking ... She should be able to understand the looks of her officers too.

Holsey spoke softly. "This isn't entirely your fault. I want you to know that."

Morden stumbled, trying to respond. "I...I made the decisions here. There is no one else to blame."

Holsey held her gaze. "I am not suggesting otherwise. You can be reckless and pig-headed, but I know you can't see the future. You couldn't have known how things would go. You are not the same person I knew."

Morden crossed her arms, unsure of what to say. "We did achieve our objectives."

Holsey leaned forward. "That's not my point. I haven't made the best decisions either, at least not where you're concerned." Holsey shifted uncomfortably. "You might set the tone as captain, but I was openly hostile toward you from the start. I accused you of not letting me do my job, but who would let someone challenging their authority make important decisions? Coming at you like that would put anyone on the defensive, and it isn't behavior of an officer of my caliber. It isn't me."

"I haven't given you the opportunity or responsibilities and trust I owe—"

"No, you haven't. But trust is earned. We could have died here. Not because of a decision, but because we were not functioning as a team."

Morden frowned. "The crew performed admirably."

"Not the crew, ma'am. You and I. The chain of command is here for a reason. The crew needs to see us agree. Your decisions might have been different if I'd given you a reason to trust my input. Instead, I gave you another problem to worry about."

Morden was the one to nod this time. Holsey was right. They hadn't been much of team. "I apologize, Commander. I—"

Holsey laughed. "That's what I am doing—trying to apologize."

Morden smiled. "This is a new situation for me."

Holsey uncrossed her legs, leaned back in her chair. "Me too. *That's* my job. To help guide decisions and run our ship. Yes, you are the captain. You have the final say, but ships wouldn't have executive officers if one person could always shoulder the full load. It's lonely at the top, and I made damn sure you were stuck up there. If you want, I will request a transfer. I haven't acted in manner worthy of the position I'm occupying."

Morden shook her head. "No, that wouldn't be fair. Assuming they don't throw me to the wolves when we get home, let's start over. We have a history, but let's bury it here with the remains of that seven-eyed bastard."

Holsey tensed. "I can't forget, can't make myself feel—"

Morden leaned forward, cutting her off. "I am not asking you to, but I know how the pain from past mistakes can trap you. I'm not asking you to be a confidante, or a friend. I just want to leave the past where it belongs."

Holsey stared at her for a long moment. "All right. I would like the opportunity to fix my mistakes here."

Morden nodded. "As would I. Now please get some sleep. I want a suitable port for our ship by 0800 tomorrow."

Holsey stood and walked to the door. She opened it, flooding the dim room with light from the hallway, and took a step into the corridor. Then she stopped and turned to face Morden again. "Captain, they won't throw you to the dogs. This mission wasn't what it appeared. Even an experienced captain couldn't have known what was happening. Realistically, the Alliance hasn't even fought a major battle against a Frontin capital ship in recent memory. They set one hell of a trap, and we still pulled it off. The admiral made the right decision picking you."

Morden felt her throat tighten. "Thank you."

Holsey nodded and left.

The admiral was right.

Morden felt lighter. Mistakes were part of life. Whatever happened when they returned home, she would learn from what she'd done here. Captain Knight hadn't been perfect. No one was. His decisions had sometimes infuriated her. She could still be the leader she knew she was.

Morden turned back to the task at hand and started typing.

Your son died defending his post, defending the lives of his shipmates, fellow officers, and the innocents we were protecting. He was a hero. You should be proud. I know I am.

The bridge was swirling with commotion when Holsey arrived. Damage assessment teams were conversing loudly across the room as they worked. The sheer number of repairs they still had to make was overwhelming.

Just cleaning the carbon scoring from the Frontin scatter guns would take the better part of a week. This was the second time those shit-for-brain creatures had hurt something she cared about. She hoped it would be the last.

Several other officers, including Lieutenant Urquhart, were working at their stations. Urquhart looked very out of place with her arm in a sling. Holsey started typing a long list of requirements into the command console. She rolled her head, stretching her neck as she waited.

Work crews were still repairing Isabelle's mainframe, slowing the computer's normally lightning-fast response time. Seeing the words, "Just a Moment Please" blinking across her screen each time she asked her console to do something was getting tiresome.

Something I care about.

It was funny to think that she actually *did* care about this ship. Maybe Morden was right. The past should be just that — the past. When she had discovered who was commanding the *Verdun*, she had been convinced this was the wrong assignment. She had been wrong. This place might be a way out of the darkness she had been living in for so long.

The computer monitor lit up, displaying a list of repair facilities with light schedules, sufficiently large facilities, and the proper inventory of available supplies. She read through them one by one, drumming her fingers on the side of her chair. She had about an hour left until the captain wanted a decision. The computer had come up with more than a hundred options, and she would need to work fast. This was such an unusual situation, a ship of the line completely off the grid. Normally, they would have just been told where to go, probably to a place where the admiralty could hold an inquiry.

Madrona? No, too close to the Milipa border.

Dunbar? No, all their larger docks were full. They couldn't handle an unscheduled ship, especially one that would need major overhauls.

Coffee. Coffee would be nice, she decided. She should have stopped by the mess on the way up. No matter where they went, it would be a long way home with the Kaehey drive barely functional, a couple months minimum just to reach Alliance space. It wouldn't shock her if command had declared them all missing and dispatched a destroyer wing to investigate.

Her eyes skipped through the other options. Titan? No way. She had been there before. The station's commander was inept, and their wet docks had barely accommodated the *Ajax*, not to mention a battlecruiser like the *Verdun*.

She kept reading.

Kent Minor. Maybe, but not perfect. No ammunition deliveries were listed, and they wouldn't have the supplies to replace the rear turret.

This would be a weird homecoming. She should organize a schedule for people to contact home. Going so long without post from the TLS or any communication with loved ones was hard on morale under normal circumstances. When so many of the crew had lost friends, it would be worse. Holsey and Morden would need to work hard to keep spirits up, especially since everyone was going to be busting their asses non-stop to get through the endless repairs the ship required. When the investigation did happen, she was determined to show the crew's diligence and dedication.

Kensington? No, that was one of those old dumps near the old Black Star Empire. Why they even maintained those old wartime outposts was beyond her. Her eyes rested on the word for a second. Then again, Morden had wanted something out of the way. Holsey opened the information panel for the facility.

It was a bit farther away than she wanted, but its manufacturing facilities were still operational, if not used very often. According to the schedule, only two ships were due for the next four months, the *Barracuda*, one of the fleet's smaller patrol destroyers, and the *Leclerc*, a cruiser, a few weeks after. Kensington's inventory listed full supplies of ammunition and parts.

Holsey fed the data to Morden's quarters, waiting for the proper approval. She had been truthful last night, even if the captain didn't believe it. Holsey didn't like Morden, and she certainly didn't always agree with the decisions she made, but Morden's actions had saved her life and the *Verdun*. Had Holsey not gone down to the laser control room after Morden, the captain would have died destroying the enemy.

A text response popped up on her screen. Morden had given her approval.

Holsey looked up at Urquhart. "Lieutenant, plot us a course to Kensington Station. Best speed."

The young woman looked up from the navigation pit. "That station is just over three months away. Are you sure?"

Holsey nodded. "Yes, Lieutenant. The captain and I want to avoid certain things, like the Milipa. Please plot a course."

"Aye-aye, ma'am."

Isabelle's voice sounded over the bridge speakers. "Captain Morden has the bridge. Commander Holsey, you are relieved."

It was nice to hear the AI's voice again, even if only performing this mundane task. Holsey almost smiled as she looked toward Morden.

Holsey had to admit it. The woman was starting to seem like a captain. It was reassuring somehow. Holsey was a marine. She wasn't the kind of person to dwell on why. She would keep it simple.

Morden sat down. "Are we ready to go, Commander?"

Holsey glanced down at her panel. "At your leisure, Captain. I just approved navigation's proposed course."

Stetler's voice followed. "Course laid in. Helm ready, Captain."

Morden leaned back, looking up at the holoports. "Take us home, Mr. Stetler."

The ship started to bank, straining against its own inertial mass. It hadn't been simple, but the mysteries of this place had been laid to rest. Holsey tried not to smile as the feeling of movement ran through her body. She looked at the holoports, at the image of the swirling asteroids, happy knowing she wasn't going to have to see them again.

M orden's eyes were fixed on the rapidly moving stars outside the observation dome as she counted down the seconds. In a few moments, they would cross back into Alliance space. She understood there was no real difference between areas in space, but the thought of Alliance · territory surrounding her was exhilarating. Morden still had excessive amounts of paperwork to do, but she needed to see the stars again, if only for a moment. This was the first real opportunity she'd had in the past month, and she was determined to enjoy it.

She was happy with the crew's progress. Everyone had been working around the clock. The ship felt almost normal again, albeit with many people in the infirmary recovering and many more missing, their bunks empty, their gear packed away for their next of kin.

The last time she had come down to the observation dome, things had been different. It was nice to come here and find it still functional, free of damage and the lingering stench of the Frontin. It was one of few rooms that the Frontin had completely ignored.

The door started to open.

Morden shook her head, looking at the door and chuckling. It was impossible for her to find a moment of peace and quiet.

Urquhart looked surprised. "Captain! I'm sorry, I—"

Morden waved her in. "We've covered this. It's public space. Come in."

The young woman smiled, shutting the hatch behind her.

Morden looked back out at the stars. "How's the arm?"

The woman's reflection in the glass rolled her shoulder slowly. "Sore. They hit me good. This stupid sling comes off tomorrow."

"Excellent. We've missed you, though I am sure you've enjoyed light duty."

Urquhart walked up next to her. "Hell no! I hate spending time in medical. That rehab tech gives me the creeps."

Morden let her gaze follow the streaking stars outside the glass. "It was never my favorite thing, either."

Morden felt a fresh wave of guilt pressing down on her heart. This woman was an exemplary officer, and the Frontin had almost extinguished her future.

"Captain?" Isabelle's sweet voice sang over the speakers. "You wished to be informed when we reached Alliance space. We have officially crossed the border."

Urquhart sighed loudly. "Thank God."

"It's always a relief to come home after a fight." Morden agreed.

"It's not that."

Morden looked over at her. "Oh? Then what is it?"

"I know we were sent there to keep people safe, and I always want to do my duty. I know I might die as an officer. I've watched enough people I love die defending our country. I just don't want to die fighting for people who hate us."

"Keeping that region safe also protects those whom we have sworn to defend." Morden tried to sound matter-of-fact and captain-like.

"I know. We all understand, ma'am. It just didn't feel right, you know?"

Morden shook her head in agreement.   Urquhart smiled. "I wanted to thank you. You kept us alive. We were lucky to have someone of your caliber leading us through it. I will learn a lot from you."

Morden tried to return the gesture, searching for something to say, but found nothing.

Urquhart looked back out at the stars. "It's just good to be home."

"It is that."

For the first time, it hit Morden that the younger officers like Urquhart would look up to her as she had looked up to Captain Knight. She had been caught up in so many things — the tone she'd set with Holsey, the decisions she'd made, and so many other elements of her position, but never this. The *Verdun* was her ship. Its future was hers to shape. The people she trained, led, mentored, and strengthened would help write that future. It was a humbling thought.

This was her ship.

My Verdun.

Somehow, it also felt right.

Urquhart's voice sounded far away. "I'm going back down to the mess hall. I just wanted to watch us cross the frontier. It felt important."

"I had the same need."

Urquhart turned to walk away.

Morden's eyes followed her. "Lieutenant, you did an exemplary job. I know your father would be proud. I certainly am."

The young woman froze, glancing back at Morden for moment, a telltale sheen forming in her eyes. Then she climbed up out of the dome and out of sight.

Morden sat down. Her ship, her crew. Why had it taken her so long to reach such a basic realization? With command came any number of stresses. Guilt was just one of them.

She would just have to learn to live with it.

Whatever happened, good or bad, she had earned her right to command.

This was a new beginning for her, she knew it. What she had told Holsey was true. It was time to leave the past behind, to let go of the fear and do her best for those under her command. She had been so caught up in the details, the tasks of how the ship ran, that she had forgotten the big picture. She would have to face her mistakes in front of others, and she would own her mistakes, but that was in the future.

Right now, they had to get the *Verdun* to port and let the wounded heal. This would be her last moment of rest until they got home. Once she left this room, she would be Captain Kim Morden of the *Royal Alliance Ship Verdun*.

This was her ship, her crew.

Captain Knight was the past. She didn't need to live up to him because she was her own leader. She would find her own way. The future belonged to her. She wouldn't let memories or other people's expectations keep her from doing her duty.

The Frontin would be back. It was inevitable. But Morden knew they were not the only threat she would face. She stood up, taking one more look out at the darkness beyond the glass and smiled. She finally felt ready to face those threats.

Head on.

Keep reading for an excerpt from *Outpost*, the next installment in the Line of Battle Series, coming in June, 2017!

An Excerpt from Outpost
Line of Battle No. 2

By W.P. Brothers

Jack Wilcox stepped out of the crowded interior of the tender and into the blinding sunlight. The late afternoon heat hit him like a wave as the tender's engine spluttered and shut off. Jack loosened his tie slightly and stepped out of the way as Major Osterman and the six marines he'd brought as escort filed off the tender. Jack watched as Osterman blinked in the light, sweat beading on his forehead.

"Didn't dress for the weather, did we?" Jack grinned, pointing at Osterman's body armor.

Osterman fixed Jack with a gaze that clearly said, "Shut up," and turned to the other marines. "Secure the docks!"

The marines scrambled up the dock toward the shoreline, Osterman jogging behind. It was good to see Gordon out and about again. His wounds from the battle with the Frontin had been so severe that it had seemed the infirmary would never let him go. Osterman's charming, levelheaded presence had been keenly missed at staff meetings, and Jack for one was happy the man was back with his marines again.

Jack turned and watched as the second tender grumbled to a halt behind the first. The hatch opened, and another six marines emerged from inside, running to catch up with the first group, their rifles reflecting the withering sunshine, their grey uniforms and armor a perfect match for the faded paint of the silent cranes and machinery up and down the dockyards.

"I think we've had the day saved for us," Jack said, bending to look back inside the tender. The dozen crewmembers buckled inside laughed and began to extricate themselves from their seats. One by one, they stepped past Jack and out of the craft, which was opening its cargo bay. The top of the tender's blocky rear section opened like a book, a small crane unfolding automatically. When Jack saw that the other tender had done the same, he turned to check on the marines, who had reached the juncture of the dock and the shoreline now, about a hundred yards away, and were setting up behind a tarp-covered pile of crates.

Jack squinted down the shoreline at the endless expanse of the dockyards, shimmering in the heat. He frowned, looking for any sign of movement. The lift cranes were unmoving, like skeletal fingers jutting up here and there from the clutter of crates, parked trucks, and palette lifters arranged along the docks. The long line of tall warehouses glowered back at him, their front cargo doors closed. Behind the warehouses, the steep-sided hills, one of them with what looked like a bunker sitting atop its cleared summit, were like silent, blue-green sentries.

Where the hell is everyone?

Jack started after the two work crews, who were walking together in a clump toward the marines, when he heard the pilot call out from inside the tender.

"Commander?"

Wilcox ducked inside, grateful for the coolness of the air-conditioned crew compartment.

"Yes, Mr. Piskorz, what is it?"

Piskorz, a muscular man with dark stubble on his square jaw, turned around in his chair to look at Jack, his eyes wide. "Commander, I'm getting a call from the Verdun. We're to return immediately."

"Are they worried we'll get heatstroke?" Jack chuckled.

"No, sir. We have a report of enemy activity in the area."

Jack's humor evaporated in an instant. "Get the engines started." He ran back out onto the dock, cupped his hands over his mouth and shouted to the rest of the group. "Pack it up!"

The sound of the tender's engines drowned out Jack's shout. One of the marines turned to look at Jack, who raised both arms and waved them toward himself. The marine nodded and turned to the other marines and the crewmen gathered around him. A second later, Jack saw him stand up, then fall to the ground, clutching his arm. For half an instant, Jack wondered what had happened. Then the boom of a rifle shot carried over to him.

Jack saw a crewmember jerk and fall as the rest of the group hit the deck. Jack did the same, dropping to the hot metal surface of the dock as the roar of gunfire split the air.

"Verdun, we're taking fire from shore!"

Jack heard the pilot calling out over the smack of bullets on the tender. Ahead of him, the marines at the barricade were returning fire. Jack followed the direction of their rifles and could barely make out the forms of people spread out behind various vehicles and crates along the dock. One of them would pop out from behind a crate, fire toward the Alliance personnel, then duck back into cover. Jack spotted an enemy trooper pointing a long tube toward his direction. It was only when the rocket burst from the front of the tube that Jack realized what it was.

"Christ!"

The rocket missed the tender by a few feet, exploding in the water. Droplets showered Jack, who covered his face and head protectively.

"Sir! I need to lift off!" Piskorz called from inside the tender.

"Not without them!" Jack pointed to the *Verdun* teams at the barricade.

"Then you need to get them here!"

Jack looked toward the barricade, then back at the pilot. "You're crazy!"

"Sir! I need to go!"

Jack nodded, took a deep breath, then stood. He dashed forward, but dived onto his stomach again as the crushing roar of machine guns erupted from behind him. Jack looked and saw that the tenders had opened fire at the enemy positions with their machine gun turrets. On the shore, the enemies scrambled for cover. Jack took the opportunity to launch himself to his feet and sprint to the pinned-down work crews.

Jack slid to a stop next to Major Osterman, ducking behind a cement barrier.

"You've got to get them up!" Osterman was fitting a rifle grenade to his weapon's muzzle. "We're stuck here until they move!"

Jack looked at the crewmembers plastered to the deck, covering their heads, shouting. Somewhere, someone was screaming. Most of them had never seen combat in the open. Neither had Jack, for that matter. The other marines popped over the barricade and fired in staccato bursts.

Jack winced as a bullet sizzled over the barricade. He shook his head.

"We'll cover you," Osterman shouted. "Get them up." Osterman turned around, aimed his rifle toward the closest enemy barricade and touched off the grenade. The barricade exploded, and Jack saw several bodies — or at least parts of them — thrown clear. His stomach turned.

"Get them up!" Osterman kicked Jack, who lurched forward and onto his feet. Not wanting to be hit, he stumbled forward toward the crewmembers.

"We're getting out of here," he shouted, but none of them seemed to hear. Jack grabbed the collar of the nearest crewmember and hauled him to his feet. Somehow this broke the spell, and the rest followed, standing up to a low crouch. Jack heard the marines touch off another grenade, another explosion. Jack glanced over his shoulder. Between the fire of the marines and the tenders, the enemies seemed to be pinned down.

Jack led the crewmembers back down the dock toward the tenders. They were fifty yards away when a jet of fire and smoke streaked by, striking Piskorz's tender full on. The craft rocked backward and exploded, ripping the dock apart next to it. Jack tasted blood and realized he had dropped to the dock again. He forced himself to his feet, dragging the crewmembers with him. But the fire from the shore had increased again, and a woman to Jack's left pitched to the ground, then a man just ahead of him fell limp. Jack stepped over the body and kept running, pushing the rest of the group ahead of him.

Marcus lowered himself into the cockpit of the Stallion he'd been given, pulled his helmet and air mask closed.

He was getting back to work sooner than he'd thought.

The cockpit slid shut, muffling the noise of the klaxons blaring on the launch deck, the rumble of the other fighters' engines spooling up.

His hands moved to the controls, punching in the settings for planetary flight mode, and an underwater launch. He hadn't done this sort of thing in a while, his mind racing back to the endless times they'd practiced this in flight school.

The bay door opened in front of him, and water flooded upward, swirled around his craft.

W.P. Brothers

"Water equilibrium in twenty seconds. Standby." The computer's pleasant, relaxed voice spoke to him.

"Come on. Come on." He activated the holodisplay, every nerve aching to get going. People — their people — were being attacked out there. Damned if Marcus was going to allow some other asshole to take more of the *Verdun's* crew.

"Equilibrium achieved."

Marcus pushed the control stick forward, his body thrown backward in his seat as the Stallion shot downward and into the inky green water.

J ack was almost to the remaining tender, was starting to reach for the door. "Shit!"

Another rocket surged past and exploded beside the tender, which started backing away from the dock.

"No, damn you!" Jack tried to wave for the tender to stop, but it was turning, picking up speed, and surging for the *Verdun*. Another crewmember fell, holding his leg. Bullets whistled and thwacked around them. Jack pulled his people back down flat against the pier. He looked back at the marines at the barricade. No longer held back by machine gun fire, enemy soldiers — at least a hundred — were closing in, moving from cover to cover. One of the marines fired toward the oncoming group, dropping two of his targets, but the surge of attackers continued unabated.

Jack saw an enemy soldier aim a rocket launcher for the marine barricade, was about to tell the group around him to swim for it. The man with the rocket pitched forward, then several more attackers around him fell as gunfire crackled from further down the docks to the left.

Jack shifted where he lay to get a look, half expecting to see more enemies. Instead, he watched as olive-green soldiers poured from between two of the warehouses and onto the docks. As the newcomers moved behind cover and blasted toward the enemy attackers, Jack felt a surge of relief.

Thank God for the Army!

Jack saw the marines, no longer pinned down, launch another salvo of grenades. Caught between the fire of the marines and the newcomers, the enemy ranks withered. Jack saw a pair of green clad soldiers drop a machine gun into its tripod and then open fire on the confused hostiles. As many as a hundred of the newcomers were on the waterfront now, some of them surging forward in short rushes to the marine positions while others ripped the enemies apart with machine gun and rifle fire. A rocket from one of the newcomers detonated among the ranks of the enemies, who turned and fled up the docks, only a few pockets of them remaining, firing blindly.

As Jack watched, a short, dark woman at the head of the group — an officer maybe — jumped over a pile of crates that two of the remaining enemies were hiding behind. She shot one of them at point blank range, and when the other swung his rifle at her, she ducked and drove the point of her bayonet through his chest. The marines were up and out from behind the barricade now, joining the charge forward after the fleeing enemies, who were two hundred yards up the dock, tossing their rifles aside and running as hard as they could.

Suddenly, the woman — yes, she had to be an officer — held up her hand. The charging soldiers stopped in their tracks and went to cover. A heartbeat later, Jack heard a sound that almost made him want to cry. It was the boom of approaching fighters.

The docks where the enemy soldiers were running were ripped to pieces in a hail of gunfire. Three enormous explosions obscured the enemies in flames, and a fourth a second later blasted the section of shoreline where they stood into fragments. Jack heard cheers and looked over at the marines and newcomers, who raised their rifles as a squadron of Stallions and Sparrowhawk fighters from the *Verdun* screamed overhead, their graceful forms catching the dying sunlight.

Jack stood, helped his crewmembers to their feet. They were in one piece, mostly. Cuts, a minor bullet wound, very afraid. Nothing serious. Jack glanced back up the dock, saw the bodies of the three crewmembers who'd been shot during the dash for the tenders. One was still clutching his leg, but the other two — and the others at the barricade...

A pair of brown boots and khaki gaiters entered Jack's field of vision. "Are you in charge here?"

Jack looked up to see the woman who had led the charge walking toward him, her rifle canted toward the ground, Major Osterman and another officer in green, lanky and tall, a few steps behind her.

"Yes," Jack said, straightening up, his voice tight from the smoke drifting from the obliterated docks. Realizing he'd only croaked the word, Jack fought the stinging smoke and shouted. "Yes, I'm in command."

"I'm Lieutenant Christine Flores."

Jack held out his hand. The woman looked at it for a moment before taking it and shaking roughly.

"We owe you infantry a big thanks," Jack said.

"We're not infantry. We're rangers. Third Company, Fifth and Third Platoons."

"Whoever you are," Jack said, taken aback by Flores' abrupt response. "We have a problem."

Lieutenant Flores pursed her lips, nodded. "That's the first smart thing I've heard all day."

Want to learn what happens next? *Outpost* will be available in June, 2017!

Also by W.P. Brothers

<u>Line of Battle Series</u>

First Command

Outpost — Coming June 2017!

About the Author

W.P. Brothers grew up in Colorful Colorado, where he filled his childhood with made-up heroes, villains, and incredible adventures in space, on the sea, and on smoky battlefields. A life-long fan of science fiction, his other passions include military history, fine cooking, competition shooting, and hiking and camping in the beautiful Rocky Mountains.

Connect with him at www.wp-brothers.com, and sign up for his mailing list. You can also join the conversation with other fans of the Line of Battle Series on Facebook at www.facebook.com/AuthorWPBrothers/.

www.ingramcontent.com/pod-product-compliance
Lightning Source LLC
Chambersburg PA
CBHW020229180626
46810CB00006B/2102